PRAISE FOR MAD MERLIN

"A distinctive and agreeable spin to the story of Camelot . . . action fans will thrill to his frequent and well told accounts of battles, both material and magical. Creative plot twists abound."

—*Publishers Weekly*

"The story never stalls, and his descriptions conjure images that are easy to visualize—with writing like this, who needs movies and special effects? *Mad Merlin* starts out great and keeps getting better."

—*Locus*

"Drawing on ancient Norse, Celtic, and Roman myths, King crafts an unusual blend of history and legend that should appeal to fans of the Arthurian cycle."

—*Library Journal*

"A nicely written and engaging perspective on the wizard's actual identity, the book's sad in spots, funny in others and a worthwhile read."

—*San Diego Union-Tribune*

By J. Robert King

Mad Merlin

Lancelot du Lethe

Lancelot du Lethe

J. ROBERT KING

TOR® fantasy

A TOM DOHERTY ASSOCIATES BOOK
NEW YORK

NOTE: If you purchased this book without a cover you should be aware that this book is stolen property. It was reported as "unsold and destroyed" to the publisher, and neither the author nor the publisher has received any payment for this "stripped book."

This is a work of fiction. All the characters and events portrayed in this book are either products of the author's imagination or are used fictitiously.

LANCELOT DU LETHE

Edited by Brian Thomsen

A Tor Book
Published by Tom Doherty Associates, LLC
175 Fifth Avenue
New York, NY 10010

www.tor.com

ISBN: 0-765-34070-4

First edition: December 2001
First mass market edition: February 2003

Printed in the United States of America

0 9 8 7 6 5 4 3 2 1

To Gabriel, my Galahad:
the son will surpass the father

Acknowledgments

Thanks, Brian, for fine editorial insights and direction. Thanks, Jim, for wise shepherding through production. Thanks, Tom, for running a company that publishes books like this one. Thanks, Mom and Dad, for the weekend of the five chapters. Thanks, Jennie, Eli, Aidan, and Gabe, for putting up with a writer in the house.

Lancelot du Lethe

PROLOGUE

Destinies Unmade

A simple spell would take Merlin across the channel, but he would have to get his feet wet. He dragged his gray travel cloak up from one boot, turned its heel, unstopped a water skin, and dribbled a slim bead of Avalon water on the scarred leather. He set the boot down. It made a small splash on the floor as he raised its mate. Another gush. He stood upright and looked around.

Though most of Merlin stood in an antechamber of Arthur's palace at Camelot, the soles of his feet stood in the waters of Avalon.

He had friends in Avalon—one especial friend. Nyneve. Wherever water was, Nyneve was. Wherever Nyneve was, Merlin was welcome. She grasped his heel and pulled him down. He descended into the floor as into a deep well. The whiteness of Camelot slipped away, replaced by cold springs and the pulses of the Otherworld.

In the tumbling darkness of water-smoothed rock, she spoke: *Where do you wish to go, Merlin?*

Even after all these years, her voice still thrilled him. He would give up the whole world for her—soon, but not yet. . . .

Benwick. We go to see King Ban. We go to gather warriors for the Battle at Mount Badon. Even here, in the chattering depths, that name brought a hush of fear. *Unless we gain the troops of Ban and Bors, Camelot is doomed.*

Camelot is doomed anyway. She seemed to wince. The words had slipped carelessly from her mind.

Merlin tightened his hold. *What do you mean?*

Only that Camelot is mortal, and so are you, Merlin. I fear what will happen at Mount Badon. I fear your death. Let this be our last favor to mortals, and then let's withdraw to the Cave of Delights.

Most beaus plucked bouquets for their loves. Merlin had made a whole world. *Don't be too eager for my heaven, sweet dear. Gates of pearl are as imprisoning as gates of iron. Mortal life's the thing. Into mortal things—blood feuds and incestuous affairs and deadly politics—even angels long to look.*

She was quiet as she drew him into the water tables of Gaul. *Into these things, I do not long to look. I'll bear you to Benwick, my love, but I'll wait in the well for you. What deadly politics you find there you find alone.*

As long as you wait for me, I will be glad.

They swam up an underground river and reached a lofty aquifer. Out into a Roman aqueduct they went, sluicing down toward Benwick. While some of the water shunted to baths and cisterns, Nyneve and Merlin followed the pipes that led to a great fountain in the court of King Ban.

From its flood, Merlin rose. His tattered cloak streamed. He was a shapeless thing amid the perfectly sculpted statues. He jutted forth like a gulping trout.

The folk around the fountain fell back and gasped. "A weird! A water weird!"

"Not so weird as I once was," spluttered Merlin. Each word sent a spray from his mustache and beard. He shook himself like a dog, wetting those around. Samite clung to courtiers. Velvet wilted on varlets. Heedless, Merlin straddled the fountain's balustrade and stepped onto the land of Benwick. He shook his head once last. White locks hurled more liquid around the courtyard. "Urgent business for King Ban. Please step aside!"

"I will not," came a bold reply. The brusque tone told Merlin who this was, "since I am he." Ban was a hearty fellow with short-cropped black hair and beard, a slender coronet in the Roman style, and a glint of humor in his eye.

Merlin smiled at his friend and grasped Ban's hand. "Hello, sire. Would that we met under better circumstances."

"Better circumstances?" Ban echoed. "What better circumstances? The wars with Claudas are done, thanks to Arthur. The land knows great prosperity. My palace has never looked so splendid. I have even the chance to entertain the court mage of Camelot, appearing here in my own fountain. Life in Benwick is so sweet, folk have been postponing their deaths to remain. It is heaven."

"Don't be so sure," Merlin replied.

King Ban's teeth flashed between bristles of beard. He clasped Merlin's shoulder. "So, why have you come, Merlin?"

"I ask your aid for Arthur against Saxon throngs."

"Arthur has given me peace, has saved thousands of my troops," King Ban replied pensively. "It is because of Arthur that I live. I would walk through fire for him, and it sounds as though I will."

"Yes, but fire of a different sort," Merlin replied. "If the Saxons win at Mount Badon, they will take the whole Midmarch. We all will be overwhelmed by foreign gods and Pagan hordes."

Ban's smile gained a bitter edge. "A horde is a horde, and a Christian horde is no kinder than a Pagan one." He clamped his teeth together. "Still, for Arthur—yes, I will send troops."

"He has saved you twenty thousand soldiers, you said," Merlin pressed. "Could he count on a tithe of that from you?"

"Oh, better than two thousand. I'll send a legion—my best legion. Why do I need soldiers in peacetime? And my brother Bors will send his best legion as well, if you ask him."

Merlin nodded in thanks. "You are most gracious. Thank you. I must go. Time is of the essence. I go even now to speak to Bors."

"Wait," said King Ban, raising his hand. "One small favor." He motioned though an archway. "Come with me, my friend, and see the future of my kingdom."

With one hand, King Ban led Merlin across the slick stones of the courtyard. With the other, he snapped a command. Nobles parted before him, and servants scurried through the arch to make all ready.

Merlin followed resignedly. His boots sucked and spewed with each step. The future of Benwick—what paltry thing would best represent it? A greased pig evading its handlers? A week-old pie with an uninviting crust? A trumpeter with a fat lip and a tin ear? Such rude thoughts crowded Merlin's mind as he stepped through the arch. A long stroll brought them to a small sewing chamber. It was warm and crowded. Bonneted and beaming, servants hovered in an angel choir about their Madonna—golden haired Queen Elaine—and her Babe.

Merlin sank to his knees. His hands opened beside his whiskered cheeks. Old eyes stared at a creature utterly new.

"Lancelot is his name," King Ban said nearby. "My son. The heir to my throne."

Merlin goggled. Not since the infant Arthur had he seen such beauty. His skin was smooth, clean, soft—so fresh from divinity. Here was a boy who would be glory personified. Merlin could not even look upon him, blinding. He shielded his eyes, but too late. Already the brilliance stamped a vision upon his mind.

He saw Camelot hung in mourning. Every white wall bore a black banner. Every garrison bed lay empty. Warriors slept row on row in graveyards if lucky, or littering forgotten fields. Some great foe had arisen to decimate the knighthood, to slay Arthur, to consign Camelot to the world of dream. That great foe lay swaddled before Merlin.

"Lancelot," breathed the old mage raggedly. "That is a lovely name."

King Ban beamed. "At last, an heir. I will give him a kingdom at peace, and he will rule when I am gone. He will change the world, Merlin."

"Yes, he will," Merlin replied bleakly.

"Then, bless him, Merlin," King Ban urged. "You've the favor of the True God and all the false ones too. Bless him."

Bless him? This child who would rise to undo all that Arthur hoped to do at Mount Badon, who would destroy all Camelot, who would destroy Arthur? Why not curse the child? Why not murder him? What were a legion of Ban's men, and a legion of Bors's men, if this one babe could singlehandedly destroy all?

Silence intruded. Merlin opened his mouth to break the hush. What he said surprised even him. "This child . . . this Lancelot . . . He will be the greatest knight who ever lives."

There was beauty in this babe, as surely as there was doom. Never before had Merlin glimpsed a child of such perfect form, physically and metaphysically. The Fates had not made him.

Lancelot was Fortune's child, the happy accident of random convergence—the perfect boy at the perfect time in the perfect place. Dumb luck made miracles as well as atrocities, and Lancelot was both.

"Bless him," King Ban repeated, his teeth on edge.

Bless him or destroy him. All mortal good is doomed. Mortal life is the thing. Into this strife even angels long to look. What a thing, to slay the infant son of an ally. What a thing, to bless the child who would destroy a nation. It was madness, all of it.

Merlin reached to his belt. He wore there a dagger, and also a water skin. Merlin grasped the skin, filled with the water of Avalon. It was arguably the more deadly. He flipped the stopper free and poured the holy water in a cascade across his wizened fingers.

Merlin placed his palm on the babe's forehead. His fingers wrapped easily around the soft skull. He could feel the gaps in forming bone, the spots that allowed a child to be born and allowed him to be so easily killed. The water of Avalon trickled down Lancelot's tiny head, pooling beside eyes of blue. "I bless you, child, as the Baptizer of old, who said 'I would not have known him, except that the one who sent me told me.' Grow, Lancelot, as is the due of every child under heaven, and become what you must become." Merlin's hand trembled as he drew it away, and he felt suddenly dizzy.

King Ban caught him at the elbow. "He makes you faint?"

"Yes," Merlin replied with an appreciative nod. "Faint, indeed."

"He will do more than that. Wonders will come from this boy—"

"He will change everything."

"He'll be more than the greatest knight who ever lived," pressed Ban. "Destiny will make him the greatest king."

"Destiny is a word for decisions yet unmade," Merlin interjected.

The king swung his arm out above his heir, as if encompassing Merlin's thought. "His greatness will rival Arthur's. Mark me."

"I do."

"King Lancelot's rule will make Camelot seem a joke."

Merlin took a deep breath. "I will not argue."

"Good," the king responded, lifting a foamy tankard from the servant who stood nearby to offer it. "Here's to Lancelot."

Grasping his own tankard, Merlin replied, "Here's to Lancelot." The metallic steins clanked together. Liquid sloshed down the sides. The two men drank.

"Thank you, King Ban, for your tremendous hospitality. Teach Lancelot hospitality. Let him keep room in his soul to accommodate anyone he encounters, especially himself."

"You speak the truth, as always, old sage," replied King Ban.

Merlin shook his head ruefully. "If I were to speak the truth, I would say that Lancelot will be Arthur's greatest champion, and his greatest foe."

A look of utter horror filled King Ban's face. He stared down at the gentle visage of infant Lancelot. "How can you lay out his future this way—half to angels and half to devils? And even if you are right, old sage, should you tell such things to my queen and me?"

"Forgive me," Merlin replied with a deep bow. He turned from the beaming visage of Lancelot and strode back down sodden rugs toward the fountain. "Thank you for the troops."

"My brother eagerly awaits you, to give you more," King Ban said.

Merlin smiled. "Good. I will tell him all that has befallen. I will tell him of Badon Hill, the Saxons, the legions, and the deaths. If he still wants to send troops, I will kiss every last one."

"That won't be necessary."

As Merlin stepped into the fountain, he snapped his fingers. "We shall see."

Nyneve laid hold of him, and the two moved rapidly through the water table of Benwick.

Did he grant the soldiers you need?

Yes, and generously, though he included one more than I needed.

She seemed to shrug. *What is one more warrior?*

In this case, one more is doom.

1

Between Fire and Water

"It wasn't a blessing, but a curse," King Ban told himself. He chewed the syllables angrily. "Those things he said over my son—they were a curse."

Ban stood in the solarium of Benwick Castle. Rare glass windows gave him a view west and east. To the west, the Atlantic Sea boiled beneath a fiery sunset. To the east, the city of Benwick burned beneath an invasion.

Claudas's soldiers swarmed the hills. They bore torches in their midst—torches for homes and swords for their owners. A thousand fires already beamed upon the hillside. A thousand hovels flamed. Smaller fires rose in flocks upon the wind. Shafts arced over the sparsely guarded wall and brought pitch-soaked points to the thatch below. As rapidly as Claudas's armies marched upon Benwick, the citizenry fled. Caught between fire and water, they crowded the docks and climbed on anything that floated.

"My best legion—off in Britannia," King Ban mused. "Bors's best legion—off in Britannia. Merlin has robbed us of our defenders. He wins, and we lose."

"What, dear?" asked Elaine. Tall and lithe, the queen had arrived silently. She held the infant Lancelot to her breast. "What did you say about Merlin?"

King Ban lowered his eyes. They reflected his burning city. "We must begin to think of alternatives, my dear."

"Alternatives?" she asked. Instinctually she gripped Lancelot closer. "Alternatives to what?"

To staying here and dying, he wanted to say, but Ban was not a cruel man. He turned toward his wife, strode to her, and wrapped her and the child in an embrace. "Lancelot has a future, a bright future, and that's what I am thinking of. Before Lancelot, I would have remained. I would have faced down Claudas myself, on this very spot. Now that I have a son, though, an heir, it would be foolish to stand against overwhelming forces—" He stopped himself too late. Pulling back from the embrace, he divined her eyes.

Question had turned to desperation. "Just an hour ago, you said the city watch could stem this tide. You said the second legion outnumbered all the warriors of Claudas."

"Words spoken in haste, to soothe, to dismiss needless worry," Ban explained uncomfortably. "Now worry is needful. It's not for me, or even for you, my dear. It's for Lancelot."

She drew a deep breath. Lancelot cried fitfully. Elaine was slender and sweet, but also strong. Even as she stared into the face of her child, her back straightened. Something hard entered her features. "What must we do?"

King Ban reached out to her. "Come with me. It's a small thing, easily done." He grasped her elbow and guided her toward the door. "Down we go, my sweet, down to the kitchens." The door swung onto a spiral stair in polished stone. Bronze lamps and olive oil filled the descent with fragrant light. King

Ban coaxed his wife down the passage. "The peasants flee the city, rats from a sinking ship. They know what befalls. Claudas lets them run, for peasants always return. One master is the same as any other. It's the nobility he is after—us, and our son—"

"Please, Ban," Elaine protested mildly.

"Claudas will reach the castle. That much is sure. Perhaps within the hour, he will stride these very steps. If we remain, we are doomed. If we flee as king and queen and prince, we are worse still, for our own folk might slay us. But if we become something less . . ." the sentence broke off midthought as the royal family shoved their way through a servant's door into the kitchen.

It was a low place. Massive beams brushed Ban's head. Wide fireplaces yawned their black throats. The remains of one beast still hung spitted above smoldering logs. Ironwork pots boiled over or burned their contents to acrid cinders. Most telling of all, the silver set and the knives had all gone missing.

Elaine surveyed the abandoned scene. Her lip stiffened. She clutched the sleeping baby with a kind of ferocity. "I will become like them to save this babe. I will become something less, anything I must become."

Ban only nodded. He gestured her toward the cellar stairs. Dark, rail-less, and patched in moss, they were altogether different from the stairs in the royal apartments. "It is not so horrible a thing, to become a peasant. They are freer than any noble. Yes, they are owned. Yes, they must serve as they are told, but who seeks to kill a peasant? No one. Who seeks to kill a king, a queen, a prince? Everyone."

Cautiously descending, Ban pushed back the cellar door. It grated open, and a cool rush of wet air emerged. Beyond the door stood cask upon cask of ale. Past the barrels and crates were pegs where peasants left their own shabby garb to don the livery of Benwick.

"You see me?" Ban asked as he drew off his ermine stole and the silken shift beneath. In their stead, Ban snatched up a weary-worn tunic of sackcloth. "If clothes make the man, I am unmade." He tried to smile at his joke, but his gaze caught on Elaine.

She stood, tall and statuesque, tears streaming onto Lancelot. "How will we regain it? If we cannot hold it when we have our armies about us, how will we regain it without them?"

"How will we regain it if we are dead?" Ban shot back. He cringed. "I should not have been so blunt. Forgive me, my dear. I am only thinking of our son."

Yanking off his canons, Ban hurled them aside. He snatched up a tattered pair of trousers with holes in knees and crotch. "Even if we cannot regain what we lose here, Lancelot can. Our lives may have been written in full, but his only begins." He cinched a rope-belt around his waist. "Merlin said he would be a knight—the greatest knight. He will regain what we lose today."

From a nearby peg, Ban grasped a crone's dress and brought it to his wife. "Put it on." He took the babe in one arm and presented the dress.

Elaine visibly trembled. Her arms, emptied of the child, clutched around her as if she were cold. "I can't wear that."

"Put it on," King Ban demanded.

She shuddered. Reluctant, tearful, angry, confused—she began to disrobe. It was a terrible scene. She seemed a woman being raped. In a way she was. Her every virtue was taken from her, dragged away like the silk chemise that pooled on the floor. Soon, she stood naked before her husband, the crone's dress still clutched in her left hand. She released a yelp of despair.

Lancelot stirred and reached for his mother. He felt his father's broad chest and tried to latch on. Only sackcloth filled his mouth. He growled, preparatory to a full-fledged holler.

Rough and insistent, Ban rocked the baby. He suddenly realized he had never done this before. "Lancelot," he muttered in sweet awe. Picking up a commoner's shift, he wrapped the child in it and kissed his forehead. "Do you see, Elaine? Already, I am a better man. Already I tend my own child, and kiss him, and protect him—a peasant's work. A peasant's freedom."

"Already, I am a worse woman." She drew the despoiled fabric down around her. Slender, strong, youthful skin was hidden beneath a shell of tattered filth. "Already I am a crone."

"Not to me, though I do hope you grow into one," Ban said. "Let us go, my darling. Let us save ourselves and save the future king of Benwick!" He snatched up Elaine's hand and led her out the kitchen steps toward the dark night beyond. "Darkness helps us," reasoned Ban. "And dirt and desperation. They will bear us along like a river." A door barked open, and his words were proved true. The bailey thronged with fleeing folk, and the street beyond had become a river of humanity. "We will ride this tide and emerge in safety."

All rivers, even human rivers, run to the sea.

The flood of refugees boiled down every street and sluiced down every alley. At last, the fleshly wave gushed out across the docks. Some few folk continued on to splash into the waters. Most churned along piers until they found a gangplank and ganged aboard. All they needed was an unoccupied square foot on deck. They didn't even need a willing captain; unwilling ones were thrown overboard.

Ships sailed. Laden with many times their typical payloads, the vessels of Benwick harbor set out in a huge and hopeless armada. Crafts collided. Boats capsized. Fights broke out. Mutinies abounded. Despite every setback, the ragtag flotilla straggled away from the burning city. The stone jetty clawed at them—the last grasp of land—and a few more folk died. The rest drifted out into the black belly of the sea.

Some vessels sailed south, toward Iberia. Others plunged west, toward nothing but doom. Most headed north, hoping for a friendly welcome in Brittany.

Queen Elaine, King Ban, and Prince Lancelot had found themselves on just such a ship—an argosy that last had borne barrels of salt fish. Everything reeked of it, everything but the captain, who reeked of other things. The old sot was half-slain by rye spirits when his boat was seized. Amiable with drink, he agreed to visit his brother in Brittany. "He'll welcome you all. He's got daughters for ever'one." The good ship *Scruple*—smelling foul with fish and fear—sailed.

In the hold, stench made the air swim. At least folk packed there were warm, shielded from winds and blackness. Those crowded on deck breathed better—or worse—in the cold night. Wind shoved them, rifled their clothes, slapped their faces, howled in their ears. The wind had a co-conspirator in the sea. Waves shouldered past the hull in an angry stampede. Deep troughs opened before the bow and hurled the ship down until it scraped its keel. Watery ridges rose thereafter and flung the craft into angry skies.

In tumult's heart, King Ban lost his own. Benwick was gone now, in flames beneath the horizon. There was only this ink, above and below, churning fitfully. He was king of nothing, in worse tatters than most on the ship, smaller than plowmen and weaker than fishwives. The woman beside him was no longer queen, but a desperate and terrified crone in rags. Worst of all, though, Lancelot had ceased to be anything but a squalling babe. Past and future were eaten by blackness, and only the omnipresent, insufferable moment remained.

Lancelot screamed. Any creature with that much rage would fight, could perhaps prevail.

Ban wanted to feel that rage. Shifting sideways, he reached for his son. Elaine seemed only too glad to relinquish him. Ban lifted the kicking boy, gray against the night. Elaine dragged Ban's arms down. He cradled the child, pressing his head to his heart. "Let that steady beat calm you, sweet child. Let it assure you."

Lancelot calmed for a moment, but then kicked sharply. Ban's arm, which had borne a thousand strokes of sword on shield, could not bear that single infant kick. An ache spread hotly from his shoulder to his elbow, and then to his wrist. It was as though the babe were made of red-hot iron. Ban struggled to hold him, but the candent ache spread toward his neck. Lancelot's protests only grew.

"It was a curse he laid on you," King Ban gasped. His left arm jangled nervelessly as his right took hold of the child and dragged him toward his mother. Take him, Ban meant to say, but he suddenly had no breath.

Elaine took the boy anyway, her face sour.

Gulping, Ban clutched his chest. It was all gone now, all but the pain. Even his own pulse was gone.

Ban turned bulging eyes toward his wife. Elaine and Lancelot floated in the center of a roaring tunnel. They seemed to be getting farther away, but it was Ban who retreated.

"Guard Lancelot, my love," gasped King Ban of Benwick, and he was no more.

• • •

The storm would not relent—not here, on land, in broad daylight two days later. Not here in Britannia (hadn't they said the boat sailed for Brittany?) on the wide plains, far from the rocks that had torn the ship apart. The storm would never relent around Elaine. It was inside her. Her ears roared with wind. Her mouth burned with brine. Her skin stung with rain. Worst of all, though, as she stared down at her child, at Lancelot, she saw black clouds tear across his blue eyes.

The boy's father was dead. He'd died of grief. Why had the angel descended to take the father but not the mother? What of her grief?

They had wanted to throw Ban overboard once he was cold, but she had not let them. "He is king!" she'd insisted. "King Ban—your king!" They had consoled her, their arms soft but their smirks hard. They thought she was mad.

They were right. She should have let them throw the body to the sharks. The rocks chewed him up just as surely.

For two days, she had wandered with Lancelot. She grew weaker all the while, and he stronger. She ate nothing but water, while he nursed upon her body and blood and bone. A woman needn't be sane to care for her infant, as long as she had milk.

Now, though, the milk was gone. She had nothing to offer him. Death would claim them both.

A seven thousand six hundred thirty-fourth step, a seven thousand six hundred thirty-fifth, and she was knee-deep in a marsh. She raised her eyes from the stagnant water, reeds jutting up all around her. Wetlands stretched out beneath sloping hills and a charcoal sky. In the midst of the gnat-filled slough rose a triangular mound. It seemed a rumpled hat, its brim sodden and dripping.

Elaine went to her knees in the muck. If she drank, perhaps her milk would come again. Her parched lips moved toward the water. She uttered an accusation, a blasphemy, a prayer: "Mother of God!"

Sudden brilliance enveloped Elaine. She looked up.

Someone approached. She strode on the water, as her son had done on Galilee. She beamed light as if clothed in a star. Her presence burned away the dry stalks and radiated through the murky flood and purified the swamp. It grew deeper, wider around her. Her footsteps made the surface silver. Angels moved in the waters and the air.

Elaine gazed into that loving light and felt the storm at last cease. Every gritty corner was cleansed, every hopeless, helpless impulse. Her arms, for two days clutching the babe, dropped loose. Elaine stood before the glorious presence.

"Mother of God," she breathed, "you have heard my prayer."

A voice of infinite love replied, "Yes. I have come to take your child."

Only then did Elaine see that Lancelot, gone from her slack arms, rested quiet and content upon the breast of the woman.

Though mad, dry of milk, and destitute, Elaine was still a mother. "You cannot take my baby."

A look of deep sadness came to the woman's eyes, a sadness that grieved Elaine. "I can . . . but I will not. If he comes with me, he will fulfill his destiny—to be the greatest knight ever to live, and to reclaim Benwick after Claudas is dead." She held out the child. "If I return him to you, neither of these things will come to pass, and you both will die mad and starved. It is your choice."

Elaine was still a mother. She bowed her head and said, "Save him, then, Mistress. Lead him to his destiny."

It was enough. Moments in dream and divinity last for hours, and a single sentence begets a whole book.

She was gone, the woman garbed in a star. The reeds had returned, and the gnat-filled marsh, the rumpled hills and all. It had been but a vision, a delirium-dream—except that Lancelot, too, was gone.

Elaine remembered her arms going limp, and she gave a cry. Dropping again to her knees, she rammed her hands down in the muck and sent fingers raking through. He had to be here. He wasn't floating on the surface. He had to be here, among the snake holes and roots.

There was no warmth and nothing solid, only cold rot.

"Lancelot!" she shrieked.

She flailed forward, to one side, to the other. The water around her roiled with filth. She dived and dragged her arms through the reeds. It was no good. This was true grief. Forgetting herself, she took a deep lungful of water and convulsed as her lungs hurled it out. Only more turbid muck flooded down to replace it.

She was drowning. It didn't matter. First Ban, then Lancelot, and now Elaine. She was drowning. Unless she touched his flesh, her child's flesh, nothing mattered. She was drowning.

A hand—she felt a hand—it grasped her, pulled her forth—not a child's hand, but a crone's, a bent old woman, her muscles like yarn on twiglike bones.

"Child, what manner of devil possesses you?" the abbess asked.

Elaine yanked her hand away and spat at the woman. Mary had not heard her prayer. Mary had mocked her, had taken her child. Elaine screamed. The sound came out in bubbling blood. She tried to throw herself back into the marsh but the ground swept up to strike her.

The abbess knelt, setting a knee on her back. "Rest, child. We will cast the demon out. You will heal. You will be yourself again."

Elaine's hiss gushed mud through her teeth.

"In nomine patri, et filio, et spiritus sanctus . . ."

He dreamed. Even infants dream. Infants only dream.

There had been waters that bore him before—the waters beneath Mother's thundering heart, the waters beneath Father's thundering sky. They had borne him from one world to the next. Now he dreamed new waters—as soft as swaddling and as deep as an old woman's gaze. The waters bore him to the next world, an old place but utterly new. . . .

2

Boyhood

He got up early. The sun slept beneath black hills. Before dawn, the lake looked like gold, liquid gold. Little waves caught the sun before the sky did.

Lancelot loved the gloaming. That was what Aunt Brigid called it. The gloaming—when day surrendered to night or night surrendered to day, the time when darkness and light were in communion and you didn't know which was which. Lancelot loved to crawl from his pallet during the morning gloaming. Adults ruled the evening, but the morning—before the cock and the kettle—was all Lancelot's.

He was barefoot. Shoes were cruel. Why cut off an animal's skin to cover human skin and bring blisters? Grass was made to slide between toes. Soles were made to be hard and full of the color of the stuff they stepped on. Lancelot's soles were green. There was a lot of grass in Avalon.

He ran across it. Dew splashed. Every leaf carried ten drops. Every drop was cold with night. They gleamed like diamonds, but soft. Lancelot ran beneath the apple trees—pretty, fierce little trees. They tried to be gnarled like oaks and lacy like wild carrots, but they were apple trees—white in spring and green in summer and red in fall and white again in winter.

How the winters passed, like the darkness when eyes blink. Twelve of them already. Lancelot grew all the while, but he marked time in the apple trees, not in his own blooming flesh.

He ran out beyond them. Not apple trees, not oaks bore the long slender boughs he wished. What sword is crooked like an oak branch? Only birches had swords in them. Lancelot leapt up to one and broke free a branch—a dead branch. Aunt Brigid had taught him not to break the green ones. He snapped off twigs and stripped old bark and lashed the sword in the air. It made a whistling sound like steel.

Here was a sword, a balanced blade meant to strike with deadly precision. Lancelot lunged. His blade caught upon his foe's. Lancelot need not retreat. His swordsmanship was peerless. He drove on, imbuing the steel with the strength of his arm and shoulder and back. His opponent could not fend such an attack and staggered backward. With a brilliant parry and riposte, Lancelot blocked the man's next and best stroke and brought his sword up to pierce his heart.

Lancelot strode onward, disinterested. He dragged the stick-sword from the fallen form, wiped it languidly on the tall grass, and slid it into a dreamed scabbard at his sword belt. He strolled toward the lake.

There was a place along the shore, what Lancelot called the Enchanted Place (he confided in no one about its existence, let alone its location) where the windblown waves of the lake swept onto a submerged burl of riddled rock. Holes in the stone produced small, animate sprays of water. Fast, fluid, chaotic, the jets were a whole band of foes. They trained Lancelot, too. He was a prince, after all, the only heir to the throne of Benwick, a city sacked by Claudas. If Lancelot did not learn to fight, he could never regain his lost heritage. The Enchanted Place trained him.

Lancelot strode out upon the burl. He stood there in the midst of the rocky holes and gathered his will. In fitful surges, little geysers rose around him. Never predictable, always fleeting, the small sprays challenged him, honed his knightly reflexes. They were not wellsprings but Claudas's men. He whirled, slashing open the belly of an invader—cutting the bastard in two before the column of water could fall again.

The first year, it had been the best he could do to turn and slay each liquid menace as it vaulted up around him. Now, he was so fast, his very gaze seemed to call forth the water, compelling the flood to fight according to his wishes.

That was the true knight—a man who not only could defeat another warrior but could make the foe fight as he wished him to.

Lancelot spun, his sword quick but his eyes quicker. He severed one column of water, stoppered a second before it could vent, and he stared a third into being. It was almost as if the water were a living creature, responding to his wishes.

Lancelot soon grew bored. Young men often do. He abandoned his watery tutors for stony ones.

The Enchanted Place was near a quarry of white stone—the compacted shells and bones of sea creatures. Cut and stacked, the dead made beautiful buildings.

Dripping from his encounter with the sea, Lancelot trooped across the wet sand and up a long, low embankment. His feet left perfect prints on the slanting stones. He climbed the rocky edge of the quarry and stared down.

There, stonecutters labored like ants—tireless and terse. Picks chuffed loudly, and saws ground stone. Figures trundled, slabs of rock clutched in powdery fingers. Gravid was the word

Aunt Brigid used for them. They stooped under their loads, bowlegged, driven into the earth. For all their stern labor, though, they were friends of Lancelot and played his games.

"Ho, there, my people," called Lancelot, trying to make his voice boom, "how fares the digging?"

They stopped, to a man, and looked up. Eyes twinkled beneath gray brows. Lips tugged into smiles under thickets of whisker. They bowed where they stood, and one of them cried, "It is the prince!" Aunt Brigid had told them of Lancelot's arrival—city in flames, father dead, mother deranged—and all these burdens borne on such young shoulders. From that day on, Lancelot had become the "prince" among them. "Work goes well, Master. Two weeks, and we'll have all the stones for the new cauldron."

"Aunt Brigid says it will be haunted," Lancelot replied. "All those sea creatures cradling flames."

The cutter replied with a deferential nod. "All of Avalon is haunted, Master. And let it always be so."

"Yes," Lancelot agreed, though his mind was already elsewhere.

On another day, he might have descended into the quarry and played a game of courtly politics among the dust and rocks. As the Enchanted Place taught him how to deal with enemies, this quarry taught him how to deal with friends. Today, though, he itched to be away. Talk of the new cauldron made him wish to see the old one. It was bronze and ancient, so green and mantled in corrosion that it seemed a living thing. Already, Lancelot could sense it, there, in the distant hills.

"Thank you for your labors, my people. I must go now, to inspect the former cauldron."

They bowed deeply again. One even doffed a dusty cap in an elaborate flourish.

Lancelot smiled as he climbed. He strode among the heather, careful not to crush it beneath his feet. As thick and green as his calluses were, he could sense the death of a single heather bloom underfoot. Such sensations grieved him.

Life is for the living, said Aunt Brigid. *Never, never enslave a living thing, Lancelot. If you must, enslave those who are dead, using the past to make the present better. In the end, we all live in the present, and if every present moment is full of living, then there will be no atrocities, past or future. Life is for the living.*

It was more than advice, more even than a credo. It was the pulse of Lancelot's blood. Why have a heart except to beat wildly? Why have an arm except to battle ceaselessly? Why have a mind except to learn endlessly?

He ascended, not panting in the slightest. The cauldron drew him up. His bare feet easily scaled the jagged black hillside. Already, the quarry with its odd little men was a distant memory. Already the Enchanted Place was forgotten. Only that wide green bowl, couched upon the soaring hill, existed.

It was a sacred place, a sacrificial place. Folk brought fine things here and knelt in prayer and relinquished their hold. For many, it was gold or jewels that slid down the blackened belly of the cauldron, awakening fire within. For Aunt Brigid, it was the green limbs she had forbidden him to crack loose, and a fish she had brought forth from her nets, and a large bundle of heather. These were her greatest treasures, and she offered them to the cauldron. Ever the sacrifices came, ever the prayers rose heavenward with the smoke, ever the fire burned. Once in a great while, a poor soul would hurl him- or herself into the flame, feeding it, and rise again in ash.

How desperate must life become to give it up in a quick rush of fire?

Life is for the living.

Lancelot reached the verdigris-covered cauldron and the wide, level ground around it. Smoke rose blackly from within the great bowl—a sacrifice, a new sacrifice in flesh.

Lancelot went to his knees. He bowed his head. The heat of the cauldron mantled his hair and shoulders. He understood the symbolism. Even to approach a divine presence, one had to sacrifice something dear, and perhaps even oneself. Always before, he had approached the cauldron with Aunt Brigid beside him, and a full entourage with her. Today, he approached alone.

What had he to sacrifice? He was poor, as poor as Aunt Brigid, who offered mere flowers and sticks. Remaining bowed, Lancelot reached to his belt and pulled forth the birch branch. He dragged it before him and stared intently at its gray wood. If only this were a true sword, it would be worthy of the cauldron, but a twig? Dry and gray?

I have nothing to offer.

"Your dreams made that stick into something," came Aunt Brigid's voice.

Lancelot remained on his knees but glanced toward her.

Aunt Brigid stood at the edge of the cauldron platform. She wore a travel gown, once blue but now the color of dust, a braid belt, and sandals, which she even now slid from her feet. She drew back the cowl of her gown, letting sunlight upon gray hair. Wisdom so shone in her eyes that it eclipsed her age. Lancelot could not have guessed whether she was old or young, but he knew she was beautiful. In her arms, she bore faggots and fish and flowers. "If it means much to you, it means much to the cauldron."

Had she heard him? Had he spoken aloud?

Lancelot dropped his gaze. "I want to offer something real, not just a dream."

"Dreams are real," she replied. "Especially when they are sacrificed."

"Then why do you offer these things, and not your dreams?"

"These things are my dreams," she approached reverently, her feet easing down upon each footprint he had left. A faraway look came to those wise eyes.

"Once I dwelt along a wider shore, a deeper sea. I had a man I loved and worshiped. He worshiped me. A fisherman, he plied his nets among the rocks and sharks. He cast and trolled and hauled until his gunwales brimmed. At dark on shore I built a fire to bring his boat back home. . . ." She lifted the bundled wood, kissed it, and sent it sliding down into the cauldron. Fire eagerly mantled the twine. It burned away. Sticks rolled apart. They crackled with sap. The sound grew to a continuous roar, like waves on a beach. "All night I cut and piled the boughs to reach above the foam, but firelight failed where he had gone. At dawn I let the flame burn down and watched in vain. Two nights of fire and fear, enough to raise a savior, but not my dear beloved. At last, waves brought him ashore aboard a boat so full of fish it nearly swamped. . . ." She slid the fish into the cauldron, and it sent up a black plume of smoke. "I kissed his lips—so cold. I pulled him from the boat and wept. I carried what was left of him toward the green plateau. My skirts collected heather in. On his grave I laid the boughs that volunteered to mourn with me. . . ." She set the bouquet of heather in the cauldron and watched it roll into the fire. Then, turning toward Lancelot, she said, "Possessions do not matter, boy, but what you love."

The words came immediately from Lancelot's lips. "I love Avalon. I know you say I am prince of Benwick, that I am destined to be a great knight in Camelot, that I must learn to read and bargain, fight and work, for the world calls me. But more than anything else, I love this place."

Aunt Brigid's eyes were profound. "Give your sword, then, Lancelot. As great as you will be at war, be willing to sacrifice that greatness for Avalon."

"I am willing." He rose at last. The prince of Benwick straightened his neck and back and stood like a man. He tossed the stick into the cauldron and watched it flare, red like a wound. Fire consumed it in eager moments, and the sword was gone.

He dreamed that night, as every night.

Like Apollo of old, Lancelot rode the sun down on its underworld journey. It sank into the lake and blazed against the quenching flood. Lancelot blazed too. He clung to the chariot of the sun, inundated, and stared at the weird world around.

Some night, he would swim these somnolent depths and rise remembering all. Some night, but not tonight.

The tides chanted his memories away, and then his mind away, and then his being away. He floated to the surface of dream and bobbed there like a dead man. The sun rose from the lake without him. Remembering nothing, Lancelot awoke.

3

Of Arms and Armor

Six summers came and went.

As Lancelot grew, Aunt Brigid's home shrank. He and the door lintel had regular clashes. This morning was no exception.

"Damn!" he barked, reeling out into the autumn morning. Lanky legs staggered—he had the height of a man, but not yet the width—and he crashed down. Lancelot clutched his head, blond shag bunching out between his fingers. He rocked gently, trying to roll both eyes back forward. "Damn it to hell!"

"Damn what to hell, dear?" asked Aunt Brigid mildly as she emerged from the same doorway.

Lancelot growled. "That damned lintel. I might as well hire a villein to stand there with a sledge and smash me every time I come out."

"So, it's training, then?" teased Aunt Brigid. She wore her gardening clothes—knees stiff with mud and back bleached from sun. It was not a kneeling day today, though. It was an apple—picking day. She walked along the front wall of the cottage, her hands drifting fondly through the ivy there before finding an old and rickety ladder. "And the swearing is training, too?"

Trying to make his smile look like a scowl, Lancelot climbed to his feet and dusted off burlap trousers. "Warriors swear, Auntie."

"A warrior. Hmm." She gave him an appraising look. "A warrior with no armor."

Lancelot clutched the homespun shirt to his young chest. "Courage is my armor."

A twinkle lit Brigid's eye as she pulled bushel baskets from a shed and trundled up the path to their orchard. "Courage is a Gaulish word. It means 'full of heart.' Your heart can't be your armor. And what sword have you got, Prince? A dead stick?"

"This sword," Lancelot replied. He brandished an old pruning knife, its blade curved and round tipped, for slicing apple stems but not thumbs.

Brigid nodded gravely and motioned him to follow. "There's a whole nation of vicious fruits ahead, boy. It'll take courage—and a strong back—to defeat them."

Lancelot gave a laugh. "I've slain legions of carrots. I do not fear apples."

Brigid plucked the first fruit of the day, held it up beside her face, and smiled. " 'The serpent told me to eat of it, and I ate. . . .' "

He would have laughed, but Lancelot was struck dumb by sudden gladness. Here was a woman who had fed and clothed and sheltered him, had raised him as her own son and bestowed on him wealth in the midst of poverty, had taught him to read in Latin, Celtic, and Germanic, had even encouraged his constant training—and she was witty too. Aunt Brigid's lintels could be damned to hell, but let the woman herself live forever right here on Avalon.

Lancelot attacked the trees with a vengeance. He filled the first bushel in mere minutes. Work slowed to a more sustainable pace thereafter. Soon, as Aunt Brigid toiled among the low branches, Lancelot ascended to the treetops. There, the sun shone hot. His shirt clung to a sweaty back, and Lancelot drew it off and flung it down. Cool air brushed across his youthful physique.

In a steady rhythm of cutting and busheling, Lancelot worked over the tallest tree in the little orchard. Aunt Brigid labored nearby, beneath the thick foliage. They spoke little and glimpsed each other less, though Lancelot felt his aunt's presence in the songs she hummed, quiet on the wind.

As he stood there, he realized he loved his life.

Though in some fabled past he had been a prince, he excelled at being a peasant. He might pine after his dead father and demented mother, but the arms that had sheltered him belonged to Aunt Brigid. He trained to be a warrior, yes, but he craved most of all the peace of this place.

Lancelot stopped cutting apples free and took a deep breath. The scent of leaves—verdant and sharp—mixed with the sweet fragrance of apples. He could stay here, on this ladder at the height of the orchard, forever.

The orchard had grown quiet. Aunt Brigid's humming had stopped.

"Where is the music to lighten this load?" called Lancelot, but no response came. "I could sing, but warriors know only bawdy songs." Still, no response. A breeze told the tale: leek stew, fragrant among the tumbling odors of wood smoke. Lancelot hurled out his free hand and rolled his eyes. "I see. Get the lad to harvest the apples, and then sneak away for some stew. Gluttony!" He smiled tightly, descended the ladder, and set down the bushel basket. He took another breath, and his jaw tingled with the salty scent of the stew. "This war on apples, waged single-handed, has given me an appetite." He raised the apple knife in mock challenge. "You'd better have made enough for two."

Lancelot descended the orchard path. A coil of gray smoke issued from the chimney. Only when Aunt Brigid cooked did the fireplace burn so. She had some explaining to do, and some feeding. Lancelot had the appetite of bones trying to grow muscle.

Flinging back the cottage door, he stepped through. He forgot to duck. The lintel struck his head and dropped him like a stone—except for all the thrashing. "Damn that thing! Damn it to hell!"

As Lancelot's vision cleared, he made out Aunt Brigid at the hearth, stirring a broad black kettle that hung above the fire. The blaze had been well-stoked with kindling and larger logs. Something was wrong with Aunt Brigid, though. She stood stiffly, her head bent down. She did not even meet Lancelot's gaze.

"So," came a new voice, harsh with the accent of the Saxons, "you've got a kid after all. Should have told me when I asked. Keep stirring. I don't want my stew ruined."

Lancelot turned toward the sound. In the single chair they owned sat a man—a warrior in full armor. Lancelot's eyes grew wide at the sight of the suit. From sollerets to gorget, it was an amazing construct of metal. Gauntlets and helm rested on the table. Most impressive of all, though, was the long, elegant sword lying across the man's lap.

"A knight!" Lancelot breathed. "A knight of the Round Table."

The warrior shot him a narrow look, and then grinned. "Yeah, that's it. A knight of the Round Table."

Lancelot felt as if he had been struck in the head again. "I can't believe it! A knight in Avalon, and we're hosting him."

"It's rude to stare at company," the man rumbled.

Lancelot bowed low. "Forgive me, great knight—you have not told us your name."

"I have not," agreed the warrior.

Aunt Brigid spoke for the first time. "You'd best return to picking apples, child."

"But I want to speak with this knight, to sup with him—"

"Listen to your mother, boy. There's not enough stew for my appetite and yours." The warrior lifted the sword ever so slightly from his legs, and it quavered hungrily. "A knight of the Round Table has many fierce appetites."

Many fierce appetites. The words ran through Lancelot like cold water.

He nodded gravely. He understood what this man wanted. It was a thing never mentioned in his studies, but Lancelot had a man's body, and he understood. Understanding gave him new eyes. Though once fine, the suit of armor had endured too many blows with too little repair. Ring-mail frayed. Plate mail was, here and there, riven. Every piece bore countless scars, and every scar bore grime.

"Get going," the warrior barked, beginning to rise. He jabbed a finger at his helm. "The last man who made me wait gave me his head."

Glancing at the battered helmet, Lancelot sucked in a breath. Only then did he smell, mixed among the odors of stew, the sharp fetor of unwashed flesh. This man was certainly not a member of the Round Table. Either he had stolen arms and armor from a true knight or, worse, had been a true knight and now had fallen. His mismatched armor told of past murders, and his quivering sword promised future ones. Lancelot knew what this man intended for Aunt Brigid, and what he himself must do.

He lifted his hands in a gesture of surrender and backed away. "Forgive my slowness, good knight. I only wished to show you my sword."

Aunt Brigid's eyes flashed in warning.

The warrior looked equally alarmed. "You have a sword?"

Lancelot smiled disarmingly and shrugged. "As much a sword as we need hereabouts." He lifted the pruning knife. It seemed absurdly small beside the sword in the warrior's hand, but at least the knife shone with use. "We have many sinister apples. Some as big as your heart."

The warrior let out a single blast of a laugh and dropped heavily back into his seat. The curved blade gleamed in his eyes.

Lancelot flipped it over in his hand, catching it deftly by its rounded tip and offered it handle-first to the warrior. "What do you think of it?"

The warrior hesitated only a moment—who would not take a weapon from a potential foe? He took the blade in his off-hand, keeping his sword ready all the while. His laughter had stopped now, and he looked over the small, worn knife. "It suits you," he growled. "No more stalling, now. Get back to work."

Lancelot leaned in, well within the arc of the man's sword, and reached out with one hand. "I'll need my knife."

The man grunted and flipped the blade over. He caught

the rounded tip in his fingers and extended the knife handle first.

Lancelot grasped the handle firmly and lunged, drawing the sharp curve of the blade across the warrior's throat. He dragged the steel deep, through skin and muscle, and heard the cluck and hiss of the windpipe severing. A red spray followed the stroke.

The warrior tried to roar, but only gurgled. He tried to slay the young man, but Lancelot had hurled himself back. Before the warrior could rise, he was dead. He slumped in the chair.

Lancelot rolled away from the crimson man and came to a halt on the rush-strewn floor. Blood mantled him.

Aunt Brigid rushed up to kneel beside him. "Lancelot, what have you done?"

Panting, he lifted his streaming face. "I have unmade a false knight, and have made a true one."

"Yes," she said, grave eyes staring at the dead form. "I believe you have. This is not child's play anymore. You've fought your first battle, and you have killed. You will need to take care of this." She nodded toward the body.

"Yes," Lancelot replied.

"And when you are done, you must begin your true training. There is a man, one I will introduce you to. He will teach you what you need to know."

The apples waited another day on the tree. Aunt Brigid prayed over the body, washed it, and layered it with spices. Lancelot dug.

He'd chosen a high spot away from water—he would not have this man's rot getting into their well or their stream. He dug deep, saving aside the fieldstone to cover the grave. The wolves would not dig it up. A fury had taken hold of him. The boy who had harvested apples that morning was as dead as the warrior himself. Lancelot was burying both of them.

The sun sank below black hills as Lancelot threw the last spade of earth out of the hole. He climbed up the side, planted the shovel, and descended the hill. A candle gleamed in the cottage window. Lancelot shook out his arms and brushed the grit from his trousers. He passed through the orchard gate.

Aunt Brigid waited in the gloaming beyond. She pointed down at a bundle of bloodied rushes. "Take those first. His blood should be buried with him."

"Yes," Lancelot said, lifting the bundle.

"And wash yourself in the lake before you come to bear him away."

"Yes," Lancelot replied.

After lining the base of the grave with the bloodied rushes, Lancelot went to the lake, washed, and returned to the cottage. Upon the table lay the body, clean and garbed in Lancelot's own sleeping gown.

Lancelot blinked. "You gave him my gown?"

"It is a small price for the armor and sword he gives to you."

His armor and sword: Lancelot glanced toward them—a filthy, ragged jumble of metal in the corner. They had once been fine, and they soon would be fine again. He would repair them and grow into them. He would train until sword and armor were part of his own body.

With a final, reverent "Yes," Lancelot bowed down to lift the body. Hauling the man over his shoulder, Lancelot strode toward the door. This time, he remembered to duck, and carried the dead man out into the dark night.

The sun had quit the world before he reached the grave. Cold winds stole the last heat from the grass. Lancelot lowered the body, lifted his shovel, and set to his dark work. Before the waning gibbous rose to stare, the nameless warrior had been covered in a foot of soil. Well after midnight, the last stone settled on the spot.

Lancelot went to the lake to bathe again. He returned to the hovel. Aunt Brigid was deeply asleep on her pallet. Careful not to shift the pile of armor, Lancelot drew forth the sword. Battered and notched, dull and filthy—but Lancelot glimpsed its fine lines even so. Hunting up a rag, he began to clean the sword. His sword.

His friends, the waters, were there. All the while that he worked the sword, the waters worked him.

They bore him to dreaming, and he dreamed an eager throng around him, country folk he knew. They stared at the tarnished sword and planished armor. They walked in gravid rows past the rocky cairn. When they turned to Lancelot, though, their bright-beaming eyes burned away his taint.

Rapt in dream, Lancelot could not have known the light in those eyes was merely reflected from the light in his own.

4

Chivalry in Avalon

A herd of horses grazed fretfully on the grassy hillside. Though their heads were lowered to eat, their ears were raised to hear. They sensed a predator in the sedge.

Lancelot was the predator. It was no wonder they sensed him; his armor clinked. It glinted through the sedge where he hid. Yes, he loved the suit. He'd polished it to a fervid gleam, had repaired every loop of mail, had buffed away every sword scar, had even mended the rents with small metal plates. The putrid armor of the putrid warrior had been transformed into a mirror-bright suit, but who would wear such a thing when stalking horses?

"Must I wear this, Master?" asked Lancelot in a hushed whisper.

The man beside him grunted. Red-haired and ruddy-skinned, Mars Smetrius was a fiery fellow. His scarlet waistcoat shone with gold medallions. "Of course you must wear it. It is your skin. Armor is your skin, and that blade at your waist, it is your all. Until they become part of you, as vital as heart or liver, you will never wield them with real power."

"But what use is a sword against a horse?" Lancelot protested. "Especially one I want to break? One I want to ride? And what use is all this armor?"

Digging the leather toes of his boots into the soft ground, Master Smetrius confessed. "The sword'll do you little good. Your truest weapon in this battle is your rope. As to the rest, though, you'll be full-armored as you ride, and full-armored as you mount, so best get used to it all now."

Fingering the rope at his belt, Lancelot nodded deeply. "I'll have a horse today. A big, powerful war-horse today."

A red brow lifted. "Have at it then, boy."

Bristling a little at that word, Lancelot eased himself forward across the grass. He gathered his muscles like a great cat preparing to spring. Such a hunter, though, would leap upon the smallest or weakest beast. Lancelot wanted the strongest—the stallion at the center of the herd.

He watched the great white steed. Its withers rose easily two hands above any other beast's. The glorious creature snorted, sniffed the air, and pawed the ground in anticipation. It sensed Lancelot's presence, though he lay downwind. A precocious creature, pure white amid piebald mares and foals. Those lesser horses would be the real problem. They would alert the stallion, and all of them would charge away across the hillside. Though Lancelot was extraordinarily quick, he would be no match for a herd of horses. Somehow, he had to inspire them to stay instead of run.

One stallion surrounded by mares and foals . . .

Lancelot drew the rope from his belt and uncoiled it. He tied a sliding loop in one end, as Master Smetrius had taught him to do, and edged nearer. He wanted that stallion, but to get it, he would have to start with a foal.

One such creature, gawky on its deerlike legs, grazed

nearby. It wandered away from its mare, seeking longer, greener grass. Near the herd, the ground was trammeled, but Lancelot lay within a thick tuft of blades. In the curling spaces of the leaves, he watched the colt browse nearer. Its brown eyes blinked as it nibbled the ground. A glint of steel showed in those eyes. The foal lifted its head, too slowly.

Lancelot surged up. The loop of rope whirled once and arced out, striking the animal behind the ears. Letting out a shriek, the horse reared back. The braid slid down its mane. With a flip, Lancelot brought the slipknot in under the beast's throatlatch. A yank tightened the noose. Bucking and wailing, the foal staggered to get away. It flung its head back and yanked Lancelot to his feet.

The screams of the foal unnerved the herd, and the appearance of this shiny man sent them charging away down the hill. Where once fifty horses had stood, now only rags of grass tumbled in the air.

Lancelot ignored their exodus, busy pinning the rope under his mailed foot. He drew the slack to his opposite shoulder and gripped it in a strong hand. The foal leapt in panic. It flailed like a landed fish. Lancelot swiftly fashioned another sliding loop at the far end of the rope.

He paid no heed to the raucous belly laughter coming from Master Smetrius down the slope. "You're going to ride that one, eh? In two years, yes? And it'll graze away garden and hillside in the meanwhile! Quite a warrior's steed you've chosen, lad! Perhaps you'll choose a jackstraw for your lance."

Paying out the line, Lancelot clenched his teeth against his master's shouts. The expression began as a grimace and finished as a smile. A rising thunder in the ground announced the return of one of the horses.

She came to the top of the hill, her mane tossing angrily as she stared down at her trapped foal. Maternal instinct had won the day. It did not matter that a shiny man stood upon the hillside, wielding the rope-magic that had enslaved countless generations of horses. It mattered only that her foal was the one trapped, bleating in terror. Like a bull, the mare lowered her head, laid her ears back, and snorted. She pawed the ground with a black hoof before rushing down the slope. Forelock first, she barged toward the man who had trapped her colt.

Lancelot held his ground, one foot keeping the colt in place and one hand lifting the next loop. He would have to time this precisely, or the mare would veer toward him.

The charging creature converged.

Lancelot stood stalwart.

Master Smetrius ceased his laughter.

The horse barreled into Lancelot—except that he was no longer there. Like silver lightning, he sidestepped the rushing creature. Only his hand remained in the space, trailing the loop. It wrapped around the mare's neck. Lancelot let the line pay out as the creature barged past. He stepped off the rope and grasped it in his hands. He had no hope of stopping the beast's charge, only of weighting the line so the mare didn't break her own foal's neck.

All the slack suddenly yanked from the line. The horse dragged Lancelot and the foal. Hurled to his face, Lancelot held on. Grass smeared across his polished armor. He bumped along the ground, determined not to let the mare loose. Meanwhile, his free hand lashed a dagger at the rope that held the colt. Three strikes. Braids of hemp severed. Five strikes. The cord was nearly cut through. Eight, and the rope snapped. The foal, freed from its mother's charge, foundered back and away from the silver man.

Master Smetrius was laughing again. "Good, soldier!

Good. You've found yourself a roadworthy horse, and perhaps battle-worthy, too! She'll be all yours, if only you can break her! It seems she has designs on breaking you."

The mare had finished her charge. She circled long and low, readying herself for another attack. She saw then that her foal was free, stumbling down the grassy hillside toward her. Anger turned to fear. She no longer wanted to attack the silver man, but to escape him. Her foal, still wearing the severed rope, trotted to her, nuzzled her cheek, and set off alongside her. They cried with plaintive equine wails.

Hauling backward on the line, he prevented the mare from breaking into a gallop, but could do little else. The mare and her foal bounced him over a couple acres. Still, they would not escape him, and they knew it. The terror of that realization spilled through their teeth.

While Lancelot held the line, coiled around his left arm, he worked over the severed end of rope. He wasn't finished. Far from it. He tied another slipknot and drew the rope out into a wide ring. If he missed the next time, it could be his death.

The mare let out a long, keen whicker, and the foal echoed it. Their cries rose on the wind. It was an irresistible sound, the distress of mate and child. Right on cue, the familiar thunder of hooves rose beyond the hilltop.

Lancelot dragged on the mare, pulling creature and colt nearer.

Above them, the great stallion appeared. He was massive. Against the quicksilver sky, the horse seemed black, though Lancelot knew his true color.

"That's the one," he said to himself.

The stallion reared. Fore hooves flashed as they spun and lips peeled back from wide, white teeth. The beast's eyes gleamed like beads of mercury. He came to ground, hooves no sooner touching than he leapt into a gallop down the hill.

Lancelot took an involuntary step back. He readied the loop in one hand and, with the other, twisted a knife into the cord that held the mare.

The stallion seemed a white comet, flaming toward him. No armor could blunt those hooves. Only a sword could cease that charge. Lancelot's hands strayed nowhere near his blade. He had come to break the beast, not to slay him.

With a weighty crash, the stallion arrived. Even nimble-footed Lancelot could not dodge fast enough. The horse's shoulder rammed his own. He flipped sideways, a straw man on the wind. His armor rang like bells as he spun above the grass. There came a strange moment of peace before impact, and then, no impact. Instead, the rope in Lancelot's hand and around his wrist snapped tight. It yanked him down the slope yet again, but not before the rope knotted around his dagger. Cords severed. The rope broke. The mare ran free.

Lancelot, meanwhile, was dragged behind pounding hooves. He'd managed to hold onto his dagger even as his other hand twisted within the vise of the rope. The stallion did not slacken his speed. He ran full-out, hauling his supposed captor across the rock-strewn grass.

This was the beast he wanted. The foal and mare had been bait. Lancelot had challenged the stallion's dominance. One of them would emerge the champion, and the other would be broken.

Even as grasses shouted against Lancelot's ears, he heard the hoots of Master Smetrius. "You've got him now, boy. Hold on! It's just a game to see if you can take more knocks than he can give!"

Insightful words, spoken by one far removed from the knocks.

A stone pounded Lancelot's head. Ringing numbness and a spray of blood followed. Lancelot held on. Nothing would slow this steed. That's why Lancelot had chosen him. The greater the prize, the greater the struggle. That insight was banged away by another stone. The smell of blood filled Lancelot's nose. He ducked his head. This thing meant to kill him, or kill himself trying. The creature would rather die than be broken. Again, it was why Lancelot had chosen him, but even this young man understood tragedy. A horse who would rather die than be broken pitted against a man who would rather die than be broken—someone was going to die.

It is the way of Mars, came a voice in his head. Lancelot never referred to his master by his first name, and that more than anything else told him this was the voice of another. *Someone always must die. How foolish to break a horse or be broken by him.*

Lancelot had had enough advice. *I'm the one clinging to this horse!*

No. I am. I am Epona, goddess of horses.

Amid the pummeling, Lancelot could not help answering. *Then you are on the horse's side. You want to break me.*

I want to keep you from breaking this steed.

Lancelot replied. *Either he is broken, or I am.*

Why must either of you be broken?

Lancelot felt the brief, bruising bark of rocks against his shoulder, but his body somehow was miles away. *I seek to be a knight. Knights ride horses. Unbroken horses cannot be ridden—*

You are wrong. You follow your master. He wants only a broad and placid back. He is content to ride a broken thing into battle. You want more. You want a horse that is an ally, a friend.

At those words, Lancelot almost lost hold of the rope. Yes,

he wanted his steed to be no mere pack mule, but a noble comrade. *Speak a quick alternative. I am dying.*

Let go, was the response. *Let go of the rope.*

Then I will lose my captive.

No captive can ever be an ally.

Lancelot let go. He rolled, bloodied and bruised, amid the sedges of the hillside. With small green hands, grass wiped his face clean. He tumbled to a halt near the base of the hill.

The rope lashed onward, trailing the white steed it once had imprisoned.

Aching and confused, Lancelot turned to his side. He clutched his stomach and began to laugh. He felt like vomiting, but laughed.

His mentor shouted, "You let him go? What kind of knight are you? Not a knight at all—not a mounted warrior! Roped three horses this day, and let all three go."

Lancelot didn't care.

"Yes, you're a great fighter Lancelot, but until you can fight from horseback, you're nothing. You're infantry." The master's voice grew slowly louder as he climbed the hillside.

Master Smetrius jabbed Lancelot in the back—only it wasn't him. The sensation was too soft, too wet, too bristly.

Lancelot rose and turned. He came eye-to-eye with the white stallion.

The beast had returned, soundless. He could easily trample Lancelot, but he did not. He could dash his brain out with one stroke of a hoof, but no. Lancelot now saw the ravages his rope had done to the horse's neck, cutting through fur and skin to bring out bright-red blood. The steed was as battered by the incident as Lancelot was.

Lancelot reached out. He grasped the crimson cord and lifted it slowly from the stallion's neck. The horse nodded, as if in thanks, and pawed the ground. Despite the capture, despite the bloodshed, this creature was unbowed.

What is your name? wondered Lancelot to himself. He felt immediately foolish, but a name came to him: *Rasa*. "Rasa," repeated Lancelot aloud. "I am Lancelot. I seek to be a knight. I seek a horse—an ally—worthy of my quest."

Rasa nodded with strange comprehension, and Lancelot got the distinct impression the creature mentally repeated his name.

Lancelot blurted, "It is good to have an ally, Rasa."

The stallion only snorted and whickered.

Lancelot answered with a snort, and then collapsed.

Rasa came to him in that watery place. As water had borne Lancelot in the past, world to world, Rasa would bear him in the future.

Rasa spoke: Have I slain you, young warrior?

I am slain, great steed.

I am as well.

Then we are spirit folk and well suited for each other. We will go, invincible, from world to world: Who can kill us, who are already dead?

You are dreaming, Lancelot.

I am.

I am as well.

5

The Voyage to Camelot

Lancelot reined in Rasa beside the deep, steaming lake of Avalon. He sighed. His breath joined the ghosts dancing above the water.

From the moment he had stepped out of Aunt Brigid's cottage, he had let Avalon imprint on him one last time. The morning dew had gleamed like gold beads on the grass. Fresh-mown thatch, which he himself had hung the day before, had set a sweet scent in the air. Apple blossoms had wrapped the hovel in a white and fragrant embrace. Wood smoke had sent its gray coil up into the wide blue heavens. Lancelot remembered every detail.

A small cough from Aunt Brigid reminded him of one more detail: his passenger.

"Forgive me," Lancelot said huskily. He dismounted, moving gracefully despite his armor. It truly had become his second skin. He lowered his oaken lance—a parting gift from Master Smetrius, carved from a tree that was "older than Christ." Lancelot doffed a gauntlet and extended his hand. "Let me help you."

She slid her fingers into his, her bony and weathered hand at once callused and tender. Lancelot looked into her eyes, and for the first time noticed how old she was. She eased herself to the ground beside him. Small, too—somehow her spiritual stature had always made her seem a giant.

Aunt Brigid averted her gaze, turning to stare out across the water. "There he is."

Lancelot followed her line of sight. A small black figure poled a raft across the misty lake. The image sent a chill through him, though he tried to make light of it. "How much do I pay Charon?"

She grimaced but still would not look at him. "Don't make such jokes. This is a death of sorts, Lancelot. You know that—a crossing from one world into another."

"I know that," he responded, chastened. "It's the world I belong in. Yes, I will always love Avalon, and love you, but I belong among warriors, among knights."

"Do you?" she replied. Her eyes welled with checked emotion. "Do you really belong among warriors and wars?"

"Yes, Aunt Brigid. I do." He watched the boatman pole the raft nearer. It was a heavy barge, fashioned of felled logs tied side-by-side. It would bear him and Rasa to the far shore. "I will not forget you, or this place. You are the only true mother I have known, and this—" he swept his hands out to take in the green-black hills and the high tor "—this has been my home. But now I have to seek my fortune in the wide world. I ride to Camelot to become a knight."

She shook her head intensely. "You are so much more than that, Lancelot."

"I know. I am Prince of Benwick, and should be king, were it not for Claudas—"

"More still," she broke in. She took Lancelot's clean-shaven face in her leathery hands and stared into his eyes. Beneath the peasant's cowl, her face was lined and wizened. "You say you will remember, Lancelot, but there is so much you never even knew. Your heritage. Don't let it lie silent. Let it whisper to you, and listen."

In all the years they had spent together, he had never before seen this desperate edge in her gaze. It was more than the natural grief of a parent for a departing child. There was something unspoken in it.

"Your kingdom's ruin, your father's death, your mother's insanity, your arrival in Avalon—this armor, this horse, this training . . . these things are not random. They intersect, curse and blessing. They form an image you have not yet perceived. An image of what you will be, my son. Grasp it, or in the end, it will grasp you."

Lancelot had no answer except to wrap her in steel-plated arms. Even through the armor, he felt the frailty of her bones and the strength of her heart. He held her that way a long while, allowing her tears on his armor if only to hide his own. At last, he turned and stared into the gaunt face of the boatman.

"He is here," Lancelot said. "I must go."

Aunt Brigid nodded, drawing back.

"I won't forget," he reiterated.

Her mouth formed a grim line. "It is not enough. You must *remember*."

Reaching into the satchel beneath his breastplate, Lancelot retrieved a silver piece and surrendered it to the boatman.

The lean fellow bit the coin, pocketed it, and waved Lancelot and Rasa aboard the raft. The young warrior couched his lance, lifted the reins from the saddle, and led his mount. Most horses would have shied from the uneasy footing of the raft, but Rasa had an almost human wisdom to him. He stomped onto the logs and stood patiently beside his man.

"Good-bye, Aunt Brigid. Good-bye, Avalon."

"Farewell, Lancelot du Lac," she said sadly.

The boatman set the butt of his pole in the muck and shoved off. Water wrinkled before the craft and broke into little white waves around its sides. Pulling the pole from the bottom, the boatman positioned it again and drove the raft onward.

Standing beside Rasa, Lancelot did not look back. He didn't need to. Avalon and Aunt Brigid were fixed forever in his mind.

No sooner had Lancelot slipped away in the fog of Avalon than Brigid, Mistress of the Mists, fell to her knees beside the flood. She let her peasant's cloak slough from her shoulders and settle about her. Also, she doffed the semblance of age that she had ever worn in Lancelot's presence. Where once an old crone had stood, now a young and powerful woman knelt beside the flood. She was utterly transformed in every outward way except her tears.

After a score of years, she at last understood how Elaine of Benwick had been driven mad by the loss of her child.

Darkness had fallen long before Lancelot reached Camelot, but the city so shone beneath the brooding heavens that he needed no sun. Camelot was a promise in white stone. Wide, beautiful, pristine, and elegant, it seemed sculpted of cloud, an ethereal city chained to the hills of Cadbury.

Through its heavenly gates flocked tens of thousands of darkling souls, avatars of a benighted land. Lancelot was one of them. He had come for knighthood. The rest, it seemed, came for celebration. Every mouth chattered of Arthur's great victory. Every eye glowed with remembered battle and hoped-for peace. Villein and serf, duke and count, knight and priest, foot-sore and saddle-sore, they flocked to Camelot. Lancelot rode in their midst. Never before had he seen so many people. The sensation exhilarated him. Not a soul there knew his name, of course, but he felt as though they had thronged the high road to welcome him.

The human flood approached massive walls, well founded on gigantic glacial stones. The boulders had been dragged some unimaginable distance and bedded deep. Still larger stones paved the thresholds of Camelot's seven gates. Lancelot approached one such gate. Though Rasa had been surefooted upon the boatman's raft, he stomped and shied on the threshold. Lancelot did not yank the rein—he trusted Rasa too much—but only patted his neck gently and urged him onward. Rasa responded with a brisk canter, wishing to be through the arched gate and beneath the massive portcullises as quickly as possible. The shadow of the wall fell cold upon them both.

Lancelot rode watchfully. In one gauntlet, he clutched a see from Aunt Brigid, sealed by some lofty signet. She had promised it would grant him passage into the city. In the other, he held a small purse that contained enough coin to bribe the gate guards. He had expected to need them both, but needed neither. Lancelot rode unchallenged through the main gate of Camelot.

The arch gave way to open courtyards and happy light. Torches painted every wall golden and tallow made the windows glow. Revelers thronged the streets—tens of thousands of them. In broad avenues they danced to fife and rebec. In narrow lanes they rolled bones or gathered about tavern doors. Thatch and slate rooftops receded in a patterned glow all the way to the palace in their midst.

When Lancelot glimpsed the palace of Camelot, he nearly fell from his saddle. It was an alabaster dream, with white walls and impossibly tall towers. Purportedly, Merlin had designed the palace in a waking delirium. He cast his sketches upon a fire that consumed paper and liberated line so that the whole insubstantial edifice took glowing shape in the midst of the city. Masons both mortal and immortal had then only to stack slabs of rock where the lines bid. So it was said, but lies about Camelot abounded. They did little harm. The city was more splendid in truth than it could have been in lie.

Rasa cantered across brick streets that, in firelight, seemed paved in gold. To either side rose half-timber inns whose wattle and daub were made grand by appointments in bronze. Greater still than lanes and buildings were the folk who conversed in arched doorways or passed wine-jacks amid bowers, or sang of Saxons vanquished and Britons immortal. They were good folk—hearty, hale, happy, and free. Any tyrant could build a glorious city, but only a great and good king could fill it with folk such as these.

Ahead rose a wondrous fountain with three women sculpted at its center—maiden, mother, and crone. The inscription at one edge read fount of the bountiful weirds.

Rasa stepped with gentle insistence through the crowd until he reached the fountain. A frisson of delight swept across the stallion's pelt. He dipped his head for a drink.

Lancelot swung down from the saddle and bowed beside his steed. He scooped a double handful of water. It seemed to laugh delightedly in his grasp. He splashed it to his face and laved away the dust of the road. It was bracingly cold, sweet as only pure water is. Lancelot gazed into the faces of weirds, Celtic deities. Refreshed, he mounted Rasa and nudged the steed back from the water.

A nearby voice from the crowd called up, "You let your horse drink from a sacred spring?"

Lancelot turned toward the voice, his own hair flinging droplets. He blurted, "He's quite a horse."

Stallion and soldier rode on. Ahead, the palace towered amid rampant gardens. These were not manicured continental affairs, but shaggy and wild bowers. Lancelot guided Rasa to a gateway of interlaced antlers. King Arthur was often depicted as antlered, the king with a Celtic mind and a Christian sword. Before the arch, Lancelot dismounted. He led Rasa across the stones, foot and hoof ringing decorously as they went. Before them, the palace's outer wall glowed with torchlight. A young man waited there.

Lancelot bowed awkwardly and drew forth the signeted scroll. "I am Lancelot du Lac, sent by Brigid of Avalon to seek counsel with King Arthur."

The young man, slim in plain shift, did not take the scroll. "Oats or hay?"

Lancelot blinked. He peered at the scroll in his hand, wondering why it had been rejected. "I am Lancelot du Lac, sent by Brigid—"

"Does your horse want oats or hay?" interrupted the varlet.

Stunned silent, Lancelot glanced toward Rasa, who rolled his eyes and nodded once vigorously. Lancelot nodded in turn. "Oats, of course."

"Thank you," replied the varlet, taking Rasa's reins. "The king, his retinue, his knights, and his warriors yet gather in the great hall. Shall I show you the way?"

Lancelot waved away the suggestion, instead saying to

Rasa, "You eat well. I'll check on you tonight." He left varlet and horse both and strode across the inner bailey.

On its far side, a room gushed light and music and laughter. Lancelot's boots rang on the stones, only too slow to carry him to his destiny. A pair of massive double doors opened from the great hall onto the courtyard. Lancelot stomped up to them, grasped the latches, and hurled them open as though they were barn doors.

Sound and heat spilled out across him. The chamber was filled with warriors and knights. All wore dress armor, lighter and more brilliant than the true armor on Lancelot's shoulders. All had eaten, as evidenced by the long tables loaded with scraps. All had toasted, as shown by their ruddy faces and loose-jointed dancing. Here were the finest folk of King Arthur's court, knights and warriors who had just won a great battle.

They didn't notice Lancelot as he stepped among them. Their dance continued, driven by drum and fife. Lancelot marched past them toward the dais at the room's end, and the throne there.

It was a massive, amazing throne, its posts seeming to delve down to bedrock and its back reaching for the skies. On the capacious seat sat two folk, man and woman, ruler and ruler, side by side.

Lancelot looked first to Arthur in his sable stole with ermine fringe. At thirty, he was a young king, youthful and handsome but wise. Unbowed by the crown that encircled his brow, the brown-bearded monarch gazed with glad but distant eyes on the throng before him. Here was the man who had built Camelot—roads and houses and people, all. Here was the long-lost son of a slaughtered king, who had risen to reclaim what by right belonged to him. Lancelot felt an immediate kinship, and wondered if he would ever be so great as this man.

He averted his eyes from the presence of the king, only to see for the first time Queen Guinevere.

Lancelot stopped where he stood. He did not breathe. Perhaps even his heart ceased to beat. All the world around him froze. Dancers posed like statues. Players held one long and piercing note in the air. Guinevere. Only she moved, brushing back her long brown hair and leveling eyes like pools of peat. It felt as though Lancelot had spent his whole life among shadows, and this woman, this queen was the first real person he had ever met. As one glimpse of Arthur had awakened noble fealty in Lancelot's heart, one glimpse of Guinevere awoke savage piety. He wanted to worship her, yes—that was the pious part—but also to own her utterly, and be owned by her utterly. The highest impulses and the lowest were unanimous for Guinevere.

He had gone to one knee. Even Lancelot had not realized it until he found himself there, kneeling before King Arthur and Queen Guinevere.

Instruments groaned to silence. Feet shuffled and stilled. Every eye turned on the young man.

With all that attention came a hush, and with the hush came Arthur's unspoken request: What do you seek?

Instinctively, Lancelot replied, "Good even, King Arthur, ruler of all Britannia. May your victory bring you boon upon boon."

Arthur bowed his head in a gesture both deferential and wary. "And what do you seek, young warrior?"

"I seek only to serve you and your queen. I seek only to become a knight of the Round Table."

Earnest though his words were, they brought laughter from the other guests—great gales of laughter.

Lancelot's ears reddened, but his eyes rested unmoving on Guinevere.

King Arthur did not laugh, though his mouth was wry. "You and every hero of Badon Hill seeks knighthood."

Lancelot shook his head vigorously. "You mistake me, great king. I am no hero of Badon Hill—if that is the battle all here proclaim." More laughter answered. "Forgive me. I have long been away on the isle of Avalon, and so am out of touch with the events of the world."

With almost paternal patience, Arthur replied, "I have many friends on that isle and would know who you are to speak its holy name."

Ashamed he had forgotten to identify himself, Lancelot said, "I am Prince Lancelot, son of King Ban of Benwick."

A great furor erupted.

"He defames our dead king!"

"How does he make such claims?"

"I kissed the babe Lancelot two seasons ago—an infant."

Lancelot spoke over them. "I am Lancelot, son of Ban, fostered of Brigid of Avalon, and trained of Mars Smetrius. I am the equal of any man in sword and horse, and so I ask you, King Arthur," though his eyes never left the queen, "to make me a knight of the Round Table."

Arthur held out his hands to quiet the uproar. "I cannot say that you are the son of Ban, but neither can I say you are not. Let your heritage and all other questions find answers tomorrow in the lists." His hand swept the assembly. "These folk around you have gathered to compete for positions vacated by my brave fallen at Badon Hill. Whether in jousts or sword fights or fisticuffs, warriors will make themselves knights on the morrow. You too, young man, will prove or disprove yourself among them."

"This imposter will have no such chance," came an angry shout above the others. A great bear of a man strode through the parting company. His ceremonial armor glinted, but a true sword raked out in his hand. The pique of his voice told that he hailed from Benwick. "I'll not stand by while a man dressed in Saxon armor impugns King Ban. Let him prove his claim in word this instant, or by sword an instant later—"

"If you won't take his word," interrupted Queen Guinevere quietly, bringing every eye to her, "take mine. He is who he claims to be." She nodded once to Lancelot. "He will vie among you tomorrow, bearing the name of his royal house."

No one could have been more astonished than Lancelot himself. He stared into the queen's eyes and saw his own reflection staring back. Even as the Benwick man withdrew in the throng, Lancelot nodded his thanks to the queen.

Her eyes brimmed with mystery, and she nodded back.

That night, he did not dream of Avalon's waters, but only of Guinevere.

6

In the Lists

Day dawned brightly upon Camelot. Sunlight made the palace a white vision against the sleepy west. Roofs of thatch glistened with dew. Wood smoke clambered out of chimneys, bearing with it scents of bacon and porridge and fried bread. Doors and shutters opened. Laughter spilled out, followed by the laughers. In samite waistcoats and tartan trews, in linen skirts and lace collars, the folk of Camelot emerged into a new day—the second day of the Festival of the Pendragon.

Lancelot rose with the sun. He had spent the night among hay bales in the stables. Though he had money for true accommodation, the inns were full. Lancelot didn't mind. His only true friend in Camelot stayed there as well. Rasa had slept standing, his pelt steaming despite the blankets laid across him. For his part, Lancelot had used the hay for warmth—the hay and a memory.

Queen Guinevere shone sunlike in his mind. Her eyes remained on him there, in that dark loft, as they had remained on him in the palace. Her gaze was knowing and mysterious.

He is who he claims to be, she had said.

How did she know? Perhaps one of her Celtic gods had told her. She was a priestess of an old faith, a healer whom some called the Power of the Land.

Lancelot rose and stretched. Hay fell away from him in a fluttering shower. He brushed off the last of it and began to don his armor. In the stall below, Rasa chuffed, impatient to get to the tournament grounds. Lancelot breathed the hay-scented air and smiled.

Guinevere would be there, beside Arthur, watching it all. He only hoped he could turn his eyes from her long enough to joust.

Lancelot hurriedly buckled on his elbow and knee cops and slung his sword on the skirt of tasses. Fully arrayed, he descended to saddle and bard Rasa for the day's fights.

Stroking the stallion's neck, Lancelot said, "Don't worry. Master Smetrius trained me well, and I trained you well." The answering snort told Rasa's opinion. "We'll win the field and a seat at the Table Round." As he fitted the halter, Lancelot smiled sheepishly. "That is, I'll win a seat at the Table Round." Rasa seemed almost let down. Lancelot rubbed his shoulder. "You might get a stall near the mare of your choice." Not waiting for comment from the stallion, Lancelot led him from the stable, couched his oaken lance, mounted Rasa, and rode toward the festival grounds.

They passed down cobbled lanes and among bright shops. Camelot wore her morning face—fresh and glad. She glowed differently beneath the sun than the moon. The same folk who had danced and sung last night now thronged the road to the jousts.

Lancelot slowed Rasa to a gentle gait to match the padding feet around. The young warrior liked humanity, he decided, now that he knew what it was.

Ahead, the road opened onto a wide and grassy plain. On one side ran the jousting lanes—long lines of trammeled earth with brief fences between them. On the other were quintains and straw men for warriors still in training. In the center, circles and squares marked the ground for sword duels. Crowds poured into the stands. Lutes, glaurs, and sackbuts played in boxes overhead. At the ends of the fields crowded the parti-colored tents of knights and warriors.

Lancelot rode out toward the competitors' tents.

His comrades—his foes—awaited him there. Stiff-backed atop bristling steeds, half a hundred warriors sat and stared at the tournament ground. Their helms shifted toward the young man who claimed to be the son of Ban. Eyes narrowed in their visors.

"Ah, here he is, the infant son of Benwick."

"Saxon armor and Saxon lies . . ."

"What does he bear—a lance or a teething stick?"

Ignoring the jibes, Lancelot rode up in their midst. He turned Rasa smartly in a space most men could not turn a dog. He offered no greeting; none would have been received. Still, the warriors accosted him.

"Where is your squire, Prince Lancelot?" asked a red-bearded Caledonian.

"I have no squire," replied Lancelot.

The man shifted atop his roan steed and pressed, "Where is your lance?"

Blinking, Lancelot stared at the dark brown spear couched beside him. "Here."

The Caledonian snorted, eyes smiling but mouth frowning. "A practice lance? Where's the paint? Where are the others? Once that one is broken, what will you fight with?"

"This is oak, from the heartwood of an ancient tree. It is as solid as iron. It will not shatter."

The Caledonian laughed. "And where is your defender?"

"My defender?" he echoed.

The red-beard grimaced. "Yes, Queen Guinevere. Only her intercession last night kept you alive. But she cannot intercede for you today."

Lancelot dipped his head. "She needn't."

"Oh," the warrior replied in a voice like a growl. "You'll wish she could. Every man here is aiming for you, seeking to throw you down. You'll need her a hundred times over today."

Lancelot nodded at this advice. "Well said, friend." With that, he nudged Rasa out of the pack, toward the viewing stands. The stallion's hooves pounded eagerly across the grassy earth. Lancelot stood in the saddle, drawing a cheer from the crowd. In truth, he cared for but one cheer, that of the queen. He rode straight for her, oaken spear standing in its couch beside him.

The red-bearded Caledonian stared after Lancelot. He dug heels into his roan and lit out in the young warrior's wake.

Lancelot reached the tilting lists. He drove Rasa up to the joust fence and gently lifted the rein. The great stallion hurled himself over the fence and came down at a gallop beyond. Half a dozen more hoofbeats, and Rasa pulled up before the royal box. The traces were slack as Rasa rose in a magnificent rear before the crowd.

They obliged with a great cheer. Even King Arthur, bedecked in white furs and red samite, smiled and nodded.

Lancelot acknowledged him only peripherally, his eyes rooted on Guinevere.

She wore white. Her strong hands were laced upon one knee, in the way of oak roots. Her feet had slipped from their sandals to rest bare upon the hewn planks. Roses bloomed in a plaited halo in her hair.

She is no acolyte of Christ, Lancelot reminded himself, but a powerful priestess of a bygone age. That fact made him love her all the more.

"My queen," he called to her, bowing in his saddle. "I beg of you a boon."

It was not Guinevere but Arthur who answered. "Already, the queen has taken your part in the disputes last night. What more boon could you ask?"

"That I might take her part," Lancelot replied without pause. He gestured over his shoulder to the red-bearded warrior who galloped up just then. "It is rumored that if I fought for myself alone, I would fall. The rumor is true. But if I fought for you, Queen Guinevere, I would never fall. I am convinced of it."

King Arthur considered this pretty speech, staring at the flushed face of the Caledonian. "You speak well, young Lancelot. And why shouldn't you fight for Queen Guinevere? Every knight should fight for her. Why shouldn't she have a chaste champion?"

"That's why I have you, dear," Guinevere broke in, her slender hand gentle on Arthur's stole. It was the king's turn to redden. Guinevere continued. "You may fight for me, Lancelot du Lac."

Again, he bowed in the saddle. "Thank you. A token, then, of your grace, that I might wear it with me like a shield."

She reached up and, with a gentle motion, freed one red rose from the circlet in her hair. She tossed the flower toward Lancelot. It arced like a crimson comet and landed easily in his mailed grip. Lancelot lifted it, drank in its scent, and deftly wove it into the visor of his helm.

"Give me a rose too, my queen," requested the northman.

Guinevere smiled, dismissing him and Lancelot both with a wave of her arm. "Go find yourself another woman whose virtue could use some defending. I have my champion."

"Yes," said King Arthur, wrapping one arm about his queen. "She has her champion. Now be off with you both."

The Caledonian bit down on his response. He whirled his horse about so violently that its rump struck Rasa's shoulder.

The stallion did not shy as would some horses. He only stood and shoved back.

Surprised, the roan tucked its haunches like a cringing dog and bolted. Its reins broke from its rider's grip, and the Caledonian nearly overbalanced backward. Hands flailing, he rode thirty hoofbeats before regaining control. His blasphemies overtopped even the hoots and jeers of the crowd. Hunkering down over the spooked steed, he pulled it back beneath him. The creature had run straight down the lists, trapped between fence and stands, and was out of ground. Growling, the man yanked the horse to a halt and spun it about again.

"You!" he shouted, standing in the stirrups and pointing at Lancelot. "You will give me satisfaction, now!"

Lancelot did not hear. He drew in the heady scent of the rose. It had still been warm from Guinevere's hair. It was as though he sat beside her, felt her warmth, breathed her air. Not even the Caledonian's shout could have broken through that moment.

Guinevere's voice did. "Lancelot . . . ?"

He looked up to her. "Yes?"

She smiled, and her expression nearly melted him. "You wear my rose," she gestured down the lane, "now defend my honor."

Lancelot stared down the lists. The Caledonian's horse

tossed its fiery mane and stomped impatiently. Lancelot turned back to Guinevere. "It would be my pleasure." He guided Rasa into a trot toward the other end of the jousting grounds.

This was irregular. Men fought by tournament rosters. Someone should have played a trumpet before battle. Someone should have made a speech before men crashed together. Such ceremony, though, fell before a challenge of honor.

Lancelot knew he should have been afraid. He could die in the next moments. He could kill in the next moments. Both were cause for fear. Somehow, though, he felt nothing except the warmth of the rose.

Reaching the end of the grounds, Lancelot turned Rasa into his own lane. He lifted the unpainted oaken lance from its couch, set his shield, and nodded that he was ready.

The Caledonian dug heels into his steed. Together they drove forward. Even through the helm he wore, the man's flaming hair and eyes shone.

Lancelot whispered to Rasa, "Let's fight."

The horse knew those words. They had initiated a thousand training sessions beneath the eye of Master Smetrius. As in those days, Rasa leapt to the attack.

Lancelot leaned into the great beast's momentum. Rasa drove forward like a ram. His leg muscles rippled. His hooves thundered. All this was background to the tilting spear, Lancelot's single focus. That venerable oaken staff was a lightning rod, drawing power to it. Only as the lance came level did Lancelot let his eye move beyond it, to the fast-approaching target. This time, it was no mere pumpkin, but a man. Within him lay not seeds but flesh and blood. Still, Lancelot did not pause. There was no time to pause, but only to strike true, as he had been taught.

The Caledonian's shaft struck Lancelot's shield, slid up its curved edge, and flung it away.

Lancelot's weapon jabbed between shield and shoulder, driving into that pumping pumpkin that was his foe's heart. No breastplate could bear the weight of lance and lancer and horse. The conic point stove steel and flesh and bone and all. It did not pierce, but landed as a hammer, crushing all beneath it.

The man folded up like an empty shirt. Through the haft, Lancelot felt muscles mash and bones crack. He let go. No one did that—no knight, at any rate—but the man was dying on the other end. He couldn't kill him, not like he had killed that Saxon.

It was too late. The horses pounded past each other. Lancelot stared, slack-jawed. The Caledonian was dead in the saddle, his chest collapsed around the shaft. Lancelot pulled Rasa up short. Horse and rider whirled in time to see the red-haired warrior slump over the mane. The lance butt struck ground and lodged. Impaled, the corpse mounted up into the morning air as its horse ran out from beneath it. It hung there as if upon a scaffold, and then fell into the dust.

Lancelot kicked Rasa—he never kicked his steed. Rasa cantered forward, bearing Lancelot to his foe. In glossy armor, the man seemed a fly on a pin, iridescent and dead. Lancelot's hands tightened around the reins.

The death of the Saxon—that had been one thing. He had threatened Aunt Brigid. This man, though, what was his offense? Since when had arrogance been a deadly sin? Lancelot swooned, sickened by the bloody corpse and his own depravity.

The crowd shouted in adulation. They loved him. The outcast, struggling to belong, strong and virtuous, skilled in the arts of war—Lancelot had suddenly become the sort of man all Camelot wished to watch. He had slain a Caledonian, yes, but had done so fairly, by right of arms. Who could argue? Such was fickle fame.

Lancelot did not listen to their rapture. It would have made him a monster. Nor could he listen to his screaming guilt. It would have made him a worm. He wished only to be a knight, a virtuous knight. To do so he would have to return to the jousts.

"You have won," said a varlet as he worked loose the lance and handed it, bloodied, to Lancelot.

Numbly, the young warrior took the weapon and couched it. The only way he could muster himself to joust again was with a promise: I will not kill again this day.

Lancelot drew in a shallow breath and nudged Rasa. The steed knew what he wanted and carried him back down the lane. Tipped in crimson, the lance seemed almost a standard. The crowd treated it as such. Folk came to their feet as Lancelot rode past. Their cheers almost shoved him sideways out of the saddle.

The shouts stayed with him all through that day, ringing in his ears. With each warrior he faced and felled, the cries grew. Somehow in the din, Lancelot kept his focus. He always won, but never slew again. The once-bloody tip of his lance grew dark and dry. He struck shields only, though with a square blow that drove their wielders from the saddle. While saving his conscience, this strategy taxed his arm. An unhorsed man without broken limbs would often demand a duel of swords, sometimes to the death. Lancelot always declined this final condition, willing to fight only to first blood. After twelve such battles on horse and foot, Lancelot was yet unbloodied, unbowed.

This thirteenth, though, might undo him—an unnecessary bout. Already he was assured a seat at the Table Round, as was his foe. Just as Lancelot had risen through the lists by prowess and finesse, his opponent had risen by blood and guile. The lad's name was Mordred—only just become a man. He was more than a lad, though, rumored to be the illegitimate and incestuous son of Arthur himself. Some even dared call Mordred "Witch-Spawn" and claimed he bore Otherworld protections. His cometary rise would support it. Mordred had squired to Sir Pellinore for only six months before this bid for knighthood. Wiry and whip-thin, Mordred slew his foes by treachery. He drew their blows aside with feints and struck them in faces and necks. He had five kills to his name, and he crowed that Lancelot would be his sixth.

"We are the same, you and I, Lancelot," shouted Mordred from across the jousting lanes. "Sons of the Otherworld, destined to destroy the over world, darkly prophesied of Merlin, and tragically vying for the love of Arthur. Soon, the only difference will be that you are dead, and I am a knight."

Lancelot did not answer. There was no response to such words. He only hefted the oak lance, urged Rasa forward, and charged the young whelp.

Mordred also charged. He seemed a fly—black and tangled in filthy loops. His steed pounded forward. His steel-tipped lance sought Lancelot's heart.

The question was not how to meet that lance; Mordred lacked precision. The question was whether to kill this man or not. Lancelot could kill him. A blow to heart or throat or head would do it. Mordred was more deserving of death than any other man Lancelot had faced. The power was in his hand. The revulsion was in his heart. Wouldn't Camelot be the better without a Sir Mordred?

The oaken lance bore in. It arrowed toward the narrow young warrior.

Lancelot would not kill again, not in cold blood.

With a shrug of resignation, Lancelot ducked Mordred's blow and tilted his own lance toward the man's shoulder. It struck on the shield.

The blow devastated. The tip smashed into metal and buckled it, cracked the shield in half and rammed through. Between armor and flesh was Mordred's hand. The oak lance impaled it like a spike, pulverizing muscle and severing tendon and crushing bone. It was a relatively small price to pay—shield arm instead of sword arm. The shattered limb took much of the impact and saved the rest of Mordred. He flew from the saddle.

Lancelot dragged his lance sharply back and rode on. He watched Mordred tumble in the dust behind him. Mordred struck ground, churned soft by countless hooves, and rolled.

Rasa ran out the gallop. Lancelot hoisted the lance, bloodied for a second time that day, into its couch. He slowed and turned his steed.

A strange sight greeted him. Mordred stood, silhouetted in black against the mounding clouds of the west. He clutched his sword. His left arm hung limp and useless. Blood visibly dripped from his crushed hand. His other hand lifted a blade in challenge and leveled it at Lancelot.

A duel of swords.

Blinking, Lancelot urged Rasa forward. He lashed his lance into its couch. As horse and rider neared the unhorsed figure, Lancelot swung down to light beside his stallion. Rasa snorted once in farewell and charged away.

Drawing his own blade, Lancelot strode forward. "I do not wish to fight you."

Mordred scowled with black brows. "Perhaps you'd rather die." He hurled himself ahead.

It was a savage maneuver, but clumsy and slow. Lancelot easily caught the jabbing blade, slid Mordred's sword down to the crossbar, and flung it away. In an after-stroke, Lancelot brought his blade skidding down shallowly across Mordred's armor to nick his neck, the only exposed flesh on his body. A stream of red snaked sullenly down the young man's gorget.

"I claim first blood," said Lancelot.

Mordred stepped back, slapping a hand to his neck. He hurled his helmet angrily from his head. "I never agreed to first blood."

"It is *all* I have agreed to."

Mordred smiled bleakly, "Next blood, then?"

Lancelot nodded, "Next blood." He too removed his helmet and let it fall in the dust.

Mordred retrieved his sword. His mouth formed a mocking twin to the red line across his neck. He began to circle, watching for an opening. "You think you cannot be goaded into making a mistake. You are wrong. Every man has a goat, and when I find it, I'll ride it and ride it."

Nothing but steel showed in Lancelot's eyes. He turned to keep Mordred before him. "Is that what you rode into the joust? Someone's goat?"

"I've ridden twenty men's goats into the joust, and killed five of them," boasted Mordred. He jabbed a dripping finger at Lancelot. "Where do you keep yours, white knight? Dead father?" He lifted an eyebrow, his sword quivering eagerly. "Lunatic mother?" Mordred's eyes became wicked crescents, but still saw no weakness. "Aunt Brigid?"

Lancelot's teeth creaked across each other. "This will not bring you victory, but death—"

"Or perhaps it is the woman whose rose you have hurled, with your helmet, in the dust?"

Lancelot glanced toward his helmet.

A hiss warned of the blade bound for his neck.

Lancelot ducked. He raised an elbow cop. It rang with the deflected blow. He turned beneath the steel and aimed a stroke that would sever Mordred's neck.

Camelot without a Sir Mordred . . .

The blow struck—with the crosspiece instead of the blade, and against the nose instead of the neck. There was next blood, yes, in a sudden, gurgling fountain from Mordred's nostrils. It was stark against his white face. The young warrior reeled and crashed.

The crowd roared in exultation.

Lancelot could only step numbly back. He was panting. He had nearly killed this man—nearly been goaded into it. And if Mordred had been smarter or faster, Lancelot himself would have been killed. This treacherous warrior would bear watching.

In reflex, Lancelot picked up his helmet and blew dust from the rose. It glowed vibrantly, as though still alive. He lifted his eyes.

Guinevere beamed amid the cheering hordes.

At last, Lancelot himself smiled.

7

Induction

Queen Guinevere straightened on the throne of Camelot. She stared intently down the long red lane of carpet. It extended from her feet to the feet of her new champion.

Lancelot took solemn strides toward her. Even garbed in thick Saxon plate, he walked with grace. He glowed brighter than the chandeliers that hung above the watchful crowd. To either side of the main aisle stood kings and princes, dukes and counts. In all their finery, none outshone Lancelot. Nor did his rivals. The other victors wore dress mail, mirror-bright. Even Mordred gleamed in ceremonial steel. Only Lancelot had donned the same dense suit he had worn in battle. He had polished the armor, doing the work of a squire, but he was none diminished by grit in his nail beds and abrasions on his knuckles. His eyes were unchanged, blue and brilliant. With them he gazed levelly at the queen.

Guinevere felt herself color. Her cheeks and shoulders were suddenly hot, as if she had downed a goblet of wine. The sensation moved through her with enervating bliss. To think she had removed a rose from her hair and tossed it to him, and that he still wore the dusty and dead emblem in his visor . . .

Reaching the stairs before the royal dais, Lancelot knelt, as did the countless warriors behind him.

Arthur rose from the throne.

Guinevere startled. The warm brush of his stole against her leg reminded her that he'd been there all the while. The seat was built for them both. She was the Power of the Land, and he the ruler of it. They were equals, bound in chaste marriage—always entwined but never touching. Guinevere watched Arthur, broad-shouldered and deliberate. She loved him. She always had. Why then did she wish for this man, this Lancelot?

Arthur reached to his shoulder harness and drew forth Excalibur. The blade sang as sunlight struck it. Silhouetted against oaken hammer beams, the sword of legend seemed a hunk of lightning. It was beautiful in the hand of the king. With it, Arthur had slain mortals and gods and tamed Britannia. The sword's purpose today was no less grand—knighting the new order of the Table Round.

With a swift stroke, the king brought Excalibur down to hover motionless above the steely shoulder of Lancelot. Arthur could have taken the young man's head. In the pause that followed, he seemed to contemplate the act.

"For virtuous prowess on the field of battle, you kneel now to receive induction into the knighthood of the Table Round. Do you promise to uphold the code of chivalry . . . ?"

"I do," replied Lancelot without pause. His eyes, like disks cut from the sky, seemed almost to beam within his slender features.

Arthur continued. ". . . to fight fairly and for just cause . . . ?"

"I do."

". . . to defend the defenseless . . . ?"

"I do."

". . . and chastely to champion virtuous women . . . ?"

Lancelot's gaze shifted from Arthur to Guinevere. He seemed to peer right into her thoughts, her desires. "I do."

For an abstracted moment, there was only Lancelot and Guinevere and Arthur. The room, the warriors, the dignitaries all were gone. Three alone remained. Guinevere and Arthur were bound in chaste marriage, a two-edged sword between them. A similar blade, Excalibur, united Arthur and Lancelot. Knighthood at the Table Round was equal parts blessing and curse. But the subtlest edge of all joined Lancelot to Guinevere. It promised both salvation and destruction. . . . In her fever dream, she and Arthur and Lancelot stood with love in their hearts but blades on their throats. If one of those swords slipped and sliced, they all would.

Excalibur dropped toward Lancelot's shoulder, touching its flat against an epaulet and ringing. "Then you are no longer a simple warrior," the king said. He lifted the sword to bring it down on Lancelot's other shoulder. "You are now a knight of the Table Round."

A cheer rose from the gathered throng. Those who days before had scoffed at this young man now threw roses. He ignored the pelting flowers. As he stood, Lancelot worked free the dead bloom in his visor. He did not turn to face the crowd, but clutched the rose to his armored heart.

Applauding and smiling, Guinevere was surprised to find herself standing before the throne. Clamping down on the hope that boiled within her, she managed to sit again. Even so, she could not wipe away the grin on her face.

Never had Lancelot seen its like. The Table Round had been fashioned from one enormous slab of wood, the cross-section of a millennial tree—a multimillennial tree. Lancelot sat in one of fifty-one seats carved from the perimeter of the table. He could count five hundred rings from his elbows to his wrists. Another two thousand would fill the space between his fingers and the hollow core of the table. There, worms and rot had eaten away a century of centuries. The tree had been far older than Christ, than David, than Moses or Abram. Perhaps it had been planted in the first Garden. Perhaps this was a slice from the tree of knowledge.

Such fancies filled Lancelot's mind. How he had dreamed of this day! Here, beneath this wooden dome, atop this marble floor, seated at the Table Round amid Arthur's knights.

Lancelot wanted to remember every detail of this night. He breathed deeply. His lungs filled with the hot aroma of the repast set before him: fresh-baked trenchers laden with thick stew; soft sweet carrots and morsels of wild boar; slivered leeks in a hearty sauce; tankards of yeasty beer; goblets of blood-red wine—a feast of savory scents in a single breath.

Lancelot tuned his ear to the music. A reedy fife danced with the song of a rebec. A drum and rasp punctuated their harmonies. A singer poured out the ardent lyrics of some ancient lay. To Lancelot, though, the sweetest music was the camaraderie of the knights and retainers:

". . . must give my glad thanks to Sir Lancelot for appearing this day not in false armor, but true—" the speaker was Ulfius, among the oldest of Arthur's retinue. Once-black shocks of hair and beard had thinned to gray. The man's propriety had meanwhile calcified to quaint fussiness. "I would like to know when we became so urbane that we needed a set of armor for show and another for battle."

No sooner had Ulfius finished his lament than he suffered

a profound blow to one shoulder blade from the knight beside him. "See, Ulfius always has it right." It was Sir Kay, adopted brother of the king. Blond and well-built, Kay had a warrior's way and wit about him. "War and show. We didn't gain the knighthood by jousts and straw villains. A whole lot of show. We rose by standing by Uther at his last battle, and fighting for Arthur at Caerleon, and marching every windswept down and peat bog between here and the Norse Sea. That was war, not show."

"Don't discount Badon Hill," interjected Sir Gawain, half-brother to King Arthur and brother of Agravain, Gaheris, and Gareth. Strapping and authoritative, Gawain had that rare combination of physical and spiritual stature. Whatever words emerged from his meaty lips were born in his ethereal heart. "Many of these new knights proved themselves there before competing in the tournament. They have conquered both in show and in war. They have proved themselves."

A wry smile filled the face of Sir Agravain. He seemed the small dark shadow of his imposing brother. "They have proved themselves, but for two."

"Which two, Brother?" asked Sir Gawain.

Agravain's smile twisted until it seemed the corners of his mustache might meet above his nose. "The two who did not fight at Badon Hill. The two who finished at the top of the lists—Sir Lancelot and Sir Mordred."

Gawain snorted. He quaffed the full contents of his stein and waved away the insinuation. "Anyone who saw that final joust would say it was war, indeed. They are proved enough to take their seats."

"Perhaps, but are they proved enough to take the Siege Perilous?" Agravain pressed, gesturing toward the empty fifty-first chair at the table. "Only a pure knight can sit that seat. If these two are such chaste warriors, let them try the Siege Perilous, and live or die."

Gawain shook his head vigorously, mats of black hair hurtling around him. "None can sit that seat—not I, not you, not this most recent cache. Only a pure knight might do it. It is too much to ask these new recruits—"

"I'll do it," broke in Mordred. "Purity is an easy enough thing to attain. What is it but fanaticism? I have purity, or its twin. I will sit the Siege Perilous."

Sudden silence gripped the Table Round. Hands ceased pulling bread from steaming trenchers. Jaws stopped chewing to hang in amazement. Gawain stared levelly at the young upstart. Beside him, Ulfius raised an eloquent eyebrow. Kay wore a look of shocked amusement, and Agravain gaped gladly. Only Arthur's eyes were inscrutable, darkly glittering beneath a solemn brow. No one seemed to breathe.

Mordred basked in their scathing attention. He smugly returned the company's stares, and then focused his own gaze on Lancelot. The other knights likewise shifted their attention to him.

Lancelot alone had continued to eat. He dragged a large hunk of bread from the side of the trencher, dipped it, and guided it to his mouth. He chewed. At last, a quaff of ale cleared his throat. Only then did he say, "I, too."

The men murmured—some shocked, some wary, some gleeful. In the midst of the rumble, Gawain stood. He held his hands out to his sides as if trying to quiet rowdy children. "This is tomfoolery. Why should we send true knights to death for a bit of sport?"

Mordred rose, slight and subtle next to the big man. His

bandaged hand seemed a claw clutched up beside him. "I slew five warriors in sport to reach this pinnacle. Why not another?"

"But look," interrupted Gawain, striding around the table. In one brawny hand, he hoisted the seat where Mordred had sat. Gawain muscled the chair around, displaying its ornately engraved back. In a large, flat amethyst there shone a ghostly name—mordred. "This is your seat. The table itself tells where you belong. And, Lancelot, your chair bears your name. Do not presume to demean this table by grasping at its highest seat." He lowered the chair, but not his baleful eyes.

Silence answered his words.

Lancelot clasped his hands together and drew a deep breath. "Forgive me, brother knights. I do not wish to offer offense—"

"Aha!" cried Mordred. "The coward backs away—"

"—but I have dreamed of this day from the time I could remember. Once I thought dreams were everything, but now I am really here, and I know dreams are nothing. The words of Kay and Agravain prick my heart. I have not known war, but show. I have not known true foes, but straw ones. I have not known honor, but tomfoolery. My prowess, my power, arise from dreamy games, not real combat. I feel a sham of a knight."

Mordred's grinning teeth ground together like chalk.

"But I know this: Dreams can provide purity. Call it fanaticism, if you must, but to hope for one thing for so long can make a soul pure. If I can sit in that seat, the Siege Perilous, I will know that I am meant to be, first and foremost, a knight."

Mordred's glee set a fine, high keen in the air.

Gawain stared gravely at King Arthur. "What say you, my king?"

Arthur's august visage clouded. Something like jealousy moved his lips against each other. Eyes narrowed with calculation.

"I would not have a knight so discomfited as this at my table. Sir Lancelot must do what he must do to be certain of his place."

The king's words only darkened Gawain's visage. He looked again at Lancelot, whose young skin beamed in the flicker of tallow, and then at Mordred, who had turned aside to hide a smirk. He said, "Sir Mordred, since you suggested this diversion, you shall sit first."

A credulous expression twisted his brows. "I am honored, and normally would not hesitate, but the choice is not mine to make. I have been bested by this one. Let him choose who first sits the seat."

"I will," Lancelot replied.

He rose from his own chair. Stepping away from the table, Lancelot straightened, and his battle armor settled. The air roared with hot silence. Lancelot stepped. Again. His feet bore him past one knight after another. Looks of pity followed him. He ignored them, heading for the empty chair at the right hand of King Arthur. The Siege Perilous. It seemed like any other chair poised around the table—broad and ornately decorated. Just now, the back of the seat was pivoted forward to merge seamlessly with the table surface. The large amethyst bore no name. Lancelot reached out and drew the chair back. The cushions within were embroidered red samite over goose down. It seemed harmless enough, but this seat had slain numerous folk who presumed to ascend to it.

If I am not pure, not destined to be a knight, I will die, he thought. But what use is a life without dreams?

Lancelot pivoted forward and brought the chair up to touch his inner knees. He lowered himself gently.

There came a brilliant white flash, and the stench of burning flesh, and Lancelot was gone.

8

Clutched in the Bosom of Fey

He was blown out of the chair and the room, through a window, into the night. His body had that boneless quality of dream bodies, and he knew he dreamed. In no true world did a man in armor flow this way, shards of stained glass tumbling all about him and striking his metal skin with little bell tones. Only in dream were falling and flying so akin. Lancelot twisted in air. The white blast that had hurled him from the palace shoved still at his feet. The black sky that caught his head was quilted with stars. He could have flown into it, but saw a more welcoming place, the waters beneath the waters. He fell down toward them.

Three women watched his descent. The Bountiful Weirds. In brassy solidity they offered loaf and cornucopia and child to Lancelot, who was in no position to accept. The statues wore long-suffering looks. He plunged into the water at their feet and made a profound splash.

That was how else he knew this was a dream. Broad and beautiful though the fountain was, it should have had a bottom. Lancelot sank as though it did not. Water wove its cinching currents around him and dragged him down. It trickled beneath plates of armor. It caressed flesh.

More than that—water loomed itself into skin and muscle. It called to cousin humors within him, lifting the warp of his flesh to shuttle new weft between. Pedals shifted. New fibers added their substance. Pedals shifted. Hues and textures changed. Pedals shifted. Someone was weaving him, patiently knitting him together.

Who are you? Lancelot asked. His voice tangled with the strands before being crimped into a regular weave. He glimpsed a figure, stooped in silhouette, working the treadle. Who was this? A woman, undoubtedly, but which woman? What Penelope so patiently, so dutifully worked the threads of time, strand by strand creating him? *Who are you?*

There came no answer, except from himself.

There had been two women. For the last twenty-some years, Aunt Brigid had worked those foot-boards, had patiently spliced any skein that raveled, had guided the colors with aged eyes. More than any other, she had knit him together. She was the master weaver, and yet this shadow was not she.

Before Aunt Brigid, there had been Lancelot's mother, Queen Elaine. If Brigid had been the master weaver, Elaine had been the spinner. She had provided the substance that would be so deftly woven. Dog's hair could not be spun. Flax made for common cloth. Wool was fine, but Kashmir finer, and samite finest of all. Aunt Brigid had given him form, but Lancelot's mother had given him substance. Still, the shadow-form was not her.

This woman was young and slender. Her figure had that unspoiled aspect of a flower first opened. The hands that worked the loom were not gnarled by time or even callused by age. Strong and elegant. Venerable Brigid had granted him form, and motherly Elaine had given him substance, but this one's gift reached deeper in time. She touched upon his soul. She had searched him and known him, even before he was knit together, even before he had lived in the womb. This woman knew what his life should be. The lazy called it destiny or fate. Lancelot could call it only love.

Who are you?

"You're safe, Lancelot, and soon you'll feel fine again," came the woman's soothing reply as she raised the warp. Frames shifted. Threads interlaced.

What are you doing?

"I'm weaving."

What are you doing . . . to me?

"I am weaving," she repeated. "It is part of this healing ritual. As I join these raveled threads of wool, your frayed tissues are made whole again."

He was rising from delirious sleep like a diver from cold depths. Through the watery surface of his dream, he glimpsed an ornate sitting room. A fire burned merrily upon a white-marble hearth. Embroidered seats gathered about the blaze. Candles glowed on the mantle. Velvet-papered walls rose to a ceiling bossed with gold filigree. Despite the grandeur of the setting, Lancelot's eyes immediately turned to the maiden seated there. She worked a large loom.

Whole again? he wondered.

"The Siege Perilous is not a seat to be sat lightly. It nearly killed you, Lancelot. For all your battle prowess and persistence, you are not pure." The pronouncement might have seemed a condemnation from anyone else, but from these lips, the words became praise. "Strong things are rarely pure. Purest gold and purest silver are soft, useless but to the dazzled eye. Purebred dogs and purebred monarchs are prone to quiver and wet themselves." She laughed lightly, and Lancelot joined her. "No, the strongest metals are alloys, and the strongest men are too."

Lancelot drew a breath and blinked. His eyes were water-weary, and the woman seemed little more defined than she had been in dream.

"Camelot was built of alloys and allies, a Christian sword and a Pagan wizard. Even Arthur is no pure creature—bastard born of a king. But what true prince has ever borne the strength of my Arthur?"

"*Y-your* Arthur—" Lancelot gagged out. He sat bolt upright and saw Queen Guinevere silhouetted before the loom candle. Then the blood rushed from his head, and the vision from his eyes, and he splashed back down in that watery place.

Gulping for air, he slapped the water with frantic hands. It was no good. Muscle fibers separated and dissolved. Air burst out of his lungs. Down he went. His mind drowned in dream.

He struggled for ground, for rock-solid reason, but this sea had no bed. Any who sought it would plunge to greater pressures and darker depths. But any who knew the fluid dynamic of dream—emotion churning free of referent—would know to swim. Lancelot swam.

There was something about this fountain—he was again drowning in the fountain—with its maiden and mother and crone, offering up their bounty. Somehow, he belonged here. Perhaps the central statue reminded him of Avalon, ringed by water. After all, Aunt Brigid had sent him across the merciful lake to Britannia. Or perhaps the central statue was the island of Britannia itself, surrounded by seas. His mother, Queen Elaine, had borne him across the merciless channel to Britannia. But there was a third. In dream, there was always a third. What greater water, what greater woman, bore him hence, to Britannia?

Her fingers worked the sinews of his shoulders. He gathered great armfuls of the flood and thrust them down. She strengthened the fibers of his legs. He kicked up from the depths. She stitched his eyelids. They drew back, and he beheld the surface. Lancelot smiled. Through the watery veil, he saw her again. He rose to consciousness and opened his eyes.

The gold-filigreed ceiling spread above. Lancelot had returned to the drawing room, to his Penelope.

Queen Guinevere leaned toward him, and he saw the sweat that gleamed upon her brow. "Are you all right? That was too quick to sit up."

Lancelot released a long sigh. "Yes, it was, my queen. And yes, I am."

Nodding, the queen leaned back in her weaver's chair. Despite her fine gown and slender form, it was obvious she had been laboring like a mason. Her feet sagged upon the treadle, and her fingers trembled as she drew them from the strands. She hadn't even touched him. Only then did Lancelot realize how literally she had spoken about his healing. She worked it through the loom before her. The strands there were somehow tied to his very flesh. Her ardent labors had saved his life.

"Thank you, Your Highness," Lancelot blurted.

Guinevere lifted an eyebrow. "For what?"

"Thank you for saving my life."

She smiled wearily. "You have become my champion. Now I have become yours."

"I only wish I had a flower to offer you. Perhaps next time I plunge to Avalon, I'll bring back an apple blossom."

Her brow furrowed. The lines made her only lovelier.

Lancelot waved away her bemusement. "It's nothing. Just delirium. I keep dreaming I'm thrown into a fountain, where I drown and visit other lands."

Guinevere laughed. "Don't be so sure it's delirium. You've nearly died, twice. A dying soul seeks whatever route it can to travel to those it loves."

"You misunderstand, my queen. I dream about splashing in a fountain. It's nonsense."

"Is it?" responded Guinevere. She sat up on her weaver's chair and worked the loom. "You're alive even now because of such nonsense." She shoved the shuttle through, pounded its thread in place, and shifted the pedals. "I am a priestess, you know. A healer, trained in the traditions of the Tuatha dé Danann. I would think a man reared on Avalon would understand the powers of the land."

A deep grin, almost a grimace, cut across Lancelot's face. "I know it is fashionable to believe Avalon is a place of faeries and phantasms, but having grown up there, I can tell you it is nothing more than a beautiful green hill beside a beautiful blue lake."

"You grew up on Avalon and never once laid eyes on anything supernatural?"

"No bogies, no faeries, no bugaboos."

Guinevere demurred. "Is it possible you grew up in the company of spirits without ever recognizing them?"

"Is it possible," echoed Lancelot, "to grow up in a meadow without recognizing the wildflowers?"

Guinevere responded innocently, "What sort of wildflowers did you have on Avalon?"

For an unguarded moment, the young knight's eyes grew wide. "Well, of course, we had dandelions. . . ."

"Of course."

Lancelot smiled tightly as he thought. "And I noted a fair bit of ivy."

"We're talking about wildflowers."

His nostrils flared. "Some of the grass sometimes got little purple flowers—"

"What kind of grass?" pressed Guinevere.

Lancelot's face clenched, a man caught. In sudden triumph, he belted out, "Clover!"

"Is it possible that you lived all that time among flowers and fey and never had names for either?" Guinevere asked.

"Possible," Lancelot allowed, "but damned unlikely."

"I am born of the Tuatha. I am studied of their lore. I am a priestess of their faith. You can believe me."

"Look," he said, cutting off the conversation, "all my life, all I've known is that I'm supposed to be a warrior, a knight. All my life, that's what I've been up to. If there were faeries on Avalon, good luck to them. I had other matters to attend to. When was the last time a faerie lent a hand on the battlefield?"

Guinevere gestured with simple eloquence at the loom. "What of this? You'd be dead now if not for the work of this contraption and me behind it and the magic that binds it to you. Do you even know what I am weaving here?"

Lancelot sat up for a better look and realized his mistake too late. Once again, light peeled from his eyes. He flopped back onto the cushioned pallet. His arms and legs hung loose.

He knew he should have felt the cradling warmth of the mattress. Instead, he endured another cold splash into the Bountiful Weirds. Water closed over him. Lancelot plunged. The currents that once had allied with Lancelot now conspired against him, dragged him deeper. His ears popped repeatedly as the air in his lungs shrank. He kept his mouth shut, knowing the black water could crush him. He tumbled. Gripped in fists of water, he bumped through antediluvian rivers beneath the world.

Their cold pulse hurled him along and up, into a nowhere

place—or rather, into three somewhere places overlaid. About his arms and legs twisted reeds, or were they eels, or were they only his own sodden clothes? And was this a hot and buzzing marsh, or a cool and blue lake, or a frigid bronze fountain? He saw all three, one atop the others in a fearsome melding of worlds. It didn't matter which was which. Lancelot was in them all. It only mattered that he was half-drowned, and that dry land lay ahead.

He clawed up onto the stony shore. Grit ground into his nail beds. He collapsed, his face pillowed in tender grass. Spewing water from his nose and mouth, he breathed in a familiar and heady scent—the fragrant clover of Avalon. Lancelot lifted his head. Indeed, it was Avalon. He would know this shore anywhere, green right to the water. A moment ago, it had been rock and grit.

A figure approached—a woman in robes. She had an ageless grace to her stride. The wind played caprice with her cloak, which seemed one moment stark black, clean and forbidding, and next moment well-worn and brown. She headed straight for Lancelot. Five paces away, she dropped to the rocky shore, knelt, and set her forehead to the ground. She groaned and muttered the devotions of a mad abbess. ". . . brought him unto me, praise thee, unto me, unto me, praise thee. My boy my boy my boy, praise thee. Bring him unto me, my boy unto me, praise thee. . . ."

"Who are you?" Lancelot asked.

The woman kept her forehead pressed to the ground. ". . . does not know me or even himself, praise thee. Does not know who I am or who he is, praise thee. . . ."

"Who are you!"

She lifted her face—gritty forehead above worry-lined eyes, a hatchet nose, and a sunken and yammering mouth. He could not have known that face, but knew it, and blurted, "Mother!"

"What are you doing here, Lancelot?" asked the woman, but she had changed. No longer did she kneel or murmur. No longer did she wear black, but brown, and her face was no longer unfamiliar. "Why have you returned to Avalon?"

Lancelot looked quickly away from Aunt Brigid to see the verdant hillside, the distant apple blossoms, the silhouette of the tor. His fingers plucked up an Avalonian clover blossom—unmistakably purple—and he drank in its scent. "I don't know why I am here, or if I'm here."

"Oh, you're here," replied the woman, changed again. Her voice was young, sardonic. "And why?"

"Guinevere?" Lancelot asked, lifting his arm. Only then did he notice he was draped across the broad stone verge of the Fount of the Bountiful Weirds in Camelot. Despite the late stars wheeling overhead, the square thronged with folk. All of them seemed to find the knight's predicament amusing. Even Guinevere. "What am I doing here? Did you carry me here?"

The queen stared at her arm, slender beneath her gown. She made a fist. "Of course, Lancelot. I carried you from the palace down three flights of stairs and across half a mile of streets to throw you into the fountain."

Lancelot's eyes traced the clinging line of her gown, across muscle and shoulder and neck. "How did I get here?"

"Your dreams. You traveled in your dreams and awoke in truth elsewhere."

Lancelot shook his head as if to fling away the words. "I don't believe you."

"Don't believe me. Believe your own hands. They have been your salvation before. Believe what you see in them, and once you believe, return to me." She turned and, clutching her arms to herself, she walked away.

Lancelot lifted his hands. Despite the spraying water, he saw the stony grit in his nail beds. As he turned his hands over, he glimpsed a more remarkable omen—a purple clover blossom from Avalon.

"Return to me," he echoed after his vanished queen.

9

Knight Errant

"Sir Lancelot!" gabbled out King Arthur, standing in the doorway to his bed chambers. The king was imposing. The candlestick clutched in his hand sent golden jags of fire across his brows. "What are you doing here? So late? So wet?"

"What am I doing here?" Lancelot echoed hollowly. Seeking Guinevere, he thought. Returning to her. He could not tell Arthur that. "What am I doing here?"

Arthur's brows stitched. "Yes."

Blood fled from Lancelot's face and flooded his heart. Suddenly pale, he dropped to one knee on the flagstones. "I-I come to see—that is, I come seeking . . . a boon."

"A boon?"

It gushed out of him, not what he truly wished, but the precise opposite. "Send me out of Camelot, away from . . . court."

Amusement and bemusement mixed in the deep gaze of the king. Arthur seemed to look right through Lancelot, to the doors behind him. "For what possible purpose?"

To escape this rebel desire I feel for your wife, he thought, but said, "To seek wrong and right it. To work the king's justice."

"Are you well, Lancelot?" asked Arthur gravely.

Lancelot nodded. "Yes. Guine—Queen . . . ah . . . your wife—or, I should say, the Tuatha priestesses know a great deal about healing. I've knitted well in their hands—care." Closing his eyes as if swallowing a stiff drink, he nodded again. "I'm well enough, yes. Absolutely. And, in fact, health is the very point of this request. Now that there is no war—now that Alle is dead, and the Saxon menace is staved off, and there is peace in Britannia—we are doomed. Warriors, that is. We'll rust and dull without a foe to whet our edges. Just because there is no villainous army on the horizon does not mean there are no villains left to smite. I ask only your leave to ride out and smite them." He ended with what he hoped would seem a triumphant smile.

Arthur blinked. The hall was silent except for the slow drip of Lancelot's clothes. "What about Guinevere?"

"Guinevere!" Lancelot exclaimed, his head bolting upright. "What about Guinevere?"

"You are her champion," the king replied, gently mocking. "Who will protect her if you are gone?"

"You, of course, my king," blurted Lancelot. "You are truly her champion, not I. That's what she called you. Her chaste—" the word flipped from his tongue and plunged between them "—champion."

There wasn't so much irritation in Arthur's eyes as fatigue, or perhaps regret. "Yes."

Footsteps came from around the corner—the light and rapid approach of feminine feet.

Arthur called out, "Guinevere?"

"Arthur, I've been thinking—you should send the knights out questing. In these times of peace—" The words stomped to a halt along with the speaker. Queen Guinevere had rounded the corner and now stood there in her wet gown, her hair dappled with the waters of the Bountiful Weirds. She stared in amazement at the two men, who returned her look.

Arthur raised an ironic eyebrow. "Send the knights out questing? Your champion Lancelot had the same idea. Have you been conferring on this?"

Lancelot and Guinevere traded shocked glances. "No," they chorused. The queen went on to say, "It must be a good idea, if we both thought of it."

"It must be," Arthur echoed. His attention shifted to the knight. "It just seems strange that, by your own admission, Lancelot, you've dreamed your whole life of becoming a knight of the Round, and now you can't wait to escape Camelot. Something must be driving you away."

"Or calling me away," ventured Lancelot quickly. "The king's justice. It is calling me to make all of Britannia into Camelot. Let each maid feel she has your protection, great king, and let each lad dream of knighthood."

Arthur studied the warrior kneeling before him. In the king's glinting eyes, his thoughts were plain: Who is this man? Why does he swerve toward Guinevere and then away? What will he do to my marriage, my kingdom, if he remains?

Lancelot did his best to remain still. He'd piled up ardent words to hide even more ardent feelings. Never before had Lancelot been at war with himself—never, before Guinevere.

Arthur shifted his gaze toward the queen. She seemed simultaneously supportive of and miffed by the thought of Lancelot's departure.

"Yes, then, Lancelot," Arthur said at last. "Ride Britannia. Mete out my justice. Quest. I'll send the others as well. Better that they wander the land and eat its bounty than that they drive poor Kay to distraction emptying the larders. Yes. Call it a mandate. Go questing."

Lancelot nodded seriously. "Thank you, my king." He bowed his head to Guinevere. "Thank you, my queen."

Darkness settled on her serene features. "Rise, then, my champion. Let me through to my chambers."

Lancelot climbed to his feet, bowed again, and backed away. Guinevere stepped quickly over the wet spot on the hall runner, swung open the double doors, entered, and drew them closed.

"Just one question, Lancelot," the king began, but when he turned to where the knight had been, only empty air remained. Arthur muttered to himself, "Why were you both wet?"

Rasa cantered easily along the Winchester Road, lifting his knees high. Summer had lain its green turf across the way. Even the ruts left by laboring war engines had filled in. Rasa's iron shoes thumped the low grass. His white shoulders gleamed. An elm brake dappled the horse with leaf shadows. Rasa's spirits were high.

His rider's spirits were low. Lancelot rode numbly in the saddle. It creaked, freshly soaped, and its fittings glinted. His armor shone with equal brilliance, testimony to the nervous fervor of his rag. His oaken lance stood proudly in its couch, and his jousting shield jutted firmly from his forearm. In all outward ways, Lancelot was superbly prepared to quest. Inwardly, though, he was shattered.

For as long as he could remember, Lancelot had been a single, simple entity. He had acted according to his words, spoken according to his thoughts, and believed according to his heart. He had been apiece.

No longer. Actions belied words belied thoughts belied heart. All worked at cross-purposes. Lancelot had gained what he had always wanted and spurned it, wanting what he could never gain. He quested in the opposite direction from the one thing he sought. Lancelot had hoped that if he got out into the country, aback Rasa the Unbroken, and slew some dragons and saved some orphans, it would all come clear again. So far, no good. Two months of errantry had proved errant. He had slain brigands and petty tyrants, defended caravans and crones, hurled game to the hungry and coin to the poor—all the good works a sword can do. But war could not fill a heart emptied of conviction.

Nor could talk, especially the talk of his newest comrade, Sir Lionel.

"—So, what it all boils down to is this:" Lionel said as his steed matched Rasa's canter, "You can't be my cousin. My cousin's a baby. You're a grown man."

Oh, this again. Lancelot knew a simple cure for such inquiries. "Are you calling me a liar?"

Lionel's eyes flashed alarm, and his short-shorn black beard bunched in dismay. "Of course not." He stared at the hilt of Lancelot's all-too-famous blade.

An even more volatile question. "Are you calling the woman who reared me a liar?"

"No! Certainly not!" Lionel waved his free hand, wiping the insinuation out of the air. "But I might ask the same of you. When I say that I was there, a year ago, at the christening of my cousin Lancelot, do you say I am lying?"

This Lionel was a fierce warrior, and shrewd. He used Lancelot's own attack against him. "No."

"Then let us agree on this one thing—the infant Prince

Lancelot I saw christened a year ago could not be you today, yes?"

Lancelot's teeth ground upon that one. "Yes, unless, of course, you are mistaken. It is not a lie to speak a falsehood that you believe is true."

"Granted. Or perhaps you are mistaken," Lionel replied. When Lancelot glared, the man quickly added, "I admit that I do not know who you truly are—"

"My sword arm proves who I am."

"The sword arm proves only itself," Lionel replied. "Men are more than their arms."

"Yes."

"I do not know who you truly are, but I would venture the possibility—only a possibility—that perhaps you do not know either." Lionel's talk was not all emptiness. Here was a man who could drive mercilessly at the truth, however painful.

Lancelot could muster only a single, expulsive, "Yes."

Rasa snorted his own affirmative. The horse sensed his rider's flagging will and sought to bolster it.

Only one thing could bolster it. Sleep. Ever since that strange dream in Camelot—the threads upon the loom, the shifting pedals, the furtive shuttle, the women who animated it all—Lancelot had lived more in dream than in truth. He wandered the waking world to stay away from Guinevere. He wandered the dream world to join her again, to recline shamelessly in her arms and confess his desire. It brought the shattered bits of him into new alignment. Only in dream was he a single solid creature once more.

"I must rest," Lancelot blurted. "Evil does not stalk days like this. Look at the bees in the field. They look like tiny suns among the flowers. What can a knight do in such a field? Joust? No. Sleep? Yes."

Lionel dipped his head in consideration. "It sounds fine. I'll give you this, Lancelot: You sleep as much as a one-year-old."

Both knights gave a brief laugh. It was a joke and a concession.

For the first time, they rode as comrades. Their beasts veered off the Winchester Road to tromp through fields of beggar-ticks and yarrow. In silent agreement, the horses headed for an ancient apple tree, whose first green fruits already hung upon the boughs. Long-necked steeds could feast from the lower branches, and knights could sleep unseen among the flowers of the field. Arriving in the tree's blue shade, Lancelot and Lionel halted their mounts and swung from their saddles.

Lionel leaned his lance against the tree, hobbled his horse, and picked through the saddlebags for something to eat.

Lancelot lashed his lance to Rasa's saddle, and the horse wandered free. Lancelot eased himself to the ground, unlaced and removed his helm, and set it under his head like a hard pillow. Aunt Brigid had told him once of a man named Jacob who used a rock for a pillow and dreamed of ladders brimming with angels. Lancelot's aim was similar—he wanted dreams brimming with Guinevere.

Taking one last, long breath of the summer air, sweet with apples, Lancelot began to drowse. In a matter of moments, he slept.

A strange, inexplicable man, thought Sir Lionel, standing beside his mount and staring at the supine knight. Never had Lionel seen a greater warrior, and never had he met so direct and earnest a man. But all that glory wrapped around a single, undeniable truth—Lancelot was not who he thought he was.

Lionel slapped a horsefly, crunching the black knot against

his neck. He lifted his hand. The bug straightened its crumpled wings and flew away. Lionel touched his fingertip to the bite mark, and it came away red.

Of course, they were not cousins, but that fact was just the start of the conundrum. Where did Lancelot gain his overwhelming prowess? He credited his teacher, Master Smetrius, but no number of lessons could teach such grace. Lancelot was a born warrior, and if not born to Ban, then to whom?

The fly returned for a second taste. Lionel cupped his hand over the bite mark. He methodically closed his fist, leaving no gap. The fly rattled in his grasp. He tightened his grip. The bug ground to a black pulp on his palm.

He had a knack for chasing down the truth, latching onto it, and never letting go.

The birds and grasshoppers grew suddenly silent. He hadn't noticed their song until it ceased. Into the lull came the low rumble of hooves on packed earth. A horse approached—more than one, on the grassy uplands east of the meadow. They came at full gallop, at least three.

Instinctually, Lionel shouldered his horse sideways to hide its bulk behind the ragged trunk of the apple tree. He glanced about for Lancelot's steed. The white stallion had wandered away among nearby elms. It lifted its queer red eyes toward the sound and darted deerlike for a thistle brake. Lancelot himself lay fast asleep on the rumbling ground, well hidden by yellow foxglove.

The riders came. They wore the purple and gold livery of the Table Round, with the rampant red Pendragon emblazoned on shield and tabard. On polished helms rode family crests. By armor alone, Lionel knew them. First over the ridge rode Sir Kay upon his frothing roan, and hard behind him came Sir

Brandeles on a bay, and Sir Galyrnde on a black. All pelted full out, as if in terror.

Lionel snorted. What monster had these knights unearthed? What beast short of a rampant dragon could put three such stout warriors to headlong flight?

Then he saw. A mere spear's length behind them came a massive man astride a sorrel beast the size of a draft horse. He wore thick and clanging iron across his broad shoulders. Sackcloth and burlap made his tabard. For colors, he had chosen maroon and black, blood and death. All this, Lionel glimpsed in a moment before the meaty man closed the spear's length.

His leveled shaft rammed Galyrnde's shoulder plate. The point lodged and drove him right up out of the saddle. Leather traces snapped taut and then broke. Galyrnde vaulted over the lashing mane of his steed. He fell, and would have broken his neck but for his laced helm. Even in his armor, he took a beating, tumbling beside the frantic legs of his steed.

The huge warrior did not relent. He drove past the veering black to smash his lance into the back of Brandeles. The point pierced, so hatefully rammed. Brandeles's arms flew out to his sides. He too slid from the saddle to cartwheel madly among the daylilies.

How he pulled his lance free, how he swung past the bay, how he sent his steed after the thundering roan that bore Arthur's own step-brother, Lionel could not guess. As that same spear caught and hurled down its third knight—Sir Kay, Seneschal of all Britannia, no less—Lionel wondered if Lancelot were indeed the greatest warrior he had ever seen.

The brawny man in black reined in his whickering bloodstock at the edge of the meadow. Three dust devils stood restless vigil above his victims. The man turned the sorrel and charged the fractious horses of the knights. With the same lance that had felled their riders, he gathered their reins to him. Halting his beast once again, the warrior dismounted. He loosed one end of the strap from its bit and strung the three steeds in a long line attached to his own. Then, as purposeful as a poacher, he strode across the meadow, reached down, and hoisted Galyrnde to his shoulder. He strode back to the man's black, hurled him over its back, and lashed him down like so much venison. He turned, doing the same to Brandeles and Kay before he noticed the tall, black-bearded knight who sat his horse arrogantly at the edge of the clearing.

"Are you a man or a monster?" asked Sir Lionel levelly. His voice was silken despite the thunder of his heart.

"What?" growled the warrior in outrage.

"I wonder, what sort of man would ram his spear into another man's back," explained Lionel. "So if you are a man, you are the basest of men. I personally hope you are one of the better sort of monsters."

The warrior flipped back his helm, and a firestorm of golden hair jutted from within. He smiled with broad and stumpy teeth. "Another knight of the Table Round. You folk line up so willingly, it is a pleasure to bring you down." The smile disappeared, replaced by a promising glare. "And I'll take you down from the front."

Tightening his grip on his lance, Sir Lionel said, "You are welcome to try. But know this—you assault the king's own men. Even if I fall, you will be hunted down and slain."

"So be it," replied the warrior. He had lashed all three of the defeated knights to their horses and had freed his own from the string of reins. He swung into the saddle. "I'll not rest until I slay the knight who is called du Lac."

Behind his visor, Lionel's face grew stern. Now, he knew

he had chosen rightly in letting Lancelot sleep. "Train your spear upon me, and let our weapons discuss this." He drew his lance from its couch and swung it levelly before him.

The warrior did likewise and kicked his sorrel into a headlong charge.

Lionel's steed bounded forward, eager to engage.

Hooves cut through the buttercups. Spears sought shields and found them. Lionel's point cracked against the shield and rebounded outward, lancing clear air beyond his shoulder.

His opponent's spear slid inward across his shield. It caught him square in the sternum and hurled him from the saddle. His horse pounded out from beneath him. With the warrior's point still lodged in his chest, Lionel plunged through unforgiving air. As he fell, all he could think was that there were more mysteries, deeper mysteries, than Lancelot.

Then he struck ground, and there was time for no more speculation. Lionel's eyes went black, and he slumped.

10

The Four Queens

Morgan le Fey rode in royal estate among her compatriots—the queens of North Galys, Eastland, and the Outer Isles. Each might as easily have been called priestess, for they knew the ancient ways. Or perhaps, they would best have been called goddesses, for their magic left no wall between the human and the divine.

The four queens rode four snow-white mules. A square banner of green silk shielded them from the sun. Four eunuch warriors held it aloft. It was the old way—female fecundity borne on, shielded with, and protected by male sterility. Eunuchs and mules were more powerful and docile than their virile counterparts. They were perfectly suited for their tasks. It was why bulls were made into steers, why stallions were made geldings. Testes were fine when properly confined, which they never could be in the presence of true feminine power. Sex of any sort carried potent magic, but the power of the genders worked at cross-purposes. A sterilized male retinue allowed priestesses to wield undiluted magic.

Morgan breathed the fragrant and fecund air of the meadow.

Great powers worked in her. Let Guinevere and her Tuatha devotees dabble in their trinities, their weirds, their divine trigonometries. The god of Abraham had long since taken over the potency of three. Even the synoptic gospels were three, the Book of John but a bone thrown to those left in hell by Matthew, Mark, and Luke.

Morgan and her comrades knew the power of four: four seasons, four winds, four elements, four phases of the moon, four times of day, four suits of Tarot—four queens of ancient magic. They rode the land in search of new power, of a young knight named Lancelot.

Testes were fine when properly confined. If all were steers and geldings, whence would the next generation spring?

Lancelot lay beneath an ancient apple tree, perhaps dreaming of his faraway Avalon. It was as Morgan had planned it. The knights who might have distracted him—Lionel and Kay, Galyrnde and Brandeles—were borne away like hunting trophies by another of their kind. Oblivious, the true man slept—and how true! His physical prowess only hinted at his spiritual powers. Though he knew it not, his was a soul that bridged Britannia and Benwick, and greater worlds.

The queens rode their white mules through the tall grass. One by one, the stalwart beasts strode to an arcing crescent around the man. The samite canopy overhead stretched out of alignment, struggling to protect the priestesses from the sun. Withdrawing their staffs, the eunuch warriors furled the awning and seated themselves among the weeds. Though sunlight threw leafy shadows across the queens, they were oblivious. They stared at this silver-garbed warrior as though he were a man of gold—young, beautiful, virtuous, potent.

"We cannot fight over him," warned Morgan, "any more than we would fight over a glass of fine wine or a select cut of steak. He is only that—made for consumption, for one of us. We cannot rip him into four parts."

The queen of North Galys glowered. Her hair was flame-red, and it made her eyes seem to burn. "Then, I'll end all argument and take him myself."

The queen of the Outer Isles, a slight and black-haired woman, said, "He is not from Britannia, and would best be coupled with one not from Britannia."

The queen of Eastland agreed. "My folk are Saxon, from the continent. Let him be my consort, and I will unite the Saxons and Angles and Gauls to rise against Arthur."

"Hold," advised Morgan. "Hold. I knew of Lancelot du Lac before any of you. I watched him. I brought you to him. If he belongs to anyone, he belongs to me. But what does it matter? He is ours. I shall place on him an enchantment to keep him asleep until he lies within Castle Charyot. Then, let noble knight Lancelot choose among us which one he would serve."

She stepped down from her mount. It was easily done. The creature was not so much a beast of burden but a living couch, bearing her with an opulent lentitude through a rushing world. She and her queens did not need speedy beasts, or brawny ones, or tall ones. As often as not, they rode trails through thin air or through nothing at all. When they deigned to ride the ground, they rode these solemn and shaggy mules.

Morgan felt the grass between her toes. She wore no shoes. She felt the humus beneath the grass—an inch for each of the six millennia that grass had grown here, and the clay beneath the humus, and the sand beneath that, and bedrock. Another step. Her mind plumbed downward yet, through miles of stone to magma—the blood of the world. Britons had forgotten the blood of the world, so enamored now with the blood of heaven. Morgan had not forgotten. Beneath all bedrock lurked red-hot desire.

She dropped to her knees, wilted by the heat in her. Brimming eyes stared into Lancelot's face. He was no ancient god, in the way of Merlin, but a young one.

All young men were gods, their blood so fast, so near the surface.

"Sleep, child," said Morgan, drawing her fingertips in a gentle caress along his jaw line. Blood trailed her touch. She had not cut him, or herself, but their blood called to each other and slipped the silken verge that divided them. She traced his cheekbones, the bridge of his nose, the brows; blood marked his skin in the outline of his skull. "Sleep, sweet son, and wake not until I call you." His face retained its serenity despite the ghastly mask drawn over it. "Sleep, Lancelot, and dream of me, and when you wake, believe."

Morgan trembled. Sitting back on her heels, she cradled her scarlet fingers in her other hand and rocked gently. The spell had taken its toll. She called to her eunuch warrior, "Bring my shield."

He obeyed immediately, leaping up from the weeds where he sat. He crossed to the mule and loosed the silver pendentive from the beast. Approaching his mistress, he held the shield before him.

"Couch him within it and bear him among you," Morgan instructed wearily. She rose, tottering. Color fled her face, but she did not sink down. "Bring him after me."

Crossing to her mule, she seated herself. Her flesh was as white as its pelt. Aback the creature, she watched the eunuchs work. Lancelot's head rested easily in the quatrefoil atop the shield. It bore his shoulders as if cut for them. His arms and legs hung free, giving him the sprawled aspect of the corpus Christi. Morgan did not mind. When men were young and virgin, let them be cast in the image of the young and virgin God. Only be certain *she* would never be cast in that image, nor should any woman, nor the world.

The eunuchs lifted Lancelot. They bore him as once they had borne the silken awning. The queens turned their mounts, surrounded Lancelot, and rode across the meadow. Though deprived of their sun shade, they did not notice. They basked in a new, earthbound sun. Morgan, most of all, drank in his radiance, for nothing felt so glorious on bloodless skin as sunlight.

Lancelot awoke in utter darkness. He had heard of dungeons. Those deep, stony pits resided in the popular mind among such things as plague, demons, and curses. Everyone knew of dungeons, but few had seen the inside of one, and fewer still had emerged alive.

This was no mere dungeon. As black as pitch and as cold as the tomb, the narrow pit was hemmed in by unmortared walls of stone. They rose sharply to a ceiling of iron bars, through which dribbled the rank waste of prisoners above. This space was, in the tongue of Lancelot's ancestry, an oubliette—a cell that opened only at its peak. The word came from the Gaulish *oublier*, and in turn from the Latin *oblitare*, the root for the word oblivion—to forget. Oubliettes were often set in the sewage runoffs of other cells, both gathering the offal and wafting the persistent scent of death.

Why do they wish to forget me? Lancelot wondered, and then, Who would wish to forget me?

The answer to the first question was plain. They wish to

forget me because thought of me causes regret and pain. The second question was more illusive. Who would feel regret and pain at thought of me?

It would not be someone he had wronged. Such folk loved to remember the injustices they suffered, especially when the perpetrator was in their power. No, it would be someone who had wronged him. There was no greater torment than the continued presence of one's victims.

So, who had wronged him and cared enough to feel regret? The answer to that, too, was plain. No man cared for Lancelot, but many women did. It might have been his mother, who had abandoned him and gone mad. It might have been Guinevere, whose simple presence made a traitor of Lancelot. It felt like neither of them—or both of them.

"Get up," said a sudden voice, the genderless sound of a eunuch guard. "Shake off the filth. You have an audience with the queens."

The queens. Were there queens without kings? Apparently. Did they regret Lancelot? Yes. Why? Because they could not own him—because Guinevere did. It was a revelation. Suddenly Lancelot knew what he must do to survive.

Two eunuch guards set their pry bars and forced the iron grate out of its frame. With a scraping complaint of metal on stone, they dragged the bars aside. A slender hemp rope dropped down to Lancelot. With it came the warrior's cry, "For Morgan le Fey! For Morgan le Fey!"

Lancelot cared nothing for Morgan le Fey, but only for that bristly rope. He reached up and grasped it. He drew himself up the cut-stone walls of the oubliette and toward a gentle glimmer of air above. The wall ran with offal and worse things, but he climbed gladly. He felt like a primordial creature clawing its way into the light of God. He dragged himself through the frame of the grate, onto the floor of a less-dank, less-dark cell. A boot shoved down on his back. It should not have been able to send him to his breastplate, but he remained weak from whatever enchantment had laid him low. Armor ground against gritty stone. The eunuchs wrestled his arms behind him. The same rope he had climbed now lashed his wrists and hands together.

Through gritted teeth, Lancelot managed to growl, "For Morgan le Fey. . . ."

They hauled him to his feet. He was hemmed in by five eunuchs: massive, clean, direct, and humorless. In their midst, Lancelot seemed scrawny and filthy. Still, they gave him space. Even bound, outnumbered, and weak, he had the power of presence among them. He embodied the species they once were.

The eunuchs led him out of the cell door, along a corridor, and up a set of rock stairs. He trudged awhile before feeling the clammy chill of subterranean air drag away. They emerged in the gaoler's chamber at the first floor of the keep. Crossing the room, Lancelot strode out the arched door and onto the springy grass of the bailey. The air smelled clean and sweet after the incessant reek of despair. Long strides bore him away from the prison and toward the palace. Ornate doors stood ahead beneath a florid tympanum. Guards swung the doors outward. Beyond shone red-carpeted stairs that led, no doubt, to the throne room of one of his queen captors.

Lancelot made no attempt to clean himself. He wore his smudges and filth with defiant pride. These had been the conditions granted him by Morgan le Fey. Let her put up with them.

Through the double doors they passed, and up the stairs, beneath a second arch, and into the quatrefoil throne room.

Lancelot and his escorts emerged in the center of the chamber. Once, it had been a Roman basilica, dedicated to the worship of the Christ. Now it enthroned his foes. In each cardinal direction opened a transept with a dais and throne, backed by a screen of oak and a window tracery. A queen sat upon each throne. Young in silk and ermine, older in linen and lace, and older still in wool and hose. All were beautiful, all powerful, and all focused entirely upon the young knight.

He returned their looks, one by one. The dark-haired, white-skinned, voluptuous one who sat on the loftiest throne could be none other than Morgan le Fey. Her husband, King Urien of Gore, had no doubt been duped into granting this church to his wife, where she might hold court with her sisters in sorcery.

She spoke, though not to him. "Even through the filth, his lines are clean."

"But it is not just physique," answered a red-haired queen, by her tone a native of North Galys. "His soul has such lines too."

A third queen, slight and dark, piped, "Perfect breeding stock—"

"Now to decide," offered the last, "with whom."

Lancelot said, "I demand to know why you hold me."

Morgan le Fey stared at him. "Douse him."

A eunuch reached down to a bucket prepared for that very purpose and hurled a glistening arch of water toward Lancelot. It struck him heavily, washing away the filth of the oubliette. The water spattered to the marble-tiled floor. It formed puddles that received the incessant drips off Lancelot's armor.

Placidly, Morgan le Fey said, "You demand nothing here, Lancelot. You are no longer a swaggering knight. You are something truer."

"What? A wet rag?" he spat back.

"Douse him," Morgan commanded.

Another bucket of water rushed over him. This time, the deluge caught his breath and made him snort and gasp.

"Though you deserve no explanation, I will give one. You are a consort, in the old sense of the term. You are the mortal partner to an immortal queen. It is why Guinevere desires you. She sees what you are, the one male in one million who must breed. The first art learned by humanity was husbandry—the art of breeding animals through the careful control of the male member. One bull, one stallion, one cock, a host of partners, a nation of offspring. That is your role. Fecundity, felicity, and every other blessing is granted by the female; fertility is the role of the chosen male. You are he."

"I chose nothing—" the words were interrupted by a third gout of water.

Morgan shook her head reprovingly. "You have but one choice. Lie with one of us—lie with all of us—or die forgotten, in misery, in your cell."

Lancelot's nostrils flared. "Understand this. I choose none of you—lewd witches that you are."

"Witchery is only a man's term for woman's power," interrupted Morgan. She scowled. "So, you choose none of us."

"On my life, I reject you all."

A look of near-grief came to the dark brows of Queen Morgan. "So be it. You are one in a thousand, in a hundred thousand, Lancelot, and you squander it in the oubliette. So be it!"

He was down again. It was that sudden. The eunuchs had thrown him to his face on the ground. They dragged him back down the red-carpeted stairs. In rough hands, they carried him across the grassy bailey, through the gaoler's chambers, down more stairs, and to the dank, offal-reeking cell above his own.

Without pause, they hurled him through the gap, and the iron grate clanked above his head.

"For Morgan le Fey," they said.

Filthy again, Lancelot gaped up at them. Darkness deepened around him as the oubliette did its work. They would forget, and he would be gone forever.

11

The Rose and the Bee

He will die, Morgan le Fey told herself, the certainty of it sending a frisson down her spine. She snuffed the candle that had glowed in her bedchamber. Darkness sucked in around her. He will stay in that cell, refusing, until he dies.

But he cannot die. He is the one. There will not be another like him within even *my* lifetime.

She drew back the flaxen folds of her bed. Cold lurked in the patiently woven strands. She slid naked legs between the sheets. Through the linen, she felt the woolen blanket prickle. It had once been a horse blanket, from when she was only a young and angry hand in her mother's stables. The thick cover still smelled of the clean oils of horseflesh. By the marriage bed, Morgan had become queen, and by another bed, she had become heir to all of Britannia. This third bed would make her queen of two worlds. Drawing a breath of cold air, she dug her nails into the deep wolf pelt that topped the pile and drew it up about her shoulders.

Urien disapproved, of course, of her sexual conquests—any man disapproved of a conquering woman—but he could not object. He was, after all, conquered. Men could never truly rule the bed. It was the ancient seat of female power. Yes, men could rape, but rape was violence, not sex. In matters of sex, men would always serve. Urien did. Lancelot would.

Morgan felt heat roll from her skin, warming the well of fabric in which she lay. Darkness poured into her eyes. She stared at a ceiling ornate in plaster figures. The embers of the fire gave them a brimstone glow. By day, the carvings depicted Eden, its inhabitants naked and unashamed—the bedchamber once had belonged to an abbot whose soul was edified by glimpses of the buxom Eve. By night, firelight, pure and elemental, gave the carvings their true aspect, and showed the true Garden.

Before Abram's patriarchy, there had been a verdant paradise. In it dwelt the goddess and her divine consort, the serpent. In that place, the fruit of knowledge and of eternal life were offered to all. Indeed, the serpent twined about the tree of life to form the caduceus—the symbol of life and healing. In that garden, every creature was naked and unashamed, and women ruled with sexual power. Night and firelight showed up the ancient truths that hid within the Apollo-shine of day.

Lancelot was the new serpent—consort to the goddess. He didn't even know it. And though the other queens knew it, lewd witches that they were, they did not know why. They knew no more of Lancelot's origins than he himself knew. In their ignorance, they could end up killing him. In his own ignorance, Lancelot could die. Ignorance was a horrid thing. Only the Tetragrammaton would have made eating of the Tree of Knowledge an offense punishable by death.

Morgan had eaten of that forbidden fruit, had come under the sentence of Yahweh. It mattered little. Once she lay with Lancelot, there would be a new goddess, and a new consort.

The audience today had gone exactly as she had planned. The events this night would unfold with identical certainty.

Morgan sighed, feeling her breath sink into the wolfskin at her throat. Lancelot did not know it, nor the three other queens, but Morgan had lured them all into her bed. Here, she never lost.

She whispered, her lips setting mist in the cold air. "Good luck, fair knight, as you attempt to escape."

A light approached beyond the oubliette's grate. It bathed the stone ceiling in a fiery glow. Eunuch heads cast shaved shadows. A guard with a lantern appeared above the pit. He lifted the beaming thing. His comrades set pry bars and hoisted the grate.

Lancelot squinted up at the light, sun-bright in that murk.

Into the radiance came a slender servant-girl. She had the childish figure of a post, with no flowering at hip and breast. Her skinny arms bore a plate upon which rested a few hunks of bread. "Leave us," she said.

The eunuchs turned querulous looks her way.

The girl returned their stares. Wordlessly, the guards withdrew, leaving their lantern beside the oubliette.

Bathed in gold, the girl was an angel. "I've brought supper," she announced in a reedy voice. "Some crusts, and a bit of fat."

The mean rations were a banquet to Lancelot—anything from the world above, anything not smeared with offal. He reached up toward the plate. His fingers trembled. It was the first time he realized how weak, how craven, he had become.

The child stooped, extending the plate down into the pit. She watched with all-seeing eyes of brown. Lancelot's fingers seemed bestial on the wooden platter. Her delicate hands let go. Lancelot drew the supper down and bit hungrily into one of the stale crusts.

"I know you have refused them—my mistresses—though it is death to do so."

Lancelot nodded, swallowing. "It is a worse death to accept them."

"Yes," she said bitterly. "I know. I serve them, a death worse than death, because my father lost a wager with one of their husbands."

Lancelot paused in his hasty meal and lifted an eyebrow. "Which husband?"

"The king of North Galys, and three knights of the Round, including the son of Queen Morgan. They defeated my father at tournament last Tuesday. Having already taken from him all else, they took me."

Across Lancelot's mind moved the flames of Benwick. Claudas had taken all from his father—all but Lancelot. "What is your father's name?"

"King Bagdemagus."

"I know of him, a great king and a greater warrior." Lancelot shook his head grimly, and he clenched his jaw. The muscle in his temple leapt. "This is the sort of injustice I am meant to right, but how can I while I languish in a cell?"

"You cannot," the young woman replied firmly. "But if you will pledge yourself to me and my cause, I will release you."

The crusts of bread dropped, unnoticed, to the floor. "Pledge myself to you and your cause? Who are you, and what is your cause?"

"I am merely a child who wants to be free. My cause is the defense of my father. If you fight for him in the next tournament, he will win my freedom."

Lancelot's eyes shone with hope. Not since he had fallen

asleep beneath that apple tree had he felt this way. "I pledge myself to defend you, my child, and to aid your father in winning the next jousts, that you might be free."

"You pledge yourself utterly," she pressed, her eyes as sharp as poniards.

"Utterly."

"Then, tomorrow at dawn, when the witches sleep, I'll lead you from this place, through the twelve locked gates, and set you on your horse. You'll ride to a monastery ten miles distant, and there prepare for the jousts."

"Twelve locked gates," echoed Lancelot.

The girl nodded gravely. "Once this was a church, with a gate for each apostle, and a single key for Saint Peter. Now, it is a witches' castle, and I have Saint Peter's key."

Lancelot smiled. "I am glad to know you, child, a creature untouched by the witchcraft all around."

Her piercing look grew more severe. "You mistake me, Sir Lancelot. I am just as these four queens, except young and not a queen. I envy their power, and hope for it myself one day. To rise to their station, I must escape them, as must you."

Mouth hanging open, Lancelot studied the girl. As straight as a pole, as young as a dream, she could ally with him because she had not yet flowered. Once she had, they would be as antithetical and inextricable as the rose and the bee. "I will await the dawn, child, and will remain utterly faithful to you."

She spoke a single word in reply. "Good."

Morgan woke with the dawn. Beneath wolfskin and wool and linen, she stretched, as languid as a cat. Let Lancelot think of her as a creature of the night. Cats were nocturnal, and yet slept and woke as they would. So did she.

Throwing back the covers, she stood beside her bed. The cold morning slapped her body. Gooseflesh stood across her skin. She yawned and stepped toward the fire. It had died to ash. Lifting hewn elm, she chucked it into the firebox and blew. In moments, flames woke. They licked the wood.

Morgan poked at it, though she was Morgan no longer. As she squatted naked there upon the hearth, her body had subtly transformed. She lost a few inches in height, and a dozen in width. Her broad breasts and child-bearing hips were gone, replaced by narrow figure of a girl. It was not fit for a queen to crouch at her own hearth. Let the maidservant do it.

The fire blazed nicely as Morgan rose and donned the shift and skirt she had worn the night before. She reached into the pocket at her waist and found the key. It would open each of the twelve doors. It would lead to Lancelot.

She sighed, allowing herself the girlish thrill of thinking of her beloved. Yes, she would open the twelve locks leading to him, and he would throw his arms about her, and suddenly the intrigues of the last decade would be made naught.

Such were the fancies of youth. Occupying a youthful body, Morgan permitted them. The truth was much more grim. Lancelot must willingly come to her bed, or he must be destroyed.

The girl shrugged away those weighty thoughts. Instead she donned a servant's shift, strode to the door of the royal apartments, listened a moment, and pulled it open. Beyond, a grand space waited. Morgan strode out beneath hammer beams and painted frescoes. She ignored them, heading for the dungeon and her victory.

She came that morning, as she had promised. Lancelot sighed gladly. How straight she was. Women were curved, and men were square, but children, all children, were straight.

"I hope only, my dear," he said in a hushed voice that was almost a prayer, "that your father's virtue matches your own."

She stared at him with doe's eyes. "My father is a great man, a great king, but the hearts of men are never as pure as the hearts of their daughters. And the hearts of kings are never as pure as the hearts of men."

Lancelot nodded at her wisdom. Had she been two decades older, he would have thought her a bitter spinster, but from her roseate lips, these words were nectar. She was right. There was something corrupt in kings specifically, and in men in general. There was something corrupt in knights such as he. "I will defend your father's honor in faithfulness to your honor, my dear—a flawed man defending a flawed king for sake of a flawless maid."

The key turned in its lock. With a strength belied by her narrow figure, the maid yanked up the oubliette grate. She stood there above him, grate hanging in one hand and keys in the other. Her silhouette was stark against the moldy ceiling. "Any man thinks any maid who saves him is flawless. Would you think the same of a maid who served you?"

Lancelot colored. No, he would not. His corruption clung to him like gangrene. Why did this maid bring outward adoration and inward guilt? He chose not to reply. Instead, he rose, leapt, and clambered up the moldy wall of the oubliette.

Oblivion. Obliteration. He was glad to be free of that forgetful place. A man in such a place was nothing at all. What did strength of arms matter to a man forgotten?

He hauled himself to his belly and brought up one knee. He climbed from the pit. His armor clanked. The stench of it seemed somehow worse in the presence of the child.

"Forgive my filth," Lancelot said. "Outward and inward. I

can offer only my sword arm, to save your father and you."

She did not answer, but only turned and walked with an iron stride beneath the dripping arch. He followed her down a long tunnel. At the next gate, bars in an ornate frame, she paused to fit her key.

Lancelot ventured again. "I will, of course, wash myself before I appear at the monastery."

"Outward and inward," she echoed.

The gate rang and swung back. "Outwardly, yes. And at the monastery, I will confess and repent—"

"You must wash your armor because it is grand, because it is meant to be clean and not filthy. You must wash your soul for the same reason. Though a lofty purpose awaits your armor, a loftier one awaits your soul. Defend my father, free me, prove yourself, and transcend the sin of man."

The words rolled out like commands. Lancelot took them as such. Here was a virtue worth defending. Yes, Guinevere also had such virtue, but to defend this immaculate child was like defending Guinevere before she was queen. To overcome the evil of man and save the virtue of woman was the greatest purpose of life. He followed his young liberator upstairs to the next gate, and the next. Twelve gates. Twelve apostles. One key. This maid, like Hercules, endured twelve great labors to free him. Lancelot would bear at least as many feats to free her.

"I will, my dear child. I will."

Rasa waited in the forest beyond the basilica. The canny steed must have followed his master. Rasa bowed once deeply, and Lancelot returned the gesture. It was fitting that Rasa should come, not a beast of burden, but one friend saving another.

Lancelot thanked his friend, washed himself in the river, and mounted.

His pledge echoed in his mind as he rode away from Morgan le Fey's palace. He wondered at the child's strange commands: "Defend my father. Free me. *Prove yourself. Transcend the sin of man.*" The sin of man? Mortal sin? And prove yourself? He would fight to prove King Bagdemagus, not himself. It was nonsense—not childish nonsense, as it should have been. This was adult nonsense—a screen of words to hide what lay beneath. Lancelot studied that roiling riddle, but it revealed only the reflection of his own eyes.

No, not his: the eyes of the child. She watched him. She wanted him to prove himself, to transcend the sin of man.

Lancelot shook away the vision. The oubliette had affected him. All that darkness, that rank and forgetful darkness. He just needed air and light, and he had plenty of both aback Rasa. He breathed. Wind washed over and into him. It dragged the last of the river water from his tabard and tunic. He rode across ten miles of sunlight—what seemed scant distance from that horrid basilica.

The thistly lowlands of Rheged passed in gold and purple panoply beneath the hooves of Rasa. Across sheep-cropped pastures spread a green maze of hedgerows, leading into a brown labyrinth in oak. Beyond it all lay his true destination: the friary of the Broken Nard.

It took its name from the great fortune in perfume broken by a prostitute over the head of Jesus, anointing him and proclaiming him the Christ. When his disciples protested, he replied, "The poor you have with you always, but will you always have me?" In emulation of their divine forebear, the abbots of the monastery advocated ritualized poverty punctuated by sporadic extravagance—mortal penury leavened by Christological intervention. It was a fitting sanctuary in which to find an impoverished petty king, who wished only to survive long enough to see his fortunes reversed.

Lancelot was that reversal of fortune. He rode Rasa up a tree-lined path and peered at the clearings around. They were peopled with inexpertly crafted statues of saints, each affixed to a cedar post that was driven deeply into the ground. The saints were as prolific as rabbits. At the end of the lane loomed the black shadow of the ancient monastery. It was no older than the basilica where Morgan ruled. Still, this structure had the pockmarked and weary-worn aspect of age. Ivy pitted limestone walls. Moss clung to brickwork. One split column of stone had been wrapped in bands of iron as if it were a splinted leg.

Lancelot reined Rasa in before a rising stair that led to the chapel. He leapt from the saddle and climbed. Rasa cantered out to a nearby garden to nibble the grass.

Lancelot meanwhile reached the top of the stair, pulled open the iron-banded doors, and strode into the decorous darkness beyond. It smelled of mildew and incense, the scent of Christianity. Beyond the narthex opened a domed chamber held aloft by four great drums. The altar lay in the east, behind a wood-worked screen. Before the screen ran a rail, and at it knelt a single figure. His velvet cloak and purple shift announced that he was laity. His sunken shoulders and bowed gray head told that he was Bagdemagus.

Wearing a secret smile, Lancelot strode down among solemn pews. The clank of sollerets against flagstones made the man at the rail startle, though he did not look up. Lancelot approached, each step knotting the king's shoulders until they clenched fistlike near his ears. Reaching the rail, Lancelot dropped to his knees beside the man, clasped his gauntleted hands, and bowed his head.

At last, King Bagdemagus turned an incredulous face his way. The beard and mustache cinched toward flocculent brows. He scowled impressively.

Without looking his way, Lancelot said, "So, King Bagdemagus, for what were you praying?"

The man spluttered. "What business is it of yours?"

"It is entirely my business," replied Lancelot, turning to stare at him, "as I have been sent to answer your prayers."

The king considered, teeth gritting beneath leathery cheeks. "You cannot have been."

"I cannot?" wondered Lancelot aloud. "Then what did you pray for?"

"Humility, if you must know."

"Humility to accept unjust defeat at the hand of the king of North Galys?"

Twin fires kindled in the king's eyes. "How did you know—?"

"What else did you pray for?"

"Patience," replied the king, his eyes faraway.

"Patience to await the return of your daughter."

King Bagdemagus gabbled. "H-how did you—?"

"And you prayed for forbearance, in behalf of your oppressor, and meekness that you might inherit the earth," finished Lancelot. He waggled a reproving finger. "Sometimes God answers such prayers by saying no."

"No?"

"No to humility, because God wants you to crush the king of North Galys. No to patience, because God wants your daughter returned by next tournament. No to forbearance and meekness, for we will rout the warriors of your foe."

A blue light trembled in the king's eyes. "I hoped secretly for such answers."

"God knows your secret heart, or more correctly, someone with godlike powers—the one who sent me."

Staring with bald amazement, King Bagdemagus could manage only to ask, "Whom?"

Lancelot smiled. "Why, your daughter, of course."

12

The Proof of Knighthood

King Bagdemagus felt like an old lion on the prowl that morning. He would win the day, thanks to an angel warrior sent by his own daughter. Bagdemagus led twenty men in simple panoply onto a dew-speckled field. At the opposite end of the meadow appeared the king of North Galys. His bright-caparisoned forces numbered two score. A third group appeared—three knights of the Round, their standards announcing their king and their pennants announcing themselves—Madore de la Porte, Gahalantyne, and Mordred.

The day would decide many fortunes.

Normally such a contest would occur upon Bagdemagus's jousting ground, but the land no longer belonged to him. Today's fight took place in a pasture three miles south of the Broken Nard. Betting on the last jousts had lost Bagdemagus his kingdom and his daughter. This time, the stakes were even higher: The very life of the king was wagered against regaining his lands and her freedom.

Such extreme stakes had brought a crowd to watch the spectacle. A few nobles came with seats and attendants, but all the others sat in the grass or milled near the woods.

King Bagdemagus cantered easily across the field. His warriors flanked him. From the other side approached the king of North Galys and his host. Bagdemagus smiled behind his helm. If he lost today, he would forfeit his life, but what was he without land and freedom? If he won—and with Sir Lancelot at his side, he would win—all that had been lost would be restored.

"Are you ready?" shouted the king of North Galys within his helm of red and black. "Are you ready to die?"

Lifting his own visor, Bagdemagus said, "I am ready to kill."

"Good luck to you, then, old man. Your time has gone. We young will pry your kingdom from your dead hands."

"It'll be strenuous work with my lance in your gut," sneered Bagdemagus.

The other king tossed his head in imitation of his great black steed, and the two of them bounded away toward the end of the lists. "Then let's have at it. No quarter asked."

"No quarter given," replied Bagdemagus in the ancient response. He, too, turned his steed. His warriors followed him to the end of the meadow. There, they spun their mounts and watched the tableau unfold.

On the far end of the field, the king of North Galys cuffed one of the Round Table warriors—Mordred—on the shoulder and shouted, "We call for challenge."

Bagdemagus stared at his own troops. None were eager to die. All were good men, outnumbered in this evil age. Still, a few had the youthful delusion of immorality, and they vied with each other to enter the lists first. Almost at random, Bagdemagus chose among them. "Defend us," he said to the young man. "Prove us."

Nodding his thanks, the warrior slapped a gleaming visor down over his face. He lifted his lance from its couch, set it and his shield, and kicked his mount into the charge. Sir Mordred did likewise.

King Bagdemagus watched, breathless. Clods of grass tumbled in the air behind the pelting steeds. On silver shoulders rode the hopes of Gore.

The foe raced up from the far side. Mordred and his beast seemed small and black. They swelled out as they approached.

Lances leveled toward hearts. Points caught and cracked upon shields. One lance—the Gore lance—shattered. Somehow, despite his gimp arm, Mordred held the shield. His spear bore on. It slid from shield to breastplate and from breastplate to neck and lodged. The point drove through.

The young immortal man, so eager to fight for his aging king, was gone in that instant. He had become a sack of skin. His neck broke. Brain and body died separately. The warrior tumbled with the piercing point of his foe. Sprays of blood coated him, and the dust of horse hooves adhered.

Sir Mordred released his fouled lance and charged past. The spear shook mournfully as the man's body hit ground and rolled. Bones broke in the next seconds, and the lance just afterward.

He had been a good man, a good warrior, King Bagdemagus thought.

Mordred rode his steed in a grand arc before the forces of Bagdemagus. He gestured to their shouts and hisses as if he were their beloved king. Standing in the saddle, he rode past the viewers and turned back toward his own end of the field. His shield arm held limply to his side, Mordred galloped by the body of the man he had just slain.

"He had been a good man," growled King Bagdemagus.

• • •

Prince Meleagaunce hauled hard on the reins of his champing steed. He turned the beast in a circle. Its hooves churned the dust of the glade. His bristly black brows jutted from the silvery helm he wore. "Did you see that? Murder, that's all. Grandstanding and murder. It's time we went."

"No," replied Lancelot summarily. Liveried in Bagdemagus's colors, Lancelot and Rasa waited patiently amid the tree shadows. The king's three best warriors—one of them his impetuous son—turned their eyes from the distant tournament grounds and looked to Lancelot. "The tournament has only begun. Let the king of North Galys and his allies think they are winning the day. Let the crowd think so, too. Then we will join."

With an incredulous glare, the meaty young prince said, "You're just going to abandon them to die?"

"They are warriors," Lancelot said simply. "We cannot fight their battles."

Meleagaunce's teeth clamped shut, and his visor after. Through both, he hissed, "I'm no coward. I'm going!" Heels and reins struck the horse, sending it bounding forward through the forest.

Unmoving, Lancelot watched him go.

The other two warriors looked between the impulsive prince and the staid knight. They clicked to their steeds and charged out after the prince.

Lancelot shook his head. This prince had none of his father's wisdom or patience but the warriors were sworn to him.

Lancelot himself was sworn to King Bagdemagus.

He snorted in resignation and patted Rasa's neck. Rasa nodded at that decision and broke into a trot behind the other beasts.

No mere trot could have caught them. Meleagaunce charged headlong. Undergrowth thrashed the horse's legs, and heels pummeled its flanks. The steed pelted through forest shadows and out onto grass. It tore across open space, leaves whirling in a comet's tail behind it.

Meleagaunce's fiery approach sent waves of shock among the crowd. Their chatter was shoved down their throats. At a gallop, the prince drove his horse into that of a waiting warrior, forcing him out of the jousting lane.

"If they want massacre, they'll get massacre!" Meleagaunce shouted, loud beyond his helm and nearly deafening within. He did not pause. His mount thundered down the lane. Meleagaunce hoisted his lance from its couch and brought it out before him.

His opponent—a man of North Galys—urged his mount to a canter and then a gallop. He too lowered his lance and raised his shield.

They came together with a violent splintering of wood and buckling of metal. Both lances struck and stuck. Meleagaunce outweighed his foe by ten stone. The Galynean's lance pounded Meleagaunce's armor against his chest—stout muscles over ox-sized ribs. The wood gave way. Meleagaunce's shaft plunged through steel, skin, muscle, bone, and heart.

Meleagaunce released the lance and rode on. His weapon tumbled groundward with his shattered foe. Only then did he pull up short. Meleagaunce stood in the stirrups, hauled hard to make his steed rear, flung back his helmet, and let out an ungodly shriek of victory.

Why must men do this? thought Guinevere as attendants bore a blood-bathed corpse away from the battlefield. They're like stags in the rut, slaying rivals and doing all to dominate.

The queen of Britannia drew her veil more tightly about her face. She did not want Lancelot to know her. She wanted to seem only another beautiful maid in the eager throng. Men did what men did, and women did what women did. Veiled but inveigling, she watched Lancelot prepare to joust.

In fact, she had not ceased watching Lancelot since he had ridden out. This quest was meant to separate them, but distance was powerless against desire. Distance was also powerless against Guinevere.

She was the Power of the Land. She embodied the ever-virginal, ever-fecund bounty of Britannia. Bounty made kings. Famine unmade them. A king might have soldiers and priests and God himself, but without the Power of the Land, he was doomed. Arthur ruled with his feet planted in Guinevere's lap.

Her own feet were planted in the wandering ways of fey. She could step like a sleepwalker through Britannia's dreamy Otherworld and peer out here or there—in the fields where Lionel fell, in the groves below the spell-warded Castle Charyot, in the abbey of the Broken Nard, and now on this jousting ground. Everywhere, she watched, with the same fascination that women have for water and men for fire. Lancelot had that sort of elemental aura, whether he knew it or not.

He did not know. He could not. This was no god astride a marble steed, but a man who rode as one with his horse. Knees to ribs and spine to spine, shoulders squared above shoulders and eyes above eyes, animal and man, muscle and bone bore toward the target ahead.

Lancelot's shaft cut a straight line in the air.

The horses converged.

The lances did too.

Spears struck shields.

The gregarious crowd rose to see. Guinevere stood like all the others.

One lance cracked. It shattered to spinning scraps. The other shaft, Lancelot's oaken one, turned his opponent's shield inside out and ripped it from its owner's gauntlet and slid beneath the man's arm and hurled him from the saddle and flung him down to the grass.

Guinevere drew in a long slow breath. It was not a gasp, for she'd seen exactly that strike countless times when first Lancelot had entered the lists at Camelot. He always struck the shield, demolished it, and let the rest of the attack slide through beneath his foe's arm. He rarely struck to kill. Guinevere breathed not from surprise, but from admiration.

If only the world had more warriors such as he: virtuous at living, efficient at slaying.

Now she knew why men must do this. Women watched and judged.

Disguised beneath scarves, Morgan le Fey watched and judged the field.

She had come to see Mordred, of course. What mother would not have come to watch her child compete and live or die? He did not die, despite his riven hand. Knives do not die, but kill. Mordred was a knife. His contests were uninteresting, for she knew who her son was. She knew what he would do.

More intently, Morgan watched Lancelot. Yes, even now, he was the one. He acted out her plan for him, the ritual proving of the male for rights of procreation. Still, Lancelot was the true mystery.

The warriors arrayed against him were nearly worthless. They rode with straight backs, jolting like dolts. Lancelot could easily have struck them dead, but he did not. He let them live. Only a lesser man would have slain these sheep—a man such as Mordred.

Mordred rode down another, the foe ending in a tangled pulp beneath a leg-broken steed. These kills of Mordred's were becoming the chime of the hour, marking the cycles of the tournament. The true interest came at a quarter past, or half past, or a quarter till—whenever Lancelot rode to fight.

The cycles of Mordred and Lancelot converged. Inevitably they mustered across each other in the lists. The great killer faced off the great savior.

Lancelot seemed so strange—young but venerable, brilliant in his much-scarred armor, honorable with every assault. He leaned in the saddle, withdrew his hand from its gauntlet, patted his mount softly, and seemed almost to whisper in the creature's ear. Stranger still, the horse responded with a deep nod. Without the slightest heel pressure, it leapt forward.

Mordred was the utter opposite. He lashed his black steed as if it were an unwilling lover. It ran to escape what lay above rather than to gain what lay before. Mordred jabbed his lance forward like an angry finger, tremulous and impotent. He roared an inarticulate growl.

Lancelot's spear came down. It soared toward Mordred. Hooves carved the earth. Lancelot's beast ran full out. Its ears laid back. Its teeth showed. Shoulder muscles flexed and pulsed. Above them, the weapon of Lancelot converged, steel-straight, on Mordred.

Morgan could not allow her son to be hurt. She reached her magic out across the jousting ground to bring imbalance to the perfect warrior.

Lancelot's spear, once perfectly aimed for the shield of his foe, now erred from its path. It jagged toward Mordred's breastplate, toward his heart.

Sometimes in nature, change meant death.

Morgan redirected her spell, toward the lance of her own son.

In the last gasp, Lancelot's spear rose true. It caught Mordred's shield instead of his breastplate. It demolished the thing and ripped it free, just as Lancelot had wished. The point sailed cleanly beneath Mordred's gimp arm, and the shaft shrieked its inevitable way along the man's armor.

Mordred's own shaft went wildly astray, bouncing from the horse's croup. It rattled out harmlessly beyond. Mordred's nerveless fingers let it fly.

The whole crowd, Morgan included, came to its feet as the young killer was raked from his steed. Tangled around Lancelot's spear, Mordred tumbled clear of his mount. He fell, crushingly, onto the hard-packed ground. Mordred rolled, reluctant and rigid.

Morgan did not need to wonder what he thought, for his mind was hers. "Here is the greatest knight ever to fight."

It was only a confirmation of what she already knew.

After a long day of fighting, Lancelot rode Rasa up before the rival kings—Bagdemagus and the king of North Galys. It was clear these monarchs had no love for each other, but love for honor and money. Both had been at stake at this tournament. The king of North Galys had lost much—honor, territory, duty, taxes, and bragging rights. King Bagdemagus had gained it all. Most conspicuous of all his prizes, though, was his daughter, restored. The young princess—no longer a maid given over to the service of Queen Morgan—stood with her father and her red-faced older brother.

Aback Rasa, Lancelot smiled to the young girl. She returned his look querulously, as though he were a stranger.

Averting his eyes, Lancelot dismounted and dropped to kneel before the kings. The day was his. His lance had slain no one, but had educated quite a few. With it, he had reunited King Bagdemagus's family. As he lifted his gaze to them, though, he saw a mixed reception.

Meleagaunce steamed within his armor. He yet clutched his lance, christened with the blood of two men, and jutted his chin defiantly. Perhaps he felt he deserved the praise for the day.

His sister, meanwhile, had gone from wondering to scowling. She leaned to her father, and whispered something against the back of her hand.

"Why, he has every right to look at you that way," King Bagdemagus replied through his smile. "He won your freedom. He is Sir Lancelot of the Table Round."

Lancelot rose, realizing the girl wanted to hide her part in his escape.

Before he could offer a word, though, a gaggle of young women rustled up to surround him. They had been following him for some time, but legs confined in lace could not keep up with Rasa. Only by dismounting and kneeling had Lancelot provided a fair target. In a bright throng they surrounded him, offering congratulations and invitations in a chorus of high-pitched voices.

Lancelot nodded his thanks. He wanted to be polite. These young courtiers were all pretty—some in full flower and some enhancing themselves with gauze—but what could he say? They buzzed about like bees, earnestly intent on things that did not interest him. Nodding and smiling, he tried to push through to King Bagdemagus. He might as well have sought escape from a constrictor. The group cinched up around Lancelot. He squirmed left, into a girl no older than thirteen. While he offered his apology, the opening to his right closed up. Always, another young creature emerged.

Then, it was she. Somehow, in that growing press of girls, there was a woman—and not just any. Though veiled, though distant, her eyes spoke to him. They told him she was proud, and that she waited. Most importantly, they told him that she watched. There was something else in those eyes, though. Could it have been jealousy at the women clustered about him?

"Guinevere!" he called, reaching toward her.

She was gone. As suddenly and serenely as stage curtains joining, women closed the gap where she had been.

He pressed toward the spot, but his hands grasped only empty air. "Guinevere?" he called amid the chatter.

Veils gleaming, she turned—not Guinevere, but Queen Morgan. Samite covered her features. Her eyes flashed playfully. "I am not she. I am much more. Not only is she watching, but I am." She grasped his hands, anchoring him in the maelstrom, leaned in, drew back her veil, and kissed him long upon the lips. "The greatest test is yet to come."

Then she too was gone—not gone, but beside Meleagaunce. With each word she spoke, she stole away his angry flame. Soon Meleagaunce looked out gladly into the throng, and his eyes came to rest where Guinevere had been. He smiled, his teeth jutting like rib bones from severed meat.

Lancelot could only shudder. He stepped backward, numb in the midst of the bellying bevy. The day was his. He had won it, and yet he had done so like a chess knight, winning checkmate not for himself but for a vulnerable king and his all-powerful queen.

13

Even Angels Fall

Lancelot and Rasa bolted away from that strange place. Ever since he had dozed beneath the apple tree, he'd tripped through unreal landscapes at the behest of unreal people. What king grants his queen a separate castle? What king bets his princess on a jousting match? What witch presides in a basilica? None of it was real. Lancelot's every step was dogged by women young and old. He was watched and measured and toted against some mystic sum. To Morgan, would he prove a good boy? To Guinevere, would he prove a worthy mate? To the princess servant, would he prove a great guardian? Weirds everywhere. They tested him, shaped him, formed him on formless adventure.

He was done with them. He'd left Aunt Brigid beyond the forgetful tides of Avalon; he'd left Queen Guinevere beyond the forgetful trails of knighthood. Let him forget them all. He was a knight—a man's man.

Hissing to himself, Lancelot rode through somnolent hills, amid tumbling clouds of bees. The thunder of Rasa's hooves drowned out the whispering wind in the evergreens. Behind him he piled up a dust cloud, its spinning motes somehow guarding him from the Morphean world he had just left. Ahead of him stretched only sky and earth and the rumpled line between. The sun edged toward that line. Lancelot raced it. He wanted to be nearer Camelot before dark. A hot fire, a secure down, Rasa's saddle as a pillow and his blanket to keep warm, and Rasa himself a grazing sentry around the camp—these things he wanted, and a tapestry of stars overhead. Lancelot ached to be on his own.

There were too many folk watching him, expecting something, sending knowing glances his way.

Lancelot lost his race with the sun. All men do. He reached a likely enough knoll and a worthy apple tree, built a fire, and made camp. He ate a few crackers and some strips of jerked mutton, and drank water mixed with a jigger of spirits to make it pure. His head settled back into the warm leather of his saddle, and he lay beneath the sky. Soon, it would be crammed with stars. Soon Lancelot would sleep. Then, in the morning, he would return to where he had left his cousin, Lionel.

A full stomach, a warm fire, a steadfast steed, and a noble deed for the morrow—these were the stuff of knighthood.

Lancelot slept before even he knew it.

As always, he dreamed of Guinevere.

A woman spoke to him, an old woman, a wise woman. The way her brows caught the firelight, the way her tongue caught the metaphors—even in dream he knew this was Aunt Brigid. She told him tales of Camelot, as ever she did at the fieldstone hearth. Her words plucked the air, and images resonated into being between them. Tonight she spoke of Queen Guinevere.

Into a leafy bower she was born. There were no white linens to swaddle her—no steaming kettles, no glinting tools. This was not a human birth. Humans struggled in all things, battling for life even as they breathed their mother's fluids. The Tuatha were different. For the fey, life began as gently as the tender stem up from the aching soil.

There, among daylilies and violets, Guinevere was born.

She cried. All creatures cry when they leave behind one life for another.

Her mother, a fey queen herself, lifted the babe from the bower where she was born and held her tightly. Her father leaned over them both and cleaned away the blue placental cap Guinevere wore. It was a sign. She would not only be a great queen of the fey; she would also be a gifted healer, and an oracle. She would marry a great king, and thereby bring peace and unity among the people.

Lancelot looked upon this nativity and smiled. In his dreaming mind, he peered at the girl through the eyes of her father, touched her through the arms of her mother, and lay in delirious identification in her own flesh. To wear her skin felt the same as to wear his own. Both had been born royalty, destined for the throne, besieged endlessly by folk who sought to test them. Both had been drawn to Arthur, to love and serve him. Their two souls converged so quickly toward the same goal, they collided. They fused.

A man leaves his mother and cleaves to his wife, for she is bone of my bone and flesh of my flesh.

Suddenly it was agony. To share the same soul and the same flesh and yet to be so widely separated—it was like being hanged, drawn, and quartered.

• • •

Lancelot awoke with a start. His heart hammered. He breathed the cold night. His fire had gone to red embers, and the stars shouted in the sky. A huge form blotted out one corner of the heavens. The figure whickered reassuringly.

"Rasa!" panted Lancelot.

He grabbed up the saddle, stood, and slung it over Rasa's back. He would be safe in that saddle, riding and fighting, not sleeping. Rasa would canter easily through night's darkest corner. Hooves would bring him to the land where this misadventure had begun. Lionel was thereabouts somewhere, and seeking him meant that Lancelot could not seek Guinevere. Any distraction. Any diversion. What had the Romans used—bread and circuses—to distract the people from hopes of rebellion?

Hopes of rebellion. Was that what this was? Did Lancelot really want to slay Arthur and steal Guinevere?

"Rasa," he said again, this time almost pleading. Saddle cinched, packs stowed, halter placed, the young knight mounted. He hadn't even jabbed his other foot in its stirrup before nudging the beast to a canter. "Take me out of here." If only he could.

Lancelot felt lost and doubted he would ever be at home again.

Rasa's legs dragged away the miles and hours till dawn. As the sun labored into the sky, he clomped down the Winchester Road. His hooves drummed steadily until he reached the precise berm where Lancelot and Lionel had left the road before. Rasa cut out across dewy fields. Morning light made beggarticks shimmer like diamonds and yarrow glow like gold.

Lancelot was blind to the beauty. He looked past dappled glades and verdant meadows to the ancient apple tree he knew must lie beyond. It was like a transplanted piece of Avalon, grown cancerous and grotesque. It was like Lancelot himself: He had grown into something horrid. Beneath that tree's fragrant bows, he had napped while some evil befell Sir Lionel. Four queens had caught him napping, had borne him away like a hunk of meat. He was done with naps and dreams. He would not be borne anywhere. He would fight, and find Lionel, perhaps even find himself.

The rangy old tree rose ahead. Rasa plunged toward it. The apples had ripened since last they had been here and some even smelled of cider. Lancelot and his steed entered the intoxicating shadow. He gritted his teeth against the scent. Rasa's final few strides ended there in tall grass. He stood and snorted.

Lancelot looked around. His heart continued the cadence of the silent hooves. He had only moments to wait before a different set of hooves took up the beat again. He looked toward the grassy uplands in the east.

A rider approached, a giant of a man on a giant of a horse. He wore coarse clothes and thick armor. His steed was unbarded. A lead trailed from his saddle to another horse. It was a gelding but seemed only a colt behind that monstrous beast. A man lay draped across its back, lashed down. He wore the fine livery of Camelot, and the crest of Lot's household, all mantled in blood. Glimpsing the shaggy hair beneath his helm, Lancelot guessed this man to be Sir Gaheris.

Lancelot's teeth ground together. He knew what it was like to be borne away like that. He stared a moment longer at Gaheris before the glint of his captor's armor drew his eye. That suit was familiar. He recognized its massive lines, its idiosyncratic details. They matched his own armor—Saxon make.

Jabbing his heels into Rasa's side—so possessed was he by fury—Lancelot sent the steed leaping forward. Rasa reared, let out an angry shriek, and galloped toward the big warrior.

The warrior lifted his head, drew steel, and hacked through the lead. His other fist wrenched the reins. The great steed whirled. Where once the man had held a sword, now he bore a lance. Gripping the horse with his legs, the warrior fetched up his shield. He kicked the beast forward. It bounded to a gallop. In scant seconds, horse and rider had gone from a quiet canter to a full-out charge.

The man was not only huge but quick, not only vicious but skilled.

Recognition flared in the warrior's eyes. His face clenched. He redoubled his speed. His lance soared in, as straight and level as Lancelot's own. The two shafts slid along each other, so perfectly aligned. They simultaneously reached out above the shields and struck the shoulders of either man.

The impact was shattering. From full gallop, they both stopped dead. Their steeds—white stallion and black gelding—rushed out from beneath them. For a moment, the two men swung on opposite ends of their fouled lances. Their legs hurled up and over the shafts like pinwheel pennants. Bloodied shoulders pried loose from the lance tips. They had spun almost fully around before they struck ground amid the weeds.

Woodsorrels clung to them like fawning fingers as the two men rose. They seemed reflections of each other, wearing the same armor, bearing the same wound, painted in blood and dust. Despite their bleeding shoulders, each man hefted his sword.

"You will die today for your crimes against the Table Round," Lancelot growled.

The massive warrior shook his head slowly as he advanced. He responded in the harsh accent of the Saxons. "So I have heard for a month of days, and yet have felled knight after knight. The only crime here is your own, Lancelot du Lac."

Blood snaked down to Lancelot's elbow, and he lifted his sword to keep his hand dry. "You seem to know me, but I do not know you."

"Oh, yes, Lancelot du Lac, I know who you are," growled the warrior. "And you will know me, Warlord Turquine of Alle's horde. I have taken over a hill fort hereabouts with the express purpose of finding you and slaying you for your crime."

"What crime?"

Stalking nearer, Turquine said, "Let me explain." He lunged. Locking shoulder and elbow in a straight line, he imbued the sword with the entire weight of his body.

Lancelot swung his own blade, barely deflecting the lunge. The two warriors turned, their bloodied shoulders bashing together. They staggered apart, each to get breath.

"For a month I have challenged and killed or captured nearly a hundred men in service to Arthur, many of them knights. Still, I did not face down the man I most hated—until today." This time, there was no attempt at surprise. Turquine only marched forward, his blade raised over his healthy shoulder, ready for a backhand blow.

Lancelot retreated. He hadn't the strength to fend off such a strike. Were he to slash at the warrior's elbow or exposed side, he would bring his own head into reach of the blade. Instead, he would use Turquine's own ploy against him. Lancelot lifted his sword.

Turquine halted in his tracks, watching with iron eyes.

Now it was a game of nerve, not brawn, and Lancelot at last had the advantage. "I have spent the last month listening to everyone argue over who I am and claim all manner of nonsense. I'll not listen to your drivel." He punctuated the comment by swinging his blade down in a half-arc.

The feint drew off Turquine. He swung full out.

Lancelot stepped back to let the man's blade slash past. Then he charged the off-balance warlord. Lancelot's sword crashed down onto Turquine's gorget, an exact match of his own. The blade cut through even that thick Saxon steel and the collarbone beneath. It plowed a deep furrow through the man's shoulder. Blood emerged from the wound and cascaded down the breastplate.

Turquine stared in disbelief. His sword hung limp in his nerveless grip, and he could only gabble an inarticulate sound before he fell backward. The warlord dropped like a tree, stiff and straight, and came to ground with a clattering boom. His sword lay far from his twitching fingers.

Smiling grimly, Lancelot strode up to stand above his foe. "You still haven't told me my crime."

Eyelids quivered over red-rimmed eyes. Turquine at first seemed to see only the sky, blue and white, above him. Then his gaze settled on Lancelot. With the last of his breath, Turquine whispered, "You wear my brother's armor. You killed him. You killed me."

Sir Gaheris awoke, lying on his side in a field of flowers. Birds darted through the nearby trees, and sunlight warmed him. Someone worked at the ropes that bound his hands and feet—no doubt his captor. There came a cutting sound, and the bonds came free from his hands. Gaheris clenched his fingers and rolled his wrists, trying to return blood flow. His hands prickled numbly. If only he could grasp. If only he could fight. Another jerk, and his feet were freed.

He would fight. He would die fighting.

Gaheris rolled to his back, struggling to rise.

The warlord shoved him back down—only it wasn't the warlord.

"Sir Lancelot! Oh, Mother of God be praised, it is you! I thought you were the Saxon."

Lancelot's blue eyes were especially piercing. "We have the same armor," he said quietly.

"Where is he?" Gaheris asked anxiously. "How did you—"

"I killed him. I killed his brother, and I killed him."

Gaheris released a gusty sigh. "Well, Mother of God be praised."

"He has a hill fort hereabouts," Lancelot said. "We'll ride there, you and I. I'll wear his cloak and ride his horse, and lead you aback yours. Whatever men he has will think I am he. We'll get inside and bring out our brothers."

Gaheris shook his head and smiled openmouthed. "You are an avenging angel, Sir Lancelot."

"Even angels fall, Sir Gaheris. Even angels fall."

Lancelot rode at a gallop toward the palisaded hill. In his wake, Turquine's cloak roiled, maroon and black like anger. On a long lead trailed Gaheris's horse, carrying the knight apparently bound in his saddle. Rasa brought up the rear, keeping close enough that he would seem to be on another lead.

Beyond the log fence, a pair of guards noted the rapid approach of their master. Jumping to, they lifted the bar and pulled the pins that held the doors. Wood creaked as the rough-hewn portal swung wide. The guards stood, one at either door, and prepared to bow to Turquine. Only in the last instant did they see, and then it was too late.

Lancelot's sword slashed to one side, Gaheris's to the other. Even as the guards fell into the gateway they once had protected, Lancelot and Gaheris pelted on toward the second palisade.

The gate guards there did not open. They had seen the fate of their comrades. Instead, one blew upon a ram's horn, and the other nocked an arrow. They trusted too much in their gate.

"Rasa!" shouted Lancelot, waving one hand over his shoulder.

The white stallion whickered in battle glee and pounded up ahead of the other horses. He bent his head toward the gate. Legs thrashed. He reached the barrier, turned a shoulder, and smashed through. The beam that had braced the doors shattered. Hinges yanked from their mountings. Doors swept inward, ending the horn call and destroying bow and bowman. Rasa emerged in a spinning cloud of splinters. Hard behind him rode Lancelot and Gaheris.

They plunged headlong through the war-clan camp within the second palisade. Perhaps a hundred ragged men staggered from tents, strapping on armor and waving swords. Lancelot and Gaheris took no time to engage these men. They let their mounts bear down any who opposed them.

Ahead rose the final palisade—a stockade really, whose chattel were the knights of the Table Round. Its gate was no wooden thing, but iron, with a key, and a gaoler. It was proof against breakout, but not against break in.

Lancelot lowered his lance. Its tip arrowed toward the gaoler. This was not honorable combat, but these were not honorable foes. The oaken spear flew with merciful speed. It impaled the man, dead in an instant, against his own stockade. Drawing the black gelding to a halt, Lancelot leapt from the saddle, snatched up the keys, and hurriedly fitted them to the lock. In moments, the iron gate swung wide. Tattered, battered, half-starved knights flooded out: Gawain, Brandeles, Galyrnde, Kay, Alydukis, Marhaus, and countless others.

"Kill a man and get a sword!" shouted Lancelot to the unarmed men. The irony of the words grated him: This whole battle had begun when Lancelot killed a man and got a sword. Still, it was a rallying cry.

"Kill a man and get a sword!" the prisoners roared. They fell on their captors with the ferocity of animals long tortured. Soon, empty hands were full of sword hilts, and bare shoulders were draped in bloodied armor. The knights of the Round Table slew their foes and climbed into their skins.

Lancelot stood numbly beside the gate. This was knighthood? Shaped by killing. He had somewhere lost track of who he was, and even of whom he wished to be.

"You've given us our lives," Sir Lionel said, clawing his way through the gate.

"No, you must fight for your lives," Lancelot replied.

Pausing a moment to rake in a breath, Lionel said, "We'll slay these brigands in your name."

It was almost more than Lancelot could bear. "No. Capture them in the name of Queen Guinevere, and take them to her."

Lionel stared at him incredulously. "What does she want with brigands?"

"She's a healer," Lancelot said. "Let her heal their souls."

14

Tribute to the Queen

"The knights return from questing!"

Guinevere lifted her head from the edge of the tub. Her eyes opened, staring narrowly. Steam rose from the bath as her body lay beneath the hot water. She had been meditating. A bath was, after all, only a cauldron, and the one within it only an offering to the land. Water was powerful, especially hot water, and it had borne her spirit far over Britannia. She sought Lancelot, but could not find him, and now, this shout—

"The knights return from questing!" the crier repeated as he strolled through the bailey below.

"The knights return. . . ." Guinevere echoed quietly. She took a deep breath, and realization came with it. "Lancelot!"

She stood. Water streamed down her body. Steam rose from her skin. She stepped from the tub, rubbed a towel across herself, and twined it around her head. The door of her chamber barked open, and someone strode in. Guinevere's heart pounded as she turned—to see her chief handmaiden.

The young woman carried more towels, a gown, underthings,

and a case that held combs and pins and salves—all the witchery that went into a proper coif.

Guinevere waved the woman away. "No time." Crossing to her wardrobe, she threw back the doors and grasped a fiery red gown from within. She dragged the towel off her head and pulled the dress on. While the handmaiden straightened her hems, Guinevere drew a comb through her hair. It dripped onto her collar.

"Your Highness," the maiden said meekly, "you cannot appear like this. You don't look like a queen, but like a woman fresh from the bath."

"That's how I want to look." Guinevere slipped her feet into a pair of slender sandals and walked to the windows.

Beyond the rose garden, beyond the palace bailey, Camelot gleamed. Through its midst marched a large retinue—perhaps fifty mounted warriors, and fifty infantry, and fifty prisoners. Guinevere made out their standards, the houses of Lothian and Chertsey, of Tintagel and Caerleon, but where was Avalon?

Guinevere turned and strode toward the door. "Thank you," she said to the handmaiden, and passed into the hall.

Her feet carried her along familiar corridors while her mind carried her on new paths. What would she say to him? At last, after long months, he was back from questing. He had sent himself away; she had sent him away. What would they say now that they were back together?

Even as her heart tumbled in her chest, Guinevere's face remained calm, serene. She would not say anything to shame Arthur or herself. She would not let anyone, even Lancelot, know the depths of her feelings.

Out of stony spaces she passed and into grassy sunlight. The first chill of autumn made the air crisp. She hurried across the bailey. Others rushed eagerly toward the palace gates, toward the approaching company of knights and warriors. Stable boys chased amid yapping curs. Cooks threw open kitchen windows to peer out. Old men left draught matches unfinished on barrel heads. Young women glided forward amid lacy veils. All the folk of Camelot turned out to see their knights' return—as if the land were at war instead of peace.

Ahead, in the tall, antlered archway that led through the palace wall, the vanguard of the company appeared. They had dismounted, leaving their horses beyond. Gawain, huge and sage, strode foremost, perhaps because his legs were longer than any others. Beside him came his brothers, and Brandeles, Lionel, and a host of others.

Guinevere smiled at them, though her eyes searched the crowd beyond. "Hail, brave knights! What adventure brings you back to us?"

Gawain approached, dropped to one knee, and bowed his head. "Little adventure, unless long languishing in a stockade is adventure. Not until Lancelot freed us had we a satisfying fight." He gestured broadly over his shoulder. "These prisoners we offer to you as spoils of that fight."

"Lancelot?" Guinevere echoed.

Gawain nodded. "Single-handed, he slew the warrior who imprisoned us. With only Gaheris's help, he overcame a hundred men to free us. And he declared the captives as tribute to you."

"Where is he?"

"Who?"

"Sir Lancelot," she replied, a bit too tersely.

Gawain nodded. "He quests still, my queen. He said that since he cannot return to you himself, he sends these fifty captives—one for each day of his absence, in tribute to his queen."

It was a brutal irony. In place of the one man she wished

to behold, she had these fifty wretches. "What am I to do with them?" Guinevere blurted.

Gawain shrugged. "He said you were a healer, that if anyone could mend these men's souls, it would be you."

Lancelot rode beneath the tempestuous skies of March. It had been a long winter away from Camelot. The days were gray, and Lancelot's heart grayer. Not even jousts, not even sword duels could lift his mood. Still, the doldrums of his soul did not stop his sword arm. He harvested villains like a man scything winter wheat. He sent them back in bunches, offerings to his queen. They approached where he dared not.

She destroyed him. It was not simply her beauty, or her mind, or her elegance. It was her identity. Somehow her mere presence made him untrue to himself and his king. She cut him in two and set the halves at war with each other. Outside of her presence, he regained his simple self, but he could not in all Britannia find something worth living for.

Rasa chuffed, his breath gray against the muddy earth. From stifles downward, he was dun colored. The great stallion had shared his master's exploits and seemed equally defeated. No one could stand against horse and rider, and yet they were losing the will to stand.

Rasa picked his way up a washed-out road—it had become a streambed after snowmelt—and entered a pass of rumpled grass between two arms of woodland. It would have been the perfect spot for an ambush, but Lancelot had ceased to care about such things. He had survived five already, and he wasn't sure if it mattered if he survived the sixth.

In the center of the pass rose a gnarled oak. Its arthritic

boughs clutched mutely at woolen skies. Even the brown leaves that clung through winter had been ripped off by vernal winds. Still, it was not devoid of life. In its branches, a feathered form struggled. At its trunk, a woman in hunting leathers reached her hands upward imploringly.

"What is this?" Lancelot muttered to Rasa, who responded with a shake of his head.

The woman spread her arms around the fat bole, caught finger holds in the bark, and struggled to climb. Far above, the bird released a falcon's shriek.

Lancelot shook his head wearily. "Surely my assistance will be required—king's justice and all. What do you think, Rasa? Poaching? No, she's a noble, or so say the leathers—"

The falcon flapped impotently, the straps on its talons tangled in the oak's branches. As if for dramatic emphasis, the woman lost her grip, slid down the trunk of the tree, and landed on her backside.

Giving a groan, Lancelot said to himself, "Oh, I see. 'My poor bird is stuck in the tree, and I cannot climb up to get him down.' And how am I to do so, fully armored?"

The woman struggled to her feet, only then seeming to see Lancelot. She clutched her trembling hands to her chest and strode toward him—"A knight! Oh, I'm saved."

Lancelot could only smile tightly. "You seem to be having trouble with your bird."

Beneath long strands of black hair, she stared out at him. There was something in her dark eyes, annoyance or fear. "He belongs to my husband, a brutal man. If he finds out I've been hunting with the bird, he will cut my throat. And, as you can see, I can't possibly climb this trunk—"

Lancelot nodded. He rode his horse up beneath the lowest

bough of the oak and looked skeptically at its bark, still wet from winter's thaw. Past the tangle of branches, the falcon did indeed look efficiently snared.

Lancelot pulled off his helm and hung it on the saddle. Removing sword belt, tabard, breastplate, and shirt of chain, he gradually lightened his shoulders for the climb. "By the time I get all this off, I'll be able to jump up there."

The woman did not smile. She only stared intently.

Feeling much lighter and much colder in the March wind, Lancelot stood on the saddle. The lowest bough would still require a short leap to reach. Gathering his strength, Lancelot jumped and grabbed onto the branch.

A loud crack sounded below. Rasa let out a shriek and bolted. Across his rump, a long red welt showed. He pelted into the woods and down a ravine and was gone. Lancelot's sword and armor went with him.

Hanging from both hands, Lancelot craned to see who had whipped his steed.

A warrior in mismatched armor strode from concealment behind a nearby spruce. He coiled his whip into a loop and hung it at his waist. In its place he drew a sword and walked over beneath Lancelot. A black smile broke out over his narrow, bristly face.

Lancelot glared at the woman. "What have you done to me?"

The warrior responded, "Nothing more than I asked her to."

Anger lent Lancelot strength, and he pulled himself up atop the bough, out of the man's reach. "What sort of warrior are you, to strike down a defenseless man?"

"I'm a living warrior," the man growled, "which you won't be much longer."

"I can stay in this tree quite a long while."

The smile returned to the man's face. He shook his head. "Not in March, not dressed as you are."

"Perhaps I'll complete my mission and climb to your falcon, and trade its life for mine."

A flash of resentment filled the man's face, but he said, "Go ahead, Lancelot. Kill my falcon. He is a small price to pay for slaying the greatest knight of the Table Round."

Lancelot studied the lower boughs. Many extended a good distance horizontally from the tree bole. Many also were thick enough to bear his weight out to their ends.

The warrior watched his eyes. "Go ahead, Sir Knight. Take a running leap and see if you can get away."

Shrugging, Lancelot climbed onto an adjacent bough, the fattest and longest one at the base of the tree. "All right." He took a deep breath and ran. His feet landed lithely on the bough, driving him down its length.

The warrior stared, incredulous, before running beneath the bough to intercept him.

The branch thinned. It bobbed with each step. As near its end as he dared run, Lancelot planted both feet and sprang. The branch itself hurled him beyond the tree. He curled over in a slow flip, his legs spreading apart. They came down astride a familiar saddle atop a white and muscular back.

Rasa whickered and whirled.

Lancelot hauled out his Saxon sword. It sliced down where the surprised man ran, chopped through the laces of his helm, and sent his head flying from his shoulders. The body stood a moment longer before its life fountained away.

The woman shrieked, running toward her slain husband. "What have you done to me?"

"Nothing more than you asked me to," replied Lancelot,

his bloody sword leveled at her. "And now, I have something for you to do."

"And then he struck the head from my husband," said the woman. Tears pasted black hair to her cheek. With wide, imploring eyes, she stared up at Queen Guinevere on the throne of Camelot. The woman wrung her hands and sat back on her heels. Her travel cloak dripped rain on the marble floor. "And he bade me come to you on pain of death, and tell my tale."

Guinevere stared blankly at the supplicant. "Why?"

"Because he said if I didn't come, or if I lied, he would return and—"

"No," interrupted Guinevere, "why did he want you to come to me?"

"Ju—" the woman tried to respond, but the word died in her throat. She bowed her head to the marble floor. Her hair spread like a dark star around her.

Judgment was the word that had stuck in the woman's throat. She had come expecting to pay for her crime. Guinevere's gaze narrowed. Why would Lancelot send the woman for judgment? Hadn't he already judged her, punished her? Perhaps he sent her to the queen for mercy—the healing of soul and body—but why subject her to this strange punishment first?

"I don't understand," Guinevere muttered.

The woman lifted her ashen face. "I had no quarrel with Sir Lancelot, and would have done none of it except that my husband was a brutal man. He said he would kill me if I didn't help him snare Lancelot." Seeing skepticism in the queen's gaze, the woman reached up to the travel cloak she wore and pulled it apart at the neck. Linen drew back from skin striped in lash marks.

Guinevere's stomach churned. Perhaps Lancelot had sent this woman for healing. "It seems to me that Lancelot has done you the greatest favor of your life. Your husband was a monster, and he deserved to die."

"But he was my husband, and I loved him," the woman replied simply.

What strange politics ruled the marriage bed. "Law and love are no reason to remain in a marriage that is killing you." In those words, Guinevere realized the reason Lancelot had sent this woman to her. She shivered—whether from dread or delight, she could not have said. "I know you expect punishment for what you did to Lancelot, but you already have endured more than a lifetime of punishment. It isn't time to tear you apart. It is time to make you whole."

The woman's tears had stopped, but she now looked more desolate than ever. "Without him, I will never be whole again."

Summer kissed the land. Small green apples hung beneath dewy leaves. Fat hares crouched amid bluebells. Rivers settled to silence in their hardening banks.

Rasa made his grazing way across deep grass. Lancelot gave him his head. Sunlight warmed his shoulder plates and helm. Still, Lancelot's heart was cold.

He had quested for a year now, dispensing the king's justice and escaping the queen's presence. In that time, he had sent countless brigands to the majesties at Camelot, and countless blackguards to the grave. His sword had done such work that its mere reputation became a weapon. Rumor of his approach quelled even the most barbarous hearts. At one point, Lancelot and Sir Kay had switched armor for a time, so that Lancelot could find a few diverting wrongs to right. It had doubled Lancelot's reach, until word got out. Back in his own armor now, he encountered only the most oblivious villains.

One such man worked his villainy ahead.

Out of a nearby hovel whose thatch had grown a thick mantle of moss, a woman emerged. She ran limping through abandoned fields. Blood poured from her nose, down her lips and chin. Her eyes were blackened from a blow. She staggered and fell to her hands. Still she clawed forward like a fleeing cat. Despite her obvious misery, she released only panting moans.

From the hovel behind her came a man's shouts, blasphemies punctuated by the rasp of a drawn sword. Blade in hand, the man appeared at the doorway. He grabbed the post to steady drunken steps. Peering out, he glimpsed where the woman shook the weeds in her flight. A humorless smile crossed his face, and he ran after her, shouting.

Lancelot nudged Rasa. "Let's go."

And so a third joined the race. Wounded and terrified, the woman crawled in the lead. Drunken and furious, the man closed in. Disgusted and determined, Lancelot rode his stallion to intervene.

Rasa's hooves ate up ground. He fairly flew over the weeds. The mere sound of his approach should have convinced the drunk to veer off, but an unusual fury possessed him. His sword flashed with each running stride. He was almost upon her.

Leaning forward in the saddle, Lancelot urged Rasa to a full-out gallop. White shoulders and haunches surged. Ahead, only a stone's throw separated the man and woman. Rasa angled in as Lancelot drew steel and held it out for a smashing blow. Rasa leapt. Sword met sword.

The man whirled, knocked to his side on the ground. Anyone else would have lost his blade with a strike like that, but simple fury made this man strong. He rolled to all fours and pushed himself to his feet.

Lancelot dragged Rasa's head around. The stallion wheeled amid dust clouds. He shouldered forward, a wall of white flesh between the man and the woman. Lancelot leveled his sword at the man. "If you want to keep your head, you will back away," he growled through clenched teeth.

The man did not back away, but neither did he approach any nearer. His voice was as black as the grave. "This is between my wife and me."

"Not anymore. Not after you struck her."

A look of wounded anger filled his face. "She bedded my brother!"

Of course, a cuckold. No man ever fought so brutally and senselessly. "She has wronged you, perhaps," Lancelot said carefully, "but you have wronged her, certainly."

"I'm not finished wronging her," the man said. "I will have her head."

Lancelot's voice grew no louder, but it was steel-hard. "You will not. She is under my protection."

"And who are you?" snarled the man.

"I am Sir Lancelot du Lac, knight of the Table Round. And who are you to ask?"

"I am Pedivere, veteran of Mount Badon and, more to the point, this woman's husband."

And more to the point, her cuckold. "Sheathe your sword, Pedivere. You will not use it again today."

Eyes simmering, Pedivere lifted his blade and slid it into the scabbard at his waist.

"Good," Lancelot said. It seemed sometimes domestic wars could end without utter catastrophe.

Keeping his own sword at the ready, Lancelot extended his other hand toward the woman. She crouched, panting, in the weeds. Her torn clothes were crimson with her blood, and her face was as haunted as a ghost's. There was pain, yes, and terror, but also guilt, and a new sense of hope.

"Well, here is my hand. If you want my help, take it," Lancelot said calmly. When she still did not move, he said, "Shall I ride away?"

She stood. Her left ankle was sprained if not broken, and she half-shuffled, half-hopped toward the man on the white horse.

Lancelot smiled. A sigh rolled out of him.

The woman reached Rasa's flanks. She looked up. Her bloodied, bruised face was bathed in leafy light.

Lancelot dipped his hand. "Take hold and come up. You'll ride behind me to safety, and we'll see about your nose." He slipped his foot from the stirrup so that she could get a leg up.

She took his hand, put her foot in the stirrup, and rose with natural ease to sit sidesaddle behind him. One hand squeezed his in thanks, and the other slid along his waist to hold to the skirt of tasses.

The woman let out a grunt, and there was a metallic clang. She shoved up insistently behind Lancelot. His back was suddenly warm and wet. Her grip fell away from the skirt of tasses. She slewed sideways. He clung to her hand but couldn't stop her fall. The woman's headless body—now garbed utterly in red—slumped down beside Lancelot. In shock, he released her hand. Her staring head bounced off Rasa's rump, leaving a smear, and fell among the weeds that had failed to save her.

With an inarticulate roar of rage and grief, Lancelot lifted his sword and turned Rasa toward Pedivere.

The man lay prostrate, his bloody sword thrown well out of reach.

Lancelot drove Rasa up just before the man's bowed head. One more stomp of those hooves, and his brain would have been dashed out. Lancelot drew the beast just short. "Get up and fight, you filthy coward!"

Pedivere's voice was muffled by the humus. "I will not fight you, Sir Lancelot. Grant me mercy."

"I'll grant you death. I don't need this sword, this armor. I'll strip them off and rip your head off with my bare hands!"

"I will not fight you. Grant me mercy."

"I'll grant you a beating nigh unto death, and you will beg to die, and then you will die," Lancelot said through his teeth as he sheathed his sword. He dragged off his gauntlets, unlaced and threw away his helm, and pulled the breast and back plates. Sliding down from Rasa, he yanked off cuisse, jambeau, and sollerets. "Now, we are equals."

"Pie Jesu."

Lancelot ducked down, grabbed the collar of Pedivere's shirt—getting a fair hunk of flesh, too—yanked him to his feet, and brought a left-handed roundhouse in to smash his nose.

Pedivere reeled back. Blood made an identical river down his face. Black wells swallowed his eyes. He fell to his backside, clutching his nose in red hands. "Mercy!"

"Mercy?" shouted Lancelot. Stripped of arms and armor, he seemed only a shrieking animal. "You had a wife who loved you, and you did this to her?"

He was weeping. "I loved her too much."

"That's not love! Love is wanting but never having. Love is hoping in the face of utter despair. Love is denying your own good for the good of the other."

"Mercy!" Pedivere said through his sobs. "Mercy!"

Lancelot stood, his hands clenching and unclenching at his sides. "No. I said no mercy. I will not kill you, but I will give you a penance. Take up her body and her head. Keep them ever on you, even when you sleep, even when you bathe. Carry them on your back to the court of Camelot. There, appear before the queen, and tell her all that has transpired here."

"I swear I will. On my life, I swear it."

"Yes, you do. If you fail in this, I will hunt you down and kill you." Lancelot turned, his voice grim. "Guinevere will know what to do with you, mad lover. Mercy or death, she will know what to do."

He had come in the deeps of winter, a wretch with a snow-mantled bundle of twigs on his back. Only within the halls of the palace, when the flakes sloughed away and warmth worked into the bundle, did they know what he bore. By then, it was too late. Already he bowed before Queen Guinevere and King Arthur, a frozen corpse on his back. He poured out his woeful tale.

Guinevere listened with patient forbearance, watching steam rise from the tied-up bones. When at last he was done, she said, "You slew your wife for infidelity."

"Yes." The man lowered his head to the marble floor, and the empty skull of his wife swung forward on its cord to nuzzle at his ear.

"You would rather no one had her than share her."

Again, the monosyllable. "Yes."

She glanced aside at her husband, who sat mutely attentive.

"Lancelot said you would know what to grant, mercy or death."

Guinevere nodded. "Death would be mercy. No, my champion knew the best course. You would have her only to yourself. Then do so, for the rest of your days. She will be strapped to you, every hour of every day. The knights and warriors of all Britannia will have orders to check you for your wife's bones, and slay you if any are found lacking."

"Oh, no, my queen."

"Oh, yes," she shot back. "You are my missionary. Travel the land. Tell all the husbands to walk with their wives in life, or to bear their wives in death. Warn them away from the path you trod."

The man seemed deflated at this pronouncement. Scrawny and trembling, he sat up. His only strong feature was his gaze, which pierced like a spike. "I can bear this. I will be no different than your own champion. I will carry the bones of my love as he carries the bones of his."

With that, the man rose and stalked from the throne room of Camelot. He left the stench of death behind as he strode out into the tumbling blizzard that clutched Camelot.

15

To Avalon

The winding ways of spring had come to Camelot, though the winding ways of Lancelot had not. The errant knight strayed yet away from the woman he championed.

Guinevere decided to stray as well. She rode a sorrel mare in company with twelve of her priestesses. They crossed the early grass, keeping to ridgelines where sun and wind had hardened the mud. Today, the sun hid amid torn quilts of cloud, and the wind was as dry and insistent as a crone's hand. Guinevere tucked her thick green robe more tightly into the knot-work belt she wore, bent her head to the wind, and drove the mare along a grassy rill.

Despite the chill air, it was an easy ride, a score of miles up from Camelot to Glastonbury Tor. Arthur had suggested she go by palanquin, as befit a queen, but Guinevere had told him that the Tuatha ritual they would perform required the horses. In truth, she was too impatient to have other folk do her walking.

Once, she had never lied to Arthur. Once, she had confided all things in him. Now, her whole life was a lie. She could not confide in Arthur about what she felt. She could not confide even in herself. She didn't know her own mind about Lancelot.

Oh, she knew her heart. Men could go their whole lives without knowing their hearts, but it was a lost and desperate woman who spent even a month disjoined. She loved him. It was not mere lust, though lust was part of it. It was a soul-aching want. Every thought wandered his way. Every breath formed his name. She had never known such love. Yes, she loved Arthur deeply—husband, companion, friend—but she was not jealous of his every moment as she was of Lancelot's. And his every moment for nearly two years had been spent away from her.

Guinevere knew her heart, but not her mind. Why would she love him so? Why would she receive the ghastly procession of brigands and murderers he sent, as if each were a bouquet? Why would every mention of his name ache like a tooth in her heart?

The queen rode toward Glastonbury Abbey in search of answers—in search of the abbess who was Lancelot's mother.

Guinevere and her twelve initiates rode out among low hills. Ahead appeared a broad, shallow bowl that held a swamp. In its center rose the rumpled slope that was Glastonbury Tor. The hilltop had once been a Pagan holy site, but now it belonged to sheep. At night, shepherds' fires set yellows stars in the sky. The only god that dwelt on the tor these days was the Christian God, and he had established his abbey on a long plateau near the swamps.

"That's where we're bound," Guinevere whispered reverently.

A fieldstone church dominated the spot, with a small chapel at its western end and a cloister to the south. Less-grand structures clustered nearby, the wattle-and-daub lean-tos of the abbesses. Even from this distance, Guinevere knew which one she sought. Removed from the others, shabby and precarious, a hovel dribbled smoke skyward. Its roof sagged as if shrugging, and its walls slouched like legs tired of standing. The real worry was that smoke, though. A madwoman should not have tended a fire, and by all accounts, Elaine of Benwick was surely mad.

The queen and her retinue rode the eastern hills. They approached the Ponters Ball, a dry isthmus across the encircling swamps. The abbey had set up a palisade gate there, and guards normally stopped and questioned any who sought entry. Seeing priestess robes and Camelot barding, the guards knew this to be Guinevere. They swung the gates wide.

Guinevere and her retinue rode through. They passed along the swamp, heading toward that single unkempt hovel. Smoke oozed from thatch and window and door. It wafted to them, the clean, overpowering scent of incense. Guinevere slowed her mount on the approach. The sorrel even seemed to soften her tread. A hush took possession of the group. Forming a semicircle before the door, the company reined in and sat silently.

Guinevere dismounted. A rag of smoke dragged across her and brought with it another smell—human waste. The two odors warred for dominance. Unwilling to cover her face with a scarf, Guinevere strode toward the door. Desiccated wood hung in a gaunt grate across it, but only white smoke showed within.

"Sister Elaine?" she called tentatively. "Elaine of Benwick? Are you within?"

No answer came except the quiet hiss of incense burners. Guinevere was about to call again when she heard rapid muttering. ". . . the queen, the queen of . . . of Benwick, praise be—

once queen, but proud no more, great God. Bowed, not proud. Proud bowed, praise be . . . Elaine queen bee, praise to thee. Gloria in excelsis."

With a grim smile, Guinevere spoke again. The muttered litany did not cease, only forming a nervous counterpoint. "I am Queen Guinevere. [*I am not Queen Guinevere*] I've come to speak with you about your son, about Lancelot. [*the sun had set on my Lancelot, oh, my baby Lancelot, son of God, son of Man, et filio, et spiritus sanctus*] I want to know how you came here, how old he was, what drove you and him."

"On the rocks it drove us, the wind, like the spirit of God over the face of the deep calling things forth in avera cadavera, calling us forth out of the burning city, out of Jerusalem, by the waters of Avalon, we sat down and wept when we remembered thee. Praise be."

"How old was he? How old was your son?"

". . . I have no son. . . . God gives and God takes and praise be the name of God. . . ." Her figure was only vaguely visible in the rolling smoke. She seemed very old, very gaunt. "I never had him in me. I had another child in me, not Lancelot. There was a womb child and a cradle child and now no child. . . ."

"How old was he when you came to Britannia?"

"I held him. I carried him, like the Madonna, like her at the creche, at the cross. Creche-cross. Creche-cross. I had them both in one year. Anno Domini. Creche-cross. Praise be the infant king, wrapped in swaddling clothes and hung upon the cross."

"He was an infant then, when you came, when you lost him?"

"I found him I lost him . . . he never was mine . . . I just held him. Where did he go? Can you find him? Help me find my baby boy."

Letting out a groan of compassion, Guinevere stepped toward the doorway. "He is in Camelot. A knight in Camelot. The greatest knight who—"

Then she saw through the thinning cloud, not an aged woman, but a young one. She was thin, yes, and she trembled, but she was no older than Guinevere herself. She could not possibly have been Lancelot's mother.

Guinevere stepped back. "Forgive me, Sister. Forgive me for intruding—"

"Can't you find him . . . can't you find my boy? Can't you? Can't you?"

Numbly, Guinevere turned back toward her sorrel, walked to it, and climbed into the saddle. "We'll not find our answers down here." She lifted her eyes to the abbey. "Only there, if at all."

Guinevere backed her horse, and the others did as well. Even as that watchful arc of priestesses dissolved and drifted away, the woman in the hovel stood. A couple of shaky steps brought her to the threshold. She clung to the posts, her voice rattling out of her. ". . . everything taken in one night. Castle, husband, self, and son. Everything, praise be to God! Everything. Praise everything. Praise everything. . . ."

The mad heckling followed Guinevere, tangling in her thoughts. The poor woman—to have suffered so in truth is horrific enough. To have suffered so in fantasy—needless and baseless and inescapable fantasy—is piteous. *To think I went to her seeking answers. . . .*

The woman could not have been Lancelot's mother, but Guinevere couldn't shake the thought that she was.

Lancelot left madness in his wake. He touched women, and they were destroyed.

The horses climbed an easy hill to a wide, grassy plateau

where the abbey stood. It was not a grand place—a fieldstone and mortar miniature of a Roman basilica. It had no stone vault, but a wooden one. Reaching a low fence, Guinevere dismounted and tied up her horse, along with the others. As the queen headed for the main door of the abbey, her initiates formed up on her like ducks in flight.

They reached the entryway—double doors beneath a lovingly but inexpertly carved tympanum. Guinevere was about to knock when the doors swung inward, revealing a prostrate acolyte, and an elder nun, beaming gladly. The acolyte wore white with gold trim, and the nun wore simple black, covering all but her face and hands.

"Welcome, Queen Guinevere," said the old woman, bowing in obeisance. Wizened hands flicked outward in a flourish. "We have been watching you."

The queen smiled and inclined her head slightly. "I would like to speak with the highest-ranking abbess."

"I am she," replied the woman serenely. "I am Mother Brigid, namesake for Saint Brigid of our beloved Britannia. How may I help you?"

Guinevere said levelly, "I wish to speak with you in private."

Nodding, the abbess said to the acolyte, "Dear, would you mind taking these guests to the great hall? The bread should be ready, and the stew."

Rising, the young girl gaped for a moment. "But, Mother, what will the sisters eat?"

Laying a gentle hand on the girl's shoulder, Brigid said, " 'Man cannot live by bread alone, but by every word that issues from the mouth of God.' I imagine women can do likewise. Let them know I have called for fasting and prayer, for the health and well-being of our visitors."

The acolyte tucked her shoulders and shuffled away down a hall. With a nod from Guinevere, the initiates followed.

"You are quite generous to give up your meal for us, Mother Brigid," Guinevere said. "Thank you."

"Fasting is good for the bowels, and good bowels are good for the soul." She smiled. Waving her hand, she said, "Come. Let me take you to my private chambers."

Brigid led Guinevere down fieldstone hallways. They passed beneath groin vaults that smelled of mildew. At the end of the hall stood a stout door in banded iron, its oaken lintel at forehead level. Brigid fished within a pocket of her robe, pulled out a large key, set it to the lock, and turned. With a clink of metal, the bolt slid back. Brigid pushed the door open.

Beyond lay the interior of a quaint cottage. A simple table and stools furnished the room. To one side glowed a hearth and fire. Wild herbs hung to dry in the rafters above. To the other side lay a pair of straw pallets. The floor was strewn with dry rushes that gave off a sweet scent. Brigid shuffled through the doorway and gestured toward the table. "May I get you something—cider, perhaps? We have a lot of apples on Avalon."

"Yes," Guinevere whispered distractedly. "Cider." She stepped through the door and hit her head squarely on the lintel. "Damn!"

"That's just what Lancelot used to say," Brigid replied. She crouched beside a small keg that rested in a stone niche. In the light of the fire, her clothes seemed more brown than black, and much more threadbare.

"What Lancelot used to—" began Guinevere, her head throbbing. "Wait, let me close the door." She turned. Behind her, instead of a long and musty hall, there was a bright hillside descending toward deep and dappled waters. A springtime wind breathed over her, bringing with it the scent of apple blossoms. A footpath led away from the front door, and in the dirt lay the bare footprint of a man.

"He left just last night," Brigid said wistfully as she bore two goblets of cider toward her guest. "Always in such a hurry to grow up. Just a boy in a box of tin." She set down the goblets and gestured for Guinevere to be seated.

The queen waved away the suggestion. "I don't understand. What has happened?"

Shrugging, Brigid took her seat and sipped her cider. "That's why you came, isn't it, because you don't understand what has happened—here today and two years back when you met Lancelot and three years back when he was but a newborn prince? You don't understand."

"No," agreed Guinevere, shaking her head. She took a sip of her cider. It was cold and sharp, gently fermented, and it warmed her shoulders. "No, I don't understand."

Brigid took the queen's hand and directed her into a seat. "First, introductions. I am indeed Brigid, and I am an abbess, but that is only one of my manifestations. Lancelot knew me as Aunt Brigid, an old woman living in a hovel on Avalon. Christians know me as Saint Brigid, long dead but thought to intercede for them, which I do. Lancelot's mother—yes, that was she whom you met—knew me as the water goddess who took away her child."

"And which are you?"

"I am all of them and none of them, both more and less. As far as you are concerned, I am the Mistress of the Mists, part of your Tuatha pantheon."

Queen Guinevere could only stare blankly for a moment. Then she slid off the stool to her knees and bowed her head. "Forgive my presumption, Great Goddess."

"There is nothing to forgive, child, and up, out of the

rushes with you. This is good cider, and you should drink it while it is still cool."

Blushing, the queen rose to her seat. "This only adds to the questions."

"I know," soothed Brigid. "Let me simply tell you the tale, and all your questions will be answered."

A sigh escaped Guinevere. "That would be wonderful."

"No, not wonderful, not in this case. There is a reason that Yahweh forbade eating of the Tree of the Knowledge of Good and Evil. Once you have knowledge, you must act accordingly. The knowledge I give you today could destroy you and Lancelot, Arthur and Camelot. It also could save you, empower you to heal yourselves and truly live. The choice will be yours—if you still wish me to answer your question."

"I do," Guinevere replied without pause. "Tell me."

"Lancelot is not who he thinks he is. He thinks he is the son of Ban and Elaine of Benwick. He was their son by adoption only, a faerie changeling placed in their crib."

"He is Tuatha?" blurted Guinevere in sudden realization. "He is like me?"

"Yes, more so than you know. He was born a Tuatha prince, as you were born a Tuatha princess. Each of you were changelings, set in cribs hundreds of miles and moons apart. Ban never knew. Elaine suspected, but never spoke her fears—until now."

Guinevere pieced it together. "It explains so much—his grace, his strength, his prowess—"

"It explains why I took him in as my own when Elaine went mad, why I reared him here, helped by the nymphs and the etter caps, the dryads and even the war god Mars-Smetrius."

"Master Smetrius," Guinevere whispered. "Yes . . . but Benwick fell only during the Battle of Badon Hill. Lancelot appeared at court six months later. How could he have grown from infancy to adulthood in six months?"

Brigid dipped her eyebrow. "You know the answer to that."

"Avalon."

"Yes, Avalon. Time here is not measured by sun or moon, but by the rhythms of one's own heart. It is why this place is so perilous to mortals. Some spend an afternoon here and leave to find their friends in moldering graves. Some spend a lifetime here between blinks of their eyes. The heart is the muscle of time, and Lancelot's heart beat wildly, recklessly. He was eager for Camelot and knighthood."

The queen seemed not to have heard this last, her mind mired in its own byways. She looked up. Rings darkened her eyes. "It is why I love him, isn't it?"

Brigid stared out the door. A cloud-shadow blackened the hillside. "You will have to answer that one for yourself."

Guinevere's eyes widened in fresh realization. "He is not like Arthur—not a mortal man like Arthur. I cannot be joined to Arthur because he is human, because I would lose the power of the land. But Lancelot is not human. He is Tuatha. He is like me. I would not lose my power. . . ."

Brigid rose, clearing her throat with a sound like a growl. She took her goblet, now empty, and the queen's as well, and filled them at the cask. "This is the knowledge I told you of. Now you know. Now a choice lies before you. Do you cleave to your husband, a man who has united all Britannia, even the world and Otherworld—though you must hold to him chastely—?"

"Always entwined but never touching—"

"Or do you join yourself with a prince of your own people, in a love that will not destroy your power but may well destroy everything else."

Guinevere had gone white, and a tear trembled, not yet full-formed within the lids of her eye. "I must go with love."

"Yes, but which love?" Brigid said, seating herself again and pushing a goblet toward Guinevere.

The queen eagerly took it and drank deeply.

"There is one thing more you must know, if you can bear it."

"If I can bear it?"

"It will make your choice harder still."

Guinevere took another mouthful of the cider and winced as she swallowed. It seemed to have gone bitter. The tear gathering in her eye raced downward. "Tell me."

Brigid nodded and stood. "Let me close the door."

No one in Glastonbury Abbey was happy. The abbesses had been fasting for three days, their meals given to the visiting priestesses. The priestesses, for their part, couldn't eat for worry about their missing queen.

On the morning of the third day, a locked door at the end of the hall opened. Out came Mother Brigid and Queen Guinevere. Elation greeted them, and questions about where they had been. The noise ceased, though, when Guinevere shoved her way, teary-eyed, through the crowd.

"Queen Guinevere, what happened?"

"Get your horses," she said, and her breath smelled of bitter cider. "We have to go find Sir Lancelot."

16

Being True

Nothing from the outside world penetrated Merlin's paradise—nothing short of an earthquake. This felt like one.

The old mage sat back from the bed of petunias he had been weeding and lifted fleecy brows toward the sky. Whenever he gardened, he wore an old body. Young bodies were too impatient to tend plants. He studied the firmament, which he himself had carved from living rock. It did not move. Something else did, something enormous, like old Saturn shifting in his underworld asylum.

Footsteps came on the grassy verge. It was Nyneve, bearing a tray with a crystal pitcher and two goblets. She had drawn water from the sacred lake and was bringing it to her beloved. Still, her young brow was knotted, her lithe figure trembling.

"There is grave news," she began, kneeling on the grass beside Merlin. She eased the tray down as well. The liquid shivered in its pitcher. "The waters buzz with it, straight out of Avalon." She began filling the goblets.

Merlin clenched fingers on his knobby knees. "I sensed it, too. What is it?"

"Guinevere knows," she said simply.

The wizard's eyes clouded. "She knows. . . ."

"Everything. Brigid told her."

His beard waggled, and he clucked. "Why would she tell her?"

"Because Guinevere asked." Nyneve studied the face of her beloved. She sought an assurance that was not there. "It's in their hands now, Merlin. You cannot interfere. Don't go to them."

"What was Guinevere's response?" Merlin asked, trying not to sound gruff.

Nyneve bowed her head. Through curtains of dark hair, she murmured, "She has gone out to find Lancelot."

Suddenly, Merlin was on his feet—not the narrow, mud-crusted feet of the old gardener, but the strong, booted feet of a young man. "It's the doom of Camelot. I have foreseen it. I have to go."

Nyneve stood, too. She gripped Merlin's arm. "No. It's in their hands. They can still save themselves if they choose rightly—"

"How can they choose rightly? Could you choose rightly?" Merlin scowled, black brows bristling. "I have to stop her, stop them. I must at least give Arthur something, some power to resist them. They will tear Camelot apart."

Nyneve released his arm. She shrugged bleakly. "Perhaps you are right. How could Guinevere and Lancelot choose correctly when even the great Merlin cannot?"

His eyes flared at her, but he offered no reply.

Nyneve lifted the water goblets, giving one to Merlin. "At least drink this, so you will know all the particulars—where Guinevere is, where she is heading. . . ."

He tossed back the drink. The sacred water scintillated

within him, telling him everything. Merlin shook as each grim fact sank into his flesh and permeated him. Oh, this would be disaster. Handing the glass back to her, he pulled Nyneve to him, kissed her, and said, "I'm off." He strode up the path toward the cottage they kept.

"I could carry you through the water. It's the surest way, the fastest," she volunteered behind him.

He waved off the suggestion. "I'll find my own way." Then, midstep, he was gone.

Nyneve shook her head and sipped slowly at the water in her hand. She said quietly, "Only find your way back."

Lancelot rode to the top of a barrow and gazed out.

In the middle of a springtime field stood a small castle—the estate of the petty King Pellas. Shepherds grazed their flocks on the parklands all around the walls. Within, lean-tos poured smoke skyward. Boys hammered a wheel onto a cart axle. Girls fed hens from the seed in their skirts. Men gutted a hog. Women worked magic about a boiling cauldron—

Puzzled, Lancelot rubbed his eyes. There they were, four women tending a huge drum full of some rolling red concoction. Could it be the four queens, the four witches? One stirred the stuff with a long, crooked stick. Another rammed logs into the blaze beneath the cauldron. The third and fourth occasionally reached in and dragged hunks of something from the pot—what were they? A torso? Legs? Chunks of meat?

"Let's go, Rasa," Lancelot whispered.

The horse leapt as though he had been jabbed. Rasa knew the tones of his master, and just now his master was deeply disturbed. Hooves hurled back the barrow. The white stallion descended the hill and pounded out across the meadow. Sheep looked up at his thundering approach. Bleating, the beasts shoved at each other in retreat. Dogs struggled to contain them. Rasa pelted down the cleared aisle, heading straight for the castle gate.

It was not much of a gate, a formality, really—two large doors meeting in a pointed arch, with a small human door cut into one of them. The guard, an old man who drowsed in a chair to one side, awoke with a start. He stood. He stared for a shocked moment as the horse and rider hurtled his way. The guard drew his sword, which waggled in his hand, and he seemed to mutter a prayer. Then he glimpsed the barding of Camelot and the standard of Sir Lancelot. Leaving his sword across his chair, the man retreated through the door, popped the bolt, and drew the gates wide. He was just in time.

Lancelot barreled through the gate and into the bailey. He glimpsed bloody bodies hung on a wire, and rode up to the huge cauldron that boiled in red. Dragging Rasa to a halt, Lancelot shouted, "What is this witchery?"

The four women—they didn't seem like witches so much as scullery maids—stood and stared in openmouthed amazement at the young knight.

"You heard me," Lancelot snarled. "What are you doing?"

"Dyeing," muttered the youngest woman in the group.

"Dying? What do you mean, dying?"

The woman shrugged and said hesitantly, "Well, we put a shirt in the pot, and it boils a bit, and then it is all red."

Lancelot glanced toward the stained stirring stick and then toward the line where clothes dripped. He barked a loud laugh. They were dyeing. He guffawed. It had been so long since he had laughed. It felt like coughing, like hacking up all the blackness that had gathered around his soul.

The women stared at him a moment longer, and then one by one joined him.

Red-faced, Lancelot tried to explain. "It's just that, there were these four witches and . . . well, one of them has been dogging my trail and . . . Ha! Ha!"

"No witchery here, great knight," replied the young maid as she smiled.

"I thought you meant dying—" Lancelot pantomimed a slit throat, his head lolling to one side and his tongue jutting out. "No witchery here—"

The next moment belied his words. Amid the boiling red heads of bubbles came a human head—a woman's head. Dye streamed down long, dark hair and over staring eyes. Robed shoulders dragged up from the clothes that tumbled amid them. Her arms remained at her sides as she floated higher. The hem of her skirt dripped a circle in the dye. She breathed. Her eyes blinked. She showed no sign that the liquid burned her.

The four maids recoiled, shrieking, from the sanguine figure that hovered above their dyeing vat. They ducked their heads and clutched their hair and ran.

Lancelot did not retreat, for he recognized this woman. He dropped from the saddle, his knee kissing the ground. "My queen."

Guinevere stared down at him, her eyes as red as beets. "Forgive my arriving this way."

"There is nothing to forgive," he replied in awe.

"I had to find you. I came the quickest way. Water is the quickest way, and this, the nearest water." With dreamy movements, she strode through the air, away from the cauldron. Descending a set of invisible stairs, she reached Lancelot. She extended a scarlet hand. He took it, and she lifted him from his knee.

Lancelot looked down at the red hand in his grip. "Your skin is so hot."

She swallowed, and her arm trembled. "Yes, I was protected by Otherworld magic when I emerged, but now this clinging stuff is starting to burn."

Lancelot swept her up in his arms. Dye obliterated the crest upon his tabard. Heedless, he ran toward the palace keep. "In the name of King Arthur, take us to the royal bath!"

Most of the dullards only stood and watched, assuming he spoke to someone else. One young stable boy obeyed. He ran eagerly up before them and said, "Follow me."

Guinevere was beginning to shudder. She clutched Lancelot's shoulder, leaving a red handprint. "It's really burning now."

He whispered, "Only moments more. Only moments . . ."

The boy led them down a narrow set of steps to a garden. At the far end, near a natural spring, stood a small bathhouse. It was a quaint thing, Roman by the looks of it. On one side, a large cistern hung above smoldering coals. The entrance was a rounded arch with an oaken door. It led into a tiled chamber. At its heart was a square bath, perhaps four feet deep and ten feet on a side.

"The water is cold," the boy warned.

"All the better," Lancelot said. Passing among stone columns, he leapt, plunging himself and the queen into the pool. It was indeed cold, prickling like needles against Lancelot's skin. It must have felt like knives to Guinevere.

She shook violently and clawed at him. "Hold me! Hold me!"

"Yes," he whispered, clutching her tightly. "The cold will ease the burning." Dye spread in red ripples out from them.

"I'll go stoke the cistern fire," offered the boy. "Turn that spigot there, at the end of the clay pipe. Hot water will pour out."

"Good. And close the door. And stand guard, by order of the king."

The boy raced excitedly away.

"Too cold," Guinevere said, nearly climbing him to get out of the water.

"Here." He turned the spigot, a wooden bung like the tap on a keg. Out gushed steamy water. Lancelot paddled the surface, dragging the warmth nearer to them. "You're going to be fine."

Guinevere pressed herself against him, trembling. "It stings. Anywhere that it touches, it stings."

He cupped water in his hand and lifted it, gently washing the queen's face. The liquid that rolled away was the color of blood. He lifted more water and caressed her cheek, her brow. The wash ran pink. A third handful dripped down clear.

Breathing deeply from exertion and cold and everything, Lancelot bowed her in his arms. Her hair spread out upon the water and bled into it. Lancelot gently drew his fingers through the silken strands. He felt the water growing warmer. The tension in her body was easing.

"Does it still sting?"

"Yes," she said, "everywhere." Her hand rose to the laces of her gown.

Lancelot rolled her into his arms and held her tightly. Staring beyond the red pool, beyond the tiled walls to some unseeable future, he said, "What was so urgent that you would come to me this way?"

"This," she said, lifting her mouth to his. Their lips met. She slid her hand into his hair and clung to him. He tasted her mouth, and she tasted his.

Lancelot broke away and held her to him. He trembled. "What are we doing?"

She whispered into his ear. "We're being true to ourselves. At long last, we're being true."

The heat of her breath tingled on his neck. This time, his lips sought hers. His hand fell to the laces of her gown. Red fabric parted over a wet bodice. As he loosened its straps, she dragged the armor off his shoulders. The cares of war went with it. His breastplate fell away to her eager fingers. He was no longer a knight, no longer anything but a man. He drew her bodice away and cupped one smooth breast. She was no longer a queen, but a woman.

He pulled her to him. Crimson waters crashed between them. He rained kisses on her neck.

Even as she clung to him, her hand reached down to his waist and loosened the straps there. She wrapped him in her legs and settled down atop him. A long, thrilled sigh escaped her lips.

His hands grasped the edge of the pool, and he held on in ecstasy. Still, the words spilled out. "What are we doing?"

"We are being true."

"True to ourselves . . . but false to everything else. . . ."

"What else is there?"

"What of Arthur? What of Camelot?" he gasped out.

Guinevere's voice was a purr. "They will take care of themselves."

Then there were no more words. The water deepened its hue. The pool began to steam. Nothing remained beyond that vermilion place. Time ceased its tyrant tread. Space folded its pavilion. All that existed were two red bodies moving together like the halves of a beating heart.

At last, he wrapped her in his powerful arms and held her

tightly. She held him too, waiting, breathing against his neck. When he released her, tears stood in his eyes.

She looked sweetly at him. "Don't be sad."

Lancelot said. "It's too late. This is what we wanted, but now we've destroyed everything. Everything we are, everything we love. We've destroyed it all."

Guinevere hadn't a chance to respond. Outside came the rumble of horses' hooves. Someone hailed the stable boy. His response came clearly through the heavy door. "Yes, he is in there, but you can't go in, by order of King Arthur."

A woman's voice responded. "By the order of Queen Guinevere—by *my* order—you will stand aside!" The key turned in the lock, and the door crashed open.

In strode Guinevere. She stopped beside the bath, a seeming pool of blood, and stared at Lancelot and the woman with him.

He stared back, confusion and guilt filling his eyes. "What—who are you?"

"Who do you think I am?" the queen replied tartly. She gestured at the other woman, "And who is this?"

"I thought she was you," Lancelot blurted.

Fury, jealousy, confusion, and embarrassment swept in quick waves over Guinevere's features.

Lancelot looked at the red woman in his arms. "Who are you?"

She pulled away from him. She suddenly looked nothing like the queen—shorter, darker, with a round face and brown eyes. She withdrew across the bath from him, clutching her clothes where they floated, and climbed from the water. "I am Elaine, daughter of Pellas, the king of this castle."

"It *was* witchery, from the very beginning," Lancelot said as he retrieved his clothes from the water. "You lured me here and took on the guise of the queen and seduced me. Why?"

"I am not a witch," Elaine replied, pulling on her sodden gown. "And I did it for love. There are a thousand maidens who would have done what I did."

Lancelot's eyes narrowed. "For love, you destroyed me?"

"For love, she saved you," said a new voice. The man had not entered the room, but suddenly, he was there—stoop-shouldered and wizened, his eyes dark beneath a storm-cloud brow.

"Merlin," breathed Guinevere.

"Yes. It is I—and so, not witchery but wizardry that accomplished this deception."

Lancelot stared at the old legend, unsure what he saw was true. "But why? Why all of this?"

The old man scratched his beard and stared down into the crimson pool. "Elaine did what she did for love. I had a grimmer purpose: to warn you away from the path you walk. You were right to realize, Lancelot, that coupling with the queen would destroy everything you both love—Arthur, Camelot, and each other. Now you know it before it is too late."

Lancelot's head ached from all the revelations. "How dare you deceive me?"

"I foresaw you would come to this. When you were in the cradle I saw it, and I foresaw worse things for you, too. You must heed my warning."

As he snatched up the last of his armor and clutched it in his arms, Lancelot said, "All that I heed is the realization that I have been away from Camelot—and from my king—too long. Whatever errors my errantry has wrought can be undone by devotion to Arthur and to God. You, Merlin, are as bad as Morgan le Fey. She seeks to destroy Arthur at all cost, and you to save Arthur at all cost. What of honor? Yes, what of it? I have been so long immersed in others' dishonor I don't remember what it is."

He climbed from the pool and strode toward the door. He stared unapologetically at Queen Guinevere as he passed her. "I head back tonight. Pentecost is coming, and I will use it for repentance."

Her gaze was equally unapologetic. "If you seek salvation in Camelot, I will, for the sake of both our souls, seek it elsewhere."

Merlin trudged up out of the sacred lake in his Cave of Delights. He was looking very old indeed. Water drooled from his beard and travel robes. He headed up the hill, toward the petunia patch and his beloved.

Without looking up from her spade, Nyneve asked, "How did you fare?"

"Poorly," grumbled Merlin as he slogged by.

"Did you accomplish what you wished?"

"No."

Under her breath, Nyneve said, "No good comes from meddling with mortals."

Merlin whirled. "You are wrong there, my dear. Something extraordinarily good will come from my meddling. Someone who is utterly good. And he can save Arthur."

Nyneve lifted her brow. "Oh? Who?"

"His name will be Galahad."

Turning again, Merlin ascended toward their cottage above. That single name had changed him. Though his clothes still dripped, Merlin himself had changed into a square-shouldered young man.

Lifting an eyebrow, Nyneve shoved the spade in the earth, dusted off her hands, and went to join her beloved.

17

Fire of Heaven

Lancelot had never done this before—had never truly prayed. There had been no reason. As a child on Avalon, he had been suffused with divinity. Why kneel to gods that dwelt within? There were no gods within him anymore. There wasn't even a soul. It was easy to kneel. He had already collapsed on the inside.

He knelt in a large but little-used chapel in Camelot. It was a beautiful, dark, warm place. Thick carpets in maroon absorbed even whispers. Tall lancets poured colored moonlight across an altar in white marble. The vault above seeped old incense. It was a decorous spot, the perfect temple for a proper God.

"As of old you came to the apostles and poured upon them your fires of heaven, come to me now. Pour upon me your cleansing flame. Burn every impurity away. Anneal my heart to serve you, to serve Arthur." He did not mention Guinevere, though her name clung to every word. "Heal my sundered self, and return to me the unity of my being."

He didn't know how to pray. He only knew how to fight—and how to love Guinevere.

"I do the thing I do not wish to do. I am the man I do not wish to be. Wash me in the blood of Christ and transform me by the renewal of my spirit."

The words dribbled from his lips and soaked into the carpet, going only down. He had thought celibate Christ would understand his torments—he who supped with prostitutes and did not partake. But how could he understand? His Mother was a virgin. His Father spoke him into being. Even the Holy Spirit conceived him through Mary's ear. How could a God who chose celibacy understand a man who railed against it?

"Lead me not into temptation, but deliver me from evil. . . ."

Beneath his backplate, gooseflesh rose. A Presence reached out for him—a summons. This was no call from Christ, no Word spoken in darkness. This was a sensual summons, like pollen on the wind. While Christians waited for fire out of heaven, everyone else waited for lustier flames.

Desire roared through Lancelot. He steamed in his armor. His hands trembled. Words yet poured out of him, words for the God of Words, but every wordless impulse reached for Guinevere.

On the other side of Britannia, Guinevere felt it too. Through a nighttime window wafted the first scent of summer. Even here in Westminster, even through the smoke of countless chimneys and the miasma of open sewers, she smelled that fresh smell. Guinevere rose from her bed, drifted toward the balcony, and looked out. Night swathed the city. Overhead, the clouds were pregnant with rain. Folk loitered in the streets. They filled their lungs and spoke with eager voices. Warm breezes burrowed among the ivy. Guinevere had cloistered herself in the city, hoping to escape the call of summer. She could not. It rose, imperious, within her. She was the Power of the Land. The land summoned, and she had to answer.

Reaching beyond the balcony, she touched an ivy vine that twined there. The plant's green flesh scintillated. The tendril coiled about her finger. Power met power. That touch carried memories of vine-garbed forests, of grasslands redolent in heat, of swollen rivers and cicada skies. The solstice was still three weeks away, but summer knocked at the door. It invited her to come out and play. It required her to.

Impulses ached in Guinevere's blood. The cycle of seasons plucked at her own cycles—denied though they had been. May called. She had refused the calls of her being for so long that she almost did so again. Almost.

Crossing the darksome chamber, she drew the latch and hauled open the door. The knights standing guard outside startled and turned inward. They bowed quickly, nearly butting her with their helmeted heads.

Guinevere wore an amused expression. "Sir Sagramour, spread the word to the rest of the knights—tomorrow we go a-Maying. Sir Brandeles, spread the word to my retinue. Every knight and knave, every matron and maid, will be decked in green, with bright-shining armor. Every horse will bear green barding and a man and a maid. We will go with swords sheathed and lutes singing. Tomorrow, we will turn this war party into a peace party and ride the woods as of old."

The two men stared baldly at her, and Sagramour said, "We cannot both spread the news, my queen, for who will guard your door?"

In answer, Guinevere drew a deep breath. "Do you smell that?"

"Smell what, Your Highness?" asked Brandeles.

"That wind. That delicious wind. It will guard my door. No evil can befall me tonight, so long as that wind lasts—and no evil on the morrow."

The knights traded nervous glances. "But your husband ordered us to guard—"

"And I order you to cease," Guinevere interrupted. "Now, go, and trust in my power. No harm will come this night!"

" 'No harm will come this night,' " mocked Morgan le Fey. Lips drew back from teeth clenched in a smile. Her hand flitted above the cauldron where she worked. The image of Guinevere rippled, but did not dissolve. "No harm this night, but plenty tomorrow."

Another sweep of her hand stirred the humors in the cauldron, making the image craze and vanish. The humors were blood—Morgan's own mixed with Lancelot's, which she had sucked through a hollow needle when he lay enchanted, and the blood of Guinevere gathered from discarded gauze. It was a potent combination, and it bound the three inextricably together.

The blood stilled. Waves of light resolved. A new image knit itself together: Lancelot knelt, abject and sweating, in a chapel at Camelot.

Morgan's sanguine smile grew only deeper. The power of spring was to bring beasts together for the rut, and that of summer was to keep them rutting. The reason to go a-Maying was to find a mate in the forests. Guinevere sought her mate, sought Lancelot. That was danger enough, but Morgan had dangerous ideas of her own.

She reached up to a peg above her cauldron and pulled

down a bloodied shirt—the "trophy" she had coaxed from Meleagaunce at the joust where he and Lancelot had battled. The garment stank of old sweat and blood. Morgan kissed the largest stain and lowered the shirt. It settled across the cauldron, blood wicking through its fibers. It spread out like the death rose that blooms from a stabbed heart.

"Only, she does not know what mate awaits her," Morgan said darkly. The shirt sank entirely beneath the blood. The cauldron stilled once more. In its mirror surface shone the blunt and brutal features of Meleagaunce.

"She will have her mate, and I will have Lancelot."

The day dawned gloriously over Westminster. Amid wattle-and-daub hovels and half-timber pubs marched a green host. Strings set a song in the air, and carefree voices rose. The procession seemed Summer incarnate, passing between hunched buildings. Where they went, gray retreated. Faces appeared at windows. Smiles followed. On a single horse, Queen Guinevere rode sidesaddle behind Sir Kay, Seneschal of all Britannia. Neither seemed royalty, though. Kay's blond head bore a wreath of ivy instead of a helm. Guinevere's dark hair reached unbound to her waist. Emerald-green gowns draped them both—the traditional garb of the May queen. Soon the hems of those robes would bear rafts of flowers.

In the laughing space between songs, Queen Guinevere called out, "Who knows this one?"

In May we climb the summit slopes
Of spring. We find the summer there
And gather in the bloss'ming hopes

That turn to faith. We slay despair
With joy. Our songs adorn the air:
Oh, derry derry do, oh, derry derry do.

Voices joined hers in the second verse. Together they sang:

Now come to me, O summer's son,
Whose pollen makes the flower yield
Its fruit. Yes come, O antlered one,
And pour across the wood and field
The bounty of the pow'r you wield.
Sing derry derry do, oh, derry derry do.

The whole company bawdily sang the coda:

So cast aside your cares and woes,
And cast aside your weighty clothes,
And feel the grass between your toes,
While all around us grows and grows
And grows and grows and grows and grows.
Sing derry derry do, oh, derry derry do.

The throng had threaded its way out of the mazy streets. It had shucked the world of the city—the dust, the smoke, the hard stares and shoving crowds. Even the children who had flocked in a glad group at their heels remained at the gates. Beyond, the parade abandoned the road. They spread across fields of green grain. One bloom at a time, the folk mantled themselves in the world of plains and forests. Lively tavern tunes gave way to the rhythmic songs of field hands, redolent in sweat and swinging blades and backs too strong to break.

Sir Pellas drew forth the ribbons that they would use for

the Maypole. He tossed their spools rider to rider. Strips of samite made colorful arcs in the air. Fellows caught them and tossed them back. So they rode, bound in cloth and song.

The horses chuffed up the long hillside. In the days of the Tuatha dé Danann, the whole Westminster Valley had been woodland. Then came the Britons. Trees had fallen and houses had risen. London had carved itself from the forests. Even now, more trees poured their ashes up its chimneys. The remaining woodlands began a few miles ahead—a day's walk for the beggars who sold faggots, but an easy ride for a royal retinue.

"We need the perfect tree," Guinevere announced as another song drifted away. "Straight, tall, and easily trimmed for the bonfire. A pine, I think. They are the straightest, and the sap burns well."

Kay, her saddle-mate, said, "You know, my queen, what the Maypole is meant to symbolize? So tall, so erect."

"I do," she responded.

"The question then is, whose is it supposed to symbolize?" Kay replied lightly.

Guinevere would not rise to the bait. "Whose do you suggest? Perhaps we could find a crooked one oozing sap if you'd like to be the honoree—"

"Ah, I would not think of trying to insert myself into the already crowded affections of your heart," replied Kay glibly.

"Crowded, indeed," replied Guinevere, "for I love my life, and my king, and my land, and this clover field, and that bounding wren, and two or three of those birch leaves drifting there, and . . . well, dear Kay, were I to include you in the long list, you'd number deep in three digits."

They reached the verge of the woodlands, a place of nettles, palisaded against incursions. Knowing the ways of plants, Guinevere grasped the reins in Kay's hand and guided the horse along the root lines. They reached a deer path, wide enough for a horse. A strange deer path, but Guinevere was glad and ready to believe. Leading the host single file, she entered the woods.

Mossy boles encroached upon the path. Boughs reached in a green tangle above their heads. The omnipresent sun was shattered to tiny triangles that dragged across the company. Soon, no sunlight penetrated. In murk, the revelers rode.

Ahead, the way opened. It was the sort of break that normally signaled the fall of a forest giant. Here, though, the clearing was conic, a wide base rising to a narrow hole in the canopy. At the center of the space stood the stout, straight bole of a mighty fir. Its boughs had been shorn away and lay in a pile to one side. The needles were yet green. The stubs wept sap. Someone had been by here recently, perhaps a-Maying, but if so, where were the samite strands?

So strange was this site, so perfect the tree, that Guinevere once again clasped the rein-hand of Kay and pulled the mount to a halt. She sat the horse silently as her comrades, approaching up the deer path, split around her. They spread in a crescent before the great tree.

Sir Kay turned toward his queen. "We could not have hoped for so perfect a tree, even had lightning struck it."

"Had lightning struck it, the tree would be dead. A dead tree cannot be a Maypole. No, this tree is perfect. That's what frightens me."

The final member of the company—a mere squire striding quickly to keep up with the horses—walked up beside the queen.

Kay mocked, "You fear leisure, Highness?"

"The best cheese a mouse will taste is the cheese that triggers the trap," Guinevere responded. "Get back, all of you," she said, her voice uncertain. "This is a trap."

She was too late. Ten knights, ten maids, and a couple squires—and none of them had noticed the dark figures that now stepped from behind the trees. Brigands suddenly surrounded them and outnumbered them ten to one.

"A trap!" Guinevere shouted.

Kay wheeled his steed.

The woods rushed at him—not the woods, but men garbed in bark and lichen. One ran toward the seneschal, a twisted oak limb in hand. The makeshift club rammed Kay backward. With a grunt, he smashed against Guinevere. The horse tucked its haunches and kicked free. Together, seneschal and queen fell to the pine needles.

The horse bowed its head and charged. A sword smashed its forelegs. The beast folded up, thrashing spastically.

All around, the scene was the same—shadowy figures converging on the green-robed party, horses falling and dying, men and women dropping to the dust to gasp for air, chains gleaming and shackles ringing as they snapped about necks and wrists and ankles. Three knights were dead already—Ladynas, Persant, and Ironside—and more fought for their lives. It was no use. Anyone who offered a fight was slain by the brigands. Anyone who even seemed a menace was swarmed.

Still panting from the first blow, Guinevere laid eyes on salvation. Young, gaunt, horseless, terrified—the squire had been utterly ignored by the attackers. He stood in a trembling crouch, as if awaiting orders. Guinevere gave him some.

"Go!" she commanded in a hissed breath. She drew off her signet ring and flung it to him. "Flee. Take a horse. Give this to Lancelot. Tell him to return to me!"

Nodding, the squire slid the ring on his own finger. One moment, he ducked away from bandits and horses. The next, he was gone. Nettles shivered with his passage, but then grew still. He would escape. He would leap on the first horse that got away. He would go to Westminster, provision, and ride full-out for Camelot. Guinevere knew it, even as the weeds settled in his wake.

"What are you looking at?" growled one of the ruffians. Knuckles backhanded her across the cheek.

Guinevere reeled, catching herself on one hand.

Kay leapt to his feet. He swung a right cross, but fist and body were caught in a swarm of brigands. With his left arm, he pummeled their heads and backs, to no avail. In moments, the dark tide of warriors had overwhelmed him and swept him under.

Guinevere struggled to reach Kay, but a brigand wrenched her arm up behind her and held a knife to her throat. The fighting died down. Only Guinevere remained from the Maying party. Kay and the other knights were incapacitated—some dead, some chained. The other women had been dragged away into the thickets, where muffled screams told a grim tale.

Into the clearing lumbered the leader of the brigands—the meaty, crude man who had set this trap: Meleagaunce. "Ah, my queen," he said through lips stubbled in black beard, "you have come to visit. Since the time of the joust, I have not been able to stop thinking of you."

Staring levelly, Guinevere replied. "Oh, really? And you are—?"

"Don't toy with me, Your Majesty," replied Meleagaunce. He wore the same thick armor he had during the jousts. "You know precisely who I am, and precisely what I want."

"You are Prince Meleagaunce, son of King Bagdemagus, of

course," said the queen. "As to what you want, though, that is less certain. You are indebted to my champion Lancelot, who fought beside you, for your father's honor. I would think just now you would be wanting such honor."

His hand flew, and the knuckles would be sure to bruise her face. "Shut up. What I want is very simple. I want you."

He had lain before this altar for three days. He had fasted and prayed all that while. Yes, for the first twelve hours, he had needed occasional moments to relieve himself. Since then, though, he had nothing to relieve, and only the judging darkness to hem him in.

Lancelot still did not know how to pray. Instead of flowery words, he offered his own life before the altar of the jealous God. If only he could be purified, could be a single, simple thing once more.

Into the hushed little chapel came a panting, sweating young squire. The boy knelt before Lancelot and, weeping in exhaustion and relief, poured out his news. "Queen Guinevere has been captured by Prince Meleagaunce. He's taken her to his castle." The lad drew the queen's own ring off his finger and held it before Lancelot.

Lancelot rose. His legs prickled as he stood. "What are you saying?"

Angry, the squire said, "The queen asked that I deliver this to you, along with a message."

"Yes, and . . . ?"

" 'Return to me'," the child replied with a purity of tone that chilled Lancelot.

"I will," said Lancelot, taking the ring and slipping it onto his smallest finger. "I will return to her."

18

What Lovers Choose

Rasa galloped full-out across the plains of Westminster. He was tireless. He knew Guinevere was in peril, and he ran for her.

The horse's keen gaze matched Lancelot's own. He cared for Rasa, yes—checking for froth, fording rivers to cool his hot hide, requiring him to graze and drink for precious minutes of every hour—but his eyes were turned toward Guinevere.

She languished in some dark cell beneath Meleagaunce's castle. Who knew but that she languished beneath the meaty man himself?

Lancelot's teeth clamped. With a gentle nudge of his heels, he urged the galloping stallion all the faster.

"Guinevere," Lancelot groaned through his teeth. "Guinevere."

"Guinevere," said a deep, dark voice at the cell door.

The queen stirred amid her chains. She hadn't been sleeping—couldn't sleep within those iron teeth, upon the wet stone floor. Neither had she been truly awake. Now she was. She sat up and pressed against the wall. Meleagaunce was at the door. He was calling her name.

"Guinevere." His voice was husky and hushed.

"Go away," Guinevere managed in queenly tones.

Silence came, broken only by deep breaths. "You do not rule me. I rule you." More sounds of iron—the clink of keys. Tumblers shifted. The lock opened. Hinges creaked, and the door swung inward.

Meleagaunce entered the cell. He seemed a beast, as massive and musky as an ox. He stared at her with dumb intensity. Breath filled him and emptied him—gray mist in that dank place.

"What are you going to do?" Guinevere asked.

Wordlessly, he clomped toward her. He reached out.

She pressed back into the unforgiving wall.

He grabbed her arm and yanked it toward him.

Shrieking, she kicked his knee, hoping to break it. The limb was as solid as a tree trunk. Her foot jangled. She kicked again.

Meleagaunce wouldn't stop. He grabbed her other arm. Iron clanked. He yanked on her kicking feet and pulled her away from the wall. His fingers jabbed. What was he doing?

The shackles clicked open and fell away. Meleagaunce backed up.

Panting, Guinevere scrambled back against the wall and glared at him. "What are you . . . what are you doing?" Inexplicably, he turned toward the cell door and stood beside it, gesturing down the corridor. Guinevere shook her head. "You're letting me go?"

"I'm letting you run, so I can chase."

• • •

"Guinevere!" shouted Lancelot in battle cry. Rasa pelted down the hillside toward Westminster Bridge. Lancelot marked the archers on and beyond it—a score of men wearing the colors of Meleagaunce. Below, the river was deep and swift, its banks choked with trees. The only way across was straight through the gauntlet. "Guinevere!"

Rasa curled his neck and barged for the bridge. The first shafts rose upon the wind. Eyes narrowed as he watched them. The stallion leapt to one side. A pair of arrows thudded into the packed earth beside him. Hind hooves kicked deep divots out of the ground and hurled him on. A third arrow grazed his tucked haunch. He bounded aside again. Two more shafts shot past his ears.

The next, though, was dead-on, too quick to evade. The point jabbed between his eyes. Iron cracked. Steel flashed. The arrow ricocheted harmlessly away.

Lancelot lifted his sword from before Rasa's eyes and deflected two more arrows with it. The Saxon blade might have been too slow on any other day, but Guinevere waited beyond that bridge, and nothing could slow Lancelot today. He swept the sword through a hail of shafts. Three bounced from the blade. Two more glanced from his armor.

The lead archer on the bridge nocked two shafts on one string, aimed, and let fly.

The twin arrows jabbed out, rose, and struck. One hit Rasa's shoulder. The other struck Lancelot's. Each buried its head deep in muscle. Lancelot roared out, his sword arm dragging loose for a moment. Rasa only snorted and bore toward the archer.

The man dropped his bow, stepped back, and hauled on his sword. Too late.

Rasa's fore hooves struck and shattered the man's pelvis. Rasa's hind hooves came down upon his chest and staved it. The archer was only a trammeled blot on the bridge. Rasa's hooves left red curves on the stone.

Lancelot grasped the sword in his off hand, drew it up, and brought it down. The blade sliced the next man from shoulder to side. The two halves fell away. Horse and rider barged on. Another man leapt from the bridge, only to be swept away by the river. Two more died by hoof and steel.

Rasa's feet came to ground beyond the bridge. He bolted upward. The remaining archers sent shafts after them, but the stallion's charge stole their speed away. The few that struck flesh only jabbed shallowly. Rasa carried his master out beyond reach of the warriors.

Growling, Lancelot sheathed his sword. He reached up to the shaft that jutted from his shoulder and drove the point out his back. A quick twist snapped the shaft, and he dragged the bloody ends away. He'd have to stop for Rasa once they were well beyond Meleagaunce's men, but he could dress his own wound here in the saddle. Reaching to his helm, he drew forth the scarf twined there—Guinevere's scarf—and poked it into the entry and exit wounds. His blood spread out through the perfumed cloth. The touch of the fabric invigorated his flesh.

Closing his eyes, he breathed the scent of her before it was lost in the stink of blood.

Guinevere ran through the bailey. Her gown clung to her—sweat and blood. Warriors upon the wall looked idly down at the terrified woman and spoke smiling words behind their hands. She did not call out to them. The predator had ordered them not to let her escape, not to help her.

The predator. That was all he was now—no ox but a dire

wolf, a monster. He could have caught her already. He'd had his hands on her. The skin of her thighs was rolled up beneath his thumbnails. He was having too much fun, though.

Panting, wide-eyed, Guinevere bolted for the courtyard well. If she could only reach pure water, she might call on its potency to escape. Three more steps showed that the well had been covered with planks and nailed shut. Someone had helped the predator prepare for her, someone who knew Guinevere's Otherworld strengths and weaknesses.

She turned and ran toward a turret that led to the castle wall. A guard stood there. He did not bar her way—there was no escape from the wall. Grasping his arm, she pleaded, "Give me your sword."

The man's fist tightened on the pommel. His eyes were steely. "No." Something entered his gaze—the reflection of a new figure.

Guinevere looked over her shoulder to see Meleagaunce emerge from the keep doorway. He scanned the bailey, spotted her, and loped forward.

"Please," Guinevere begged the guard.

"No. Good luck, Your Highness."

She fled past him, up the spiraling stairs. Her breaths were loud, but not as loud as his boots below. He would catch her here. He would rape her on the stairs.

Light shown dimly above—the top of the wall. There would be another guard there, though he would not grant his sword either. She would have no time to ask. Meleagaunce was just below. His hands groped around the corner.

Guinevere scrambled up the last of the steps and darted out through the doorway. She wheeled, grasped the soldier standing there, and hurled him backward down the stair. In the twisting darkness he met his master, and both men tumbled. It would slow Meleagaunce, but not stop him. It would only stoke his rage and his lust.

Numb, Guinevere staggered away atop the wall. He wouldn't have her. Whatever happened now, he would never have her.

He will not have her, thought Lancelot, struggling to pierce the red clouds that rolled about his eyes. He will not touch her. Only such thoughts kept him going. The ache in his shoulder spread down to fingertips and out across his chest and up to the balance center of his ear. He was weary, unsteady.

What sort of poison did those arrows bear?

Rasa was little better. The great stallion bore forward at an unsteady canter. He favored his wounded shoulder and ran like a three-legged dog.

The castle of Meleagaunce lay two miles distant. Its turrets showed above the old-growth forest that loomed ahead.

Lancelot patted the horse's healthy shoulder and felt foam beneath his fingertips. "We're almost there, Rasa. Then you can rest. I will challenge Meleagaunce afoot."

The horse whickered in reply. Together, beast and rider picked their way down the forest road. Foliage closed darkly above. Cold stillness replaced the summer winds. Rasa's hoof-beats grew muffled. All around, oaks crowded the road, and their gnarled roots grabbed at Rasa's hooves.

Something worse moved among the boles. A golden tail flicked. Leaf shadows gathered and sprang. Something stalked them—two things, one on either side of the road. Eyes watched, and fangs glinted.

Lancelot leaned to Rasa and whispered into the horse's ear, "Let's go, boy."

Rasa understood and broke into a trot, and then a desperate gallop. Tree boles flew past.

The predators paced them. One—a she-lion the size of a plow horse—bounded onto the trail and charged after them. Her golden fur rippled across vicious muscles. With each leap, she closed the distance to Rasa. The other predator—a leopard with the sinuous grace of a snake—hurled itself through the treetops overhead. It closed on Lancelot.

"Faster!" he hissed, but Rasa was already spent. The stallion ran on nerve alone. Still, a mile of forest remained before the road opened again.

The lion bounded once last, within striking range. It leapt. Its claws stabbed down and buried themselves in the horse's haunch. Blood poured in eight lines down the white pelt.

Rasa screamed. Claws dragged him down. The lion grasped him again and sank its teeth into his side. Rasa fell and flailed.

Lancelot turned to slash the beast with his sword, but a great weight struck his back and flung him away. He landed on a gnarl of roots, rolled twice, and then smashed into a tree trunk. The leopard leapt upon him and gripped his neck in its fangs and bit.

The predator's dagger bit into Guinevere's neck. She clung to a merlon of the castle wall. She could flee no farther. This was the highest bartizan at the end of the longest wall. She had fought and fled and bled, but could not escape.

Her pursuer loomed, hateful and shadowy, above her. He panted. His eyes were white rings of excitement. They hungrily studied her. Her gown was mere rags. The slits revealed every scratched and bleeding inch of her skin. The blood seemed only to pique his desire. His hand trembled as it reddened from the flow across his knife.

"Choose, Guinevere," he said huskily. "You are beaten. You will be penetrated, one way or the other. Choose how. . . ."

She stared into his hateful eyes.

His hand tightened on the slick dagger. "Choose now." Slowly, the point sank inward.

The leopard's wicked fangs sank into his neck. With one snap of those jaws, the beast could have torn Lancelot's throat out.

The teeth never closed. Instead, the great cat lifted its wet fangs from Lancelot's throat and sat down upon his chest. It fixed him with sharp, smiling eyes. One of the creature's foreclaws glimmered a moment. Curved claw became curved metal—a ring. The paw around it transformed into a hand, the leg into an arm. Spotted fur smoothed into clean, white skin. Feline features shifted only slightly to the face of a woman—a beautiful woman who straddled him and wore only the glinting ring.

"Morgan le Fey," Lancelot growled out.

Her voice was a throaty purr. "I am your faerie guardian."

"You are a witch," Lancelot spat, struggling to get up. He couldn't move, pinned beneath her inexorable magic. Only his head lifted, and only to glimpse the corpse of Rasa, torn open by the gorging lion. "What do you want with me?"

"You know what I want with you," she replied. She ran a long fingernail along his jaw. "The same thing I wanted last time."

Lancelot struggled for breath. "Get off me."

Morgan shook her head slowly. "No. This will end one of two ways. You will give me what I want, or I will rip your throat out. It is your choice."

"Give you what you want? Give you another bastard child like Mordred?"

"Oh, no, not like Mordred. Your child would be something more, something greater. And there will be great pleasure in creating it." Her voice dropped to a low growl. "Or great anguish otherwise. Choose."

"Choose," growled Meleagaunce once last.

"I choose," Guinevere said, clear eyed. She flung herself back, out of the crenellation, over the wall. She fell, blood trailing like a ribbon from her neck.

Blood formed a collar about Lancelot's neck. "I choose." He reached up toward her. His hand traced along her cheek. She was magnificent, voluptuous, powerful. Her smile of triumph was dazzling.

Morgan le Fey shifted her hands down to the laces at his waist.

His fingers met hers, shivering and eager.

She laughed at his fumbling hands—and then her face darkened to a furious scowl.

He had yanked the ring from her finger and rammed it on his own.

Suddenly, all the illusion was dispelled. No longer was Morgan a nubile creature, but a middle-aged woman. Every trace of her feline grace was gone. She leapt up, away from him, and fled into the woods.

Lancelot staggered to his feet and lifted his sword. The lion, too, had transformed. It was once again the plow horse she had stolen from a nearby field. She had granted the thing a glorious aspect and sent it galloping after Rasa, bearing her to Lancelot. Rasa was no longer torn open, but stood stunned nearby.

Lancelot looked at the ring—perhaps a ward against magic, perhaps a means to control magic. Either way, it would guard him from Morgan. He peered among the gray boles, seeking the witch. She was gone, fled away with the speed of a hart.

It didn't matter. Morgan didn't matter. Only Guinevere did.

Sheathing his sword, Lancelot strode gravely across the root-riddled ground. He pulled himself into the saddle. His shoulder ached. The wound there was only too real. Still, with this ring, he would know for certain that the woman he rescued would be his Guinevere.

Heels nudged the steed to a trot. Rasa picked his way through the last mile of forest. Sunlight broke over their backs, and hooves came to ground on sheep-shorn grass. Rider and steed rushed toward the castle, which stood in defiance atop the hill.

The battlements seemed stumpy teeth against the sky. Guinevere smiled as she fell. Meleagaunce was only a fly crouched there, staring angrily after her.

She didn't even look to see whether she would strike berm or moat. It didn't matter. Either way, he would never have her.

Her head struck. There was a wet sound like a melon shattering, and then only blackness.

Upon the black waters of the moat floated a white figure. Rasa tore toward it, across the green belly of the land. Were it not for the ring Lancelot wore, he would have thought this yet another delusion. But no—it was Guinevere. She lay bare amid brackish weeds.

"To her, Rasa. Return to her."

Despite the steed's wounds, he cantered with a stately tread to the edge of the moat. Lancelot threw himself from the saddle and into the water. It was as fetid and cold as death. Weeds clawed at him. He pulled free, stroked toward her, and grasped her. She was warm. Her breast rose and fell. "I have you, my queen. I have you."

Kicking to stay afloat, Lancelot stroked for the shore.

Shouts came from the wall above. Arrows followed. They plunged into the waters all around.

Lancelot rose in their midst. He carried Guinevere across his arms. Rasa bowed his head before the queen and dropped to his knees, that they might mount. Lancelot rose upon the noble steed. Rasa stood and galloped away, his neighs like laughter. Shafts peppered the ground behind his hooves, but none could reach the queen or her champion.

The white stallion topped the green hill and was gone.

19

Who Are We?

They were nearly dead when they reached the Castle of Astolat. All three of them were nearly dead.

The snow-white horse staggered up to the gates. An arrow jutted from its breast. Its left foreleg was brown with blood. It snorted at the guards and glared with eyes both imperious and imploring. Its ruddy hoof dug a divot from the ground. Bowing a tangled mane, the horse revealed its ravaged riders.

First, there was a woman, battered and bloodied. She wore only a tabard emblazoned with the Pendragon. It garbed her like a ceremonial robe. She lay across the beast's white neck, a sacrifice on a marble altar.

Behind her slumped a man. His chest was crossed by a deep line of red. It was not pure blood that wept from that wound, but poison. Beneath blond knots of hair was a face as pale as ivory.

The guards stared dumbly at these strange figures. Astolat was no grand castle—merely an earl's house fortified with a palisade—and these guards were no grand warriors. Within hauberks of boiled leather, old eyes goggled. White knuckles gripped rusty hilts. One guard snorted a question at his comrade, and the other shrugged his reply. Surely it would be improper to slay sleeping folk, but who were they, and why were they here?

As if sensing the stillness of his steed, the man drew a breath, cracked an eyelid, and uttered a command. "Aid us."

Those quiet words crashed against the guards. They shuddered visibly. One managed a question. "Wh-who are you?"

The answer came from the woman. "Queen Guinevere . . . and her champion . . . Lancelot."

One guard gave a strangled cry of despair. Both dropped their swords and leapt forward. Each caught one of the visitors as they fell from the saddle.

They lay head to head, their toes pointing to either end of the great hall banquet table. It was the only surface clean enough, sturdy enough, and well enough lit to allow the chirurgeon his examination. In truth, Valisaeric was no chirurgeon, but only a barber, and not a very good one. Still, he had dressed wounds at Badon Hill, and he wasn't afraid of blood. He ordered from the room everyone who was—and that meant everyone. Even young Elaine had to go. Though she was a skilled healer in her own right, she was smitten with the knight, and it wouldn't do to have her washing his wound.

Lancelot bled from one deep, poisoned wound struck in an instant. Guinevere bled from countless wounds gained piecemeal through long travail. Both were near to death.

Valisaeric did what he could. He stoked the great hall fireplace until it was wroth with flame. Pots steamed, and he poured his cutting implements into them. He stripped both his patients to their skins. Taking a kettle of water that had boiled and cooled, he washed their wounds. He even drove one of the kitchen funnels down into the knight's shoulder and poured two gallons of water through the gouge. Rye spirits followed afterward, for that wound and all the others. The stinging stuff made his patients wince and shudder. Their bodies grew rigid. Gooseflesh swept in waves across their skin. Still, they did not awaken. They were gripped by some strange force. Not since the gate had they been awake. Ripping bed linens into long strips, Valisaeric bound their wounds.

He stepped back. They might as well have been corpses, cleaned and dressed for the grave—lifeless except for the wan rise and fall of their pallid breasts.

Valisaeric drew a blanket up across the queen, from toes to shoulders. He left a large enough fold at the top that he could cover her face.

Lifting his head, he prayed, "Great Healer, save her." The tallow chandelier sent blond circles of light out among dark rafters.

Valisaeric gathered another blanket, walked to the feet of the knight, and began to cover him. At Lancelot's hand, he noticed for the first time the strange, glimmering ring. It drew the eye. It drew the hand. Without even willing it, Valisaeric reached down, pulled it off, and lifted it. The band scintillated with power. It tingled in his fingers.

Suddenly, the queen and the knight breathed easily, their flesh the pink hue of health. Stranger still, something drifted around their heads, a ghost, or a pair of them. The two troubled faces had begun to smile.

Clutching the ring to his chest, Valisaeric backed away. He sat heavily in a chair and stared at the whirling apparition.

Perhaps this was the Holy Spirit, with the gift of healing. Yes, that's what he would believe. Any other thought would have sent him fleeing the room.

At first it had all been isolation and agony. He didn't even know who he was. He knew only that he was dying alone.

Then something changed. The wall of souls tumbled. The bulwark of skin—so thin and yet so inviolate—crumbled. Over its wreckage, Lancelot climbed. He was Lancelot. He knew that now. And he climbed toward the single other entity in his consciousness. Sharp-edged stones cut his feet, but he climbed, and he found her: Guinevere.

She was beautiful. Always she had been beautiful, but now she was quintessentially beautiful. It was as though she wore her soul on the outside. Long cascades of brown hair, almond eyes, high cheekbones, lips as red as apples—she was tall and slender and robed in power. Her eyes, as brown and deep as highland peat—held his gaze. There was love there, and longing, and mystery.

Lancelot approached her. No longer did stones cut his soles. What he walked on, he neither knew nor cared. He only approached her: Guinevere.

Where are we?

Not where, Lancelot. Not even when. But who? Who are we? she replied. The words seemed to pour from her eyes. *Once we know who, every other question will be answered.*

He drew a deep breath, and the scent of her—not her perfume or her clothes but the scent of her very flesh—filled him. *I am Lancelot du Lac.*

Yes, but who is he?

You are my queen—Guinevere.

And who is she?

Yes, who is Guinevere? Who is Lancelot? Names, words—such thin things, disturbances in air or stains on a page. They masked the surface of things and gave them illusory form. When pierced or peeled or dissolved, words left only formless mystery.

Guinevere reached out to take his hand. Her fingers were attenuate, her arms graceful. Lancelot extended his arm and saw that it too was lissome. A kingly robe in red samite draped his body. It was cinched above a velvet doublet and a flaxen shift. Trews and boots—but he had been barefoot when he emerged, barefoot and naked.

You were bare but not naked. Your soul had not yet garbed itself in flesh, let alone clothes.

Looking down at the fey clothes he wore, Lancelot said, *I didn't garb myself. I would not have chosen such.*

Guinevere smiled gently. *But you did.*

Lancelot nodded. *Is this a dream? Are we truly here?*

We are true. As to whether we are here—she gestured out beside them.

Lancelot's eyes followed the sweep of her hand. Until that moment, he had seen only Guinevere and himself. Now he saw the world all around him. He knew immediately it was not the world he was used to, and yet also that this was a world where he belonged.

The grass beneath his boots was tender and fine, almost like carpet. It extended across a broad plateau that reached into the near distance. A sheer drop led then to the plains, broken by blue ridges here and black crevasses there. All ended at a wide and spangled sea. On its far side, on the very horizon of the world, stood purple mountains, so tall and sharp that they bridged the firmaments.

The sky was a deep blue, the color of dawn or dusk. It was ruled not by a single tyrant sun, but by a dancing host of heavenly bodies. Stars, comets, planets, meteors—all whirled in silent symphony, moved by the calculus of desire. They cast multiple shadows around Guinevere and Lancelot.

This is a dream, Lancelot said.

It is, and it is not. If by a dream you mean something less real than the waking world—no, this is not a dream. If instead you mean a realm that lies beneath the waking world, where we store all our eternal truths, then yes, this is a dream. This is the Otherworld.

Lancelot ground his teeth grimly. *It is the poison. It is killing my mind, and this is what I see as I die.*

Guinevere laughed. The sound came from her lips, not her mind, and for the first time she spoke, "You could not be more wrong."

"You speak—*we* speak."

She shrugged, "Words are the clothing of our minds. You had no clothes until you needed them, and no words either."

Lancelot shook his head. His hands gripped his hair, and he gasped as if bedeviled. "I am a simple warrior—"

"You are not a simple warrior. Come."

Clasping his hand, she began to stride across the dewy grass. Her feet touched ground lightly, like a dancer's. His followed. Each step bounced as from a sponge, and each next step lofted them higher than the last. Lancelot sensed what was coming. He could feel the motes of potentiality gathering beneath his feet. They neared the sheer edge of the plateau. Grass gave way to empty air and, below it, descending fists of stone. He held tight to her hand. Their feet came down together. The ground lofted them.

They flew.

The world dropped away. It was as though the yawning

crevices of stone were folds in a paper fan. They came together and diminished. All the land shrank. Only the shadows of the fliers grew. They swarmed across the grasslands. A breeze began, growing to a sharp wind. It blew the grains in long waves. It was more than wind, though. The crest of each wave was mature grass. The trough was newborn blades.

We are flying across space and through time, explained Guinevere. *We are revoking the years.*

I did not know you had such power.

I do not, but the land does. I am only its servant, its priestess. It bids me walk these paths made for gods, and I walk. It bids me bring you along, and I do.

They veered down sharply. It seemed they had flown but a few miles, but as they dropped toward the lowland plains, Lancelot realized that hundreds of miles had scrolled away. Now they flew above tumuli piled up by ancient peoples. One particular prominence swelled up toward them. Lancelot watched it rise. Any moment, Guinevere would pull up to let their feet light upon the ground. Any moment. It soared upward with skull-crushing power.

Lancelot closed his eyes in the instant of impact. He felt it—a profound blow—and yet it did not hurt, did not pulp his brain. Instead, he clove through the ground like a diver through water. Grit and dirt sifted past him. Lancelot clung all the harder to Guinevere's hand. She dragged him deeper into the tumulus.

Suddenly, it all was gone—the grit, the darkness, the motion. Guinevere's hand had changed too. It was now the tender hand of an infant.

Lancelot knelt there beside her bower. She was beautiful, unmistakably Guinevere. Her brown eyes regarded him gladly, though she was but weeks old. Tuatha children, he somehow knew, were never the puling, oozing things that human children were. The baby wore a gown of thistledown. A golden circlet ringed her head. Ivy and lily held her. Already, he loved her.

Someone approached. Lancelot looked up. Only then did he see that the bower lay beside a tall, gentle waterfall. It dropped a smooth curtain of water, as silvery as a mirror. Mists played ever about it, dampening the rock walls. From that mirror flood emerged an elf—tall and regal. His robes were untouched by the water that cascaded around him. His hair was the same color as the falls, and his eyes were like silver coins. Without looking, he placed his feet perfectly on the slick stones. He had rehearsed this moment. His limbs were stiff with resolve.

Lancelot sat back, though he did not release Guinevere's hand.

The elf-king—there was a signet ring on one finger—took no note of Lancelot. He knelt by the bower as if he and the child were alone. The old elf drew in the scent of the baby and smiled. In ancient but strong hands, he reached down around her and lifted her.

Lancelot released the infant's hand, though he immediately felt Guinevere's adult hand return to his own. She knelt beside him and watched with equal rapture.

It was as if the Tuatha king cradled a star, so bright was his face. Then, a shadow came across one side.

My mother died after my birth.

Lancelot stared at Guinevere.

My father could not rear me alone, and so he chose to give me in service to the land, give me into the cradle of a human king.

The monarch's down-turned face was now awash in shadows.

He gave me in betrothal to Arthur.

The elf-king rose and turned. He walked back across the slick stones. Child in hand, he stepped through the mirror falls. As his robes broke the skin of water, Lancelot glimpsed the candlelit nursery of a human castle beyond. Then the falls closed over king and babe both.

The daughter of King Lodegrance of Camelaird had died in childbirth. It seemed a fit thing to let one family be whole. My father gave me to that empty cradle, to that wanting breast.

A tear stood in Lancelot's eye. As it spilled down his cheek, Guinevere touched it and drew it away.

"Come," she said aloud. "There is more. Across the waters, in the lowlands beneath those purple mountains—we will find another nativity."

"Up again?" he asked, looking toward a sky that was blue and speckled with stars.

She shook her head. "No, down."

Clutching his hand, she dived for the rocky pool. There was not a foot of water above jagged stone, but she dived and dragged him after. He went, and closed his eyes. There came another impact, this one wet and cold and vital.

Everything solid in him dissolved, leaving his watery being to seek its way. Side by side they coursed. Through chattering shallows and swollen pools, through silty deltas and the briny deep, they swam. It was miles in mere seconds, for time obeyed the whims of their beating hearts.

They were there. They emerged in a deep, dark well, and swam into a bucket. It rose on its rope. On one end of a shoulder pole, they rode into a castle, and were poured out into a basin.

They stepped from the shallow water onto a floor of gray stone. It had been fretfully scrubbed for decades. Everything in the small chamber bore that ardent attention—the drapes as white and straight as columns, the cradle polished and spotless, the toys arrayed upon shelves awaiting a child who could play with them.

Fear lashed Lancelot. He clung desperately to Guinevere's hand. Everything had changed. He was the infant now. His were the beaming eyes, his the head that bore the coronet, his the helpless body. He was the babe.

More had changed. In place of lilies and ivy, he was bedded in linens washed in alcohol. Instead of waterfall mist, he was bathed in the fist-wrung water of that basin. He lay upon a sickbed. He languished in his cradle. Ten years, twenty years, thirty years, he languished, the eternal infant.

Lancelot cried out in terror. Guinevere held his tiny hand.

His parents had ceased being parents. The king and queen were so maddened by their child's state that they had all but disowned him. He was the ward of nursemaids—servants or slaves. He was a duty, like the shoveling of stables or the slaughtering of hogs.

How strange, this dream. His parents were not this way. His room was not this way.

In stalked a man, a Tuatha man. Anger clenched the elf-king's face. Madness wept from his eyes. Bashing aside the young woman who had been washing him, the man snatched up Lancelot and snarled. Guinevere lost her hold, and there was only the grip of those furious fingers. Five strides, and Lancelot felt himself thrust down into the basin. He sucked water, felt its swelling pain in his chest, tried to scream, and inhaled only more.

Then, he was through. It was a mirror portal, like the last, and he was through, squalling in the cradle of a king. His infant eyes recognized the beams overhead, the trappings of his first days at Benwick. He also felt, for the briefest instant, the shoulder of the other boy who occupied that cradle. A human boy—blue-eyed and blond-haired, his double. The mad hands grasped the other child and drew him away, through a mirror membrane and into fey.

You were a changeling, too, Guinevere said into his mind, though Lancelot could not see her, could not feel her. He screamed in a foreign cradle. *You were brought to the overworld because of the madness of your parents—because of a curse that left you a babe for decades.*

Lancelot kicked and bucked. Through the door came a woman, her brow shadowed in sadness. His mother. She lifted him from the blankets and looked wonderingly at him.

We are both children of the fey, Lancelot, came Guinevere's thoughts. She drew him upward, away from the Otherworld. *We are both children of fey royalty. We are both changelings in the cradles of kings. It is why we love each other. It is why we live in a world of statues, populated only by we two.*

Her voice was soothing, the words eager to smooth over the dread revelations of the last hour—the madness, the drowning, the abandonment, the betrayal. Words failed.

Lancelot awoke on a table of oak. Though Guinevere lay head to head with him, though she clutched his hand, he once again felt as if he were dying, as if he were utterly alone.

20

Two Kinds of Love

Midsummer had come. The sun ponderously climbed the hills of Surrey. Morning breezes whispered sultry things to the River Astolat. It ignored them, sliding onward—silent and black and imperturbable. Willows hunched beside its banks and dragged their grieving fingers in the water. A broad-beamed boat worried at a long and crowded pier.

It was a morning of farewells.

On the gangplank stood Guinevere, queen of Britannia. She had almost fully recovered from her ordeal, and the Astolat chirurgeon would be shipping out with her to make sure she would be well. Guinevere wore the gowns and veils befitting a queen on her homecoming to Camelot.

Before her knelt her champion, Lancelot du Lac. He, too, was hale and whole, regaled in the samite and steel of his knighthood. Even so, he looked toward the boat with an expression of deepest dread. He would not be returning with his queen. Since their flight together through the Otherworld, since the revelations of that flight, they had contrived not to be alone together. They had discovered the fountainhead of their desire but still were bound by oath and love to their king. It was a difficult thing to know the truth and yet remain true.

Guinevere smiled sweetly down at her champion, uncaring that the earl of Astolat and his family watched. "It is a gentle river, Lancelot. It will bear me gently away, back to Camelot."

"It will bear you away," he echoed emptily.

She stroked his jaw, the fey lines of it unmistakable now. "We are like brother and sister, my champion, borne out of like cradles and brought to this land we love. Let those you battle and those I heal make Britannia stronger."

He could not even answer this time.

Taking his hand, she lifted him to stand beside her. "I leave you with a sister's love." Leaning in, she kissed him chastely on the cheek. His eyes closed. She pulled away, stepping down from the gangplank into the beamy boat.

Lancelot opened his eyes and backed off the gangplank. The boatswain heaved the heavy plank onto the deck. It seemed almost a dragon boat, with oars stowed straight up along its gunwales. In the center, a square canopy in green waited for Guinevere. It would be a gentle and stately ride.

Beneath his breath, Lancelot whispered, "It is my funeral barge."

Someone beside him overheard—the young Elaine, daughter of the earl. At sixteen, the dark-haired lass could have been Guinevere's kin—eyes so wide and lips so red. "Don't speak so, great knight. I can't bear to hear you speak of your death."

He turned to her, his cheeks flushing, and bowed his head. "Forgive me. I spoke only to myself. Don't fear. I won't die. I'll prevail in your brother's name."

Her sweet face was querulous. "In my brother's name—?"

"The joust," prompted Lancelot. "You asked me to joust for him tomorrow, since he is ill—?"

"Oh, yes, yes. The joust," she said, blushing.

He turned grave eyes on the boat as it slid slowly away from the dock.

Elaine lingered near him, as if hoping to say more, but Lancelot had ears only for the plaintive splash of oars in the water.

Trumpeters played the royal welcome. Elaine of Astolat, at the hand of her father the earl, ascended to their box in the jousting stands. They were petty royalty in a petty land. Elaine felt her position deeply. The lane fence wasn't even straight. The quintains had been chopped to shabby stumps. The royal box needed a second coat of whitewash, and everything else needed a first. Mired in this shabby backwater, how could Elaine ever draw the eye of the one she loved?

Reaching their seats, Elaine and her father sat. The standing throng of peasants cheered. She waved to them, as she had been trained. Perhaps none saw how weary her smile was. They were trapped too—some of them fine folk—but none of them were in love with Lancelot.

Here he came. Even in her rheumy brother's armor—some of it was made of painted wood, carved to look like metal—it was obvious who he was. At full gallop, he sat his horse as though it were still. He held the crude wooden shield in regal trim. Everything he touched, he elevated. Elaine only wished he would touch her.

In company with her father's other men, Lancelot rode up before the royal box. He was the only one on a real horse. Next to his steed, the others looked like asses. Asses astride asses.

Elaine's younger brother, Robert, flipped up his visor and addressed the earl. "Today, as always, we ride for you, Father."

Behind his white beard, Earl Ducet smiled. "Make me proud."

"I will," Robert said, his eye twinkling, "though I cannot speak for my brother." He motioned to Lancelot beside him. "He is not feeling like himself today."

"Off with you, then," the earl said.

Flipping his visor down, Robert turned his steed and rode away. The other horsemen did the same—all except Lancelot. He merely sat astride his mount and stared out his helm at Elaine.

Her cheeks burned, and she wished she could die. She opened her mouth, not to speak, but to breathe.

"What is it, Erik, my son?" asked the earl, his own voice holding quiet mirth.

"I am not accustomed to riding, except as the champion of a highborn woman," replied Lancelot. His voice was rich, even in that kettle of a helmet.

Elaine gripped her seat. Her heart thundered with hope, but her head echoed the word *highborn*. How could it be anything but mockery?

Her father spread his hands. "With the queen's departure—"

"What of Elaine?"

She trembled. He knew her name. He spoke her name.

Blinking beneath white brows, the earl said, "You mean your sister?"

Lancelot nodded.

"Well, why not?"

"Excellent," Lancelot replied. "Some token then—a rose from her hair. A scarf from her neck."

Oh, damn! What a day to be caught without a rose or a scarf—not that there was a single rose garden in the palisade.

What did she have? Oh, it was torment to be so poor! She would give him her head if he asked for it.

Standing, overwhelmed with desire and dread, she grasped the lace at her bosom and ripped it from her gown. The resultant hole revealed nothing—not that she had much to reveal—but it did leave a ragged scar above her heart. Elaine was poet enough to appreciate the symbolism. She held out the torn lace and said, "Ride for me, my champion." She threw the rag to Lancelot.

He caught it with his bare hand, as if he were eager to feel her warmth in the fabric. His hands were strong and rough on the ravaged lace—and yet graceful as they wove it into his visor. He was breathing her scent. It was as if he lay his head on her breast. The whole time he would be fighting, he'd be breathing her. He'd be riding the horse, bouncing in the saddle, leveling his lance, breathing her—

She was sitting down again. She didn't remember sitting down, but here she was, and there he was, wheeling away to join the others.

Her champion. Lancelot du Lac was her champion. She didn't know what had happened between him and the queen, but after all, Guinevere had left him. Literally, she had left him. He was looking for someone to fill the emptiness. Elaine could fill it. She could. And he could fill the emptiness in her. She blushed at the accidental innuendo, but of course he could. In both ways, he could.

She was sweating a cold sweat. It dribbled down her and made her shiver.

Father was talking. How long had he been talking? "—want to maintain this charade, however obvious it is, it would help if you wouldn't throw yourself at your supposed brother."

"Shut up, Father," Elaine replied.

"Fair enough."

Her champion. Guinevere had tossed him away, and Elaine had picked him up, and now she belonged to him.

Even now, he entered the lists. His steed—muscular and white—stomped. Dust streamed up from its hooves. Lancelot waited. Perhaps he breathed—certainly he breathed, and if he breathed he remembered her. Then with a sudden surge, horse and rider hurled themselves forward. They were powerful. Everyone else looked like he was playing, but not Lancelot. For him, this was war. His lance tilted down. His shield rose. His foe—she hadn't even noticed he had a foe—was so frightened he dived out of his saddle.

Elaine stood and cheered and laughed. She had been afraid he might get hurt. Imagine that, Lancelot getting hurt! It was absurd. The relief of seeing that man roll from his saddle as her champion rode by—Elaine was shouting like a regular wench and she didn't care who heard. After all, she was merely professing her love.

To imagine she had laughed at the thought of Lancelot hurt—and now he lay, split open like this! Oh, that wretched Sir Hector, Lancelot's own cousin! How could he have struck that way? And it was her brother's fault too, not having a decent helm. Lancelot might as well have been wearing a stew pot for all that he could see out that damned thing. And even so, Lancelot prevailed. Hector lay now under the ministrations of lesser healers. Elaine would allow no one but herself to heal her champion.

Sweet Lancelot. A crown of blood ringed his golden head. Elaine's fingers grew red as she gently but thoroughly washed the wound. All the while, she sang a hymn to the land. That was her true power—stirring the spirit to heal the flesh. Even as her rag worked through the wound, tissues behind it knitted together.

The cut was clean, the gory work done. She set her fingers on his cheeks. They adhered. She closed her eyes and sang on.

This moment would prove everything. It would prove that she, not Guinevere, was the true healer. It would prove that Lancelot needed her as much as she needed him. It would prove that they were meant to be together forever.

She sang. Her voice—pure and bright—filled the great room. It resonated in rafters and shook tallow from the chandeliers. Red and hot, the droplets fell around them. They were not two creatures but one. Her song drew his pain out of him and into her. Her heart could bear it; it could not be destroyed. Love washed away pain. Healing flowed from her into him, and tissue by tissue, the horrid cleft closed.

The cleft between them healed as well. It was as if Elaine and Lancelot were the severed halves of a single being. Now they were joined.

The song ended. Its ancient words—the strange and beautiful words of Tuatha devotion—had simply run out. Elaine opened her eyes and saw. He was healed. The blood in his hair had turned brown. The cut in his head had stitched closed. He slept now, not at the ragged precipice of death but in gentle slumber.

Sighing, Elaine stretched her arms in ecstasy. She reached beneath the knight's bare shoulders—she had stripped him to his waist—and drew him up into her arms. She rocked him gently and hummed her healing song.

"Yes, my love. We are together now, forever."

He stirred, at the verge of waking, and said, "You have saved me."

Her heart ached gladly. "We have saved each other."

Reaching up, he cupped her head and rose to kiss her. That kiss set her body on fire. At last, he drooped away, cradled in her arms.

"I love you, Lancelot. I have always loved you."

He nestled against her and smiled. "What are we to do? Where are we to go?"

"Love writes its own tale. Love makes its own world," she said. She had composed those lines two years before, and had waited all the while to speak them to him. At long last, she had reassembled her broken life. At long last, everything made sense. "Tell me you love me, Lancelot. I want to hear it from your lips. Tell me you love me."

He drew a deep, happy breath. "I love you, Guinevere."

She had had a moment of bliss. It was more than many folk ever had. Now it was over. That very instant, she began to die. Her heart was young and strong and could bear any agony but that one. Hearts cannot survive hopelessness.

"I am not Guinevere."

"What?" he replied blearily, his eyes opening for the first time.

"I am not Guinevere. I am Elaine of Astolat. I am nobody."

He stared at her, and the look of shock and dismay in his face almost killed her. "I have been dreaming."

"I have been as well."

"Forgive me, Elaine. I had thought your healing hands—your voice—"

"Yes, I had thought so, too."

He sat up and pulled away from her. They would never touch again. Another bleak realization swept across his face. "You had said you loved me."

She shrugged, tears already streaming. "The things one says."

Lancelot shook his blood-caked head. "You deserve someone who can love you in return. My heart is not my own. It belongs to one whom I can never have."

"I know."

His eyes gleamed, but there was no true light in them. "We are so alike, Elaine—two hearts aching for a person who is pledged to another. We are like brother and sister. Do you remember Guinevere saying that?"

She could not answer.

"Oh, now, sweet child. Don't cry. You are beautiful and young and wise. You will find another love, one that is not forbidden."

She mustered herself somehow. She had not thought any poetry remained in her soul, but there was one last shred. "There are only two kinds of love, Lancelot—forbidden and tragic. Forbidden love is not consummated. Tragic love is."

He stared a long while at her. He was memorizing her face, her words. Then, bowing his head, Lancelot du Lac turned away and headed out the door.

After he left, summer was hot and weary. There were jousts, of course, and feasts, and the buzzing heat of bugs among green stalks. Everything buzzed. Everyone busily pursued life.

Elaine had no more life to pursue. She had loved him since first she glimpsed him at the Festival of the Pendragon, three years before. She loved him still, but she could never have him. There was no reason to rise, to eat, to drink, to live. One by one, she had ceased those activities. She had lain abed as wheat whitened. She had lain abed as it fell to scythes and ground to flour and baked to bread. Now, as the first snows fell upon hoarfrosted fields, a page brought hot bread to her sickbed and found it empty.

Elaine walked. Barefoot, gaunt in her nightgown, she walked beneath skies of torn fleece. River Astolat was a black snake nestled in the valley. Its smooth back steamed as Elaine approached it. There were brambles amid the spikes of ice. She left red footprints in the snow.

The pier was a white wedge against all that blackness. Snowflakes fell to strike the river and dissolve to nothing. Alongside the pier, her father's royal barge bumped quietly. It had been battened and left empty; who would want to ride an ice-edged river? Elaine dragged the mooring lines from their blocks and stepped aboard. Already, the silent current dragged the boat sideways, away from the pier.

Stepping to the central pavilion—its awning was taken down and stowed—Elaine lay down. Flakes churned above. They landed like cold kisses on her skin. They melted and wept. She lay couched in snow. It dragged her warmth away. It turned her flesh to ice. Soon, the snowflakes no longer melted on her face. Soon, her tears were twin trails of silvery ice.

It was as though the cruel hand of God had beached the craft there above Camelot. First, a girl with a bucket found it. She stood there weeping when a pair of villeins happened along. They dropped their loads of firewood and gaped. More folk came—a hunting expedition with a doe strung on a pole, a tinker and his rattling pans, a knight on a champing steed. The snow was trammeled and brown by the time Lancelot arrived.

He dismounted Rasa and let him roam. Striding down

through the crowd, he could not take his eyes from the boat and the figure within.

She was beautiful, mantled in the thinnest layer of snow, like a gossamer shroud. Through it, he could see her blue skin, her wide-open eyes. There was no mistaking her.

Lancelot couldn't breathe. It was as if he had been pounded in the chest.

Lancelot climbed onto the boat and went to her and brushed the flakes from her face. A few remained in the corners of her eyes—they seemed tiny and brutal spikes. He could not get them out. Lancelot shook his head.

There are two kinds of love—forbidden love and tragic love, she had said. *Forbidden love is not consummated, and tragic love is.*

"Yours was both, sweet Elaine." He stared a long while, memorizing her face. Then he looked up to Camelot, to the palace tower where Guinevere would be. "Mine will not be."

21

Dead Brothers and Living

Poison was a sweet thing. It could make an apple as deadly as a lance.

Sir Mordred polished just such an apple against his waistcoat. Liquid death lurked beneath the apple's skin. He studied his reflection in it. The fruit's contours distorted his smile into a grimace.

Poison was better than a lance. The victim's own hand bore it in.

Mordred slipped the ruby fruit into his sleeve and strode into the palace kitchens. In the steamy chamber, cooks turned spitted boars above licking flames. Others peeled carrots and boiled leeks. Still others stood at a sideboard and arranged apples on platters. As they finished, Mordred wandered over. He leaned idly against the shelf and extended his hand as if to pick up an apple. From his sleeve he produced the poisoned fruit. He looked it over one last time and placed it atop one of the piles. It was the largest, reddest apple—the most desirable and most deadly.

Giving a lazy sigh, Mordred wandered out of the kitchens

and into the great hall. The court of Arthur was gathering for the Feast of Fat Tuesday. Poisoned or no, apples were a delicacy this time of year. Mordred made his anonymous way among the long tables and the chatting courtiers, going to his accustomed spot—well away from the king and queen. He needed no throne to rule. Beneath a gently luffing banner, he sat and watched the folk—his folk—arrive.

For years now, Mordred had been secretly studying the alchemist's arts, specializing in substances that could alter folk—make them happy or sad, confused, brilliant, garrulous, lovestruck, insensate, dead. He often administered doses of this or that to his fellow knights and the maids they championed. A truth serum in the cordial of an unfaithful knight produced an interesting confession. An analgesic poured within a knight's gauntlets insured his loss in the lists. A rage-making potion on a sword pommel could inspire a cold-blooded murder. The results were amusing, yes, but also very useful. Mordred gradually learned which potions to administer, in what quantities, and through what means.

By assiduous use of such substances, Mordred had gained a silent but strong sway over the court of Camelot. Rivals turned to gibbering fools, virgins to trollops, fierce foes to craven cowards. His compounds subtly shaped every member of the court, shaped their actions. He worked like God. Let his mother practice her sorceries. With a few pinches of powder, Mordred could slowly take over Camelot.

Today would be the first time, though, that any of his serums directly killed. It would be interesting to see whom. He did not plan regicide; there was too much to lose. He had no intention of killing anyone in particular, but someone—anyone but himself. He would let fortune decide. It was time for his alchemical hold on the court of Camelot to become lethal.

The pleasant babble in the great hall died away to a hush. A page announced the king and queen. Everyone stood—even Mordred in his dark corner. Varlets spread green rushes before them.

From the archway came Arthur and Guinevere, an august couple. Arthur's ermine-trimmed robe seemed to be seeping its whiteness into his beard. Once he had been an approachable young man, one of the crowd. Now he was the reticent figurehead, absent even in his presence, ruling merely by being. Arthur's eyes were hidden in his bushy brows and beard.

Beside him, Guinevere was as radiant as ever. Her bright beauty cast her husband's face in shadows. Her brown hair curled elegantly on a lacy bodice and gown in purple.

Behind them came Guinevere's champion, Lancelot. He too beamed.

These three formed a triumvirate, with all the power and problems therein. They lay beyond Mordred's reach. The king and queen had personal guards for their chambers, and food tasters. Also, Guinevere's healing powers would make her aware of even slight changes in her personal alchemy. As to Lancelot, he simply had been gone from court too long, and was too assiduous in the cleaning and care of his armor and weaponry. It didn't matter. These three languished from a natural poison—love.

King, queen, and champion made their way to the dais where the royal table was spread for banquet. Perhaps the Table Round was egalitarian, but the feast table told clearly who was loved and who was not. Prince Mordred resided in the cold shadows of his father's gaze. Arthur, Guinevere, and Lancelot took their seats, and the rest of the company moved solemnly to take theirs.

Out came the apples, blood-red on silvery platters. Unknowing peasants carried them. They might as well have been serving up heads.

Mordred smiled. He spotted the vessel of his violence. The largest plate with the grandest apple made its way straight to the royal table. Mordred's smile faded. His gaze grew keenly intense. He did not want to commit regicide, but he had let fortune choose for him. It would be interesting. . . .

The tray of fruit settled onto the board. Candlelight bounded off the mound and painted Guinevere crimson. She would choose. She leaned toward Lancelot, who whispered something that made her laugh and blush a little. Then her eyes came to rest on the course set before her—on the very fruit that bore poison. She seemed Eve of old, wanting that fruit. Her hand reached up. She plucked it from the pile and held it admiringly before her.

Mordred swallowed. A prickle of sweat broke out across his brow. His eyes remained fixed on that single, great fruit. It would be interesting. . . .

"Ah, so fine an apple. So grand and round and red," said the queen as she held it aloft. "Who would be worthy of so great a fruit as this?"

She had drawn the ear of all those around—Lancelot to her left and Arthur to her right. Even the burly Hebridean princes who sat in Angus-leather cowls leaned in to listen. The queen had begun a game, and they all wished to play.

Prince Patris bowed his freckled face and said, "Great queen, already the apple resides in the fairest and most exalted hand in the room. Rightly it is yours."

Her face warmed with the compliment. "But I could not eat half such a huge fruit, and it would be a waste to leave it only gnawed. By rights, it should go to a hearty man. But whom?"

Prince Mador, the younger and darker brother, said, "Then let it be for Arthur the Great, who is the heartiest man not just at this table but in all the isles."

"True enough," said Guinevere. She turned and gave Arthur a look of genuine love. She presented the fruit to him.

The king of Britannia's eyes glinted darkly beneath his brows. There was desire in that gaze, both for the fruit and the hand that held it. Also, there was playfulness. He didn't want the game to end. "Were I to partake of this fruit, I would have to be the second. A taster would get the first bite, and that seems unworthy of such a specimen. Thank you, my wife, but surely there is another great man here." He looked to the Hebridean princes.

Prince Patris said, "Even on our remote isles, no knight's name rings with such renown as that of Lancelot du Lac. Surely he is worthiest after the king and queen, and surely he does not have a food taster."

Guinevere's hand swung the other way, and she presented the fruit to the shining knight.

Lancelot smiled and waved his own hand. "I could not eat of such a fruit while my sovereign sat hungry." There was play in those words, and Lancelot's color deepened.

"Who then?" asked Guinevere.

Prince Mador spoke up. "Of all of us here, my brother has most often placed another man before himself, and so—his being great—I humbly suggest it be given to him."

Guinevere passed the apple to Arthur, who in turn conveyed it to the prince.

Looking around, Prince Patris beamed through his freckles. "Well, then, I accept." He gave a big laugh, and all the others joined in. But the game was not truly done until Patris opened his chops wide, rammed the fruit between his teeth, and bit down with a force that cleft straight to the core of the thing. He chomped gladly. Blond chunks of apple flipped from his lips. Juices ran down his ruddy beard.

The laughter only deepened. Prince Mador tried to shout some happy thought through the roaring throng, but his voice was drowned out.

Even Patris was laughing, though wedges jammed his gullet. No, he was not laughing, he was sputtering. He spewed out the chewed stuff and grabbed his neck.

"He's choking!" shouted Mador. All fell silent.

"Not choking," said Patris as blood poured up his throat. He coughed, spattering the table. "Poisoned!"

It was his final word, but his final act was to turn and glare at Queen Guinevere. Patris then slumped sideways off his chair. He fell next to his brother, who half-caught him. Patris's head struck the floor, and from his mouth poured blood in a foamy river.

Mador clutched his brother and felt every convulsion move through him. "Patris. Oh, Patris!" He shouted, "Call the healers!"

"I'm a healer," said Queen Guinevere suddenly beside them. Her face was ashen, and tears stood in her eyes. She reached toward him.

Mador struck her hands away. "No, not you. Not his killer!"

In a very small voice, she said, "I did not know. You must believe me—"

"So cruel to play your games, to dangle death before the men around you. So vicious, slaughter wrapped in samite—a murderer hiding behind her station. If you were but a man—"

"I am a man," interrupted Lancelot, "and know her to be none of these things. I will defend her honor, and pay with my life if I am wrong."

Prince Mador's eyes were very dark. "Oh, you will pay, Lancelot. You will. And when you die, I will be proven right and will demand the burning death of the queen as well."

A single votive candle glowed in the chapel window. It struggled to illumine the stained glass. It could not. This was the dark midnight of Ash Wednesday. Beneath the failing candle, a man knelt and whispered prayers to God. On the morrow, he would face Lancelot, and death.

Prince Mador prayed—perhaps for his dead brother, perhaps for his grieving family, perhaps for himself. Honor had demanded that he challenge Guinevere. History told that anyone who faced her champion would die. Prince Mador was in a spot. His shoulders twitched with rage and grief and dread.

Mordred watched delightedly at the chapel door. He did not wear his armor, but the sackcloth garb of a monk. He did not carry a sword, but something more deadly—the bread and wine of Christ, with Mordred's own modifications. He had not poisoned them, but had made them more fortifying. Why let Mador die in the jaws of fate? Why not make him Lancelot's equal, perhaps his superior? With one taste of Christ's body, Mador would become stronger, smarter, faster, and more agile. With one swallow of Christ's blood, Mador would be whipped into an utter fury. The effects would last for the better part of a day, long enough for Mador to kill or be killed.

Mordred shuffled into the chapel. He affected the penitent

posture of a monk. Flagstones chilled his leather-shod feet. He reached the front altar and set down the silvery tray. It rang lightly.

The prince looked up, startled. Sweat beaded his forehead.

In reverent tones, Mordred said, "Do not take the Eucharist until the sun has risen, lest you break your fast."

Prince Mador nodded his thanks. Red-rimmed eyes shifted to the bread and cup.

Bowing, Mordred backed away. "It is best to be armored and ready before you do, that Christ's grace might cleanse your accoutrements too."

"Yes," replied the man quietly. "Thank you." And he prayed.

On the second day of Lent, Lancelot rode Rasa out upon the parade grounds. Cheers bloomed from the stands. Pennants snapped brightly in the cool air. Pastries baked in field ovens, and ale casks flowed freely. For the folk of Camelot, this was a festival.

Not for Lancelot. He would kill a man today. Lancelot would kill Prince Mador or die by his hand. And if Lancelot died, Guinevere would die. How had all become so twisted? None of them deserved to die. Guinevere was innocent of the poisoning. Mador was guilty only of grief for his brother. Lancelot had to defend the life of the one against the life of the other. Three good and virtuous folk, and at least one would die today.

Prince Mador stormed onto the opposite end of the jousting grounds. The horse beneath him, a dappled gray, seemed a boiling thunderhead. Hooves rumbled amid the hissing of the crowd. Dauntless, Mador dug heavy heels into the beast's flanks. The prince bent in the saddle as if in a charge. His red-crested helm turned toward Lancelot. Epaulets pivoted, and shield, and on down until the horse itself veered his direction. Lightning-bright, Mador's lance tilted. This was a charge.

"Let's meet them," Lancelot said gravely to Rasa.

Flipping down his visor, he inhaled the scent of Guinevere's rose. Rasa bounded to a gallop. Lancelot dressed his shield. His oaken lance leveled. Its point sought out the man's neck. No, Lancelot did not want to kill this man. Perhaps he could batter him to surrender. The lance shifted toward Mador's shield.

They hurtled together like a pair of rams. The concussions of hoof joined the glad bellow of the crowd. The riders converged. Lances smashed shields. Metal failed. Straps snapped. Men hung in air a moment as their mounts ran out from beneath them. They fell to the dust.

Lancelot tried to gasp, but his lungs were dead. He dropped his riven shield and fouled lance. He staggered to stand. It had been a long while since he had been hurled from the saddle. This Mador was formidable.

Already, the prince stood. He too had dropped shield and lance. A naked sword waited in his hands—a great sword.

Grimly, Lancelot drew his own blade. He took his first shallow gulp of air, and two more before he advanced.

Mador came at a run. He was not a huge man, but he wielded the great sword with ease. It arced over his helm and flashed a triangle of sunlight as it fell.

Lancelot angled his blade to deflect the braining blow. The great sword plunged like an ax. Metal rang. It jangled Lancelot's fingers. He held to his blade, but only just. He stepped back from his foe.

Mador lunged. His sword rammed out.

Had he not dodged, Lancelot would have been skewered.

As it was, the sword passed just beneath his arm. His own blade bashed it down, but not before Mador could drag an edge across Lancelot's side. It came away red. Lancelot staggered back. A long, shallow cut lay along his ribs.

"First blood," called Mador within his helm.

Lancelot panted. "I'll not surrender the queen's honor to first blood."

"I wouldn't want you to," Mador returned levelly as he closed again.

Lancelot backed away another step. "Never have I fought so powerful and skilled a warrior as you, Prince Mador."

"Nor I any better than you, Sir Lancelot." He sent a chopping stroke toward Lancelot's neck.

Batting it away, Lancelot said, "It is a shame one of us must die."

"Yes." Mador wrenched his sword in an eviscerating stroke. "One of us must die."

Lancelot's steel struck, tangling with his foe's. The weapons clanged and rebounded.

It was going to be a very long duel.

Mordred marveled at the power granted by the body and blood of Christ. He marveled too at the power of the body and blood of Lancelot.

By late afternoon, there was little more than body and blood. Mador's helm had been split, and both men had doffed them. Then in succession had gone breastplates, gauntlets, and greaves. Now, even Mador's sword was shattered. Lancelot set aside his own. They fought with bloody knuckles. Neither could prevail. Neither would submit.

It was getting boring. Mordred could stand anything but boredom.

He spotted Sir Pynel nearby. The man had a guilt complex. The right contact poison on his sweaty hands would turn complex into conscience. Then just a few words about innocent men slaying each other needlessly, and things would once again get interesting.

Staggering and bloodied, unwilling to submit, the warriors grappled each other. They were not so much foes now, but brothers, forever wrestling, but neither truly intent on slaying the other.

"The queen . . . is innocent. . . ." whispered Lancelot, not for the first time.

"My brother . . . is dead. . . ." came the all-too-familiar reply.

A new voice spoke. "I cannot allow this to continue."

Lancelot and Mador looked up from their grapple. With bloodshot eyes, they saw Sir Pynel kneeling beside them. His hands were clenched in supplication, and his features were wrought with guilt. "I did this terrible thing."

"What?" chorused Mador and Lancelot.

"I poisoned the apple. I conveyed it atop the pile to the queen. I sought to kill her. I have nearly killed you both instead." The young knight stared at them, his eyes like twin pits in his ashen face. "Do with me what you will."

At last, Lancelot and Mador broke their grapple. They seemed comrades in war paint. They approached the man. Lancelot stooped to retrieve his own sword. Mador drew Pynel's. With a unison motion, the two men struck, their blades meeting in Pynel's neck.

Even as the perpetrator's body fell, Prince Mador went to his knees. "Forgive me, Lancelot, for the battering I have given you for sake of the queen."

"Forgive me, Mador," replied Lancelot, kneeling as well, "for the same. You did what you did only for loss of your brother."

"This day, I have gained a brother. His castle will not stand empty, Lancelot, for this day, I grant it to you."

Beneath the blood, Lancelot grew white. "I could not—"

"It will fall to reivers and petty dukes otherwise. It is a fine castle upon North Uist, middle isle of the Hebrides. And a fine people. They would follow you, Lancelot, if you would lead them."

Lancelot heaved a profound breath. Dropping his sword, he reached out a sanguine hand. "Yes. It is the least I can do for so valiant a warrior. Brothers in battle, then."

Mador took the hand and clasped it. "Brothers in blood."

In the hushed stands, Mordred watched and heard it all—and smiled.

22

The Raven and the Rose

At the ship's prow, Lancelot stood beside Prince Mador and Queen Guinevere. Behind them, their retinues crowded the fore deck. All the folk wanted to see the Isle of North Uist, the new land that Lancelot had won. He had come to claim it. Prince Mador of the Hebrides and Queen Guinevere of Camelot had come to represent their united peoples on this auspicious day.

"Reef the main!" cried the captain. Crew clambered aloft to gather cloth. The sail spilled autumnal air. The ship lost the fervid momentum that had driven her across the heaving sea. It was well. She approached a fjord between two black sentinels of stone—a dangerous passage. Five months before, this same ship had almost smashed upon those rocks. Then she had borne the body of Prince Patris to funeral throngs. Today, she carried the new ruler to his eager people. "Steady as we go."

The ship hove up between the two head walls. There was a perilous moment when the waters shoved her keel across a ridge of stone. Knuckles whitened on gunwales. With a swooping motion, the vessel shot down into the rocky fjord.

"We should have waited another half hour," Prince Mador said. "It's a tidal passage. We had just enough draft to clear."

Lancelot only nodded grimly, looking around at the steep valley. Sea-battered cliffs bunched on either side of the passage. The ship threaded the needle. Dead ahead, the valley widened just enough to allow a small harbor. Two large ships waited there—one a dragon ship—and numerous small boats as well. Gulls wheeled in shrieking flocks above.

Prince Mador went on, "The channel goes dry at low tide, but the bowl ahead never fully empties. It's an excellent harbor—twice a day."

"A nice trick against sea invaders." Lancelot looked to the harbor's single pier, their destination. Folk in bright finery lined it, a reception committee. Beyond them, workers poured fish into brine barrels. Farther back, wagons labored up the switchback path that led to the top.

"It is a harsh land," commented Lancelot.

"Yes," said Mador, smiling and nodding. "But a good one, with good folk. But you aren't looking high enough." He pointed up the looming cliff. "There is your new holding—the Dolorous Garde."

Lancelot's eyes widened at the name and still more at the black severity of the fortress. Built from the same dark stone all around, the castle seemed an extension of the cliff. Uneven battlements topped the curtain wall, and turrets gnarled the corners. Two towers jutted up on either side of the square central keep. It seemed more a carbuncle of stone than a castle.

"The Dolorous Garde," repeated Lancelot.

Prince Mador shrugged. "It's not the palace of Camelot, but it is impregnable, and within, it is quite fine."

Guinevere's hand slipped into Lancelot's elbow, and she

said, "You'll have your own castle at last. A twice-born prince, but only now will you have a castle."

"More than a castle," Prince Mador said. "You'll have the fealty of all the souls on this isle—nearly twenty thousand, and two thousand of them are fighting men. Look, here, the chiefs are waiting to do fealty right there on the pier."

As the ship approached, Lancelot studied his new subjects. They were Hebrideans, mixing Norse blood with Pictish, short with tall, fair with ruddy. Their finery was no samite and sable, but rather the fierce panoply of half-wild or half-fey folk. Wolf skins, stag horns, raven feathers, trophies of war, blade belts with barbarous assortments—they were a grand and fierce lot. Lancelot's fey subjects could not have been stranger.

Prince Mador studied Lancelot's grim expression. "Why are you sad, my friend? I am not. Nor are the people. I have buried my brother, and we have mourned. Now it is time to welcome my new brother. Do not be sad, Lancelot. You are gaining a nation and an army. You are saving a land from lawlessness. You are allying the Hebrides and Camelot. It is a joyous day."

"Yes," said Lancelot.

The ship's last sails reefed. She sloughed up alongside the pier and bumped once. Mooring lines leapt out among the chieftains, and they caught and secured them. Lancelot stood now eye to eye with his new subjects. He gave them a forced smile.

To Mador, he said, "Forgive my dolorous countenance, here beneath my Dolorous Garde."

The feasts began the moment Lancelot strode through the gates of his new home. A great cheer arose from the Hebridean chiefs. The castle dogs answered with throaty baying. Children ran giggling across the bailey to meet him, their arms filled with heather boughs. To this general din, five pipers added their strange skirl.

The whole company began to dance. Lancelot had never seen such a thing in Camelot. The city was too decorous for such unseemly displays. Not here, not at the Dolorous Garde. Farmers jigged, their sticks of link-sausage shuddering and making the dogs go wild. Guards turned circles and seemed only the more formidable for the weapons whirling at their belts. Brewers bounced their rumps as they rolled casks into the yard. Bread maidens stepped gladly. Even the crows on the ramparts scampered in anticipation.

Lancelot could not help being swept up in the din. The music of the pipes and drums was irresistible. It didn't enter through the ears, the way court music did. It came through the toes. Feet bounced with it, and then ankles and legs and knees. It took possession from below, as if the very spirits of the earth rose to manifest in human bodies. Lancelot's dour mind was taken captive by his gleeful legs. He stepped and turned and stepped and kicked in emulation of those around. Panting breaths turned to laughter. He felt good for the first time since—since Avalon.

In the wild turn of the dance, she came into his arms. Lancelot had not been looking for her, or Guinevere for him, but suddenly, they were clasped together—queen and champion. The crowd saw and cheered. Every man grabbed a woman. Every couple spun. Girls formed long daisy chains while boys forced dogs to dance. The pipes blared. The drums struck double-time. The fifes reeled.

Five months before, these same folk had solemnly marched

their dead prince into this same yard for burial. Now, they danced as though to wake the dead.

Lancelot laughed, holding Guinevere to him. "Why am I suddenly so glad?"

"Better to ask why you spent so long being sad," put in Guinevere.

Though still he danced, Lancelot's expression grew long. "We both know the answer to that."

"Not the whole answer," she replied, and she peered intently into his eyes. "Not both of us."

Brows knitting, Lancelot said, "What do you mean?"

"There is one thing I didn't tell you about our past. One thing I didn't dare tell. But we have been unhappy for too long."

"Tell me, then."

"Tonight, after all this," she said, stepping lightly to swing them away from listening ears. "Tonight, I'll come to your chambers and show you."

"Tonight," he affirmed. A wondering gladness fluttered in his heart as the dance whirled them away together. "No longer will this be the Dolorous Garde, my queen. Henceforth, I will call this the Joyous Garde."

The words "after all this" took on a greater significance than either the queen or her champion could have expected. The music and dancing, feasting and drinking did not cease until dawn. The reeling did not cease until well after that. It ended only when the reelers flopped into their beds or someone else's and fell fast asleep.

Lancelot and Guinevere had more right than any of them

to be exhausted. They had danced each dance, though only the first one together. They had drunk the toasts and sung the lays. In all ways, they had been the master and matron of the celebration. Very quickly, Lancelot had realized that to rule these folk, he had to seem an avatar of bounty and glad times. Now, retiring to the oak-paneled royal chambers, he should have simply fallen fully dressed into bed. His heart still fluttered, though. He pulled off his sodden clothes, bathed quickly in the washbasin left for that purpose, donned a sleeping robe, and waited. He didn't have long.

Guinevere's heart must have been fluttering too. Garbed in the homespun clothes of her handmaiden, Guinevere stole quietly through the doorway. She turned, eased the door shut, and set the bolt. Leaning there, she sighed gustily.

Lancelot watched the fabric stretch tight on her mature physique. "And what is your handmaiden wearing?" he asked quietly.

Guinevere turned slowly. "My sleeping gown. She is me—within my curtained bed. Only she knows, and she has perfected a none-too-flattering imitation of my voice. No one else will find out." She walked slowly toward him. Even in a handmaiden's clothes, she was beautiful.

His eyes did not leave hers. "What did you wish to tell me?"

"To show you," she said, sitting beside him. Through the homespun, he could feel the feverish warmth of her flesh. Guinevere bowed her head and leaned against him. With one slender hand, she drew her hair away from her neck. "What do you see?"

He was trembling. He wasn't sure what he was supposed to look at.

"Here, on my neck, just beneath the hairline."

He saw it then—a tattoo, stretched and faded. It was a rose, clutched in the beak of a red-winged blackbird. "When did you get this?"

She stood and crossed to the washbasin. Taking it to the window, she set it on the sill. Guinevere beckoned to Lancelot. "Come here."

He did.

She drew him tenderly into an embrace. Her hand rose gently up the back of his neck, into his hair. She leaned him back over the basin, as if to kiss him. Instead, though, she lifted a small, silvered glass in her other hand. It blazed for a moment with the risen sun. Guinevere shifted her hand.

Blinking, Lancelot looked up into the glass and saw his own head reflected in the basin. He saw his hair, and Guinevere's narrow hand, and just beneath, a faint tattoo. It was identical to the one on her neck.

"What is it?" he asked.

Guinevere drew him up away from the basin and the window. She pulled him into her arms and held him. Very quietly, she spoke into his ear. "When a child is born into a royal house of the Tuatha dé Danann, he or she receives the sign of that house in a tattoo that will forever remain."

Lancelot paled, and he shrank away from her. "We are of the same house—the same lineage?"

She did not let go, pulling him close again. "The same house, yes, but not the same lineage."

He could only shake his head in dismay. "What does this mean? What does any of this mean?"

At last breaking the embrace, Guinevere reached her hand to the basin. "Wet your fingertips."

"Why? What is any of this?"

"Pure water is a conduit between the world and the Otherworld. It is what joins them. It is a forgetful ocean—what has been called Lethe—so that those who travel one world to the other will forget where they have been. Those tides wash away memories, yes, but the memories are not lost. They remain forever, swarming in the water. For one who can navigate that terrible flood, the knowledge of all the foregone world awaits." She lifted her fingers, and water ran slowly down. "A conduit."

Unsure what else to do, Lancelot dipped his own fingers in the basin.

She reached to him, embraced him, and lifted her wet fingers to the tattoo behind his neck. He reached to her neck and did the same. Skin and water and skin touched and—

An antediluvian battlefield spread out before them. There was no solid ground. Protean plains drifted and piled and reshaped. Figures moved across the boiling landscape—two armies in two lines. Some scampered. Some swam. Some scuttled. Some flew. All converged upon a central lowland of cloud where they would battle.

Distance collapsed, and suddenly the creatures were all around. Here in the vanguard were horrid, looming things—ogres trudging like sacks of skin, leanan sidhe singing ghostlike above, boggarts and barghests bounding in flesh-eating frenzy, ouphes and trolls, hobgoblins and spectres and worse things without names. One was a man made entirely of maggots. Another was a great wet muscle that moved with convulsing slaps across the ground. Packs of dire wolves the size of horses loped in their midst, eyes drooling fire. Watery lizards covered the ground underfoot and parted like gelatin with each tread.

It was a horrid army, and on the other side of the ever-shrinking battlefield marched one just as wretched. So many hooves and claws and scales upon the livid ground churned it into life. It added monsters of its own—mammoths and giant ground sloths and enormous carrion birds. Mounds of earth welled up and took form, and beasts lumbered forward. Some would reach battle. Others would dissolve away like piles of sand.

As terrible as these Otherworld vanguards were, the regular armies behind them were worse. Row on rigid row, Tuatha dé Danann soldiers ranked to both horizons. The tall angularity that made these folk so lithe in dance made them knifelike in war—cold and brutal. Slender fingers seemed spikes. Tender eyes seemed pits. Pallid flesh seemed ice. Unlike the beasts before them, the elf folk would kill dispassionately, efficiently.

With a roar, the vanguards ate up no-man's land and sank teeth into each other. Claws and fangs and gobbets of meat and shrieks of dread or delight and the mass madness of melee erupted. Those at the head slew and were slain. They slumped one atop the other in a ridge of corpses. Those behind climbed and slew and died and built the ridge. It was a bloody and mangled mound the Tuatha at last climbed, a place of shattered flesh below and keening spirits above.

Like the monsters that had come before them, those fair warriors fought. Their silken flesh split. Their eternal hearts burst. The star glow in their eyes faded to nothing. They fell upon the pile, their swords and spears and tabards intertwined. They fell, the red-winged raven emblem of one army alongside the coiled rose of the other.

The battle was a soul fountain. Souls burst from their bodies below and flew high and white into the sky. They curled, as waters do, and arced back toward the place of their birth. Half fled one way, and half the other. Two great rivers of souls diverged and poured across the sky.

Clinging to each other, Guinevere and Lancelot rode one of those great rivers. Wraiths, ghosts, and spectres surrounded them and bore them along. Below, the torrid world fled away like a windblown sheet. Hours passed in agonized moments. The souls poured over an aerial cliff and plunged. Churning brightly, they turned their heads toward home. From the white cascade streamed one, and then another, and two more—spirits following their own paths to the places they would forever haunt.

Guinevere's spirit dragged her, and she dragged Lancelot. Her home lay below—that pillared palace. It was not the white marble dream of Romans, but a living home formed of trees. Lancet towers, roseate balconies, viney rails, and foliate archways. It was a warm home, fragrant and alive. It was Guinevere's home.

Tugging impatiently on Lancelot's spirit, she delved down through the air, along walls of ivy and through a clover-shaped window. There below was the nursery, the bower she had seen before. It was full of cries.

Losing hold of Lancelot, Guinevere rushed down to look upon the babe that was her.

In the arms of a druidess, the infant Guinevere lay on her side and cried piteously. The druidess's other hand reached back to bowls of thick stuff, saffron and woad and ochre. . . . She slipped a needle into one bowl, drew it out again, and stooped to the child.

Guinevere glided insubstantial beside the druidess and her own infant self, but she could not shield the child. The druidess's hands moved right through her and pricked the babe's neck, adding more detail to the raven of her tattoo. Already a rose showed, full-formed.

In sudden decision, Guinevere beckoned to Lancelot.

Come. She grabbed him and pulled him aloft. They flew through the open window, away from that warm home and into the teeming sky. Guinevere turned them against the spirit tide. She set her brow for a distant land. Above the ghosts, they flitted.

Where do we go? Lancelot asked.

To another home, to another cradle.

Below them, they saw the wicked battle. Dead bodies formed a long altar to some mad god.

That battlefield, Guinevere sent, *I know it now. In ancient times, there was no channel. Britannia and Brittany were joined. It yet is so in the Otherworld. That battle takes place on the isthmus that joins my lands to yours.*

Your lands to mine? wondered Lancelot. *Mine?*

Yes, Lancelot. A fey princess of Britannia and a fey prince of Brittany, born to two great Tuatha nations at war.

We were born years apart, protested Lancelot.

We were born at the same time. When I was taken out of the Otherworld, you languished. You did not grow. Time did not flow for you until you were made changeling. Then the spring of years, so tightly wound, uncoiled—thirty years in six months. We are the same age, Lancelot, only we have floated on different tributaries of time.

He understood suddenly. The whole of his being ached.

They plunged now toward his home, his castle. Grand and stately, it was built of standing stones. They rose in rings like gods' teeth. At the heart of the concentric lines stood a massive building. Once, it had been grand, with soaring traceries and fluted columns. Now it might have been a mausoleum. Grim stone filled every window. The building had made itself unassailable, trading beauty for security. Yet in all that lightless stone, there was one beautiful glow of gold. A candle shone through a long low window. Treading upon the glowing beam, Lancelot and Guinevere entered the window and came to a nursery.

It was a similar scene. A druidess knelt there beside the cradle of a baby. This time, though, the baby lay asleep as the woman prepared her rose-colored dies. None of her needles were yet stained. Already the raven was clear on the baby's neck.

Yours was the House of the Raven, mine the House of the Rose. We both bear the Raven and the Rose because we were betrothed as infants. We were given to each other to bring peace to the Otherworld. We were meant to be joined.

Lancelot could not think. The words seared his mind like branding irons.

Before I was betrothed to Arthur, I was betrothed to you, Lancelot. You and I together were meant to end an ancient war and build an Otherworld Camelot.

23

Standing in the Way

The water conduit broke. Fingers rose from tattoos. Memories vanished, and minds separated. Lancelot and Guinevere pulled apart.

They stood and stared at each other. Neither looked regal now. Lancelot seemed a boy in his night robe, and Guinevere a girl in her handmaiden's clothes. Both dripped with sweat. The world of flesh mocked the world of spirit.

"How can we remain faithful now?" Lancelot whispered feverishly. "If we cleave to Arthur, we betray our own betrothal. If we cleave to each other, we betray Arthur."

"I know," Guinevere replied miserably. She seated herself on the bed. "I have known since the Mistress of the Mists told me."

"You spoke to the Mistress of the Mists?"

"Yes."

"Take me to her, then. We'll speak to her, learn what to do."

A grim smile formed on Guinevere's face, and she nodded. Rising, she straightened her shift and headed for the door.

"Once your rule is firm here, and once I have spent sufficient time again at my husband's side, I will take you."

This isn't Avalon, thought Lancelot. He sat astride Rasa and gazed at a swamp that steamed in the springtime sun. If anyone knows Avalon, I do, and this isn't it. He tried to keep a frown from his face. Guinevere needed all the support she could get.

She had brought a whole bevy of her priestesses along for this expedition. They wore springtime green and sang songs to awaken the land from its wintry slumber. All the way from Camelot, they had serenely embodied their love of the land and of Guinevere. Still, Lancelot had overheard the whispers. Last time they rode to Avalon, Guinevere had ditched them there. They had spent three days battling nuns and searching swamps, only to find her holed up with the abbess. That was the time she supposedly had spoken to the Mistress of the Mists. Now, despite their soulful songs, the priestesses were at least dubious. Some even trembled with fear.

Lancelot shared their concern. He didn't want Guinevere to be shamed. Still, how could it be avoided? She insisted on calling Glastonbury Avalon. She insisted this fetid swamp was the lake, and the treeless mound at its center was the island. The whole place wasn't a hundredth the size of Avalon. It was ugly instead of beautiful, petty instead of grand.

Clicking his tongue, Lancelot urged Rasa forward among the singing priestesses. Their smaller mounts—geldings and mares—shied instinctively from the stallion. He came up alongside Guinevere's mare. His flank brushed hers, making her pelt shiver. Lancelot spoke quietly beneath the thready song. "Guinevere, this is Glastonbury, not Avalon. If you want me to lead—"

"Dismount," Guinevere called to her priestesses. "Hobble your steeds and gather beside the marsh."

Intently, Lancelot whispered. "There's no shame in admitting a mistake—"

"Then you won't be ashamed when you do," she said, smiling sweetly as she dismounted. Guinevere crossed the spongy ground, marsh grass dragging at her robes.

Lancelot patted Rasa's neck and climbed down. The stallion snorted and cantered away along the shore. Giving his own snort, Lancelot trudged to Guinevere's side. Behind him, the priestesses gathered in a semicircle.

"Pray," Guinevere instructed without turning around. Her eyes remained on the low, rumpled hill beyond. "Pray to the Mistress of the Mists, that she will come to us. Chant the lay of water."

Lancelot began to protest again, but Guinevere held up a staying hand.

"Please, just wait. Allow me that one courtesy."

He clamped his mouth shut and stood. The chants of the priestesses had begun, a watery devotion that flowed around and over him. Lancelot was unmoved, a stone in a stream. The chant spread out across the swamp.

It was absurd—rank water, choked trees, a little hill, a shabby abbey. That last thought almost made him laugh. To think any divine entity would dwell in this muck pit—

He caught his breath.

The Lake of Avalon suddenly spread before him. It was as dark and clear as sapphire beneath the azure sky. Within it towered the island of Avalon, resplendent in apple blossoms. Strangest of all, though, a beautiful woman robed in gossamer light and power stood upon the water. She shone like the sun.

In reflex, Lancelot lifted his hand and winced away from

the light. Only then did he see that the priestesses were gone, that the hillside was a short-shorn carpet of grass. He went to one knee on the grass, except the grass was gone, too, replaced by rushes—dry rushes on a cottage floor. The world had changed again.

He found himself within the hovel of his Aunt Brigid. All the smells—the wood smoke, the fennel and mint and wild carrots—returned to him, the scents of childhood. In one breath rode a thousand memories. They filled his chest and warmed him. He looked about. The rafters bore a load of yet-green thatch. The table held a pair of cider goblets, just used. The linens upon the pallets had been flung back as if by waking sleepers. What did it mean?

Guinevere and the Mistress of the Mists stood before him. They watched him like parents nervous of their child's response.

He tried to speak, but his voice was hoarse. Coughing into his hand, he managed to say, "Where . . . where is Aunt Brigid?"

"Right here," said the divine woman. She swept her hand gracefully down her glimmering form. It peeled away the glory that enfolded her. From within stepped a wizened woman, her eyes twinkling in the folds of her face. "Lancelot, you have come home."

"I don't understand," he rasped. "How could you be—?"

"You do understand," Brigid replied. "Now is the first time you can understand. Until you knew who you were, you could not have understood why I had reared you. Now you know."

Guinevere's voice was grave. "He knows everything. That is why we have come."

The old woman seemed suddenly older. She nodded and dropped slowly onto one of the stools. "I know. I have been watching."

Guinevere's face brightened. "We want to know what we should do."

"First, perhaps," Brigid said gently, "you should see your lands, your people, see the fey kingdoms that await you. Take my hands. It'll be no more than a step."

It all was happening too fast for Lancelot. Only a moment before he had found out his Aunt Brigid was divine—though in truth he had sensed it all the time. Now, she was offering to take him to the fey kingdom he was meant to rule. First things first.

He stood, approached Aunt Brigid, and wrapped her in an embrace. Even though he knew this old flesh, this gray hair, was only a semblance for his sake, it still felt good to hold her. "It was all an illusion, then, Brigid? You, the hovel, the orchards, the rocks by the lake?"

"No child," she soothed. "I am never an illusion. I have many forms, yes, and this one is genuine, just like all the others. All the rest of this is real too." She gestured toward the doorway. "See for yourself."

He turned. On numb feet, he walked toward the door. Its old metal latch felt exactly as he had remembered it. His own hand had changed more. Slipping the hasp, he swung the door wide and stepped through.

"Damn!" he shouted, and then laughed, and waited for his vision to clear.

Before him spread Avalon—green and lush, with apple trees in bloom. The sun shone glad and golden in the deep sky. Breezes rustled the grass like fleeing fey. Lancelot glanced toward the high grave where he had buried the Saxon, and saw the mound and its marker. Above even that, far up the slope, the sacred cauldron stood whitely. Just now some of the quarrymen who had cut the stone for it offered their sacrifices.

"Dwarfs!" gasped Lancelot in realization. "I just thought they were pounded down by hammers and rocks."

Aunt Brigid came up behind him and set her hands on his shoulders. "None of it was illusion, but only now do you truly see it. Only now that you know yourself can you know them."

Lancelot's mouth dropped open. Sprites ran in tiny chains across the grass at his feet, their wings shimmering in flights of fancy. Seelie hounds chased them, yapping beneath the apple trees. The blossoms buzzed not with bees but brownies. The choppy lake gleamed with creatures—selkies and kelpies, naiads and merfolk, leviathans and lurkers. The whole place teemed, and he had never seen it.

"Always around me?" he asked.

"Always."

He inhaled and saw only then the welkin spirits that whirled in the air. One sylph winked at him and dived between his lips, slid down his throat, tickled his lungs, and laughingly rode his sneeze back out again.

"Etter caps and thrummy caps and blue caps, boggles and bodachans and bogeys—and worse things too. You couldn't see any of them truly—you couldn't see anything truly—while you were standing in the way."

Lancelot sneezed out one more sylph. "I'm ready. A moment ago, I wondered how I could be a king of the fey when I had never really seen one. Now I know I've grown up in their loving arms. They taught me to run, to swing a sword, to ride a horse, and—" The hairs prickling at his neck made him turn.

Lancelot's old master waited amid the apple trees, his arms crossed over his chest. He was not just red-complexioned. He was actually red. Hair, beard, skin, nails—all but his teeth and eyes, which smiled at him. "Trained by the very god of war. It's no wonder you are the greatest of knights."

"Master Smetrius!" breathed Lancelot. "Master *Mars*-Smetrius!"

"I did as Brigid did—migrated pantheons when my own was eradicated," explained the god of war. "Lived to fight another day."

"And lived to train another Ulysses," Brigid put in.

"Ulysses!" Lancelot said.

"Let's not get too proud," Mars said. He waved Lancelot over. "Come here, King Lancelot. Let me see that sword of yours."

Lancelot approached his old master and dropped to one knee. He unsheathed his Saxon blade and handed the sword over.

Mars took the blade in his powerful hand. Motes of red fire seeped from his knuckles to trace out the lines of the weapon. "All the tools of war respond to me, and I to them," he said. His eyes were twin flames, studying the scintillating weapon. He ran his thumb along one keen edge. Blood flowed, divine blood. It wicked out across the lines of the sword, from tip to hilt, and sank into the steel. "This blade will strike true against any creature, human or fey. You will need it." Reverently, he lowered the blade.

Lancelot took it wonderingly. As his eyes drank in the new aura of the weapon, he said, "I only wish I had brought my lance. I left it at Camelot."

"It is plenty sure already," said Mars. "Now, rise and go. You have a journey to make."

"Thank you, Master," Lancelot said. He rose and sheathed his blade. "Thank you."

Turning back toward the hovel, he smiled at the two women who most had shaped his life: Brigid and Guinevere. They waited, side by side, types of each other. Aged wisdom, beautiful youth—but their eyes contained the same divine spark. Lancelot held out his hands and walked toward them. They reached out and received him.

With that touch, the hovel and the hillside vanished, replaced by another green space. Trees rose in ancient colonnades. Ivy draped enormous boles. Vines formed a verdant web tree to tree. Sunlight poured through the lofty canopy, and slanting rays etched leaf-shadows on the forest floor. Furtive creatures moved in the undergrowth. Those faint rustles were the only sound in the whole wood.

Releasing their hands, Lancelot, Guinevere, and Brigid gazed in wonder at the primeval forest. Their feet shifted on spongy carpets of moss.

It seemed almost sacrilege to speak into that hush. Lancelot's whisper sounded like a shout. "Where are we?"

"It's the castle—my birth castle, from our dream," Guinevere said.

Lancelot lifted his hands toward the woods all around. "Castle? I don't see a castle."

"*This* is the castle," Brigid explained. "Centuries have passed since you were born here. The castle has grown."

"Centuries?" Guinevere asked. "What of my parents?"

Brigid lowered her head and said in a level tone, "They are gone."

"That is why the castle is overgrown," Guinevere lamented. "No one rules."

Brigid shook her head gently. "No, my dear. You rule."

"What?"

"You are the Power of the Land. From the throne of Camelot, you rule world and Otherworld, both. Every creature beneath Britannia listens to your prayers. They watch you through shallow dewdrops and deep pools. They serve you and Arthur as do the mortals above."

Guinevere's eyes seemed like mirrors, reflecting the vast and stately beauty of the forest castle.

"It is the power of Camelot," said Brigid. "It unites the worlds. It is the power of your union with Arthur—always entwined but never touching." She spoke softly, but her words struck hard. All of this—the serenity of this place—would be in jeopardy if Guinevere's union to Arthur were ever ended. Brigid regarded the downcast faces of the queen and her champion. "Go ahead, my queen. Call them out."

"Call whom out?"

"Call out your subjects. They are all around. They only wait to be invited."

Shrugging uncertainly, Guinevere said, "Come out, then, all of you."

It was as if a great wind gusted through the forest. Every tendril and branch and bud swayed to life. From the canopy descended spirals of leaves—not leaves, but fey creatures. Gold and gray, green and yellow, the arboreal spirits chased each other through the air. They descended toward their queen and swirled around her and mantled her shoulders. Sprites glinted through her hair as if in a living coronet. They covered her lips, kissing her, and stood at rigid attention across her robes. She was transformed by them, clothed in fey panoply.

More creatures approached from below. Groundlings emerged from rings of mushroom. Brownies clambered up vines for a better look. Dryads slid from folds of wood. Tuatha lingered among the massive trees.

In moments, the empty forest was full. Every leaf held a craning family of fey. Every burrow showed gleaming eyes.

Even the distant oak sentinels hid gregarious giants. All looked to their beloved queen.

"My people," Guinevere whispered in awe, and her words were carried on myriad mouths to the ends of the wood.

Whenever you wish, Guinevere, you may come here, they said into her mind. *Wherever there is pure water, we will wait and watch. Through deep wells, we can bring you here, to your castle.*

She answered them in her own thoughts and somehow knew they heard. *Thank you, my friends.*

And where there is pure water, you can summon us. We will emerge and fight for you. We will always fight for you.

Thank you.

Lancelot was awestruck too. He would have fallen to his knees in obeisance, though he feared to crush the folk who crowded there. Instead, he whispered breathlessly, "My queen. I never knew your true power."

"Nor I," she said. Turning toward Brigid, she added, "And Lancelot has such a kingdom as well?"

The old woman's expression darkened. "Not such a kingdom. Not anymore."

"What do you mean?" he asked.

"Your realm is a dead one now."

"What?"

"Take us there," Guinevere said, extending her hands. Pixies flitted away from her fingers as Lancelot and Brigid took hold.

Next moment, the fey folk and the forest castle vanished. Only Brigid and Guinevere and Lancelot remained. They emerged in a gray and dusty plateau. Standing stones jutted like broken teeth from bare ground. Wind moaned among the stones and lifted ghosts of dust to chase each other.

On numb feet, Lancelot started forward. He passed through the first and widest ring of megaliths; beyond stood a second and a third. His boots brought more dust devils spinning up around him. Ten more strides, and he could see the castle.

He fell to his knees, head shaking blearily.

Fire had eaten away its roof. Giant shoulders had battered away its walls. All within was soot and ash. No—not all. Even from this distance, he could see the long white bones lying everywhere.

Brigid and Guinevere approached. They stood behind him, one on either side.

With ashen lips, Lancelot said, "The armies of the Rose did this?"

"No," said Brigid gently. "The long war between your realms did weaken you, though. Your betrothal to Guinevere ended hostilities all too briefly. When she was made a changeling, the battles resumed. You languished, an infant without her, and would not grow. After decades of desperation, your father made you a changeling, to go seek Guinevere. He then sent his greatest forces to the isthmus to stop the Rose advance. Those forces were gone the night your nation was invaded from the south."

"From the south?"

"Another old foe. They waited until you were undefended, and then marched and sacked the castle."

"The night Benwick fell."

Brigid nodded. "It was the same night. Both your Tuatha father and your human one died that same night—"

"All because the betrothal was broken," finished Lancelot. He closed his eyes, unwilling to see the horrid castle.

"If ever you are to regain Benwick, you must regain this kingdom too," Brigid said softly.

He lifted his face to her. Ash caked his tears. "There is only one way to regain this kingdom—one wonderful, dreadful way."

"I know."

"Would you perform the ceremony?"

"I would . . . if you wish me to."

Remaining on his knees, Lancelot turned. He took Guinevere's hands in his own, dirtying them. "Queen Guinevere of world and Otherworld, Power of the Land, will you marry me?"

Tears stood in her eyes. "And betray Arthur? And betray Camelot?"

"Why does Arthur need the Power of the Land? Why does Camelot?" He gestured out toward the blighted landscape all around.

Through trembling lips, she said, "I will."

24

A Dream in Midsummer

The Castle of the Rose was resplendent with summer. Word of the wedding had moved through the wood and had brought the season spinning into being. Every plant put on flowery finery. Every animal wore a sleek summer pelt. Every fey arrived in samite and lace.

They all arrived. Pixies glittered in the air. Thrummy caps watched from within lady slippers. Bodachans made benches of fungus heads. Tuatha stood in long rows among the trees, golden lanterns hanging from their sleeves. Beyond the trees lurked bigger things, darker things—dire wolves and ogres, trolls and giants.

Perhaps the most exotic guests, though, were the Hebrideans. Prince Mador was a guest of honor, and all the folk of North Uist were invited. In kilts and pelts, they belonged. They could not talk a straight line or shoot a straight arrow, but in their reeling way, they were the truest folk Lancelot had ever met. Only by spinning had they found their center. He loved them and they him, and they showed up in whirling hordes at the wedding of the centuries.

World and Otherworld, all had come to see the promised union of the Raven and the Rose.

Through the colonnade of ancient boles, the bride and groom would pass. Even now, sprites dropped rose petals and raven feathers to flutter down upon the mossy lane. Nixies sent raindrops pattering in tiny music across the grass. Welkin spirits danced in knot-work figures in midair.

Out of the deep woods they came—Queen Guinevere and Prince Lancelot. They walked hand in hand. Their bare feet pressed together in the moss. They had doffed their mortal clothes, and wore instead the finery of the woodlands. No human could weave so tender a cloth as a spider. No tanner could make as slender a skin as a snake. Lancelot wore a black cloak of woven feathers over a web-work shirt and leafy trews. Guinevere wore a gown of gossamer down, with a bodice plaited from her own long, brown hair. On their heads they bore crowns of crystal. Pure glass gathered up the faerie lights and cast the radiance back upon the people.

There were smiles, yes—it was a wedding—but there was no laughter. A grave joy filled every face. Centuries of fey had yearned for this day. Generations had been born and lived and died without seeing the union of Raven and Rose. It was teleology. Every footstep the bride and groom took down that aisle pushed the old world farther behind them—the world of Camelot and Arthur, the fusion between thing mortal and immortal—and brought a new world nearer. No one could see that new world; it lay beyond a blind threshold. The future remained dark until it was irrevocably reached.

Lancelot clutched Guinevere's hand. She squeezed back. Their hearts were thundering in their fists. How strange that love and terror should feel the same.

Beneath aerial troupes of dancing spirits they went, up to

the sentinel oaks. The trees formed a sacred ring at the head of that sanctuary. Within the ring, standing barefoot on the tender grass, was Brigid. She wore a divine aspect—tall, willowy, robed in holy power, with eyes like candles. Bride and groom knelt side by side and bowed their heads.

The Otherworld held its breath, watching, listening.

"You have come here to be wed."

Keeping their heads bowed, Guinevere and Lancelot answered in unison. "Yes."

"One of you already is given in marriage." It was not a condemnation, only a statement of fact.

Both bride and groom looked up, and Guinevere said, "Yes."

Brigid nodded. "Polyandrous and polygamous marriages are not forbidden in fey, but you must know they are perilous unions."

Their understanding was written in grim lines on their faces.

"It is best for all parties to approve—" her eyes flashed down their objections "—but as long as the ruler and the new spouse wish it, that is enough. Queen Guinevere, Power of the Land, do you wish it?"

"I do," she replied without hesitation.

"And Lancelot du Lac, prince of Benwick and knight of the Round Table, do you wish it?"

"I do."

Brigid stared a long while at the two of them. "Be it so. Queen Guinevere, you are joined with Lancelot du Lac. Lancelot du Lac, you are joined with Queen Guinevere. Queen Guinevere, you will remain joined also with Arthur until one of you breaks the union—and he will once he knows, and he will know sooner than later. You have until then to work whatever wonders in the Otherworld you might, and use whatever Otherworld powers you gain to save Arthur and Camelot."

Guinevere gazed at those luminous eyes. "Are they so truly doomed?"

"You knew they would be. You have doomed them; if they will be saved, you must save them."

It was a bleak pronouncement, heard by every last one of the myriad souls gathered.

"You are one now, Guinevere, Lancelot. You are wife and husband. Let this pledge be consummated." So saying, Brigid withdrew. She did not walk away, did not even float backward across the mossy earth. She merely diminished, fading as a flame does before the wick goes dark. Gone.

Gone too were the countless souls who had witnessed all. Some had gone of their own will. Others had been borne away by the will of Brigid. As the centerpiece of any union, consummation was the private rite of those at the center. Moments before, millions had gathered and watched. Now only two remained. Two who were to be one.

They rose from their knees and turned to each other. Their hands met, and eyes. Trembling, they embraced as children lost in the woods. A monumental change was moving through them, through world and Otherworld. They had begun something very big and were ending something even bigger. They clung to each other as if no one else existed. So begins any true consummation.

As the dread and fear ebbed, other emotions welled up—love and desire.

Guinevere slid her hands beneath his raven cloak and pulled it away. His web-work shirt clung to the sculpted warmth of his shoulders. Her fingers glided along the fan of muscles behind his neck, down to the solid ridges of his shoulder blades, and inward to the crease of his spine. Lean and powerful, perfectly proportioned, his was the body of a god.

Lancelot caressed her back through the gossamer gown. He bent his head to kiss her long, slender neck. Each touch of his lips to her skin brought a warm tingling. Reaching the top of her neck, he nibbled her earlobe, kissed her cheek, her temple. He lifted his hand behind her head and guided her lips to his and kissed her deeply. How long they had waited, with nary even a kiss. This kiss promised deeper and greater communions.

She reached to her chest, where her own hair had been plaited into a bodice. With quick motions, she loosened the braids. Her hair fell loose across the gossamer gown. Beneath her fine locks, beneath the translucent fabric waited virginal breasts. Never had a man tasted of them; never had they fed a child. Lancelot gently caressed one and then the other. He knelt before her, kissing them.

In ecstasy, she ran her hands down the back of his shirt and drew it up, off his shoulders. He was more beautiful than she could have imagined—smooth and muscular and elegant. Her hand caught him beneath the jaw and lifted him.

Lancelot rose gladly to taste her mouth again. As they kissed, he undid the ties of her gown. It slid with slow seduction from her. She stood, naked, before him. She was magnificent—the hollow of her neck, the shape of her navel, the sweep of her hips. He trembled in her presence as if she were a goddess.

Guinevere meanwhile worked loose the laces of his trews and slid them downward. They dropped to the ground. "Let us be joined, my husband." She lowered herself to the ground.

He followed, flesh to flesh. Kissing her, he gently eased into her.

She shuddered once. Her nails dug into his back. Tears stood in her eyes.

"What have I done?" Lancelot whispered in dread.

Guinevere smiled despite the tears. "I was a virgin, Husband. That's all. I was a virgin."

King Arthur awoke in a cold sweat, as he had done countless times since Guinevere had disappeared. Clutching his blankets, he sat up and looked around the dark bedchamber. It was not that he missed her at his side. She had never slept at his side. It was that he missed her in every other way. Camelot was not the same without her.

"Who's there?" Arthur growled. He could sense a presence, someone watching.

Out of the night shadows where Excalibur slanted, lines intersected. Planes aligned. A face formed. Ancient, kind, wise, and inestimably sad.

"Merlin," whispered Arthur in awe. "Grandfather. . . ."

A voice built itself from silence. *It has been six years.*

"I know, Grandfather, but she is not dead. I still have the land's power. She must be in Avalon. Time moves differently in Avalon. She will return to me, to us. . . ."

The old wizard's visage stared bleakly into the darkness. *You cannot count only upon the Power of the Land.*

"Guinevere is half of this throne. Without her, Camelot falls."

You must find new power. Seek the Grail, Arthur, the Grail and the Lance.

"What grail? What lance?"

The Holy Grail is the cup of Christ, used upon the night of the Last Supper to hold his symbolic blood and used upon the afternoon of the crucifixion to gather his true blood. It will heal this wounded land, this wounded king.

"Where is it, Merlin?"

It is here, in Britannia, brought by Joseph of Arimathea, but where, I do not know.

"And what of the lance?"

The Lance of Longinus is the centurion's spear that wounded Christ upon the cross and brought forth his blood. The Grail will heal your land, and the lance will make you invincible in battle. Send your knights to seek them, and pray that they might find them. Only with these relics and Excalibur can you save Camelot.

Arthur blinked into the darkness. "A Christian sword. A Christian grail. A Christian lance. Your old foe, the Tetragrammaton, has conquered Camelot after all."

Better it be conquered than utterly destroyed. . . . With that, the whispers ceased, and the sad, ancient face slumped into shadows.

Aback great seahorses, Queen Guinevere and King Lancelot rode to the northern extremity of their realm—the Isle of North Uist. Prince Mador straddled a merbeast behind. In rolling white waves, selkies and kelpies swam. They carried sodden Picts. Kilts and braids streamed brine. Red-bearded mouths pulled from the breath-conches that had sustained them. Laughter and song bellowed out. Hundreds of Hebrideans had attended the Otherworld wedding. Now they returned to the world, and to the thousands who had remained behind.

Picts shouted up the cliff face to their kin. Caves above lit. Scraggly figures stood silhouetted there. They bleated welcome. Even the wheeling gulls called greetings.

Dryad throats piped with reedy melodies. Rorquals emitted

profound harmonies. Sprites shimmered like tiny chimes and weirds bent the waters in odd arpeggios. A grand celebration had begun.

Hebrideans understood nothing quite so much as celebration. If Lancelot could only convince them that fighting was festival, they would be the fiercest warriors in Britannia.

The company churned its way inward, past the ship-breaking headlands, across the keel-scraping tidal channel, and into the bowl of the bay. Above, the Joyous Garde shone in white glory. Per Lancelot's orders, the lichen-encrusted stone had been bleached. Once-black walls gleamed as if new. Garlands festooned them. Folks' smiling faces lined the battlements above—more festive even than the garlands.

Lancelot breathed a glad sigh. Here was the one real-world place where he and Guinevere could be husband and wife, king and queen. These Hebrideans were not merely his subjects. They were his confidantes, his friends.

Trumpets sounded from the walls. Voices answered from the deeps. Merfolk beached themselves on the rocky shores of the bay, and Hebrideans descended from the snaggled cliffs above. The songs united them all. All began the dance.

King Lancelot and Queen Guinevere strode to the southern extremity of their realm—a great gray heap of bones. They had come for war.

On this fey plain centuries before, the armies of the Rose and Raven had met and slain each other. Corpses great and small had piled one atop another. Giants, ogres, and trolls had made their bones the bedrock of this hill. Tuatha in tens of thousands had turned their flesh to mud and cemented the stones in place. Sprites, sylphs, pixies, and all the other wee folk had become the innumerable dust. The king and queen of fey climbed a hill made of their own dead folk.

Behind them, the land teemed. They led a green army of more than just fey. They had brought flora—marching fungi for eating the dead and voracious grass for covering bare earth and even lumbering oaks for rebuilding the forest. They had brought fauna—bounding harts, watchful rabbits, darting birds, wild horses, loping wolves. It was an invasion force, to be sure, but made up of a different breed of warrior. There were no armies to conquer in the lands beyond the ridge. There was only death itself.

Lancelot stared out at his faerie homeland. Once it had been called Dalachlyth, which meant, quite simply, abundance. Now it was a wasteland, ruined by war and want and wrath. It had been decimated the very night Benwick itself was decimated. While Claudas had burned the world above, monsters had burned the world below. All was gray and dead to the horizon. Nothing grew. Nothing moved. And somewhere beyond the horizon lay the ruins of his former castle. They would march until they reached it. They would spread across the shattered rock and empty dust and bring the land back to life.

"Let us begin," King Lancelot said quietly. He took his first step down the far side of the mound.

Queen Guinevere matched his stride. From her mouth a song began. It was wordless, like the chant of bees or the gossip of rivers. It poured from her out across the dust and bones. Tones resonated among them. Skulls hummed like crystals. Dirt jiggled and aligned. Seeds borne by centuries of wind began to grow, for to them, the song of Guinevere was sun and rain both. Tender shoots rose amid the tangled bones, flourishing with the touch of her bare foot.

They were Adam and Eve, driven from the garden into a

world of thorn and thistle—and yet they brought the garden with them.

Called forth by song, grasses swept out past the monarchs and spread across the lowlands beyond. Where grasses went, deer did too. They bounded in a glad dance over the new meadows. The oaks could not wait to join the flood. On lashing roots, they ambled ahead to plant themselves where the water and light would be best.

Lancelot and Guinevere strode onward. Her song preceded them. Their folk rushed gladly ahead. Once this had been a blighted and forbidding place. Soon, it would be a paradise. Hand in hand, the king and queen of fey created a new world.

At last, they rested. There was no more marching to do. One step at a time, Queen Guinevere and King Lancelot had returned Dalachlyth to life. It had taken months of fey time, and who knew how long in the world, but now the land was green and bountiful. Its rulers sat resting while their new castle grew itself upon the ruins of the old.

Amid tumbled stone column rose trees. Straight, tall, and broad of bole, they unfurled branches at their crowns to form a dappled vault. In the rubble of the outer walls grew thistle brakes, impervious to flesh and green enough to rebuff fire. Vines stretched out to sketch the inner walls, and from them hung curtains of lichen. Pixies coaxed leaves from every shoot, and etter caps dug wells below. Wood creaked, wings buzzed, feet scurried. All this industry would soon produce a castle as grand as Rose Castle—in fact identical. The two palaces were, after all, only halves of a whole. They were the home of the Otherworld's Camelot.

In the midst of the pleasant clamor, Brigid appeared. She

wore her divine form, though this day her eyes did not beam. They looked fretted. "It is time. You must return to Camelot."

"Hello, Great Brigid," said Lancelot, rising from his seat to kneel before her. He took her hand and kissed it.

Guinevere knelt too. "Do you see that the palace is nearly done?"

"You must return to Camelot. It has been twelve years since you left."

"Twelve years!" Lancelot echoed, astonished.

"Arthur has sent his knights on a fool's errand—on Merlin's errand. Merlin knows of you two. He has warned Arthur not to depend on your power any longer, Guinevere."

The queen grew very pale. "Arthur knows?"

"No. He pines for you. He knows only that you are in Avalon, and that time here moves strangely. Emerge as his wife and his wife's champion. Return to him. He needs the assurance of your power. He has sent his knights seeking the Grail and Lance of Christ, and should they find them, Camelot will welcome us no longer."

Lancelot rose. "Yes. We must go. I will seek the Grail and Lance and make certain they are never found."

"How can we leave our lands?" Guinevere asked.

Brigid smiled sadly. "You will not be leaving them—every dewdrop is a window between the worlds. If you need us, seek a deep well and return. If we need you, we will draw you back across." She lifted her hands, and suddenly in them she held clothes and armor. "I brought your things. Dress in them and go. Tell Arthur none of this. Say you were captives of time. He will believe you because he wants to believe you."

"Yes."

They did not wait for privacy. There was no need of it here, among their folk. They stripped off their fey regalia and slid on the coarse clothes of mortality. Even as their own castle rose around them, they could think only of the castle at Camelot falling.

They reached out, grasped hands, and stepped up to one of the newly dug wells. Etter caps scrambled up the stony sides to get out of the way. The king and queen of fey leapt. They splashed into the cold veins of the earth and ceased to be—and reappeared upon the swampy shores of Glastonbury.

The air was sharp and dead. No creature moved on the green hills. None spun through the air. This was Britannia, as verdant as ever, and yet after the fecundity of fey, it seemed a desolation.

"How are we to reach Camelot?" wondered Guinevere flatly. "Walk?"

Then came a flash of life in a nearby wood. Something large and white barged among the ash trees. The ground trembled, and from a brake of leaves burst Rasa. He galloped down the belly of the land, straight for Lancelot and Guinevere.

"He waited for us for twelve years?" Guinevere asked incredulously.

Lancelot shrugged as the beast clomped to a halt before them. Saddle and reins were gone. "With Rasa, who knows? He is, after all, a horse from Avalon. Who knows where he has been?" Lancelot patted the creature's gleaming side. He seemed not a day older. "Hello, boy. It's good to see you again."

Rasa nodded.

"Let's get us back to Camelot."

25

The Grail and the Lance

Lancelot rode Rasa among northern lakes. Evening sun made the hills into folds of green velvet. Below lay waters that glittered like gems. Rasa cantered easily along a rill and then descended across spongy ground. He leapt a meadow fence, clomped across the short-shorn grass, and vaulted the wall on the far side.

It felt good to ride this way, a human knight instead of a fey king. The limits upon mortal eyes and minds were mercies. One could not enjoy the present moment while staring down eternity. Lancelot enjoyed the present moment.

Late sunlight rippled over him as Rasa charged through a glowing glade. The cool sweet air of the forest told of violets in bloom. Horse and rider broke out upon the brow of a hill. Low mountains spread to the Eire Sea.

Everything felt right. Arthur was in his castle—twelve years older. All of them were except Guinevere and Lancelot. She sat beside him, and world and Otherworld were one again—always entwined but never touching. The king and queen belonged together as much as Guinevere and Lancelot did. Their chaste union actually soothed the ache of her absence—and the guilt of their betrayal.

It was good to quest again, knowing what Lancelot knew, and knowing the prize would be so great.

Already, knights had encountered the Grail in hundreds of places across the land. Always it had appeared in glory and healed those who might approach. None had laid hands on it, though, and it vanished as quickly as it had come. Some knights had been driven mad and come to wretched ends. Some had shucked armor and weapons and donned monk's sackcloth—wretched ends. Nearly half the knighthood had become casualties to the quest. They had sought the Grail for the wrong reason—personal glory. Lancelot sought the Grail to save Camelot.

Rasa cantered along the crest of a blue valley. A village lay below, nestled nearby Grass Lake. Its chimneys emitted the smell of smoke and food. Lancelot wished he could go down to the village, perhaps spend the night. He could not. His errand was too pressing.

An hour back, Lancelot had encountered an old shepherd whose broken leg had been healed by the Grail. It had manifested itself within a shepherd's cairn in the uplands. The man was so overjoyed, he told all those he met, that they might go and be healed. He directed Lancelot to the spot—the highest mound west of the lake. Even now, Rasa trotted from the valley ridge and onto the base of the mound. He climbed eagerly.

Shadows enfolded them. The sun sank behind the mountains. Dew settled on the grass. Rasa's hooves dug into moist soil as he bounded up the hillside. Sheep scattered, bleating. There at the crest stood a pile of stones, which evening sunlight laved in gold.

Rasa slowed to a walk. Lancelot stood in his stirrups and stared.

That was not the glow of sunlight. Something *within* the rock shelter shone. Not a wisp of smoke stained the air. Could it be the Grail? After months in the saddle, could he at last glimpse the Grail?

Lancelot halted Rasa and dismounted. His boots came down lightly on the grass. He let the horse go. Rasa took lance and packs with him. Lancelot still had his sword—his god-blessed sword. He kept it sheathed as he warily approached the cairn.

Like all such rock piles, the cairn was a shelter for shepherds. It seemed almost a crypt, fashioned of fieldstone and large enough for two men. Just now, the stone beds to either side of the cairn held something other than shepherds. Six great candles glowed, filling the chamber with brilliant light. In their midst rested a cloth of red samite that held a silver tray. On the tray stood an ornate cup of gold.

Was it a trick? Who would risk so fine a cup on a trick? But it had to be. How could the poor son of a carpenter afford so great a goblet? Perhaps it had been a present from Joseph of Arimathea. Lancelot peered more closely. The six candles convinced him. They alone could not account for the sunlike radiance that poured from the cairn. It was more than radiance. It was holiness.

This was no trick. He stood on holy ground.

The sensation stopped Lancelot in his tracks. He feared to approach, lest the Grail flee from his unworthiness—as it had from so many. He feared to halt, lest he never lay hold of it. To his knees he went. His hands fumbled at his boots, struggling to remove them. Scintillating power suffused the air.

Though the sun had set, the hilltop shone as at midday. It baked Lancelot in his armor. It perfused his muscles. He sat.

It was a beautiful place. No wonder shepherds chose the spot. No wonder Christ chose it.

Lancelot lay down. Why not? What rain could fall through this blaze? What harm could come to him here? None.

He slept.

He slept.

There were figures moving around him—dim figures. Men and women. Most were peasants. Shepherds. Farmers. Vagabonds. They entered the radiant nimbus that spilled from the cairn. In they went broken—hobbling, bandaged, blind. Out they came whole. They passed by Lancelot respectfully, glancing down at his curled figure. One old man, whose hands were as gnarled as oak roots, reached out to him, beckoning. Lancelot tried to lift his hand but couldn't. He couldn't move. He could only stare up in mute sadness. Shaking his head, the old man pressed on into the ravening light. Moments later he emerged, rubbing fingers that were straight and smooth.

Lancelot was paralyzed, trapped. This power exceeded any he had ever known, even the might of Brigid. This holiness, pure and unyielding, would not be admixed with even the slightest evil. In its presence, Lancelot was as good as slain.

He lay there as more folk came to be healed. He was a stone at the threshold to heaven, forever bathed in its glow but forever outside.

Suddenly, he understood. He had approached wrongly. It wasn't that his heart held more evil than that of any farmer. It was that his intention was wrong. The Grail had come here to heal, and all those who approached with infirmities, wishing to be whole, were made so. He had not approached to be healed.

"Heal me," Lancelot murmured, stunned he could speak.

"Heal me," he repeated. His hand rose, his whole arm tingling as if with needles. "Heal me!"

Another supplicant, a white-haired woman who wore an eye-patch, reached down to haul him upward. She took his hand and, with surprising strength, lifted him.

"Thank you, Mother," he said to her, panting. "Please, go before me."

Without a word, she turned and crept nearer the glowing place.

Lancelot followed in her shadow. He peered past her shoulder, and could only just make out the glories within. The Grail blazed like a star upon the tray that held it. The power that poured out of it sent currents to push him back. Only in the umbra of the old woman could he make his way.

She reached the threshold to the cairn and went to her knees. She bowed her face to the ground and lay there a long while. An occasional tremble of her shoulders showed that she still lived. At long last, she rose again. When she turned to go, bright tears streamed from her eyes—both eyes. She fixed them upon Lancelot.

He nodded his thanks to her, stepped forward, and knelt where she had. The moment his face pressed to the stone, he understood.

There was no more light, no more heat, no more Grail—only an omnipresent mind.

Only ask, and you will be made whole.

He could not lie, not in that light. *I am not broken.*

You are broken, Lancelot du Lac. You have broken yourself.

You are powerful, Christ, but you have come to mortal men. I am not a mortal man. You do not know the ways of fey.

You are wrong, and you are broken. Only ask, and you will be made whole.

He felt his own shoulders tremble. *What would you do to make me whole?*

Only you can make yourself whole. Renounce your wedding. Repent your warfare. Devote yourself to the cross.

I am not broken.

Words did not answer, but visions—of a truly unbroken soul. He saw a pure child arise from utter deceit. Merlin's trickery had arranged his conception. Bastard-born, the boy would never be bastardized.

Do not wave Arthur in my face. . . .

More visions came, of a noble young man who sat the Siege Perilous—the very seat that had flung away his father.

It is not Arthur you show me, but a nearer soul. . . .

And last, a future vision—of the young man laying hold of the implacable Grail, laid hold of by it, and borne away to infinite light. *The son will surpass the father. The son will rise.*

Galahad. . . . The name poured out of Lancelot like breath. *My son.*

Go, Lancelot du Lac. You will not be made whole.

Suddenly, it had all returned—the radiance, the heat, the Grail. Lancelot rose. He reached out toward the cairn, but the golden energy thickened around his fingers, flinging them back. The Grail remained inviolate within.

He turned to go. Through tears, he saw more supplicants approach. He had knelt, broken but unrepentant, before paradise and been turned away.

The son will surpass the father. . . .

Lancelot rode through autumn and into the bitter winter. Ever at his back rode dread, an unwelcome saddle-mate. He had met the foe—the coming Christ. Yes, Lancelot had known the stories of Christ and of the Bible. Aunt Brigid was also Saint Brigid, after all. Never before, though, had he encountered the mind of Christ as he had at that shepherd's cairn. Guinevere and Lancelot had surrendered Camelot to this rapacious God. The land would never be the same.

To Christ, knighthood itself—warfare and pride and honor—was sin. Christ commanded men not to strike back at those who struck first, but to turn the other cheek. He forbade pride in one's own deeds, but only in the works of God. He required that honor go unavenged, and that wrongdoers be forgiven. Christ was antithetical to knighthood. Already, he had sent a score of knights cringing for the cloisters.

Without the Power of the Land, without the melding of world and Otherworld, Camelot would become a theocracy—the tyranny of the One God.

Lancelot's mind reeled. He wandered. He had lost track of the day and the month. He had even lost track of where he was. Once, he had ridden Rasa into a deep pool and willed them both by sheer mania to the wells of North Uist. It had become his true home. Ill folk orient toward home. There, he had forgotten his madness and had eaten regularly. Now he ate only because villagers shoved pastries and pears and cheese into his hands. If he had not been on quest, he would likely have starved.

But Lancelot didn't want food. He wanted the Lance of Longinus.

Of course he couldn't lay hold of the Grail. It had laid hold of him. It was a healing thing, offered by Christ to his disciples and bearing both metaphorical and actual blood. A healing thing could not be taken by violence. This lance, though, it was a killing thing. It had stabbed the Christ. It could stab any man. It could be taken in a violent hand and used for violence.

Still, so far, he had heard no word of it.

Rasa clomped down a berm laced with morning hoarfrost. He trotted out onto a narrow lane. It was treacherous footing—the muddy ruts had frozen overnight—but Rasa rarely stumbled. The horse led this quest. His master only rode quietly along. The lane led into a village of thatched cottages, most in wattle and daub, but a few half-timbered. At the far end stood a mill, its waterwheel gleaming with ice as it turned. Every shutter was closed, and every door was dark. Sleeping in.

Just the sort of village the Christ would have liked.

Rasa cantered to the center of town and halted, knowing what would come next.

With a cold gauntlet, Lancelot struck the shield that rode on Rasa's rump. The riotous clangor echoed down the street. Lancelot kept it up until shutters flew open and faces popped out. From one doorway came a couple of adolescent boys in nightshirts, wielding fireplace irons. They stopped dead when they saw the mounted warrior.

One was agitated enough to shout, "What is it!"

Raising his visor, Lancelot said gravely. "I seek the Lance of Longinus."

"Who?" ventured the same boy. His older brother cuffed the back of his head.

"The spear that stabbed Christ in the side—the Lance of Longinus. It is what I seek."

The older boy—lanky, with haystack hair—said, "We're sorry to hear your friend got stabbed, but we never seen him."

"Christ is not my friend. He is the Christian savior—"

"You're trying to find his killer?"

"No, I'm trying to find—" Lancelot stopped. Even in his muzzy state, he could tell he was making no headway. "Have you heard rumors of strange visions, lights in mountain crypts, miraculous healing, anything like that?"

The younger boy blurted, "We had a cat come back to life." He ducked, avoiding the blow of his brother's hand.

"That cat wasn't really dead, just breathing real slow."

"For three weeks, breathing so slow you can't see it?"

"You never should've tried to stab him—"

"If I'd not, he'd still be breathing slow."

Eyes rolling, Lancelot shouted to the rest of the villagers. "I am seeking a miracle that flits across our land. The Lance of Longinus could save Camelot."

A pillow-faced woman in one window said, "What's wrong with Camelot?"

"Nothing. Have you heard any rumors of visions or miracles?"

"Not aside from their cat—oh, and the fact that my Bert didn't snore last night. That's about as miraculous as we get."

Laughter poured from windows and doorways. Bert even poked his red face out to show the pillow marks. He laughed the hardest, with a snort that told he would be an atrocious snorer.

Amid the general hilarity, Lancelot clucked, sending Rasa forward at a slow clop. Useless, like a hundred other villages.

A sound came dead ahead. Another horse and rider approached at a heady gallop. Judging from the man's size and his regalia, it was none other than Gawain. He thundered down the lane, his eyes on Lancelot. Gawain reined in his horse, which had considerable difficulty stopping on the icy road. The beast actually skidded past Rasa and only barely remained upright.

"Lancelot!" Gawain called out in surprise as he struggled

to bring the beast up beneath him. "What are you doing here?"

Lancelot watched him placidly. "Seeking the Lance of Longinus."

"By Christ, you had the vision too!"

"What vision?"

Gawain flipped back his visor, giving a view of his beaming face and black beard. "An angel of God appeared to me in a dream and told me it was here, in the village of Millsdam, but that I must ride with all haste, lest its secret owner bear it away."

Lancelot considered the words and the ingenuous face of the knight. Suddenly the laughter seemed mocking.

Lancelot whirled Rasa tightly about, raked free his sword, and shouted, "Someone here is hiding the Lance of Longinus. Your laughter tells me that perhaps all of you are. Sir Gawain and I will not leave without that sacred lance. Any more mockery will be answered by the sword."

Gawain looked askance at his comrade, and black brows bristled uncertainly.

" 'The Kingdom of Heaven is taken by violence, and violent men bear it away.' " Lancelot said. "Now, surrender the Lance to us, or pay for your insolence."

The younger boy gaped incredulously and then broke into an all-out run for a nearby barn.

A cat came back to life when he tried to stab it. . . .

Giving a yell, Lancelot sent Rasa bounding after the boy. He sheathed his sword, instead drawing his spear from its couch and leveling it. He bore down on the running kid. Gawain galloped just behind him. If the boy got into the barn, he could lose them, slip out some lower window. With the utter precision of the joust, Lancelot sent the spear point out to snag the boy's nightshirt. The shaft plunged through, missing flesh, and lifted the boy. Slowing Rasa, Lancelot pinned the kid against the barn door.

"Surrender the Lance!"

"I don't know nothing about your damned lance!" the boy spat, his feet kicking above the ground.

"What did you stab the cat with, then, to bring it back to life?"

"A pitchfork!" the boy growled. "I wanted to get him off the hay without touching him."

"You're lying."

"Lancelot," said Gawain gently, "he's not lying."

Eyes blazing within his helm, Lancelot said, "You're the one with the vision. If this boy isn't the bearer of the Lance, who is?"

"You are," replied Gawain. He gestured toward the oaken lance that held the boy suspended.

In a rush of memory, Lancelot understood. He had never seen a lance the like of this one—straight and unbreakable, fashioned of oak older than Christ. It had always struck true, and never needed honing. Of course Master Smetrius would grant him such a weapon. Who would be more likely to own the centurion's lance that slew Christ than the Roman god of war?

Staring at the Lance—it even seemed to shimmer with a power he had been blind to before—Lancelot said, "All this while, I had it and didn't know."

"It has been serving Camelot all this while," Gawain said.

"It will serve Camelot as long as I live to wield it," Lancelot answered.

Gawain's beard bristled. "I am glad to hear it. Now there is only one thing you must do."

"Find the Grail? No, I have found it and failed it. My questing is done."

"No, I didn't mean that. I mean, you must let the boy down."

26

The City in Embers

Mother came to him in a fitful dream.

Do you see what they are becoming, Mordred? She asked, her hair coiling like tentacles about her beautiful face.

What, Mother? Mordred wondered absently, rolling over and covering his head with his pillow.

They are becoming what we are supposed to be. They are becoming queen and king of world and Otherworld, both.

It was really annoying to be a grown man and have his mother still plague his dreams. *So what?*

If Lancelot and Guinevere gain the hearts of Camelot, none of your poisons and none of my enchantments will drive them from the throne. If they do so while simultaneously ruling the Otherworld, from the Hebrides to Benwick, they will be unassailable.

Mordred gave up, rolling on his back and releasing a gusty sigh. "So, I imagine you've got some simple plan that will bring them crashing down."

You know me too well, Beloved Son.

• • •

"Here it is. It was among us all this while, Your Majesties," said Lancelot. He reached to the table before the throne of Camelot and drew back the cover of purple velvet. Beneath lay his own oaken lance. "It was a gift to me from my weapons master, who had the deepest of connections to the Roman army."

Arthur stood, eyes sparkling, and approached. "The Lance of Longinus. It always strikes true. It never fails the will of its wielder."

"Yes," Lancelot said pensively. He glanced over Arthur's shoulder to Guinevere, who remained upon the throne. Both excitement and sadness shone in her face. She did not approach her champion, her husband.

Arthur lifted the lance, testing its heft in his hands. "Yes. We've been blind not to see it before. And you—no wonder you have always been so indomitable."

Lancelot smiled wanly. Arthur knew only the half of it.

"Well, you can go right on wielding it, being indomitable on behalf of Camelot. To think we sought a weapon we already had. I wonder what Merlin was thinking."

"Had we not sought it, we would never have recognized it for what it was," pointed out Lancelot.

"True enough," Arthur replied, setting down the weapon. "Excellent work, Lancelot. And what of your other questing?"

The knight's face darkened. "If the Grail is to be gained, it will not be gained by me."

"You encountered it, then?"

"Long enough to learn I can never hold it."

"That is bleak news." The king's eyes were nettled. "One folly after another. Discovery of this lance is the only good to come of these quests. Five knights slain outright, another score committed to monasteries, and a handful . . ." Arthur stared levelly at Lancelot. "I fear, among the casualties, was your own son."

"My son?"

"Yes, Galahad. The child born to you by Elaine, Daughter of Pellas. He grew much while you were captive in fey. He was old enough for his first wisp of beard, a fine warrior with a true heart."

"Galahad. . . ." whispered Lancelot.

"He found the Grail, and it slew him. The knights told a longer tale than that, but it came down to that. The Grail slew him."

Lancelot's face was ashen. "I never knew him. I never knew—"

"He was a great knight—in many ways greater even than you, Lancelot," said Arthur gravely. "I wish I had never assigned the quest. It was Merlin's doing, really. He feared my queen was dead. He said I would lose the Power of the Land. Does she look dead to you? Does her power seem in doubt?"

"Certainly not, sire," replied Lancelot.

Lifting an eyebrow in irritation, Guinevere said, "You were gone a long while, Sir Lancelot. What other news do you have from your quest?"

Lancelot looked up toward her. "I went to the Joyous Garde. Prince Mador kept it dutifully during my absence. He told the people their ruler was off making alliances in fey, which was not truly a lie. Mador has even raised a small army to help me retake Benwick. Of course, his hope is to extend the power of the Hebrides onto the continent. I don't mind. I will not disparage any aid in regaining my kingdom."

"Yes," King Arthur said, turning back toward the throne, "and you can plan on our aid as well, Lancelot. When you are ready to retake your homeland, only give the word, and the armies of Britannia will muster to you." He seated himself beside Guinevere and clutched her hand.

"I will be ready sooner than later, great king."

"We are glad to have you back in Camelot," Guinevere said.

Lancelot bowed low to his king and queen. "No one could be more glad than I."

The moon rose, a half-deflated ball, above the balcony of Lancelot's chambers. When he had been a young knight, he had lived on the ground floor, sharing quarters with squires. Now, his rooms were loftier, set just below Guinevere's. The thought was that, should any trouble come to the queen during the night, she could strike a chime in her room, and her champion would come running.

Her balcony was an easy climb above his.

It had been a year since he had been alone with his wife. For that matter, outside of fey, they had never been together. How could they here, now, with Arthur sleeping across the hall, with the Round Table half-emptied by the Grail, with Camelot itself verging upon a cliff? And yet, they were husband and wife. To deny their union was to deny their Otherworld nation. If Camelot was already doomed, what good was it to doom Dalachlyth—and Benwick—as well?

Lancelot looked out across Camelot. It spread in twinkling beauty below, as if Arthur had brought the stars down to reside upon the hillsides of Cadbury. Always at night, the city showed her true aspect—part earthly, part Otherworldly. Above the torch-lit streets radiated the faint lines of ley where faerie folk walked. From cellar bars drifted songs from fey throats. Across roofs of living thatch and along sills of dwarf-quarried stone capered wee folk on their way to one mischief or another.

No. Doomed or not, Camelot was a miracle. If Lancelot were to climb to that balcony tonight, he would be destroying a miracle.

Lancelot turned his back on the shimmering city. He stepped into his chambers.

Someone dropped down onto his balcony.

Lancelot whirled. "Oh, Guinevere!" he said rushing onto the balcony to wrap his arms around her. She was warm in her nightgown. He pressed her to him. "Guinevere! I so wanted to climb to you."

"I know," she said, breathing against his neck. "I know. It has been so long." She kissed him tenderly upon his neck.

"We shouldn't, not here," he said even as he returned the kisses.

Their faces rose. Their lips met.

The taste of her was exquisite. Hot and clean and soft and willing. She desired him as much as he desired her.

She held his head and kissed him, long and eagerly.

Lancelot's hands reached down to her breasts, smooth beneath the shift.

Guinevere worked loose the ties of his tunic and drew it down over his shoulders. She kissed a line down his neck and along his chest muscles.

Pulling his hands free of his tunic, Lancelot drew Guinevere's gown up over her head. He leaned against her, pressing her naked buttocks against the stony rail. Clutching her tightly, he rained kisses on her shoulders and arms.

"I love you, Guinevere," he said huskily, leaning back to look at her.

Her figure—beautiful as it was—blotted out the lights of Camelot. "I love you, too."

Lancelot held her. "Let's go inside."

"Did someone see us?" Guinevere asked, stiffening in his hands.

"No," Lancelot said. "No one sees what we are doing. No one but you and me."

They lay long in each others' arms as the deflated moon made its wobbly way across the sky. For a time, one would lie awake and listen to the other sleep, and would weep secret tears before nodding off. Then the other would wake and do the same.

The moon was low in the west when Guinevere slipped away from her sleeping husband. She stole cat-footed across the cold floor, lifted her nightgown from the balcony, and donned it. She climbed, balcony to balcony, slipped into her own chambers, and curled up in cold sheets. She shivered for a long while, and did not sleep again, though she lay in bed until long after sunrise.

"Thank you, Your Majesty, for granting us this private audience," said Sir Mordred, bowing just within the doorway to King Arthur's chambers. He always kept his ruined hand clutched up against his waistcoat, which gave his bow the impression of being one part curtsey. "I have taken the liberty of requesting tea and cakes for our meeting. They will be arriving soon. May we be seated?"

King Arthur glowered awhile at Mordred and Agravain. The aging king seemed lost behind his bushy beard and brows. "Sit," he said simply, indicating a pair of chairs beside the door. Arthur himself sat on his bed, crossing arms over his chest like a shopkeeper unwilling to bargain.

Leaning forward with a grave but conspiratorial air, Mordred said, "Now that so many of your great knights are gone, only a few of us remain with the experience and will to advise you, my sire." He said the last two words pointedly. "And we wish only to do what is best for you and for Camelot."

"Get on with it," Arthur said.

Smoothing his black beard with the fingers of his ruined hand—a move calculated to evoke pity—Mordred said, "It has come to our attention, and more importantly to the attention of much of the court, that since Lancelot's return from questing, he and Guinevere have been trysting."

"What?"

"They have been secretly meeting for the purpose—"

"I know what trysting is!" roared Arthur. "I also know what treason is, and bearing false witness!"

A knock came at the door.

"Oh, that would be the tea," said Mordred, eagerly rising. He greeted the servant pleasantly and asked him in to place the tea tray on a low table. "You may go. We have important matters to discuss." The servant bowed and withdrew, closing the door. Mordred meanwhile fiddled about with the kettle and cups, saucers, and squares of cake. He conveyed a plate and cup to Arthur, who had no place to set either, and said, "Try the cakes. They are quite light."

"You've just accused my wife—your queen—of infidelity, and you have the audacity to offer me cakes?" growled the king.

"The tea is quite fine too—honeyed."

Despite himself, Arthur took a sip. A look of surprise registered on his face, and he took another sip. "Honeyed?"

"Yes. An agreeable mixture. Makes even bitter things easier to swallow."

The king's shoulders slumped in relaxation. "Fine, then. What were you saying? Something about Guin."

Delivering cake and tea to Agravain and taking some himself, Mordred sat. "Well, it is widely known at court that the queen spends many of her nights with Lancelot. Either in his chambers or hers."

Arthur's bluster left in a long, sad sigh. "There have always been suspicions. I've had my own. But what of proof?" He took a long drink from the tea, and seemed almost pained by its sweetness.

"There is none," Mordred said, "as yet."

"Then why did you come to me?" he asked wearily.

Mordred donned an almost wounded look. "I, well, I assumed it would be best to speak with you first about it. See what you wanted to do. It really is your decision—whatever is best for you and Camelot."

A rueful smile flashed within the king's beard. "What's best for Camelot. . . . What's best is that I—and all the rest of you—turn a blind eye. Why destroy what we have for sake of pride?"

Mordred nodded deeply, obviously having expected a different reply. "Yes. That would be best. Let us continue on as if nothing has changed. You are beloved, Father. You'll not be much diminished by this. Even as a cuckold, you are the greatest ruler this land has seen since Caesar."

"A cuckold . . ." echoed Arthur.

"I mean, the ones who are truly diminished are Guinevere and Lancelot, to do such a thing. To pretend at loving you but all the while mocking you this way."

"Mocking me this way . . ."

"If only we had the Grail," Mordred went on ruefully. "Then you wouldn't so desperately need the power Guinevere used to grant you."

Arthur could hardly breathe. His hands trembled, so that the cake fell to the floor and the tea cascaded in red lines down his leg. "What should I do? Suddenly, I can't seem to decide anything."

"Don't worry, Father," Mordred purred. "You said that you needed proof. That's what we do next—get proof."

Lancelot lay sweating on his bed, thinking of the queen. It was a hot night after a dog day, the sort of night to get one's blood up.

He wished he'd chosen this night to launch his Otherworld attack on Benwick. Soon enough. He and Guinevere would recapture his homeland soon enough.

As always, his thoughts curved in upon Guinevere. Where was she? Most often, she came to him. It was better that way. No guards waited outside his doors—no king across the hall. Sometimes they had dared her chambers, which were more sumptuous, complete with a bath that remained ever warm. Tonight, if there would be a tonight—it would be in Guinevere's chamber.

Lancelot rose. He was bare to the waist due to the heat and wore only a loincloth. Soon he wouldn't wear even that.

The stones felt cool and good beneath his feverish soles as he walked out onto the balcony. Camelot spread before him, gleaming with thousands of red flames. They didn't seem stars tonight, distant and blue, but a bed of embers. Heat rose in waves off the city. It was as if he stared at Benwick after Claudas was through with her.

The thought almost stopped him. What was he doing? Dooming Camelot and Guinevere and Arthur and himself. He no longer had delusions about that. But damnation lay not in a single act. A thousand small choices had led him this far. What was one more night of faithless betrayal after so many others?

"Good-bye, Camelot. Take care of yourself this night."

Lancelot climbed to the rail of his balcony. He reached up. His hands fastened on stone balusters, and he pulled himself up. Legs hanging free in the still darkness, he climbed with arms alone. He reached the rail and leapt over it. He was trembling, though whether with desire or nerves he could not tell.

"Guinevere," he called softly through the open door of the balcony. "Guinevere, it's me. Don't be afraid."

There came no answer from within except the soft sound of breathing.

Smiling, Lancelot crept quietly across the sheepskin carpet. "Sweetheart, don't be afraid. It's your Lancelot. Wake gently, Guinevere."

Still, there came no reply from the bed—only that quiet, slow breathing.

Lancelot sat down on the bedside, reached gently to the figure lying there and stroked her shoulder—but it was metal.

A hand—a man's hand—grasped his wrist and twisted it behind his back, and a sword clanged against the bed-frame. "We have you now, traitor."

He held his hand clamped over her mouth. His breath came in long, hollow draws across her ear. Even nearing fifty, Arthur was still a powerful man.

"Don't fear, my dear," Arthur said in hushed tones. "I just want to hear what is happening across the hall."

Arthur's chambers were dark, and the roughness of her abduction, the anger in his limbs, made her tremble as she never had in his presence.

She let out a moan, which hissed through his fingers.

"If you promise not to cry out, my dear, I will move my hand."

Guinevere nodded her head deeply.

Arthur immediately moved his hand from her mouth to her shoulder. "There, that's better." There was something in his breath—not intoxication, but a similar, piquant odor.

"What will they do to him?"

"Only capture him, let us sort things out," he said quietly.

"What are you going to do to me?" she asked. "Rape me?"

The king was silent. When at last he spoke, his voice was deeply grieved. "I would never rape you, my dear. You know that."

She did know it, and she was ashamed for having said it.

"So strange," he said, "that with your husband, it would be rape, but with your champion, with him it is—different."

Guinevere swallowed. Tears that had waited long in her eyes flooded downward. She wanted to tell him that Lancelot was Tuatha, a king, her husband—all the things that had made her betrayal seem right at the time. But nothing could make this right, and she could not slip away from the king. She could only wait in his chaste arms for sounds of battle across the way.

27

Immolation

Lancelot's left arm was pinned behind his back, but his right was free. With it, he reached over his shoulder, grasped his assailant's collar, and pulled. In full armor, the man rolled up Lancelot's hunched back.

A desperate sword cut empty air before Lancelot.

Yanking his left arm free, Lancelot caught the sword by its crossbars. He held tightly as the man flipped. Gauntlets pried loose from the pommel. The man crashed headlong to the floor.

Panting, Lancelot stood above him. He held the sword steady in the reeling darkness. "Who are you, and what business have you in the quarters of the queen?"

No answer came. Not even breathing.

"Who are you? Answer the queen's champion!"

The silent stillness that replied could have meant only one thing.

Lancelot drew a jackstraw from the bedside stand—damning himself for knowing where they were kept—lit it at the embers of the fire, and transferred the fire to a candelabrum. Light sketched the wretched scene.

Sir Collgrevaunce slouched upside-down, his neck broken, his head kissing his chest. He had been one of the newer knights, a young man who had fallen under Mordred's spell. . . .

Muffled boots filled the hallway beyond.

Lancelot hurried to the door and threw the bolts. He also hoisted the twin beams into their brackets. Nobody would be coming through there.

Someone tried the latch. A weight pushed tentatively against the door. It returned with more force. The beams held.

"Open up, traitor. We know you're in there."

Once again, the word traitor. The whole thing was a trap laid by conspirators. They could not have done this without winning over Arthur.

"We'll batter the door in," warned the voice, and Lancelot recognized it to be Mordred's.

Without answering, Lancelot strode past the body of Collgrevaunce and out onto the balcony. He need only return to his own chambers—

From below came the sound of kicking boots, and then a door failing. Chunks of wood crackled and bounded through his room, and in their midst pounded a dozen pairs of feet.

Greater and greater, this conspiracy, he thought. His heart ached with fear, not for himself, but for Guinevere—where was she?—and for Camelot and Arthur. He feared the death of all he loved.

Only fighting banishes fear. Lancelot withdrew to the body of Sir Collgrevaunce and dragged it out beneath the staring stars. Quickly, he undid the man's armor and donned it—chest plate, back plate, tuille, cuisses. It paid him well to have been his own squire.

Already, the men were climbing from the balcony below.

"Stay back," Lancelot called out to them. The ones who had been struggling up the wall paused. "We will sort this out under sunlight, not in darkness."

"We will sort this out now. Your deeds make this matter dark, Lancelot."

"I do not wish to harm any of you, but whoever sets foot on this balcony tonight will die," Lancelot warned.

That gave them pause, too, until Sir Agravain replied, "We have the king's own orders to apprehend you dead or alive. Do you so brazenly oppose your king?"

That almost took the fight out of him. Lancelot wanted to harm no man, least of all Arthur—and yet look at what he had wrought. Guinevere gone. Knights fighting knights. Conspiracy and treason. Infidelity and fratricide. Lancelot might have surrendered then.

"We have your precious Guinevere. Come with us, and it will be easier on her."

Lancelot knew the punishment for infidelity. He suddenly had plenty of fight in him.

Agravain was first to reach the balcony. He dropped down like a giant roach, glossy and black on the parapet. His sword tasted the air before him.

Lancelot rushed him, as if to bull him from the balcony. He batted aside Agravain's blade and rammed his own into the man's throat.

Agravain grasped the impaling sword and struggled to produce a last few words, but could not. He dropped, nerveless.

Withdrawing his blade, Lancelot spun.

Another figure clambered over the rail, Sir Gyngalyn. A year ago, the young man had been a squire. Now—

Lancelot's jaw knotted. He lunged. The stroke cut Gyngalyn's sword from the air, and then rammed beneath his gorget.

Now he was dead. "I beg of you—do not come, any more of you. Agravain and Gyngalyn lie dead. It grieves me to have slain them. It will grieve me to slay you."

Still, they came. One after another, he slew them. It was as if distilled rage moved through their blood. It made them fearless, but it did not make them better fighters. What could inspire such hate?

Not what, but whom. The last man to rise was Sir Mordred, son of Arthur himself. Mordred was a poor climber. His shield hand had never healed after the Lance of Longinus had shattered it. Still, he had made up for it with the poisons he reputedly used upon his blades. Even a glancing blow from Mordred could kill.

Struggling up the final foot over the baluster, Mordred slung his gaunt form onto the balcony. He was as ungainly as a bat. Standing, Mordred spread his twisted limb. He gazed first at the bloody corpses of his co-conspirators—twelve of them. Then, without a hint of fear, Mordred lifted his eyes to their slayer.

"Very sporting of you to let me get my feet." Mordred sat down on the rail.

Lancelot did not respond. This was part of the duel. Mordred never lost the verbal part of a duel, and often it won him the whole.

"Where is your lady, though? I thought you never fought, except for her. It looks as if you've fought pretty well for yourself."

"You know where Guinevere is."

Glad to have drawn a response, Mordred let his sword idle in front of him. "Yes, I do. Arthur's got her. He's teaching her what it feels like to have a real man inside her."

Mordred won.

Lancelot lunged. His blow, ill prepared, glanced away from waiting steel. Mordred tangled his blade with Lancelot's, spun it, and wrenched the sword free. Unarmed, Lancelot stood before the leveled blade of Mordred.

"So easy," Mordred said, still sitting on the rail. "I should have reached you first. It would have saved a few sides of meat." The man's sword lingered just beneath Lancelot's jaw, ready to jab. The metallic scent of poison rose off the blade's tip. "Now, the question is, do I take you captive, or do I kill you here? Which would be more fun?"

Lancelot did not answer. He only stood amid the bodies.

"Either way, I might as well have you kneel. I'd like to see the great Lancelot on his knees before Sir Mordred." His glib tone hardened. "Kneel."

Breathing deeply, Lancelot stared at the deadly, poisoned sword.

"I said, *kneel!*"

With a sigh of resignation, Lancelot dropped down to one knee. He grasped the corpse of Sir Melyon, yanked it from the ground, and hurled it. The body missed Mordred's blade but struck the man. He tumbled over backward, falling from the rail to the rose garden three stories below. The thud and screams that followed told equally that Mordred was not dead, but neither would he be able to fight.

Breathing heavily, Lancelot looked around at the carnage. He bowed his head. "Brothers, forgive me for what I have done." The words felt feverish on that night air. The moonless sky wavered with the departing spirits of the dead.

Mantled in blood, Lancelot rose and climbed down to his own chambers. He quickly washed himself and donned his armor. Strapping on his Saxon sword, he strode through the shattered door.

He yet had friends among the knights. They would help him escape. They would help him rescue Guinevere.

He had not raped her. Guinevere knew Arthur was incapable of it, even with Mordred's poisons running through him. Still, the feverish way he held her through that night of battles and blood made her sad. Always entwined but never touching—it was madness to live that way. Guinevere had found her way out, but Arthur was yet trapped in it.

Now, they were both trapped. Through the main streets of Camelot, Guinevere rode, bound and gagged, in a prisoner's cart. Dust rolled up behind the wheels but could not block the accusing sun. All along the way, folk gaped, hurling insults and rotten fruit. The looks they threw were worse still. Some folk wore devilish grins, cheered by the anguish of the queen. Others frowned in blistering reproof. Many more seemed wounded: Her betrayal had stung them to the core. Here were the folk who once loved her, whom she had destroyed as surely as she had destroyed herself.

Unable to look any longer in their eyes, Guinevere let her head loll back in the cart. She saw the sweaty tunic of the drover, walking beside the horse. He was a simple yeoman. His load was dumped and his vehicle pressed into service. He walked with heavy steps, and tears made muddy tracks down his cheeks. Whether he wept for his lost cargo or his lost queen, she did not know. She could bear him no ill will. Nor could she muster resentment for her honor guards, Sir Gaheris and Sir Gareth. Sons of Lot and brothers of Gawain, they walked unarmed to either side of the cart. They had requested this position out of love for their queen. She could not even hate these jeering multitudes. They did what they did only for love of Arthur.

There he sat, in a pavilion at the end of the parade route. His own guard surrounded him. Sitting on a makeshift throne amid ruffling canvas, Arthur seemed no longer a man, but a statue. The twinkle in his eyes had receded so far as to have disappeared entirely. His face hid in a thicket of whiskers, and his heart beneath layers of fabric and fur. No, not even him could she hate. This end was her own doing—hers and Lancelot's.

Guinevere allowed herself a secret smile. He had escaped. That very night, he had killed twelve and escaped. Rumor said that he had even spoken to his friends—Lionel, Hector, Bors, Galyhud, and others—in hopes of rescuing the queen. Three attempts on the dungeon had proven fatal for many knights. If Lancelot and his folk could not prevail against a handful of guards and a jail cell, how could he against the massed knighthood, Camelot itself, and the stake and flames?

The stake loomed up beside the pavilion where her husband would watch. It was a tall, rough-hewn thing, driven deeply into the ground. There would be no tugging it out, no breaking it loose. The rope they would use was rigging line for ships—stout and tightly woven. It would wrap her waist and hold her immovable. Even an ax would take many blows to part all that cord, and there would be no time for such blows. And the fire—oh, she made out that wicked stack, cord upon cord upon cord. It would have been enough to immolate a whole village, though it was meant for just one queen.

Hope of escape melted away. Guinevere's heart was bare and sad. If only there were dew somewhere, anywhere, her folk could rise and take her back with them. Morning had dawned dry and witless.

The cart stopped. So did the hail of refuse. Crowds jostled to see what would happen next.

With great solemnity, Sir Gaheris slid the heavy rope over one shoulder and knelt in the street before the hog-tied queen. "Your Majesty, I am going to lift you now."

She nodded, uncertain how to reward his decorum.

Gently but firmly, Gaheris cradled her trussed-up figure in his arms and raised her from the cart. His brother used the corner of his tabard to wipe the refuse from her face and hands.

"I thank you for your kindnesses," she said to them both.

"Forgive us, great queen, for our part in these things," Sir Gareth said as his brother set out for the pile of wood.

Gaheris was damnably sure-footed on the shifting stack. He rose like a ram on a scree slope, gaining with each step. At the top loomed that giant and horrid stake. He meekly set her down with her back against it, uncoiled the rope from his own body, and wrapped it around hers. He tied a massive knot, wound the rope many times around her waist and the stake, and ended with another great knot behind.

"Can you breathe, great queen?" he asked as he finished tying.

"Does it matter?" she replied.

"It is better to die of smoke than of fire. The more you can breathe, the sooner you will die of smoke."

"I can breathe," Guinevere assured quietly.

Gaheris nodded. "Good-bye, Guinevere."

"Good-bye," she said. She watched his broad shoulders as he trudged down the pyre.

Now, she was truly alone. Those were the last words she would exchange with anyone—though they were not the last words she would hear spoken:

"Behold," cried Sir Mordred from the parapet below. "The wages of sin." He had recovered remarkably from his near-fatal encounter with Lancelot, and had volunteered to speak for Arthur during this traumatic event. It told how far the king had fallen. "She who was sworn in the bonds of wedlock to our own king, to our own nation, has betrayed both in the arms of another. Passion burns hot, but fire," he lifted a torch with one hand, and it burst into flame, "burns hotter still. Let her soul be salted with fire!" He flung his arm out.

The torch arced, end over end. Every eye in the crowd watched its waffling flight. It struck the pyre. With a preternatural whoosh, flames leapt skyward. They spread in a wide ring all around the stake. Mordred must have doused the tinder with one of his foul concoctions. Flames stood in a cylindrical curtain all about Guinevere. White smoke poured skyward.

Even through the ropes, Guinevere felt the searing heat. Each breath baked her throat and poured poisons into her lungs. She blinked repeatedly to keep her eyes from going dry. Through the flames, the faces of the crowd twisted into demon masks. Their hoots became a banshee keen. Nothing was true anymore. Even Arthur, watching on the other side of the flame, seemed a straw dummy.

A new figure appeared. On his white horse, he arrived. Lancelot rode full gallop down the filthy lane. In his left hand, he lifted high his sword. In his right he couched his unfailing lance.

Lancelot! It was a delirium dream, surely. But dreams do not fight like that.

A man who lunged out to bar his way was flung aside by that seeking lance. Another who brandished a board at Lancelot had the thing split down to his white-knuckled hands. A third, who swung an iron bar to kneecap Rasa, got iron back with a horseshoe in the gut. None could stop Lancelot.

These are peasants. What of the knights? wondered Guinevere through her mind-haze. Staring out past the curtain of fire, she saw many familiar knights—Lionel, Hector, Bors, and many more—restraining their fellows. Lancelot had not asked his friends to fight the other knights, but only to hold them out of the fight. There had been death enough that first horrible night.

No peasant could stand before Rasa as he crashed down the lane, toward the pyre, and no knight attempted to—until Gaheris and Gareth. Though unarmed, the brothers stood side-by-side, directly in Lancelot's path.

He bore down on them. Perhaps he did not see that they were unarmed, did not know who they were. Perhaps he cared only for Guinevere.

The Lance of Longinus, which never missed its intended target, struck Gaheris in the chest. It burst through plate and mail, fabric and flesh, meat and bone until it shattered the heart that had animated them all. Gaheris was a limp sack of meat on the end of the lance as Rasa trampled down his brother. Four hooves, four great cudgels—they left only a trammeled spot in their wake.

Bloodied, Rasa climbed the burning side of the pyre. Lancelot yanked on the spear, but it was hopelessly fouled. Gaheris's corpse would not relinquish it. Lancelot did. He cared less for it than for Guinevere. He and Rasa plunged through the flames. Their hair and pelt burned. They seemed avatars of death.

How could Lancelot save her, even with steed and sword? Already, smoke had made her lips and nose black. She languished. There was no time to chop her free. She would be dead in moments.

As Rasa crossed the final few feet of burning wood, Lancelot reached beneath his burning tabard and drew out . . . a rose bouquet. What madness! They would all die together, clustered about peeling flowers.

Without dismounting, Lancelot swung down—face literally burning with intensity—and thrust the bouquet up for her to breathe in.

Gasping, Guinevere drew in the sweet, cool scent of the roses. They were not simply roses, but Otherworld roses, from her castle garden. They brought with them dew. It splattered her face from every red fold. It coated Lancelot's arm and Rasa's snorting nose. Like ten thousand minute hands, it lay hold of them. It drew them insistently out of the world of fire and hate. Horse and rider disappeared amid the conflagration. The ropes around Guinevere went slack as she too was gone.

Only the roses remained, red and curling in the furnacelike heat. They turned to ash and wuffed away.

28

The Battle of Benwick

Burned and blistered, Lancelot, Guinevere, and Rasa emerged in a snowmelt stream. Guinevere sat in the flood, as she had at the stake. Blue waters rolled over her legs. Soot formed a black shroud in the water. Lancelot dropped into the stream beside her. It swallowed him to the waist. The cold at first burned, but then brought blessed numbness. While the lovers clung to each other, Rasa cantered up the rocky river to a deep, circling pool and plunged in. His pelt steamed.

They had been dying a moment before. The miracle of fresh dew in an inferno had saved them. Fey hands in fey waters had brought them away from Camelot. They would never return. But where had they arrived? This was not Avalon or Dalachlyth or the lands of the Rose.

It didn't matter. They were together. Nothing mattered now.

Lancelot washed the soot from Guinevere's reddened face. Her hair had not burned, and no blisters marred her beauty. Smoke had been her slayer. Still she coughed it from her lungs.

At last, she lifted her eyes to see Lancelot. A deep groan escaped her.

Blisters covered his lips and eyelids. Black spots on nose and cheeks oozed blood. Every hair follicle was burned to a nub, including eyelashes and brows. Armor and clothing had given some shelter to the rest of his body, but his face was ravaged.

Hearing the groan, Lancelot soothed, "You're all right, Guinevere."

"Yes, but you aren't."

Filling her hands with chill waters, she lifted them and gently pressed them to his face. She hummed an ancient Tuatha healing song. Life flowed from her flesh to his. It rebuilt burnt tissues. Desiccated membranes moistened. Particles resumed the Maying dance of life, and the stuff of death washed inexorably away. Guinevere pulled her hands back to see two distinct prints of healthy flesh where they had been. She moved her fingers deftly and gently over his face, as if she were sculpting him. In moments, it was done. Only his baldness told of the travails he had endured.

"Lancelot," she breathed, wrapping him in a tight embrace.

He closed his eyes and held her. All the pain and terror melted away. For a time, nothing existed beyond that embrace. Only when Rasa nudged his back with a wet muzzle did Lancelot open his eyes.

Both banks of the stream were filled now with folk—ruddy-faced and beaming in their trews and kilts.

"I know where we are," Lancelot said, beaming back at them. "We're home."

• • •

The Joyous Garde presided, white and glorious, above the armies of North Uist as they stood arrayed around the rocky bay. Every warrior had turned out. So had a few sons too young to be warriors but too old to be denied. All wore their fierce tartans—red and blue, black and green. All bore fiercer weapons, from great swords that could down a horse to boot daggers that could blind a guard. Others had brought threshing flails or pitchforks or axes—whatever lethal thing came to hand. They would need all of them this day.

Lancelot reviewed the troops. His boots crunched mussel shells. His hand scrubbed the short shock of hair atop his head. These were fine troops and eager, but would their backcountry fervor prove a match for the skill of Claudas's men?

Guinevere, sitting nearby, wore a dubious expression.

Lifting his voice, Lancelot addressed the troops. "Today, we fight. We fight for North Uist and for Benwick and for all that lies between. We fight for world and Otherworld. Camelot welcomes us no longer, but we will make our own Camelot. Most battles are fought for the past—old squabbles and outlived grudges. Not this battle. This battle we fight for the future."

A hearty cheer rose from the troops. It reverberated in the bay's stony throat and blasted out among wheeling gulls.

"We are but two thousand, true," Lancelot said, "but our fey allies will be ten thousand more. Surprise will make each of us worth ten of our foes. We will overwhelm them!"

Another cheer, louder than the last, shook the bay. Polearms thudded eagerly on the gravel.

"Remember—slay only the soldiers of Claudas, those in orange and black heraldry. They are an occupying army of a nation that is ours. Kill no citizens of Benwick, but slay the soldiers of Claudas and take up their posts. From the lowest to the highest, we will take back the city."

The third cheer was nearly deafening. It made blood thunder in every heart. Even Guinevere stood, her face red with excitement and her eyes glittering. She walked to Lancelot and took his hand.

Raising their fists together, the king and queen cried, "To Benwick!" They turned at the head of their troops and commanded, "Forward!"

They marched down the rocky shore and into the shallows. From their belts, they lifted breathing conches—great shells bristling with white spines—and placed them over their mouths and noses. The waters were cold upon their legs, knees, thighs. It stabbed at them as their torsos began to submerge, but the king and queen did not slow. Even in the frigid grip of the water, they sensed the warm caresses of their folk.

The same creatures that had pulled them through rosy dew now clutched them in salty shallows. Their heads sank below, and the pull of fey was complete. They disappeared beneath the waves, borne on immortal hands toward faraway Benwick.

Rank on rank, the army of North Uist marched into the bay. Rank on rank, they disappeared. In scant minutes, only the spinning gulls and the beaming castle remained.

"What is that?" wondered King Claudas to himself, staring out the solarium of his palace. He lifted an aged but steady hand to his brows to block the sun and gazed down upon his city. Something was pouring out of the fountains and wells and sewers. Something big and alive.

Claudas ground his teeth. In the twenty years he had ruled

over Benwick, he had seen numerous infestations—rats, roaches, fleas, mosquitoes, frogs. Indeed, the folk of Benwick themselves were the largest and most obtrusive vermin he had had to endure. They had never embraced him or his warriors, and were good citizens only at knife-point. But not rats, not roaches, not even Benwickians could compare to what poured from the aqueduct and seashore and river.

They seemed giant beetles, and they scuttled quickly, spreading out across the city. Citizens cringed back from them, but the things gave no care. They went right for Claudas's men—the garrisons, the walls, the guard posts. They killed the stunned warriors and moved on.

The door behind Claudas barked open. The old king turned angry eyes. "Well? What is it?"

A messenger spilled inward. The boy groveled low, shrinking from the man's gruff voice. "The guard captain sent me. We're under attack, sire."

"I can see that! Do you think I'm blind?"

"N-no, sire," stuttered the boy.

Wheeling to glare out the windows, Claudas asked, "What are they?"

The boy blinked blankly at him.

"What is attacking us?" demanded the king.

"Why, men are. Wet men, in skirts—but they are vicious warriors."

Claudas's brows bristled. Though he was an old warrior, he was still ferocious. "Men don't climb up from wells and out of fountains."

"Actually, the Vandals invaded Rome through the aqueducts—"

"Shut up!" shouted Claudas, waving away the discussion.

"Whatever they are, call out all the guard. Sound the civilian trump. Every man, woman, and child in the city is to fight these . . . these things!"

"Yes, sire," the boy said, bowing once last before slipping away out the door.

Claudas knotted his fingers behind his back and stared out the long bank of windows. No doubt Ban himself had stood here on the night of Claudas's invasion. The solarium offered a commanding if unnerving view. That had been a fiery night, and this would prove to be a watery day. Claudas would not do as Ban had done, though. He would not flee like a rat down to the wharves. He would remain and fight, even if he were the last man.

Turning, he strode from the solarium toward the keep where he would make his stand.

Lancelot and his contingent of Hebrideans arose within the central courtyard of Benwick Palace. They emerged from a brimming fountain. Heads, shoulders, arms, all broke the surface, and men clambered forth. They dropped their breath conches and raised swords, axes, flails, cudgels. . . . Behind them, a marble god wrestled a giant serpent. Before them, the warriors of Claudas wrestled their fear.

"Charge!" cried Lancelot. Streaming water, he leapt from the fountain and pounded across the courtyard. His sword stabbed out before him.

At his shoulders came ten of his men. The others split off in groups to take down nearby guards.

At least the first of Claudas's men stood his ground. That was about all he did. His sword swung out to deflect Lancelot's blade, managing only to knock it down into his own knee. The man cried out and crumpled.

Lancelot swept by, tapping one of his men. "Take his place. Dress his wound. Convince him I am king."

The warrior at first seemed downcast by the order, but the final part of it made a sanguine smile spread across his face.

Lancelot and his nine swept inward. Already, other teams had secured the rest of the courtyard and were driving into the garrisons. The fighting there would be bloody and to the death. Once the garrison was cleaned out, the rest was only a matter of housekeeping.

"This way!" shouted Lancelot, waving his sword toward the looming tower at the center of the castle. "To the keep!" If Claudas was here—and sources had said he was—he would be in the keep.

Lancelot led the charge out from beneath the marble promenades and across a practice ground. Hebridean boots kicked up dust as the contingent advanced among quintains and practice dummies. It was exhilarating to run full-out from one fight to the next. The warrior beside Lancelot let out a ululating war-cry.

Next moment, it ended in gurgles. The man crashed to his face in the dust. An arrow jutted from his neck. Blood flowed bright red. Lancelot looked up in time to see a shower of arrows pelting down from above. It struck in their midst. Shafts thudded into the earth and shuddered. Two more men cried out and fell.

"Find cover!" shouted Lancelot, diving behind bails of straw.

His men did likewise, behind practice dummies and stone mounds. They cringed there as another hailstorm of arrows peppered the ground around them. Every quivering shaft pointed back toward the source of the arrows—the top of the keep. There was no way to clean out that nest, and no way to advance while it remained. A dozen archers with countless arrows could keep them pinned down forever.

"What now?" shouted a Hebridean.

"Yes," Lancelot repeated quietly to himself. "What now?"

Guinevere and her contingent emerged within the spring-fed pools of the palace gardens. She did not lead kilted warriors, but forces that were altogether more lithe and lovely. Naiads took form from the deep pool and strode out on a rose-strewn shore. Dryads scuttled in driftwood bodies up to nearby groves. They soaked into the bark, livened the quick, and animated the boughs. In moments, dozens of cherry trees pulled their roots from the earth and strode toward combat. Lesser warriors in plethora poured past Guinevere's feet. Boggles scurried across the lawns to snatch the footing from guards. Boggarts clambered up the castle walls and fouled the bowstrings of archers. Sylphs woke life on old ivy vines and sent them racing up the walls to drag warriors down.

Even as Guinevere stepped fully from the pool, her fey warriors had secured the gardens and moved in a great green wave deeper into the castle.

Claudas's men stood stunned as will-o'-the-wisps circled around them. Others could not keep their feet from dancing to the enchanted fifes of fauns. Still more had laid down weapons, thinking they lounged in green fields instead of a castle at war.

All went well, and yet, Guinevere sensed that something was amiss. Not here. With Lancelot. He was in trouble.

Her soul fled toward his, drawing her body. Running

across the garden, she reached a wall rampant in ivy. She clutched the vines and climbed. Her folk followed, wondering what she sought. With the eager speed of a spider, she scrambled up that wall. Her heart pounded for her to go faster. Clawing her way to the top, Guinevere stood and saw.

Lancelot and his men were pinned down beneath arrow fire from the keep. Already, four men had died, and a fifth squirmed, his leg impaled by a shaft. Atop the keep, the archers laughed as they craned their bows down and let fly.

"Take the keep," Guinevere commanded in low tones. The words fell upon countless leaves.

Ivy grew voraciously, reaching down the wall and spreading across the practice grounds below. Under its cover, armies of little folk—brownie and bogey and boggle—advanced. Some brought succor to the trapped and injured warriors. Most, though, were intent on the keep itself.

Behind the ivy carpet, cherry trees thrashed their way through the garden gates. They strode straight for the keep's main doors. Storms of arrow fire from above fell on them, availing nothing. In moments, the cherry trees reached the doors. They sank tendrils into any cracks they could find, and then grew. The stout doors shattered. Wood flew out in shards, and iron bands rattled to stone thresholds. Guards goggled within. The trees grasped them and dispatched them mercilessly.

All around, ivy climbed the keep walls. Minute warriors rose on the tendrils. Leaves rammed themselves into arrow loops, clogging them. Vines roped off murder holes. The main mass of foliage surged up to the battlements above. Tendrils twined around bowstrings and shafts. Branches wrapped around archers' necks. With a vengeance, little folk attacked big.

On the wall, Guinevere could only smile. Her expression intensified as Lancelot rose below, pointed his sword toward the shattered doors of the keep, and shouted, "On! On to Claudas!"

Lancelot and his final three warriors ascended the keep stairs. They had secured each level below, and King Claudas had not yet turned up. Only one level remained.

"If he is within," whispered Lancelot to his warriors, "we will offer him every courtesy due his office."

"Why not just kill him and have done?" asked a red-bearded warrior. "If he lives, there will be a question of legitimacy."

Lancelot shook his head slowly. "Not after today." He was right. The people of Benwick had joined Lancelot and his liberators, not caring who they were. Anyone would be better than Claudas. When they found out it was Prince Lancelot, returned after all these years, there had been elation in the streets. Fry pans had felled a good portion of Claudas's forces. No matter what the final disposition of Claudas, the folk were already proclaiming Lancelot king.

"Get ready," Lancelot said. "When I kick the door in, I'll go straight, you two go to either side, and you watch the rear. Ready?"

They nodded.

Lancelot lifted his boot to kick.

The latch clicked. The door swung slowly open.

"You may enter," came a wry voice.

Lancelot peered through the door into a guard station. It was meant to house the archers atop the keep. It held two cloth bunks, pegs for clothes and armor, a wash basin and pitcher, a pantry of dry rations, and bundles of arrows. A ladder led up to a closed hatch and the roof parapet where the archers had been torn asunder. Half in the ladder's shadow stood an old but hearty warrior. His face was haggard, but his eyes sparkled.

Lancelot advanced through the door and took up a position in the center of the room. His men fanned out behind him as he had requested. "King Claudas, surrender to us, renounce your claim to Benwick, and we will treat you with civility."

"No," the man replied curtly.

"No?" Lancelot echoed.

Claudas's eyes glimmered. "If I surrender to you and renounce my claim to Benwick, I have lost everything—"

"Except your life."

"Even my life, for it would be yours to do with as you wished. If, however, I challenged you to a duel, I might slay you and regain the throne and win all."

"King Claudas, understand this: You stole this land from my father. In effect, you slew him and sent my mother raving. You orphaned me. You sit a seat that is not your own, and if you persist in challenging me, I will have difficulty controlling my wrath."

Claudas shrugged. "It matters little, in a contest to the death."

"So be it," said Lancelot. He lifted his sword into position before him and set his feet. His eyes bored into King Claudas's.

"So be it," answered the old warrior. He emerged from the shadows of the ladder and advanced. Just before reaching Lancelot, he let out a great roar and swung what should have been a decapitating blow.

Lancelot slammed the blade aside. His next stroke rose with hungry speed. It caught King Claudas beneath the jaw and rammed through. Claudas lurched up off the floor. The blade bit through his palette. He wriggled in shock and pain. It cracked through sinuses and slid behind eyes and pierced brain and blasted through the top of his skull. The stroke was complete only when the blade bit into the wooden ceiling above and hung Claudas there.

Letting go of the streaming hilt, Lancelot turned to his men. "The issue of succession is secured."

That night, Lancelot was crowned King of Benwick. The name of Claudas was struck from the royal rolls. Lancelot's new subjects were in a celebratory mood, and his old subjects, who had won the day, were only too happy to teach them how to celebrate.

Every wall in the city glowed with firelight. Every square thronged with revelers. Candles floated upon the black bay, and songs charged the air.

Lancelot watched it all from the windows of his father's solarium. He had chosen not to remain long among the festival throngs. Guinevere had retreated with him. From this height and this distance, it was difficult to tell glad fires from killing ones, to tell shouts of celebration from shouts of terror. This was how the city had looked the night his father had died.

"It is a weighty thing," Guinevere said at his arm. "After all this time, to regain what your father had lost."

"Yes, it is," replied Lancelot. "But that isn't the reason for my mood tonight."

"What then? Your people love you. They have pledged to fight beside you to regain the rest of your lands. It is only a matter of time now."

Lancelot watched the fires below. "Yes. It is only a matter of time until Arthur comes. Then I must make horrible war."

29

Preparations for War

"Greetings, Sir Lionel!" King Arthur said heartily. He clasped the knight by the arm and smiled, his teeth white within his beard. "First at the feast, as always! Ha! Take your seat. I see the others are lining up behind." Arthur bodily pulled Lionel through the doorway and reached with his other arm to greet the next knight. "Sir Bors! So good to see you here. Some said you were more faithful to your cousin than to Camelot. Ha! Well, everything starts new today. Everything! We're rebuilding the city, the knights, everything." The knight furrowed black brows. Arthur drew him on and hailed the next arrival. "Gawain! Oh, it's good to see a seasoned knight. Tell these pups how we built Camelot the first time. Tell them we can build it again."

"Can we, Arthur?" asked the big knight levelly. "Can we truly?"

The king's smile became a portcullis across his mouth. "Of course we can. With the sword Excalibur and the scabbard Rhiannon, with the Lance of Longinus, with the oracles of Merlin—"

"He took your wife," Sir Gawain interrupted.

Only then did the king's mustaches close over his teeth. "He saved her from execution. He was right to do it. I must have been mad—"

"No, sire. He took her long before that. He took her the first day he rode into Camelot. Your honor demands—"

"This is a festival, Sir Gawain," interrupted Arthur with forced gladness. "Let us throw off the shackles of the past and lift our hands to the future!"

Gawain lifted his hands, but in resignation.

Arthur was already clasping the arm of the next knight. "Sir Mordred," he said, accidentally laying hold of his crippled arm. Arthur gazed downward, releasing his hold. A decision was forming in his mind. "Mordred . . . we're starting over now, starting fresh. It's an all-new Camelot and . . . of all my knights, I'm most hopeful for what the future might hold for you. You're not just a knight. You're my son. I've acted as if you weren't, and I regret—"

"Sire, I understand what you are saying," Mordred assured. "I too wish to make amends. In the new Camelot, I will give up my caprice for sake of the throne."

Arthur lifted his eyes. Hope glimmered in their depths. He clasped Mordred's good arm. "Yes. It *is* a new Camelot. A new day!"

The same words gushed out as each knight arrived. Arthur's hands trembled. The fever that had brought him to this moment had broken. Each greeting grew louder than the last. Each hope grew grander. The future of Camelot burned brighter than the past ever had. Arthur seemed never to exhale, only drawing in great gasps. His chest inflated, growing bigger and tighter and emptier. At last, he could not breathe at all and had to sit and pant, his face buried in his hands.

By the time he recovered, all the knights had arrived. Perhaps half of the seats at the Round Table were filled. Arthur's mind supplied the ghosts of those gone—Lancelot, Gaheris, Gareth, Galahad, Agravain, Gryfflet, Brandeles . . . some lost to treasonous battle, some lost to the Holy Grail, some lost to the merciless years. . . .

"That's the first thing, the first order of business," Arthur announced as he strode toward his seat, "to induct new knights. We can't have a feast like this at a table half full! We'll send out the runners in the morning, a call to all landed warriors, summoning them to Camelot for tournament."

"Yes," Sir Mordred said, "an excellent programme. We'll summon the warriors of the nation to Camelot, and we'll test them at tourney, and induct new knights. Once again, our company will be full."

Arthur reached his seat and eased himself down into it. The doors to the chamber swung open, and servants emerged, bearing platters heaped with steaming loaves. A maidservant set down wooden plates and large spoons, and a manservant followed behind, placing and slicing open the loaves. A third servant poured a thick stew of eel and onion into the trenchers. Aromas of yeast and fish mixed in the steam that rolled upward.

Arthur breathed the scent greedily. "Do you see how easy it is, you doubters, to rebuild the knighthood? A game. A simple tournament."

"To rebuild the knighthood and to rebuild the nation are two different things, Your Majesty," said Sir Gawain. His comment caught Arthur with a full mouth.

Mordred spoke up. "No. It is simply another game—only on a larger scale."

Gawain scowled. "What game can restore the honor of Camelot?"

"The game of war, of course," Mordred said. "Why else would our king gather to him the greatest warriors in the land except to make war?"

Gawain turned toward Arthur, who was still swallowing. "Is this true? Is this your plan?"

"The k-king's justice is my plan," sputtered Arthur, reaching for a tankard set before him. He drank deeply. "Knight errantry."

"Send me errant, seeking injustice, and I will sail to Benwick to take the head of Lancelot," Sir Gawain said.

The words were tangling in Arthur's ears, in his mind, on his lips. "Forget about Lancelot—"

"He slew my brothers Gaheris and Gareth. He killed them in cold blood—unarmed and guarding your queen—"

"He did not know them, did not know they were unarmed—"

"He stole your wife and destroyed your knighthood and your nation—"

"Can we forget Lancelot?"

"No! I cannot, the nation cannot, and you cannot. Camelot cannot live while Lancelot lives," Gawain said firmly. "Do you love him more than you love Camelot?"

"No."

"Then call your warriors, and fill out the Table Round, and ship for Benwick to take the traitor."

The words were twisting. Arthur looked to the trencher, eel meat gleaming blackly within the dark stew. His peered at the knights. Their eyes reflected his figure—shattered, piled upon by misfortune. "This is the only way to restore Camelot?" Silent nods answered. "Then, yes, of course. We gather the nation, and we sail to make war on the traitor. I myself will go.

I will leave my son upon the throne. He will hold it until Guinevere and I return."

For the first time in that strange feast, there came a cheer from the remnants of the Table Round.

Lancelot stood on the steps of the palace and lifted a quarterstaff into the air. "Behold, folk of Benwick, a simple weapon, but one that will make you powerful."

The wide square before him thronged with peasants. Warriors moved among them, handing out staves. Folk fingered the poles absently. One young man decided to clout his brother in the head.

"It makes you bigger," Lancelot said, grasping the haft by its end and whirling it in an arc around himself. "This is my space. As long as I wield this weapon well, no one can enter my space."

Staffs began whirling within the crowd, and folk began falling.

"Yes, that's the idea—just move farther apart. Don't break any ankles. That's it. Sweep the feet, and retreat. Even knights can't fight when they are lying on the ground." Lancelot paused in his demonstration. He set the butt of the polearm on the step beside him and leaned on it.

Peasants whirled their staffs, knocking each other off their feet. There was so much laughter and so many growls of irritation that none of them could hear him.

"Well," Lancelot said to himself. "At least Guinevere will have volunteers for her healing demonstrations."

• • •

Unfortunately for many ankle-sore peasants, the queen was nowhere nearby. In fact, she was twenty miles from the city.

Queen Guinevere, a retinue of Hebridean guards, and a whole company of fey attendants traveled dusty farm roads. Guinevere rode the buckboard of a big wagon. She clutched leather reins, driving the six-horse team. Within the wagon's bed lay a number of bulging sacks, labeled with the names of the grains they carried—rye and wheat and barley. More empty sacks jiggled at the base of the wagon, occasionally bunching up against the fey workers who squatted there.

Most were bodachans—industrious household creatures who were used to laboring among humans. A few red caps had set aside their picks to help with the farm work, and of course there were the pixies whose job it was to tend plants in all their stages. While the smaller fey rode in the wagon, Tuatha warriors walked alongside it. Wranglers brought up the rear, driving a motley herd of cattle, goats, and pigs.

Another farm appeared on the hill ahead. Guinevere did not even flip the reins, but only spoke to the horses. "There it is. That's where you smell the sweet grass. That's where there's water. Take us up there, and you'll graze and drink."

Nodding, the horses shouldered their way up the slope. Guinevere stared past the tall grasses, toward the farmhouse. It was a small, dilapidated place, built of fieldstone, undressed logs, and mud. The thatch roof was thin and gray. Behind the house loomed an even more ramshackle barn of similar construction.

The wagon pulled up before the building. Guinevere climbed down, with the aid of a Hebridean guard. He placed the back of his hand beside his mouth and called into the hovel. "Announcing Queen Guinevere of Benwick."

"What?" came the reply from within.

"Announcing Queen Guinevere of Benwick."

"Yeah, and I'm King Lancelot," said a toothless old farmer as he drew back the curtain that served as his door. He stared, his eyes and mouth making a trio of circles on his face. "I'll be damned."

"No, not if we can help it," Guinevere said. "We've come for your grains and your livestock—anything you don't need to get through the winter."

"What?" he barked.

"King Arthur and his army are coming. They will be laying siege to Benwick."

"Why do I care about Benwick?" asked the old farmer.

"Because you'll be in Benwick. Everyone will be. The army of Camelot will sweep through the land, seizing anything they can eat and burning anything they cannot. They'll kill anyone they find."

"So you've come to seize it instead."

"In exchange for your harvest and home, you'll have accommodations in the city, and food for as long as the siege lasts. When it is broken, you will have help rebuilding your farm, and food until your first crop comes in," Guinevere said easily. "We are offering the same deal to all the farmers."

The man scrunched his pruny face. "And if I refuse?"

"Keep your food and try to fight off Arthur yourself. You won't be welcomed in the city."

Spreading twiglike arms in surrender, the man said, "All right. You can have what's in the barn—well, two of the cows. Leave the third, and the mule. And leave enough hay to feed them. I've got two bins full of feed grains, and another two full of wheat. You'll never fit it all."

"Water them as well." Guinevere nodded to the drovers, who led the horse team back toward the barn. The queen meanwhile reached into her travel cloak and produced a scroll, a quill, and a small pot of ink. "Your name, then—as you will give it when you present yourself at the gates of the city, seeking sanctuary."

"Antoine."

She pressed her lips together. "There will be hundreds of Antoines."

"Antoine of the Hill, then," he replied.

As she wrote, she said, "A rider will come by at least a day before the ships land, calling all to the city. You are advised to set out immediately upon hearing him pass. Have your belongings packed. You can bring one wagonful into the city."

The old farmer was repeating his royal moniker quietly to himself: "Antoine of the Hill, Antoine of the Hill . . ." A smile crept around his lips.

The sound of the wagon wheels announced its return.

"Is there anything more you wish to know, Antoine of the Hill?"

The man gabbled at the wagon—done so soon, and it looked as if they hadn't taken but two sacks of grain. Distractedly, he said, "In fact, there is one question. Why's a queen out doing a seneschal's work?"

The wagon rolled up beside Guinevere, and she lightly climbed aboard. "My friends and I are efficient packers." Clucking to the horses, she sent them on down the road. Two of Antoine's cows waddled in the herd behind.

The old farmer stood in his threshold, scratching his head. He suddenly ran for the barn and threw open its doors. His mule and last cow greeted him. One corner of the loft held enough hay for their winter. The rest of the barn had been picked clean.

"I'll be damned."

• • •

On that frosty morning, the wintry sun burned with much light but no heat. Refugees jammed the roads. Laboring beneath loaded packs, they should have been warm, but nothing could cut the chill.

War was coming. War with King Arthur of Camelot.

Only sight of Benwick warmed them. Her five landward gates were thrown wide. Warriors manned them, checking every name against the scroll. It was the Lamb's Book of Life. To be written there meant lodging, food, safety, and hope. To be excluded meant shivering on the streets and begging. No one was turned utterly away. Anyone outside the arms of Benwick would simply die.

King Lancelot and Queen Guinevere themselves oversaw the disposition of the refugees. Aback Rasa and a snow-white mare, they rode from gate to gate. They passed judgment on those found lacking, and served hot cider and bread to those called to enter. They had encountered no great difficulties—

Until a war trump blared from the dockside gate.

Lancelot stood in the stirrups and craned above the heads of shuffling refugees. He lifted a hand to his brow to shield out the sun's glare. Against the black curve of the port gate, he saw swords flashing. "Stay here," he told Guinevere even as he urged Rasa to a gallop.

"Not likely," she replied, and her beast leapt to pace his.

With an irate grunt, their personal guards charged afterward.

Over frost-rimed cobbles they rode. The way descended through the mazelike lower ward, and then rose just slightly to the gate where the fight had broken out.

Benwick's guards stood in a wide and wary semicircle, their

swords hemming in a group of noble warriors who had taken the gate. As Lancelot neared, he made out the livery of Knights of the Round.

"King Lancelot," called out the guard captain. "These Knights of the Round Table are demanding entry."

"Lionel!" Lancelot greeted them. "Hector! Bors!" His eyes swept the rest of the company, perhaps a score of them, all friends. Lancelot halted his steed. "What are you doing here? Is this the much-feared invasion?"

The company laughed. Lionel spoke for them all. "Sadly, no, Lancelot. Arthur is coming, and with a huge army. Nothing is the same. Gawain and Mordred are running things. The Round Table is full of strangers. We've left Camelot. We've come to join you."

The guard captain interjected, "They could be spies. Assassins."

"Oh, shut up," said Queen Guinevere crisply as she reined in beside her husband. They both dismounted, pushed blithely past the wall of swords, and walked to their former comrades.

The guards of the king and queen let out shrieks and hurled themselves from their horses. They scrambled forward, but couldn't reach them in time.

Already, Lancelot and Guinevere were in the arms of the knights, embracing them and welcoming them to Benwick.

Arthur stood at the prow of a Saxon-style long ship. Its single sail bellied full of a late-winter wind. The mast creaked as it drove the craft through white-topped waves. Drums boomed out a relentless cadence. Between surges of wind came surges of oar. Fifty men, half the ship's complement, drove the craft through wave upon wave. Ten horses stood in uneasy stables aft. Abeam of the ship sailed two hundred more such craft. Each was full to the gunwales with hungry warriors.

It was madness. Throughout fall and winter, when men should have stayed hearth-side with their wives, they instead had ridden to Camelot. They had jousted on frozen lists, had fought with coats over their armor, had sometimes surrendered only to get indoors. Those who prevailed became new knights—Arthur did not know their faces. They sat in seats that still bore the names of the departed. Those who did not prevail became enlistees for Arthur's invasion army. Through a long winter, they had depleted Camelot's every store. They had to invade Benwick if only to find food to feed the men. Armies must eat to fight, and must fight to eat. As soon as he had called this army to assemble, Arthur had made war inevitable. It was madness.

Beside Arthur stood Gawain, as stoic as a statue. The cold, long winter had only whetted his desire for revenge. It was piteous to see so great a man turn himself to so petty a pursuit—piteous, but all too common these days. Nothing grand and noble remained for any of them.

"This is grave business," Gawain volunteered, as if he could hear the king's thoughts. He looked to skies the color of dirty wool. "Gray and grave business, but necessary. When it is done, and Lancelot is dead, and Guinevere is returned to you—then all will be light and colorful again."

Arthur bunched his beard. "You truly think so?"

Gawain winced, as if caught off guard. "Yes. Truly." He gave a vigorous nod of his head.

Arthur only turned his eyes again to the tossing sea and the slender gray line beyond it. "There it is. Our gray destiny. There is Benwick."

30

The Siege Begins

Grim-faced, Gawain rode in company with the Knights of the Round Table—such as they were. Only a handful of the fifty had served Camelot for more than a few months. Still, they were more honorable than the deserters, the traitors, the cowards.

Gawain stared up at the figures on the city wall. One lifted a bow, narrow and violent against the sky. A shaft leapt from it. The arrow rose in a high arc. Gawain and the others watched it come, instinctively bunching their horses up around the king's. The shaft plunged, dropping a few hundred feet short and shattering on the frozen earth.

Cowards. Not a boat launched to challenge their blockade. Not a warrior opposed their landing on the beaches near Benwick. Not a boy with a stick remained to defend the countryside. The hooves and boots of Camelot made a muddy highway inland. Gawain and the knights rode in the vanguard of a column of twelve thousand troops. They marched to surround the city, yes, but even more importantly, to terrify the foe.

Ahead stood a farmhouse, solid in brick and timber, right

beside the road leading south. It had its own short wall, and a granary tucked behind the house. It was a small estate in the perfect location. Whenever the company had reached a road, Gawain had ordered a division commander to encamp. This particular road would house the royal encampment.

"There it is, sire," Gawain said, gesturing toward the large building. "Your palace away from Camelot."

The king nodded, though he looked peaked in the wintry light. "Looks cozy."

Gawain sent two of the new knights to secure the structure. "Soon we'll have a fire on the hearth and meat frying—all the comforts of home." Even to Gawain's ears, that conceit rang harshly. There were no comforts anywhere these days. Still, he felt he should go on. "Siege warfare needn't be chaos. It is all about precise deployment, predictability, and resource management. It is winning not with swords but with ledgers."

Arthur nodded, waving his hand beside his ear as if to shoo a fly.

One of the knights stepped from the front door of the structure and waved the all-clear.

Gawain smiled tightly. "Ah, see. There we go. Predictable." He called out the names of the ten best knights, ordering them to remain with the king and his personal division. The rest would lead the remaining divisions in the march to surround the city and close off every roadway. Even as the companies split, Gawain barked orders: "Set up camps. Assign runners. Send ax men to the forests for firewood. Await orders."

Arthur quirked an eyebrow. "You seem to be enjoying this."

"Appearances are deceptive, sire," Gawain responded. "I am not enjoying this. I'm glad that at last we are bringing the traitor to account. I'm glad my brothers will be avenged. But this is grim work. War always is." His face lightened as the companions halted their horses before the farmhouse.

It was large enough for the king to have private compartments and the eleven knights to sleep in other rooms. The lower courses were made of stout red brick, and an upper story in wattle and daub jutted three feet beyond the lower. The thatch roof looked new and solid.

"No doubt, the interior is just as pristine," Gawain said as he dismounted.

Arthur stepped down beside him and strode toward the door. It opened easily, pivoting on one edge. The king ducked his head beneath and stepped into the front room. Gawain followed.

There wasn't a stick of furniture in the main room, though the walls showed the outlines of where table and benches had been. Even the smooth patches of the scarred wooden floors showed where rugs had been rolled up. Arthur looked grimly at the empty room and stalked into the next. It was just as bare, and someone had piled the fireplace full of rocks. Up the stairs the king went. No beds, no cots, no pallets.

"None of the comforts of home."

Gawain, who had kept uneasy pace with him, said, "We'll send out men to pillage the countryside. We'll send them right away. By the end of the week, this will seem a royal residence."

"What if the other farms have been cleaned out as well?"

"We'll burn them to the ground," Gawain said spitefully, "and we'll send boats back to Camelot to bring furnishings."

A shout came from downstairs. "The granary is empty."

"We have rations," Gawain said, his hands patting the air as if to prevent an eruption. "And we'll send back to Camelot for more food. These are simply supply-line issues."

Arthur strode to a window and looked out at a garden dead

with winter. "They've moved every particle of food into the city. They've spent as much time preparing as we have." He turned toward Gawain, an angry light in his eyes. "In this war of ledgers, we are already losing."

"A rider approaches!" shouted someone below.

With a wordless nod, the two men turned, descended the stairs, and emerged from the front door of the estate.

The rider was a young man on a pony. The trail of dust behind him led back to the city. In blue and white, he wore the livery of Benwick, but the flag that snapped at the top of his spear was the sign for parley. The messenger's face was very serious beneath his blond flop of hair. He rode directly toward the company of knights and warriors. Hands rested on sword hilts as the young man pulled his steed to a stop. It reared once but, after another tug of the reins, settled its hooves.

He cupped a hand to his mouth. "I have a message for King Arthur."

Gawain strode gravely toward the messenger. "I, Sir Gawain, will take it to him."

Reaching beneath his tabard, the man produced a small scroll case. He tossed it to Gawain, bowed once in the saddle, and said, "I was told to await a reply."

Gawain examined the case—tool-worked metal, the two halves joined by the seal of Benwick. He carried it to Arthur, who cracked the seal and pulled out the roll of paper within. He read:

> "To King Arthur of Camelot, ruler of all Britannia,
> my friend, and my sovereign.
>
> "From King Lancelot of Benwick and North Uist.

"Greetings.

"I am greatly saddened by the arrival of your armies upon my lands, and would be only more greatly saddened to do battle against my countrymen. I sue for peace. Let our nations ally, that both might rebuild. Enough harm has come between us. Now let us heal.

"I eagerly await your reply.

"King Lancelot"

Arthur stared long at that missive. He smoothed his thumbs across the letters, as if testing their ink. When at last he looked up, a fragile light shone in his eyes. He said simply, "It would be good to heal."

Gawain glowered. "The man has your wife."

The light in Arthur's eyes flared to twin fires. "I killed my wife, at the stake, don't you remember? She is dead to me."

"And my brothers are dead to me."

The two men stared at each other. Slowly, light died in Arthur's eyes.

"I await a reply," the messenger reminded from the back of his pony.

Arthur looked down, and Gawain called out an answer. "Tell Lancelot that we will not cease until he is dead." Holding up the roll of paper, he added, "And thank him for the fire starter."

• • •

As spring crept slowly over the land, King Lancelot and Queen Guinevere invited their knights to a very strange banquet.

"Behold," cried Lancelot, sweeping out arms robed in red. To one side stood a long table laden with glorious fare: roast boar, pheasant, prawns, loaves of rye and wheat, jeroboams of wine, and casks of ale. To the other side stood an old wagon heaped with identical foods. Lancelot looked past them, at the crowd of confused knights. He beamed. "This feast is one we shall eat with our enemies. I am sending them one of everything, and this note, which reads:

> "To King Arthur of Camelot, ruler of all Britannia, my sovereign.
>
> "From King Lancelot of Benwick.
>
> "Greetings.
>
> "I know you have refused my many overtures of peace. I know the wine keg I sent you was smashed, and the pig was flogged until it ran off. I know you think little of these offerings. But this night, share a feast with me. My court and I will be eating its exact like even as you do. Be assured that nothing is poisoned, and all is of finest quality. And as you eat, I ask only that you remember fondly the days when we feasted together at the Table Round.
>
> "Your humble servant, King Lancelot."

No one dared move. This was war—siege warfare—and to throw a single banquet was extravagant. To throw two, one for the enemy, was ludicrous.

Sir Lionel spoke for the rest of them. "You know what is going to happen, cousin? You know what will happen to all this food?"

Lancelot tilted his head. "I have a fair guess. The wagon will roll into a dark camp. Warriors, lean like winter coyotes, will rise and follow, drawn as if by strings through their noses. The driver will halt the wagon outside King Arthur's quarters while someone runs the message within. Out comes Arthur, holding the scroll loose in his trembling fingers, eyes gleaming. Behind comes Gawain, who won't say a word, but sets his shoulder against the wagon side and shoves the whole thing over." Lancelot demonstrated with his own shoulder, and his hands sketched a calamitous crash. "After which, he will expound a while, 'It just goes to show . . . cowards hide behind gifts . . . you'll thank me tomorrow. . . .' while simultaneously kicking away the heads of knights who scramble in to salvage something."

By the time he had finished, all the knights were laughing. The company drifted eagerly toward their seats. Lancelot motioned for the servants to haul the wagon away and dispatch the horse team.

"A very funny tactic," admitted Sir Lionel as he seated himself before the steaming boar. "But isn't it foolish to waste food—the single most important commodity in a city under siege?"

Lancelot guided Guinevere to her seat. "Oh, this food isn't wasted. Once the wagon is spilled and the contents are ruined, that camp will be twice as hungry as it had been before."

"What if they don't spill it? What if they eat it?"

"Then we have won. Then, they have feasted with us."

• • •

Spring deepened to summer. Never did King Arthur feast with King Lancelot. The siege armies had endured the worst months of privation. Soon, they could take the first harvest off the land. Then the scales of want and plenty would shift in their favor.

Lancelot and Guinevere knew other fields to harvest, though.

They descended a dark spiral of stairs. Only the lantern in Lancelot's hand gave light to the stony shaft. Its tepid glow could not reach the bottom. They were below the dungeons, deeper than the foundations. This single dank shaft beneath Benwick Castle was its greatest weapon against siege. A pure well that could not be reached by any foe meant the city would never want for water. The castle's designers could not have imagined, though, the other great use of this well.

At last, they reached the base. A stone walkway encircled the wide, black water. Its surface rolled silently with deep currents.

Lancelot set the lantern on the stair. He stripped off his kingly robes and laid them aside. He did not want to be encumbered in the water. Guinevere did likewise. They stood only in samite underthings.

Lancelot smiled. He reached out to her and drew his finger along her jaw. A similar smile grew on Guinevere's face.

They had not intended this, but there was something about the primeval power of water and the deep thrumming darkness and the simple glory of human bodies. Often, in the midst of union, Lancelot and Guinevere spontaneously wandered fey realms. It was a cynosure point between bodies and souls, world and Overworld. It was only right that they would observe the ancient rites now.

Twined together, they plunged into blackness. The cold pulses of the earth grabbed them and yanked them under. The lantern light vanished. Then, even the insistent shove of the water was gone, and it was only the two of them. That was enough.

They resurfaced in Dalachlyth Castle, amid tumbled pillars of limestone and towering columnar trees. They had come here countless times since the siege began, seeking solace among their own kind. This time, they had come for more than solace.

Yet entwined, the king and queen of fey did not rise to address their people. They remained in each others' arms, lying amid clover berms and sparkling pools. This was their court. Their people attended from every hanging vine and drooping leaf. Even the air was charged with welkin spirits, silently hovering to await command.

"It is Midsummer, good folk," Guinevere said placidly. Her voice resonated richly through the palace to every waiting ear. "A season fit for festival."

"Arise this night," Lancelot continued, "in the lands around Benwick. Make sport with all you find there."

Guinevere laughed lightly. "Let laces be knotted."

"Let wineskins be emptied."

"Let horses be spooked free."

"Let young men follow visions of young maids."

"Let old men see their frowning wives."

"Let mayhem rule the ranks of Camelot."

Already, the fey folk were streaming upward, away from their rulers. The air bubbled with laughter—myriad voices saying simply, "As you wish."

It had been a rotten night. Screams and shouts came from all quarters. Men chased phantasms. They staggered off beneath the glaring moon. Horses broke from corrals and bolted who knew where. Sticks leapt and spit underfoot like snakes. Sleepers awoke in treetops. Guards slapped themselves unconscious from imagined bugs. From moonrise to moonset, there was only madness.

When at last the sun brought sanity, Gawain was not ready to be sane. He struggled out of his sheets (which had tied themselves around his ankles), drew off his nightclothes (which somehow had become a woman's gown), dragged on a shirt that smelled suspiciously of cheese, gathered the pieces of his armor from the corners where they had danced all night, and donned them. He had to cut the laces out of his boots and restring them before putting them on. He found his sword, sheathed in a noisome eel, cleaned it, and slung it through his sword belt. It took two more hours to locate a reliable horse and a rideable saddle, but plenty of the morning remained.

He tied a parley flag to the tip of a lance, set it in its couch, and rode toward the city. For six months, none of the besiegers had ridden within bow fire. Gawain almost wished they would shoot at him. The cowards probably would.

It was strange how quickly the land rolled away beneath his horse's hooves. They had spent so long staring at that deadly swath, it had seemed larger than it truly was.

Gawain rode his horse up, almost into the shadow of the city walls. He had marked out a sally port, where he might lure his prey, and shouted up to the walls. "I would speak to King Lancelot and the so-called knights who flocked to him."

The man upon the wall considered for a long, long while. "Your tone does not suggest that you wish to broker peace."

"True enough," roared Gawain. "I do not wish to broker peace. I wish to broker war. So far, all we have learned in these six months is that King Lancelot is quite skilled at sitting on his hands—more skilled than King Arthur. When it comes to fighting, though, he leaves the work to his impish minions, his little people. Where is his courage, his honor? Here is a man who slays my brothers—my unarmed brothers—in cold blood, steals the wife of his king, corrupts the hearts of his comrades, and flees away with them all to hide among faeries. I do not want peace with this man! I want war!"

The guard upon the wall answered laconically, "This seems a strange parley."

Gawain stood in the stirrups, cupped his hands around his mouth, and shouted for all Benwick to hear. "Bear my message to King Lancelot and his so-called knights—is any one of them man enough to ride out this morning and joust with me? I will gladly face down every last one of his so-called knights just to win the right to face him down. And when I do, I will kill him." Gawain's face was red as he sat back down. He clutched his lance—the unpainted oaken Lance of Longinus, which struck ever true—in a sweaty hand. "You tell him that."

"No need," said a new voice. Gawain looked over to see Lancelot himself standing on the wall. "He already heard."

31

Dark Tidings

Dawn came red to the channel that morning. It was as though Britannia and Benwick were separated not by water but by blood. Upon that sanguine flood labored a small craft. Its single lateen sail rattled angrily with the shoving wind. Its prow punched through the waves. The water that slapped in over gunwales came back again from a flung bucket.

A single figure manned the craft. He left his bucket in the bilge and checked the cleated sheet. He drew it tighter, and then retreated to the rudder. Wedging a different block beside it, he climbed back down to his bucket in the bilge. Occasionally on his rounds, he would glance with longing at the oars shipped to one side, as though he wished he could muscle this boat across the water. His rough-woven tunic and trousers were wet with sweat and sea spray. Salt caked his forehead. He had many cuts on arms and legs. A long one made a rust-colored stripe across his shirt back, from shoulder to hip.

He soon would doff these clothes. In the high stern rested the folded livery, armor, and weaponry of a Knight of the

Round Table. He was Sir Ronwyn, among the newest knights, inducted just before the siege of Benwick began. The accoutrements of his office were precious to him, of course, but less so than the sealed scroll case in a locked box beneath them. Ronwyn was sworn on pain of death to deliver the missive to Sir Mordred.

Britannia was near now. Near at last. She had grown all morning from a gray rill to a brown one. Now, sunlight cast all in relief. To the left rose the natural rock archway called the Turtle's Door. To the right opened a sheltered inlet known as Conroy Bay. It bustled this morning with fisher folk, some going in while others were coming out.

Ronwyn's boat dipped as she passed the arms of the bay and entered fresher water. He retreated to the sheet and paid out line. The sail spilled. The boat lost some of her fever. Ronwyn cleated the line and trimmed the rudder. He cruised up between the fishing boats. They held loose-laid nets, curled above desiccated floats. Farther in, he approached docked craft. Men hauled prawn bags up from buckets.

Ronwyn let the sail luff. The boat had enough headway. She slouched in along the pier. He tossed the stern line first, letting the wind bring the bow in against the dock.

No sooner were the lines lashed than Ronwyn was tearing off the bloodied, sodden underthings he wore and tossing them to the deck. The fisher folk stared, baldly amazed. With stern dispatch, he donned his knightly clothes, his armor, and his livery, and belted on his sword. The watching eyes grew wider with each new item added. He transformed from a ragged seaman to a rugged knight. Last of all, Ronwyn took up the lock box and held it to his breast.

He stepped onto the pier. "A horse," he demanded in a voice raspy from the sea. He strode toward land, where a pair of men loaded a wagon with fish. "A horse!" he shouted more loudly.

The two men did not answer. They only stared dumbly.

"In the name of King Arthur, I demand your horse," Ronwyn said.

The older of the two men—gray-grizzled and powerful—said, "You cannot take our horse. We've no other, and no way to pull the wagon otherwise."

"I am to bear an urgent message to Sir Mordred on pain of death."

The man crossed arms over his chest and planted his boots. "Find another horse."

Without moving the lock box from his breast, Ronwyn drew his sword and lashed down. The first stroke severed the man's neck through to the bone and sent blood spraying. The second stroke ripped open the belly of his partner. Neither was a particularly well-aimed blow, but both killed. It took four or five more sloppy chops to cut the leads on the horse. With an almost vengeful motion, Ronwyn yanked the harness from the beast, leaving only the reins. He grasped them and swung himself onto the horse's bare back.

While fishermen gaped, the young knight rode away, toward Camelot.

"Behold, Gentles!" cried Sir Mordred as he lifted a chalice of cut crystal, filled with a wine as red as blood, "the bounty of Britannia."

All along the great tables, chalices rose in noble hands. Guests drank. It was the finest vintage in his father's cellar, and it rolled upon and pleased and loosened the tongues of his finest nobles.

"Feast then, all of you, this third night of Midsummer. A new season has come to our land—a season of welcome and plenty!" Mordred's call reverberated among hammer beams and wafted down banners.

The revelers echoed, "Welcome and plenty!"

Sir Mordred seated himself in the double-wide chair that once had held Guinevere and Arthur. He did not feel diminished by its size. Mordred was in his heaven.

In the name of his father, away fighting Lancelot in Benwick, Mordred had invited every great duke of the land, every petty king, to come to Camelot for the Midsummer feasts. Almost all had come. There were no jousts to draw them, for the warriors were away. There were untended women in plenty, but even Mordred knew that was not the true enticement. The dukes and kings had come because the land was in turmoil. They had come in fear of losing what they had, or in hopes of gaining something more. Mordred, as was his particular talent, made certain to promise each and all what was wanted.

The wine had natural properties for making friends of enemies and letting rulers worry a bit less. Mordred had enhanced its charms, though, with a compound that heightened emotion and dulled reason. With such libations, he had plied his people for three days, and he knew he had them. Every last one.

Even as they began their course of stew, Mordred rose from his seat to address the company. Their faces lifted from the food before them, and their eyes were eager.

"All that surrounds you, my friends—the Babylonian tapestries, the ceilings in gold-bossed plaster, the marble fireplaces, the velvet draperies—all of the splendor of Camelot is the flowering of Britannia's wealth. You, each of you, have made this city the glory that it is."

Polite applause answered that statement, but Mordred was far from finished.

"It is time for this city to repay the favor. It is time for Camelot to glorify the land. Let the bounty of Britannia that wells up here in Camelot pour back outward to enrich the lands that produced it."

The response to this was hearty and glad. These folk had heard such promises countless times in the past three days, and lapped up each one.

"When my father returns victorious from Benwick, I will beseech him endlessly on your behalf. I will not rest until he assigns a large portion of the annual taxes to return to your kingdoms and dukedoms, that you might have Babylonian tapestries and gold-gilded ceilings."

It was not just an ovation that returned, but a kind of mad, wordless joy that rang in the rafters. The sound mounted and redoubled. It might have trebled but that the huge doors barked once and swung inward.

The revelers turned, smiles still half-formed on their faces. They had learned to expect dramatic surprises from their host. None, however, could have expected to see what they saw.

A mounted knight rode through the open doors. As he emerged into the light of the chandeliers, the group noted how manifestly dirty he was. The knight hunched on the bare back of the beast. His hands were dingy with blood from gripping shorn reins. The steed was no war horse, but a hackney, accustomed to farm work. Its haunch was raw where a wooden box had ridden. The knight halted his mount, but the smell of sweat and worry walked on before them.

The nobles' excitement turned to disgust and not a little fear.

Mordred stood, livid. "What is the meaning of this?"

The knight seemed roused by Mordred's voice. He bowed aback his steed. "Forgive me, great Mordred. I am Sir Ronwyn, late of the Benwick siege. On pain of death, I have traveled here at all speed, bearing news from the battle."

"News!" Mordred echoed, excitement entering his tone. "Well, then, let's have it!"

The knight reached to the wood box on the horse's haunch, untied it, and dismounted. His legs trembled stiffly, as if he had ridden all day. Ronwyn gritted his teeth and bore the box forward. He reached Mordred's place at table, produced a key from a chain on his neck, and opened the box. Within lay a sealed scroll case.

Mordred reached reverently down and lifted the case. He studied it carefully, examining the wax seal. "It is Gawain's seal, and it is intact," he confirmed quietly. He broke the wax, opened the case, withdrew the scroll within, and unrolled it. Taking a deep breath, Mordred began to read:

> "To Prince Mordred, Acting Sovereign of Britannia and True Son to the True King Arthur.
>
> "From Sir Gawain, Commander of the Siege of Benwick.
>
> "Greetings.
>
> "My heart is near to riven, not just from the vile stroke that has laid me low, but from the viler news I must report."

Mordred looked up, sober-eyed. He studied the faces around him, asking their permission to read the rest in private. Grave looks answered, requiring him to continue.

> "On Midsummer morn, wishing to press the siege to a conclusion, I rode to the walls of Benwick. There, I proposed a contest to Lancelot and his traitorous knights, that the siege would be decided that very day in the joust. As champion of the cause of King Arthur, I would face whatever knights proposed to challenge me, and down them all, one by one, until only Lancelot remained. Then he would be required to face me. Should I throw him down—as King of Benwick—his nation would surrender to King Arthur and Camelot. Should he throw me down—as champion of King Arthur—the siege would break, and we would return defeated.
>
> "It was agreed, and all morning, as my powers waxed, I faced knight after knight, and threw them down. I wielded the holy Lance of Longinus, which strikes ever true. At last, none of Lancelot's knights remained to challenge me, and he himself came down to do battle.
>
> "He knew he could not defeat me, not as I bore the Lance of Longinus, so he contrived a wicked ruse. As we rode our horses together, our lances leveled, an archer from the wall shot an arrow that pierced my horse's throat and made it stagger and fall."

A groan of terrified amazement came from the listening crowd. Mordred lifted a hand to hush them, that no one miss the words that came next:

> "The Lance of Longinus grounded itself in the muddy earth and ripped from my hand. Even as I plunged, Lancelot rode past and rammed his own lance through my side."

Someone wailed piteously. Men gripped their sides.

> "I was slain in that moment, though it is taking hours for the pollution of my bowels to claim me. Even now, my innards gape from the holes in belly and back. I lie here and dictate these words to young Sir Ronwyn. He has sworn to convey them to you at all haste, or die trying."

With new respect, the nobles looked to Sir Ronwyn, who knelt before Mordred in a posture that told of his panting weariness.

> "Would that this tale of woe were done with my death, but Lancelot's wickedness was not yet spent. While I writhed upon the trammeled earth, he returned to gloat over me. He hefted the Lance of Longinus, which once he had pledged to wield forever in defense of King Arthur. Like a wild wolf, he howled his triumph. His wolf pack—the honorless knights who defected to him—did likewise from the wall. Indeed, all Benwick rejoiced at the triumph of evil.

"But then, out of our own ranks rode a regal figure—King Arthur himself. He was mounted on a white stallion, and wore not only his raiment but his armor—the very plate he wore to conquer all of Britannia. On his back, he bore Excalibur in Rhiannon, and his eyes flashed like lightning. Oh, he was a magnificent sight. I thank God I lived long enough to see him and hear what he said next.

" 'Lancelot, you creeping worm, you who steal the wife of your king, steal his knights, his nation—how dare you exult in your depravity. You have not won this day. You have felled the champion of King Arthur, but not King Arthur. Now, put away the Lance of Longinus, which you swore always to wield in battle for me. Let us just fairly, and one of us slay the other, and be done!' "

Proud smiles filled the faces of those listening. It was as though each of them looked upon the glorious face of the king.

"But Lancelot was ever the coward, and said, 'I will put the Lance aside, but only if you put aside Excalibur and Rhiannon.' Our king had no cause to put them aside, for they were his rightful weapons, granted him by Merlin and the Mistress of the Mists. He refused. Lancelot said, 'Then let us fight with these titanic weapons, and see who wins.'

"King Arthur agreed. Though the Lance of Longinus would undoubtedly strike true and hurl him from the

> saddle, the scabbard Rhiannon would let none of his blood be spilled. Arthur would be pierced but not slain, and once the two men were on foot, Excalibur would slay the rebel. And so, the two men rode opposite ways, preparing to run together."

Mordred glanced up, licking his lips. The long scroll trembled in his hands. All around him, the nobles stared, their faces as white as paper.

> "King Arthur set heel to his horse. It bounded to the gallop. Sir Lancelot set heel to his. It hurled itself forward. In city and siege army, not a whisper came. The thunder of hooves shook every heart. Lances leveled. Shields dressed. Our king rode as he had against Lot of Lothian, against Alle of Sussex. His lance struck true, catching Lancelot's shield and sparking upward and slamming into his shoulder.
>
> "Lancelot's spear struck truer, as was its divine mandate. He aimed not for our king's heart or head, as would a true warrior, but for a precise spot just right and below the notch of the throat. The lance struck and caved armor. It pierced skin and muscle. It crushed ribs and tore through lungs and emerged from our king's back, where it did its most heinous work. There, it slammed into the scabbard Rhiannon—that is what Lancelot sought to destroy with this strike, for to destroy it was to slay our king. Rhiannon split, and Excalibur shattered, and the blow of the Lance turned King Arthur into a fountain of blood."

Tears stood in eyes all around the room. They had not yet burst forth, for the final word remained unspoken.

> "I saw it all where I lay, from the bloodied place whence Sir Ronwyn found me and bore me away. I see it even now as I lie here in death's couch and speak these last words to that same young knight: There was so much blood, and our king fell so loose of joint, I am sure that before he struck ground, he was dead."

The tears flowed now, even from the eyes of King Arthur's son.

> "King Arthur of Camelot is dead, and never have we needed him more. While Arthur and I lay side by side, Lancelot brought his knights and his army forth from the city. They routed us, killed many, and pressed the rest into their service. We are destroyed.
>
> "The slayer of King Arthur now commands what remains of his army, of his knighthood. He has sworn now, with Guinevere at his side, to return across the channel and conquer Camelot itself. He is coming to destroy you as he has destroyed us.
>
> "These are my last words, Mordred: Stop him. Only you can save your father's kingdom."

Mordred read these words with hushed intensity, as if he wished no one else in the room would hear. But they all heard. Every last one.

• • •

Midnight painted the chapel windows black. Candles gave the only light—thousands of candles in thousands of fists. All of Camelot had turned out for the solemn ceremony. They stood tight-packed in the nave, craning around columns, whispering tearful prayers. The breath of the people was stifling, and no relief came in the black breezes of night. A bell tolled the hour, jarring the hearts of those gathered. Its doleful tone died away to nothing, and then came a second terrible stroke. Twelve tolls, each resounding like the word *doom*.

Something arrived at the back of the chapel. There was a definite sense of presence. The folk turned. Their candles came about to shine upon it. Gold greeted them. On a pallet carried between six strong men, there lay not a body, but the figure of a body. It was a golden coat, sewn together from torn tatters. It was the coat of King Arthur. On the night of his coronation at Caerleon, King Arthur had worn a golden robe. To field his conglomerate army, he had torn the robe to ribbons and given each of his warriors a strip to wear as a banner. Years later, when he had conquered all Britannia, he gathered in those strips for this new coat. It lay there upon the pallet, in the very semblance of absent Arthur. At its hand lay a golden scepter. At its head lay the king's own crown.

To have a funeral, there must be a body. This was as near as the people of Camelot could muster.

The packed throng parted before that pallet. They watched tearfully as it passed among them. Candles rose to add their light to the coat's radiance. In their motley midst, the raiment of the king passed. At long last, it reached the altar stone.

There, Mordred stood waiting. He gazed upon the items. He bowed his head. The candle he bore gleamed in a single tear that fell upon the coat. Lifting his face, he wore a mask of courage, and said, "King Arthur is dead."

The words whispered in sorrow among the crowd and fled away.

"King Arthur is dead, but his kingdom will live," Mordred said.

He reached reverently out and lifted the golden coat. He slid it over his own back. With steady fingers, he clasped the golden scepter. In his other hand, he raised the crown. Placing it upon his head, he shouted, "All hail, King Mordred!"

The crowd shouted its deafening reply. "All hail, King Mordred!"

Mordred strode back the way the pallet had come. The people split before him. As he passed, they dropped, one by one by one in fealty. As he strode through the chapel, on the way to his throne, they dropped.

Every one.

32

The True Justs

Lancelot grasped the edge of a battlement, cold with morning. He sat down in the crenelation. He had to think. Below him, just beyond the wall's welling shadow, Gawain waited on his stamping charger. Doom waited.

Gawain was a fine warrior, especially as the sun rose toward its zenith, and he was wroth with fury. The true danger, though, rested in his hand—the Lance of Longinus, carved of oak older than Christ. It always struck true. Any man who went up against Gawain this day would be thrown down. Any man Gawain wanted dead would die.

"What say you, pretender king? Can your stolen bride save you now? Your stolen knighthood? Your stolen nation? This is the blood of Gaheris calling out to you this morning. This is the blood of Gareth screaming from my veins for rectitude. Come, Lancelot! Face me!"

Lancelot gripped the crumbling edge of stone. He must answer. It would be suicide to joust Gawain, and Lancelot's death would be Guinevere's death, and Benwick's. He seemed forever doomed to be the death of those he loved.

Lancelot rose. He felt the grit of the wall eating into his fingers. He called down to Gawain. "You will have satisfaction today, Sir Gawain. Your brothers were great men, and deserved better ends than I gave them. You are a great man, and deserve the best of ends. I wish only that I do not provide it today."

Gawain laughed, a sound that began deep in his belly like a killing cough. "One of us meets a bad end this day, Lancelot. You or me."

"Fight me!" shouted a new voice. Lancelot stared down the wall to his cousin Lionel striding angrily there. "I will joust you, Gawain."

Lancelot reached to him and whispered—"Lionel, do you see what he bears—?"

"Oh, I see what the coward bears," Lionel shouted. "Your own lance, granted you by the very gods. He would bear your own lance in combat against you. Let me, then, be your lance, my king, and strike this man from his seat."

"I'll not have it!" Lancelot growled.

Gawain laughed again blackly. "He has less courage than you, Lionel. Or perhaps little faith in you. I accept your challenge. Come at me, Lionel Lance-a-lette."

That taunt settled it. Lionel turned and strode down the nearest stairs. His horse waited below. Lancelot—his cousin, his king—argued to Lionel's silvery back, but the knight could hear only the red thunder of his own anger. Leaping onto his waiting steed, he rode, steel shoes on cobbles, to the sally port and shouted it open.

Lancelot watched angrily as the guards worked the heavy winch. A block of stone that was both door and deadfall grated slowly up. The passage was wide enough and tall enough for a single rider on a single horse. Lionel's knee cops scraped the sides as he edged the beast within the port. It balked to clamber beneath the weighty stone, but Lionel drove it on. No sooner had the switching tail cleared the space than the windlass whirled, and the stone dropped with a resonant boom.

Lancelot shifted to peer beyond the wall, to the empty grounds where the two foes faced off.

Gawain trotted his steed to one end of the plain. The horse whirled and reared. Gawain was twice Lionel's size, and his mount was equally powerful. He was filled with righteous rage.

Lionel rode the opposite way, lithe and calm. He was a slight man, yes, but a favorite son of Gaul. On his shoulders heaped the weight of cheers from guards all along the wall. This contest drew them like carrion drew vultures. They crouched there and cocked their heads over the stones to see. Their eyes gleamed in black interest, and they gave out throaty calls.

The contest drew more than guards. The cobbles below crackled with hooves. Lancelot glanced down to see his knights, a score of them, arriving with full regalia and lances—as if this were just another tournament. They hitched their horses and climbed to the parapet. Their faces glowed with hope for battle.

Lancelot felt sick. He turned toward the plains. It had been a dry season, and the grass still wore the pallor of winter.

"At last, a chance to fight," came the voice of Sir Bors at his side.

"So, the blow-hard couldn't stand the wait anymore," added Sir Hector. "I'm glad. I couldn't either."

Bors stared levelly at his comrade. "I'm next."

"Yes," Hector agreed amiably. "I'm first, and you're next."

This was play for them. It was not for Lancelot. This was death itself, stalking all of them. He would not let his comrades die, but neither would he slay another son of Lot.

The rumble of hooves below tore thoughts and words from the air. Suddenly nothing existed but two men galloping toward each other on the dry plains of summer. Dust rose in pale clouds from the charging steeds. The riders leaned avidly, shields on hearts and lances leveled. They seemed two stags, antlers jutting ahead, intent on crashing. The mounting crescendo of hooves gave way to the inevitable crack of lances on shields.

Lionel's spear shattered, disintegrating against its target. Gawain's spear—Lancelot's spear—struck true. It caught on Lionel's shield, ripped it backward, and ripped the shoulder and arm that held it. Bones broke. Lionel was levered from the saddle. With a small cry he spun aside. His white-eyed steed charged away. He fell on his shattered arm in the dust.

Gawain rode on. The percussion of his steed's gait slowed to a canter. He lifted high the Lance of Longinus and shrieked to the heavens. "Blood for blood! Who will face me now?"

Bors swung his gauntlet, backhanding Hector's breastplate. "Let's both go. You can aid Lionel, and I'll joust. If there's anything left of Gawain, you can have a go."

Smiling affably, Hector nodded. He shouted over the wall. "Give us a moment. We've plenty more where that came from!" They turned and clattered down the steps toward their horses. As they went, their fellow knights shouted out to them—"Don't worry. We're right behind you." "Get him warmed up for me." "Don't let him hit you in the head—it might break the Lance."

All Lancelot heard were the words of Hector: *We've plenty more where that came from*. The fact was, he didn't have plenty more. These were his friends, his comrades. He would not send them all to the grave, but just now, they seemed happy to send themselves.

The winch worked below, and the sally port stone shifted like the door of a crypt. Out rode Bors and Hector. They rumbled onto the plains, and a cheer poured from the walls. Bors waved as if to a festival throng and pranced his steed along, gathering praise. For his part, Gawain grandstanded before his own troops, who lined up eagerly just out of bowshot to watch.

Hector rode to Lionel, dismounted, and lifted the man, cradling his arm. He positioned Lionel on his steed and led the beast back toward the sally port.

"Guinevere," Lancelot murmured to himself in realization. He reached to the nearest guard and tapped his shoulder. "Run and fetch Queen Guinevere and her healers."

The young man smiled and gestured near the sally port. "She's already here."

Lancelot smiled too, but grimly.

Guinevere stood in company with white-robed initiates, waiting for Hector and Lionel to return. She wrung her hands. As if sensing her husband's attention, she looked up at him, pointed toward the port, and shouted, "You're not going out there."

Lancelot did not respond. He only turned away. He didn't know what he was doing. For the first time in years, Lancelot did not know what he was doing. It didn't seem to matter. The world rushed headlong into destruction without his help.

On the plains, the two combatants rode toward their separate sides. The cheers from wall and field faded before the coming deadliness. Each stroke of the beasts' hooves carried crisply through the warm air. The riders turned and addressed their steeds. Across the field, they locked eyes. They seemed almost to breathe together. Heels came to flanks. Horses whickered and bolted. They surged over earth already blackened by previous hooves, toward a spot marked in Lionel's blood.

Lancelot's knuckles whitened as he gripped the battlement. His teeth ground together.

Steeds converged. They sounded like rumbling hearts. Lances leveled. The men bore together.

Bors's weapon never struck. It was a foot too short.

Gawain's lance smashed the inner edge of Bors's shield. The oaken point scraped inward and bounded to the breastplate and caught. It stove steel and struck flesh like a bludgeon. Ribs cracked in a fine network. Bors's bellow was the lance speaking, not him. He hung upon it a moment, his horse gone from beneath him, and then plunged to the ground.

Gawain rode on, wrenching the Lance of Longinus away and lifting it high. His folk cheered across the field, a sound of jubilant anger.

Bors thrashed in the dust and gulped like a fish. He clutched gauntleted hands to his staved breastplate. Metal scraped on metal. Hurling off the gauntlets, he ripped away the straps and clawed the breastplate off. It seemed he could breathe then, though blood bloomed across his white shift.

"Get to him!" shouted Lancelot. "Hector, bring him in!"

The knight had delivered Lionel to Guinevere and returned to the field, hoping to joust next. Still, he rode straight for his fallen comrade. Lancelot's hands became fists, and the grit ground within them. He flung it out in fury and barked at the guard beside him.

"Get Rasa. Get my lance. Get helm and gauntlets—all of it. You have five minutes."

"Yes, my king," the guard said, wide-eyed. He rushed away.

Lancelot headed for the stairs. He felt Guinevere's gaze. Her eyes were imploring. His were relentless. He glanced toward Lionel, whose arm was set in splints. Priestesses leaned upon him and sang lays over the wounds. Lionel basked in warrior's bliss, suffused with his body's delirious humors, wracked with a pain so great it felt pleasant, and attended by white-garbed beauties. The scene almost made Lancelot sick. All this clash of antlers and rutting afterward—there had to be more to knighthood than this.

He descended the stairs to the street and approached his wife.

Tears stood in her eyes. "You know what's going to happen, don't you?"

Lancelot's teeth were tight. "I know I must fight him."

"He has the Lance of Longinus. It strikes forever true. He wants you dead, and if you face him, he will have you dead."

"It was my lance before it was his," Lancelot muttered. "Perhaps it remembers me."

"It was Christ's lance before it was yours, and it slew him," Guinevere said. A small gasp escaped her lips, as if she had just lost something over a cliff. She flung her arms around him, and the tears fell now. "Let's away to Dalachlyth, Lancelot. Let the fey folk rise from the plains and drag him down and eat his wretched flesh from his bones."

He breathed into her neck, and he was weeping too. "Is that how I am to slay the last son of Lot?"

"Better that than he slay you," Guinevere said.

He held her fiercely. "Why not simply have the archers on the wall fill him with shafts? I cannot. You know that. I must face him."

She pulled away and stared at him with streaming eyes. "You must die?"

Lancelot returned her gaze. "From the moment you were made changeling and were betrothed to Arthur, fate has laid before us only one death or another. We have chosen, and lived all this while in the bleak choosing. This is no different. Death on the field or death on the wall. I must choose. I will live or die in the next moments, and you must let me live or die."

She could not reply, only wrapping him in desperate arms. They stood that way until Hector came, bearing Bors like a slain ram in his arms. He breathed, yes, but blood painted him from shoulders to knees.

Guinevere kissed Lancelot once last. "Farewell, my love," she said, and turned to the wounded man.

"Farewell," Lancelot said.

On the street behind him, his own destiny waited—Rasa and lance and shield, all. Beside the horse stood a guard who mopped his brow with his sleeve.

Lancelot nodded his thanks. He approached, donned his gauntlets and helm, took his shield, and mounted. He rode toward the sally port. At its narrow mouth, he met Sir Hector, heading the same place.

Smiling, Hector said, "I have spoken for the next joust, my king."

"Yes, and I am your king," Lancelot replied. "Follow me, and be ready to bear me back in, as you have borne the others."

The knight's ready smile was tinged with sadness. "As you wish, my king."

They rode, Lancelot first, through the tight channel, beneath the deadfall, and out onto the bloodied plains. From wall and field both came a great cheer when King Lancelot emerged. The sound mounted up—hope, joy, pride, excitement, dread, anger. The very air withered before that noise. Lancelot did not lift his hand or rear his steed. He only rode solemnly out across the trammeled ground toward one end of the field.

Gawain, on the other end, was jubilant. He roared to the heavens and lifted the Lance of Longinus like a lightning rod. A thunderstorm of cheers and shouts answered him. This would be it, the battle that decided the siege.

Nothing felt right to Lancelot. His lance was too light. Rasa twitched nervously. Lancelot had no will for this. He did not want to slay Gawain. He did not want to be slain, but he had ridden forth to do one or the other.

"For my brothers, Gaheris and Gareth, I fight you, Lancelot du Lac!" shouted Gawain from across the field. "For the honor of my king, Arthur, and his queen, Guinevere, I fight you, Lancelot du Lac! For the knighthood and for Camelot and for all that is right, I fight you, Lancelot du Lac!"

Lancelot could little bear to hear the bloodthirsty cheers awakened by that call. Now he must reply. His people waited upon the wall. What would he say? He did not know until the words were tripping out. "For none of those things I fight you. For sake of your brothers, so wrongly and regretfully slain, I would not slay you. For sake of King Arthur and Queen Guinevere, so wrongly and regretfully parted, I would not slay you. For sake of the knighthood and Camelot and all that is right, I would not slay you. And yet, here I sit, prepared to fight my friend, to battle my liege, to do that which has no honor only because I must. Dear Gawain, forgive me this day if my lance, my sword, do you harm, as they have done to all others I love."

No cheers answered that speech. Walls and fields were stunned silent. Even Gawain sat still upon his steed, as if waiting for something more. His horse stomped once in irritation. Gawain snorted. "Don't think you can mourn your way out of this, Lancelot," but there was sadness in his words.

"I know better than that," Lancelot replied. He brought Rasa into direct line with the hoof-marked earth, and said, "Let us do battle."

"Yes!" snapped Gawain, and he dug heels into his mount.

Lancelot paused a moment, wondering why Rasa did not

move. He felt it too, the reluctance. Lancelot pressed his heels into the beast and leaned above his neck and sent him charging. Down a black-churned trail Rasa galloped.

It all felt wrong—horse, lance, and foe—but a true warrior needed only be right himself. Mars-Smetrius spoke in his mind. A thousand jousts spoke in his blood. The shield rose to its precise position. The lance lowered and rode as straight as bow shot. Lancelot converged upon his foe, his friend. His strike would be perfect, calculated to hurl Gawain from horseback but not to slay or even to wound.

Gawain's strike would be perfect too. What he willed, through the Lance of Longinus, would be done.

The horses thundered together.

Lances reached across the emptiness.

They struck at the same moment, tip on shield. They struck the same place, at the heart of the metal. Leftward, a hit would wrench the shield away and shatter the rider's arm. Rightward, a hit would strike the breastplate and crush the ribs. At that center point, though, the blow hurled man and shield and all out of the saddle.

They both toppled backward. Their mounts ran on while the men and their interlaced lances crashed down. Dust mantled them. Shouts from the walls and fields settled in silence. Who lived? Which man would rise?

Gasping, staggering, Gawain lurched to his feet. He seemed an angry bear. His people roared their gladness.

Getting his knees under him, Lancelot rose slowly and stood. From the walls poured adulation. He was deaf to it. He saw only the man opposite him, and the Lance of Longinus lying in the dirt. "You spared me," he gasped out. "You could have struck to kill, but you did not."

Gawain smiled with gritty teeth. "Not yet. I wanted to slay

you, not let your lance do it." He reached over his shoulder and drew his sword—a mighty blade that gleamed in the morning air. "There is yet death to do."

Grimly, Lancelot pulled his sword from its sheath. The Saxon blade, enspelled by Mars, had served him well all these years. He feared only that it would serve him well again this day. "I would not kill you, my friend."

"Then you will be killed," answered Gawain. With a roar, he charged Lancelot.

Unmoving, Lancelot waited for the charge. Gawain was a big man, but his sword work was not the equal of Lancelot's. This stroke, this shrieking overhand, all-out assault, could be bashed easily aside, the tip grounded, and the man struck dead in backhand. It was what Mars-Smetrius whispered to Lancelot. It was what Lancelot grimly planned. As the two warriors came together and Lancelot raised his sword to deflect, in the triangle between the blades he glimpsed Guinevere on the wall. Her face was as white as the limestone.

There had to be good in the world. There had to be a choice other than death or death.

Lancelot bashed aside Gawain's sword. It swung down and stuck in the ground. In follow-through, Lancelot pulled his stroke. Yes, it cracked through armor and cut the man's shoulder. Yes, it brought blood gushing, and made his sword arm worthless, but it did not kill him.

Gawain's hand came loose from his sword. His other hand grasped the welling wound. He dropped to his knees and gasped, "Kill me, Lancelot! Kill me as you killed my brothers—unarmed!"

Staring down sadly, Lancelot said, "I will not, Gawain. Let Guinevere tend you. Let her heal you. Let her heal this whole war."

"No!" shouted the knight. "That witch won't touch me. Arthur's healers will tend this. I will knit, and I will come back, and I will kill you."

Lancelot only called out to the siege army to send their healers. Then he turned his back on his friend and strode toward the city.

For three months, Gawain lingered. He lay upon Arthur's own bed in the farmhouse. Gangrene spread in slow waves from the cleft in his shoulder. Not leeches, not rye spirits, not prayers could stop it. The disease had spread like hate, and now its grasping fingers slid around Gawain's own heart.

The death rattle had begun. Arthur sat by the bedside and clutched the hand of his most faithful knight. Beyond the shutters, the sun had abandoned the world. Red clouds swathed all. The other knights knelt in vigil on the autumn grass all around. They knew a great soul would pass this night.

A fit of coughing racked Gawain. He struggled to his side and spat blood in a bowl already half-full of it. Hacking, he lay back down. His eyes swam with tears. "So," he gagged out, "he has slain us all."

Arthur only held to the knight's hand.

"Sometimes evil wins."

Arthur couldn't argue. He was as slain by Lancelot as any man. And yet he still loved him. All that Gawain could feel was hate.

Gawain's eyes grew wide with new pain, and his mouth opened in a silent scream. When the agony eased, he said, "Don't bury me in this . . . pit. Send me back to Camelot. . . . Bury me with my brothers. . . . Among Guinevere's roses."

"Yes," soothed King Arthur. "I swear it."

A small smile formed on Gawain's face as he looked fondly one last time on his aged sovereign. The smile remained even as Gawain disappeared from behind it. His breath went out of him, and Arthur closed his eyes.

Releasing the man's hand, now as soft as putty, the king rose and strode to the window. He threw back the shutters and stood there, mantled in the last red glow of the sky.

On the grass below, the knights knew, and they wept.

On a crisp autumn morning, a man under the flag of parley rode toward the walls of Benwick. It was not just a man, but King Arthur himself, robed in royal finery. He approached at a solemn gait.

Word tore through Benwick. All the city flocked to the walls to see. Lancelot and Guinevere were there. They watched patiently as their sovereign approached. When he neared, the king and queen of Benwick went to their knees and bowed their heads. Beside them, the guards did likewise. In waves, the folk of Benwick dropped down before King Arthur of Camelot.

He rode to a stop and gazed at them all. From within his robes, he produced a scroll case. He drew out a scroll, cleared his throat, and called to them. "We have been fools, all of us." He lifted the paper. "While we have made senseless war upon each other, Sir Mordred has taken the throne of Camelot and crowned himself king and raised an army to keep us out."

Incredulous whispers filled the air.

The old monarch rolled the scroll and put it away. "While I have sought to capture your kingdom, Lancelot, Mordred has captured mine."

Lancelot rose, extending his arms toward Arthur. "My sovereign, my friend, you *have* captured my kingdom. The folk of

Benwick—and even I, their king—are yours in the fight to come. We will join with your army here. We will sail to Britannia and corner the rat and take back Camelot."

King Arthur only gazed back up at his first knight and his erstwhile queen.

Lancelot went on. "It is not Mordred who took your kingdom from you, Arthur, but me. And now, I will return your kingdom to you. The siege of Benwick is broken. Together, our armies will restore you to your throne. We will remake Camelot!"

In city and out, the armies cried out their gladness.

33

The Battle of Dover

As the previous winter had died, two hundred ships had sailed from Britannia to Benwick. As the new winter tightened its grip on the world, six hundred ships returned.

Waves foamed white before their breaking prows. Oars clove deep in the blue-black flood. Gunwales thrummed with the hands of the sea. The very wind that mounded wave upon wave also bellied the armada's sails. The ships drove northward on a long reach. They left a boiling trail in their wake. Horses whickered in the sterns. Lances lay alongside the keel, and swords hung from the waists of the oarsmen. They would be fighting soon.

At the prow of the largest ship stood King Arthur and King Lancelot, allies in full armor—old warrior and young, flinty-eyed as they stared at the great white seawalls. Beyond them lay their mutual objective. Beyond them lay Camelot.

In the morning sunlight, the white cliffs were dazzling, almost hiding from view the hundreds of sails that stood at their base, the hundreds of ships Mordred had arrayed against them. They seemed almost a thousand. Even at this distance, it was clear they had launched. Sails reached the opposite way across the same wind. Keels shot toward the fleet of Lancelot and Arthur.

"How has he set so many craft in the water?" Arthur wondered aloud. "We took every seaworthy vessel in our assault on Benwick."

Lancelot peered intently forward. "There are two answers to that. First, Mordred has gained many new allies, and their ships, and their men. We will be fighting strangers to win back our home."

Arthur pursed his lips grimly. "What is the second answer?"

"They may not all be seaworthy. Mordred need not cross the channel, only make certain that we do not."

The combined speed of the converging armadas brought their bows close. Each of Mordred's vessels was fronted by a large iron block. They were nearly crewless, with one man at rudder and one man at sheet and one man moving about deck, pouring something.

"We'll meet them half a mile from shore, in twenty feet of water, with five-foot swells," Lancelot said grimly. "They mean to ram us and burn us."

Arthur shouted to the boatswain, "Signal the fleet. Beware the rams!"

Word went out, but too slowly. The ships had closed to a few hundred feet.

"Head-on is the best tack," Lancelot said. "Either we miss them or we strike prow to prow. We cannot get broadside."

"Stow oars," called Arthur. In aside to Lancelot, he said, "If a ship strikes the oars, the men will be battered and thrown overboard." He shouted, "Ready archers!"

Lancelot frowned. "They won't remain aboard long enough for us to shoot."

At fifty feet, Mordred's men leapt from the gunwales into a frigid sea. The craft bore on, their lines cleated and their rudders jammed. Flames burst up from the planks. They engulfed everything. In moments, the masts and sails were mantled. Wind off the canvas only fed the blaze. Fabric flash burned. The ships needed it no longer. They roared in to strike.

A fiery vessel loomed up before the kings' ship. Lancelot felt the prow begin to turn away and commanded, "No! Head on!" The rudder man realigned the ship, and it plunged toward the conflagration.

"We'll be burned alive," Arthur shouted.

Lancelot shook his head. "We'll cut right through. We're twice as heavy, and we have the wind. Brace!"

The two kings crouched behind the dragon figurehead. Everyone on the ship caught a handhold and hunkered. Ahead, sky and sea disappeared, swallowed by a single standing flame. The prows came together.

Buoyed upon a wave, the burning ship struck too high. Its ram caught the dragon figurehead and cracked it off. The wooden sculpture plunged to the forecastle deck between the two kings. The ram pushed onward, but was levered from below. It tipped up. Wind shoved the Benwick ship forward. Its prow sawed right through burning chine boards. A rift as tall and wide as a man opened. A trough formed beneath the ships. Wood splintered. The rift widened until the burning ship lost its bow. Water gushed in. Fires turned to steam and then to nothing. Another wave lifted Arthur's ship, but Mordred's sank beneath the seas. Over its smoldering hulk, they sailed.

As they cresting the wave, Arthur looked abeam. Most of his ships had broken through the vanguard and sailed toward the white cliffs. "Oarsmen, row!" Arthur cried exultantly. They had lost headway, and another wave of vessels approached.

These were fully manned, with soldiers ready at the gunwales. "Archers, ready!"

Lancelot wore a look too fierce to be a smile. "We'll meet at a quarter mile out in ten feet of water. They'll try to come alongside and grapple us. Our best bet is to slip past, make landfall, and fight there."

"Swordsmen, ready to cut grapnels!" Arthur called. He clapped Lancelot on the back. "Why have we not fought this way before?"

Lancelot drew his sword, watching the ship as it came. "We were always too busy fighting each other."

The ships converged. Mordred's men crouched at the gunwales, grapnels in their hands. The two prows passed. Mordred's mainsheet snapped loose, and the sail luffed. The ship heaved alongside. Grapnels flew like spider webs. Their lines uncoiled, men at the other end.

Lancelot reached up, caught a grapnel in midair, and yanked. The man holding to it pitched into the water between the bumping hulls. Lancelot threw the metal claw back, cutting through the enemy mainsail. Another grapnel sailed in, grabbed the rail, and grew taut. Lancelot hewed its cord. Still, there were too many. The ship sides cinched together. Men leapt across.

Arthur caught the first such man on his sword. It impaled him through the gut. The king swung his arm down. The man slid off into churning seas. Another boarder hurled himself onto the king. They fell to the forecastle deck, the traitor on top. His sword swung in a decapitating blow.

Lancelot's blade was quicker. It caught the stroke, hurled it aside, and skewered the man through his heart. As he crumpled, Lancelot reached to help Arthur rise.

Instead of taking the hand, Arthur hoisted his would-be slayer overhead, stood, and flung him into the path of another boarder. They collided in midair. Live man and dead man fell between the crunching hulls.

The sea played havoc with the strapped ships. Wind turned them seaward. Waves ground gunwales against each other.

Hacking at the grapnels, Lancelot said, "We have to win free!"

Arthur joined him, severing more lines. "Even if we kill the men, we still have to fight the sea."

Lancelot smiled tightly. "Not much longer."

Guinevere had been gathering armies below—rorquals, cachalots, kraken, and leviathans. She and the naiads, the selkies, kelpies, merfolk, and spirits of sargasso had plumbed the deeps and gathered her greatest powers. In one hand, Guinevere clutched a breathing conch to her mouth and nose. In the other, she held the mane of a narwhal. She clung to the beast, its skin warming hers in the dark chill. It rose eagerly. Its curled horn shed water in elegant spirals. All around, more creatures ascended—dolphins in their pods, rays like ghosts of muscle, eels in wavering bands. The creatures of the sea joined their spirit kin to rise and fight the strange shapes above.

All footed folk were invaders in the sea. Every last boat above had earned the ire of the creatures below. Still, they would wait to attack until Guinevere gave the sign.

With a final surge of its tail, the narwhal breasted the waves, breaking into light. Ahead, Guinevere saw two ships, roped together and foundering. It took only a moment to make out the livery of Benwick on the one.

The narwhal dived again, and Guinevere guided it gently toward the ship to starboard. The creature obliged, swimming just beneath its keel and whapping it once soundly with its tail.

Out of the teeming depths, creatures rushed upon the waiting hull. Sharks bit, tearing away hunks of wood. Kraken reached their tentacles up to pluck men from the decks and drag them below. Whales surged up to smash the hull and stave it. Water sucked in through sudden breaches. Men leapt from the sides, only to be pummeled by dolphins. In shallow waters, the craft sank.

As Guinevere and her narwhal surfaced a second time, she saw Benwick warriors cut the final grapnel lines. Dragging away from the sunken hulk, the ship once again caught wind and edged her prow landward. Guinevere glimpsed the next pair of beleaguered craft. Arthur and Lancelot stood at one prow.

The narwhal dived. Guinevere held on, breathing the chill air of the conch.

Arthur and Lancelot. Both kings, both husbands, both beloved. How had she come to love two men? As the cold currents dragged away, she knew. What greater men than these two had there ever been?

Up from silty waters, the narwhal swam. She guided it to the foe ship. It rapped its tail upon the hull. In its wake, the denizens of the deep converged to slay. Behind Guinevere came the distinct sounds of wood cracking and buckling and disintegrating.

The narwhal leapt free again. As she rose upon its back, Guinevere pulled the conch shell from her face and shouted to her beloved husbands, "I'll meet you upon the shores!"

The kings of Britannia and Benwick steadied themselves at the battered prow of the ship. The dragon figurehead was gone, shattered. The ship needed none. Arthur and Lancelot led her up. Through waters choked with bodies, she surged. Burning boats and sunken wrecks lay behind. Before lay the beaches of Dover.

"She has a four-foot draft. We'll not get nearer than a hundred yards," Lancelot said, pointing to a line where green seas turned tan. "She'll beach, and we'll have to fight through waves to reach shore. Do you see the troops there, on the green plateaus above the cliffs? They'll be able to rain arrows on us."

Arthur nodded and smiled. Throughout the fight today, Lancelot had analyzed each tactical conundrum. Now, he missed a detail. "Yes, they have the high ground, but look at us. Look abeam."

Lancelot peered out to starboard, and saw fully two hundred ships racing toward the beach, stretched out over two miles. To port, the same scene presented itself. Only in the center did Mordred have archers.

"We'll keep the bowmen busy while our flanks sweep up and take them," Arthur concluded.

Canting his head in acquiescence, Lancelot said, "Yes. It is good. But the way to keep a bowman busy is to keep pulling his arrows out."

Laughing heartily, Arthur said, "As long as you don't leave one in, you should be fine."

The first hiss of sands came below the keel. The ship slowed. All aboard pitched slightly fore. They braced themselves. A grinding sound began across the hull. Wind battered the sail, but still the ship mired. With a final lurch, it stopped altogether.

"Britannia awaits!" cried Arthur.

He seemed a mere boy, eager to the fight, as he hurled himself from the rail. Splashing into the flood, he disappeared a moment. Silt coated him as he rose. Water streamed from the hilt of Excalibur and sloshed in Rhiannon. Ahead of him, the first arrows struck the water and bedded in sand beneath.

"You heard your king!" Lancelot shouted. "Britannia awaits!"

He jumped into the churning tide. It swallowed him as it had Arthur. Sinking feet into the sand, he broke the surface and slogged inland. In moments he had come abreast of Arthur. So had a thousand other warriors. All gritted teeth in seeming smiles. The cliffs lit their faces.

"They cannot stop us," Lancelot said to Arthur even as a hailstorm of arrows cut the water before them. They stepped over the shafts and continued in knee-deep water. "This is our land."

"Yes!" the king said as if in revelation. "This is our land!"

Next moment, an arrow belied the idea, cracking off Lancelot's helm before slapping the waves.

"Visors, don't you think?" asked Lancelot as he lowered his.

"Visors, certainly," replied Arthur. He flipped his closed, gray beard spilling out below.

The water sloshed at ankles now, and the men began to run. Arthur reached over his shoulder and drew Excalibur. Lancelot pulled his own sword. Solid ground underfoot felt good. It made them want to run. So did the shafts that thumped and shuddered in the sand nearby.

Lancelot swung his sword back and forth above his helm. "You have to wonder if you could cut these things out of the air." Another barrage fell on them, and his sword did indeed hurl away a pair of shafts. "Do you see what I mean?"

Arthur pointed at Lancelot's neck, and even within his visor his eyes were wide. "No, I don't."

Lifting his free hand, Lancelot felt the shaft that jutted up from a hole in his chain-mail gorget. Moments later, he felt the warmth of blood pour down his chest. "Yes," he gasped, and realized he could hardly breathe.

Arthur wrapped an arm around Lancelot, drew him up, and ran. He dived for a grassy break. It had gathered enough sand over the years to provide some scant cover from the cliffs above. Arthur grappled his friend, rolling him up against the roots. They lay there, panting, as another salvo of shafts ripped down from the cliffs.

Arthur said, "How's that shoulder of yours?"

"I've got kind of a pain in the neck," joked Lancelot, though neither of them laughed.

Arthur peered up past the grass brake, then pulled his head back as an arrow tore past and embedded in the sand. "I always thought the same of Mordred." That time, they did laugh.

"Didn't you say . . . we had to be careful . . . not to leave one in?" Lancelot asked, gasping for air.

"I did. And you know, I'm king. What I say is law. Let's have a look." Shifting so that both men remained in the cover of the ridge, Arthur pulled back Lancelot's blood-soaked tabard. The arrow jutted down between three metal plates. It had pierced the breastplate strap on its way. "Shoddy armor, son."

"God-damned Saxons. Can you get it out?"

Arthur shook his head. "Not here. Not yet."

"How are we doing?"

Arthur stared along the beach. Bodies lay facedown, their backs filled with arrows. Other warriors crouched at similar ridges, struggling to stay out of fire. No one advanced upon the cliffs. "Pretty well, really." He stared again at the arrow. "I just wish Guinevere were here. She could have this out in a trice."

"She said she'd meet us on the beach. I wonder where she is."

Arthur drew off his helmet, spilling white locks down around his shoulders. His face was worried within his matted beard. "I'm half hoping she doesn't try to meet us—" a fresh barrage interrupted his words, thudding into the earth "—not in this death trap."

Lancelot nodded his agreement. Both men lapsed into silence. Wind brought waves crashing onshore, and water rolled amid stones and gravel. Gulls circled over beached ships, seeking food. The setting would have been placid had it not been torn by war.

Arthur glanced along the shore. Some of his men were standing, staring up at the cliffs. No arrows came out of the sky to slay them. Shifting, the king peered up the white wall, to the figures atop it. Forces still lined the grassy peak.

"It's been a while since they've fired," Lancelot noted.

Arthur grinned. "They can't." He released Lancelot and stood up.

"What are you doing? You'll get shot."

"I said, they can't. Guinevere's got them."

Even with an arrow in his neck, Lancelot sat up, staring up the cliff. At its peak stood Guinevere, in company with Tuatha and dryads, brownies and sylphs. Once she was done marshaling the spirits of the deep, she had shifted to those of the woods. She'd sunk Mordred's ships and routed his army.

"With a queen like her," Arthur said, "it's no wonder we're kings."

"She said . . . she'd meet us . . . on the beach. . . ."

"Let's not quibble—"

Lancelot slumped suddenly, and the sand was red beneath him. "I need her. . . ."

• • •

When he awoke, Lancelot saw first the smiling face of his love, Guinevere. She drew back from him, her fingers bloody. He no longer felt the arrow that had pierced him. Arthur stood beside her. They had saved his life, the two of them. They grinned, dark silhouettes against the white cliffs and blue sky.

The armies of Benwick and Britannia had landed. They were taking back the isle.

34

Bargains

Within a perimeter of forest folk, the armies of Arthur and Lancelot camped that night. Mordred's forces, routed on sea and land, fled northwest. Seelie hounds nipped at their heels, and woodland spirits set gnat-song in their ears. They would return to their supposed king in Camelot and tell that Arthur had landed with a vengeance and was marching upon Camelot itself.

"Next, Camelot," Arthur toasted, lifting high his tankard. It foamed over, fresh drawn from a cask rolled to the fireside.

"Next, Camelot," chorused Lancelot and Guinevere.

They drank heartily. They had eaten heartily that night, too—a roast boar they shared with their commanders, and boiled fish for the troops. The army had brought provisions for a protracted campaign, but after the victory today, they knew this war against Mordred would be swift and decisive. In celebration, they ate and drank.

Around the coals of a once-blazing fire, King Arthur, King Lancelot, and Queen Guinevere sat. There were no stones or stumps nearby, so they sat upon their packs. Red-faced from wind and ale and fire, they stared contentedly into the embers. The day's exhaustion, so long denied, seeped into every tissue. Still, none of them nodded. To sit here full and quiet and free felt wonderful. They kept the silence of friends.

At last, Lancelot rose. He clapped a hand to his neck, healed but tender, and said, "That arrow took more out of me than I had thought. I'd better get some rest." He stretched, lifted his pack, and headed across the clearing to his tent.

"Good night," Guinevere and Arthur said together. They glanced at each other, smiled, and looked away.

"I should sleep as well," Arthur said. "It's a long march tomorrow."

"Good night," Guinevere replied, perhaps too hastily.

The king stood, letting the bitter insinuation slide away. He carried his pack the opposite way, to his tent. Guinevere watched him walk away, still powerful, still manly, even in his gray years. Arthur quietly greeted the guard and slipped within the flap. He lit a lantern, and it cast his image, huge and somewhat twisted, upon the canvas. He rooted through his pack, seeking night clothes.

Guinevere glanced toward the other end of the clearing. Lancelot's tent was dark. Perhaps he was already asleep.

Two kings, two men, two tents. Guinevere buried her face in her hands. Together, the three would win back Camelot, and what then? Did she sit the throne beside Arthur, or the throne beside Lancelot? Did she allow Dalachlyth and the Castle of the Rose to go empty, or did she allow Camelot to fall once more? She could not be queen to two kings.

She was more than a queen, though. Guinevere was a woman. Only in the company of Lancelot could she be a woman.

She rose, lifted her pack, breathed the sharp smell of smoldering embers, and headed across the clearing. The guard greeted her quietly. She drew back the tent flap and stepped within. Setting down her gear, she lay down beside the figure there.

"I had hoped you would come," said Lancelot quietly.

"I had hoped you were not asleep," replied Guinevere. She wrapped him in her arms and rolled on top of him.

"Do you think? Tonight, with your husband just across the way?"

She was unlacing her bodice. "My husband is right here, beneath me." The cloth came up over her head.

"You know what I mean."

Her smile showed even in the dark tent. "I know that today I won a battle and tonight I feasted and drank. There is but one more thing I wish to do, and I cannot with Arthur." Bending down above him, she lightly kissed the tender flesh of his neck, where she had healed him. "You owe me."

"I do," he responded with mock gravity. He laughed and drew off his own shirt.

"Besides, it is the surest way for us to check upon our fey kingdoms," Guinevere purred into his ear. "Much nicer than leaping into a cold puddle."

Lancelot rolled her over and kissed her. "Much nicer."

In the torrid midst of it, a vision came to them—not their glorious kingdoms of fey, but a fearsome vision.

Arthur marched. He was robed in gold. Excalibur shone like a star in his hands. All around and behind him marched the vast army of Benwick and Britannia. They seemed a fleecy blanket Arthur was drawing across the wintry earth. He pulled them behind him toward the icy banks of the Somerset Cam.

Across the river approached a single figure—Mordred. Narrow, vicious, wicked, he walked jauntily. From his hip, he drew a sword that ate light. It dragged a shadow in its wake, a shadow that spread like a tear in the world and swallowed all in darkness. Down the hoarfrosted slope he went, down to the river, resplendent in ice.

Arthur stepped into the chill waters and waded inward.

Mordred paused at the banks and dipped the tip of his sword. It ate heat as well as light. The river froze solid. Crystals raced upstream and down until all the water was rock-hard. In its midst, Arthur was frozen too. He seemed no longer a man, but a figure in ice. Only Excalibur remained.

Mordred strode out across the glassy surface. He reached Arthur. He plucked up Excalibur and held both his swords aloft—blazing light and raging shadow. He held day and night in his hands. Smiling, he kicked once brutally.

The icy form of Arthur shattered. Shards slid out in a starburst upon the frozen river. They came to a stop and transmuted back to flesh—chunks of flesh. Blood wept from them onto the ice. Arthur was no more.

Advancing over the bloody stumps of his father's legs, frozen in the river, Mordred laid into the army with both swords. He tore them apart. Night and day, he laid them in their graves.

Startled and sweating, Guinevere and Lancelot awoke in each others' arms. They panted in the darkness.

"What does it mean?" Lancelot wondered.

"It means we cannot battle Mordred this winter," Guinevere said. "If we do, Arthur, and all of us, will be slain."

• • •

Mordred stared out his tower window in Camelot. He saw a sepulchral land.

Morning refused to come. The sun never rose. It only appeared a few hours into the day, a bloody bolus wrapped in gauzy clouds. Nighttime frost had laid its shroud across the grass, and the bleak sun could not melt it. Only the feet of the refugees melted it, the fleeing feet of Mordred's onetime army. Routed on sea and land, they straggled back to Camelot.

Mordred had planned a triumphal parade for these forces, complete with chains for their prisoners—Lancelot and Guinevere. He had planned that Arthur would be dead.

The army did not return in marching ranks, but in tatters. They did not return with Lancelot and Guinevere in chains, but with them enthroned in nightmare. Worst of all, the warriors of Mordred told that Arthur lived.

It was only a matter of time before those warriors reported to their superiors, and they to the nobles, and the nobles to Mordred. Every last one would want to know why they fought against their own living king.

Mordred hated this—not because there was no way out, but because the way out was so repugnant. There at the windowsill he knelt, a child in prayer. Closing his eyes and clasping his hands, he said, "Mother, my poisons have poisoned me. I repent of trusting my own strength over yours. I had thought to make the lie of Arthur's death true, to stop the armies of Lancelot upon the channel, to bring the faerie queen in chains to my throne. All that I had accomplished is now undone. I beg you, Mother, if ever I was your son, your anti-Arthur born to end his kingdom, come to me now and help me end it."

Morgan was no true goddess, but she was a powerful sorceress. She listened with magic ears to every word her son spoke. Behind Mordred, out of his own gray shadow on the stony floor, she took form. Darkness wove itself into a sable gown draped in black lace. Only her face was white, too white within dark tresses.

She spoke quietly, "Thank you, son, for calling me."

Mordred turned from the window and stood. He warred to keep resentment from his features. "Will you do it?"

"I already have been doing it," she said, smiling sweetly. In her magic, she had remained young, younger even than he. She seemed almost a little girl in a dress of mourning, standing before a man. "Last night, I visited a vision upon Lancelot and Guinevere. They fear to face you in battle this winter."

Mordred could not help grinning. "Can they convince Arthur and their armies to camp throughout the months of cold?"

"No," she replied. "Of course not. But they will press you to surrender."

"What?" Mordred raged.

Morgan's face lost all trace of kindness. Her eyelids were edged like ceramic. "You can determine the terms of your surrender."

"Terms?"

"You will retain your knighthood, and retain the title Prince Mordred, and be granted a large see in Powys, and will be named the royal heir when Arthur is dead."

"I have to wait until Arthur is dead?"

Morgan snapped angrily, "You're a poisoner. You decide when Arthur is dead! Better these terms than that Arthur kill you tomorrow."

Dropping his gaze at her reproof, Mordred nodded. The plan was a good one. It had all the right elements—winning despite a loss, shifting the fight from fields to court, battles Mordred could win. "Thank you, Mother."

"You must draft these terms of surrender today. Couch

them amid more outrageous demands that you will be willing to give up."

"It will be easily done," Mordred said, rubbing his hands.

Morgan shook her head. Already, her body was unraveling itself into shadows. "Not as easy as you think." The last of her disappeared as fists pounded upon the door.

"Let us in, Mordred!" growled a familiar voice. "It is I, Llangolth, Duke of Gwynedd, in company with a score more of your nobles. Arthur lives! The king we thought was dead is alive! Let us in."

Steeling himself, Mordred walked toward the doorway. He consciously banished the fear from his face, donned a mask of confusion and concern, and flung wide the door. "Arthur lives?"

Duke Llangolth stalked in wolflike, and behind him came his pack of nobles. Their hackles were raised and their teeth bared. They circled Mordred. The duke said, "Everyone is reporting it! They say he fought in the vanguard yesterday. They say he fought beside Lancelot, who supposedly slew him!"

"Oh," Mordred gasped, as though the news struck him a physical blow. "Oh!" He spread his arms. "What am I to feel? If this is true, my father lives, and what joy! But if it is true, he must think me the greatest traitor of all time!"

"Not just you, but us!" snarled Llangolth. "You told us he was dead."

Mordred shook his head bleakly. "I didn't tell you he was. You heard the news the same time I did, from the same scroll." He strode to a chest and threw it open, rummaging within. "Where is the damned thing!"

"Never mind that now. Arthur lives. He is marching on us. He thinks of us all as traitors, and we would be if we fought him any longer," Llangolth said.

Mordred's hands grew still in the chest, and he gazed

beyond the tower walls. "We already are traitors, whether we intended to be or not. We already fielded armies to prevent Arthur's return. He could demand all of our heads. . . ." A strangled yelp went up from one of the nobles, and Mordred knew he had them. "Unless we surrender to him."

"Surrender?"

"Yes," Mordred said feverishly, as if the idea was only just occurring to him. "Dictate the terms of our own surrender. Indicate we did not know our king yet lived. Indicate that we surrender on condition we all retain our titles, positions, and lands, that none of us lose our heads, that there shall be no punitive taxes or other measures taken against us. Only then do we surrender and reaffirm our fealty."

The duke's face was swollen with blood as he gaped at Mordred. "Well, get writing. We'll sign it all. Get writing!"

A cold week had passed since the victory at Dover. Arthur and his allies had marched steadily inland until they camped within a mile of the Somerset Cam.

This frozen morning, Arthur sat a war horse, Excalibur, and Rhiannon at his back and the Lance of Longinus couched beside him. He waited upon the fields beside the Cam, what was called the Camlaun. He was in grand company. To his right, Lancelot waited aback Rasa. Full barded and panoplied, knight and steed never looked more glorious. The rest of Arthur's knights completed his company—Lionel, Hector, Bors, and the friends of Lancelot as well as the new knighthood who had besieged Benwick. All were united now, and all resplendent in armor and finery. Behind them waited the massed armies of the allies, eighteen thousand strong. They assembled this morning not for war, but for peace.

Mordred wished to surrender. Word first came to Arthur's camp at Dover. The initial offer of terms was patently absurd, and Arthur said so flatly. He underscored his point with a sixty-mile march inland. Another offer came, better but still unacceptable. The allied armies swept northwest toward Camelot. Only here, on the banks of the Somerset Cam, did a reasonable surrender arrive. Mordred would renounce his throne but retain the title of prince. He would be granted a tract of wild Powys to rule, and would be recognized as the royal heir. Arthur would not put to death or strip of title or lands any of the nobles who had sided with Mordred. Simply put, Arthur would regain his throne and Camelot would return to the way it had been before the siege of Benwick. The conspirators—they called themselves the bereaved nobles—claimed they had done what they had done in grieving ignorance, believing him dead. They spoke of a falsified report from Benwick, though no one now could find it anywhere.

Arthur didn't believe them, but he didn't need to. He was done with war. Let the rats live, that the people might live as well. Too many bodies floated in the channel. Too much blood turned the white cliffs red. Let war be done. Arthur would rather spend the cold corners of winter in a warm bed in Camelot.

If only Guinevere could be part of the deal. If only she were captive to Mordred and not to Lancelot. Arthur dismissed the thought. No treaty could undo what had been done there.

"Let us meet them," Arthur said simply. He pressed his heels to his mount. The horse started down the frosty slope of Camlaun. The company of knights followed, leaving the infantry on the field. Arthur and his escort headed toward the river's ice-choked banks. The Cam flowed cold and clear between gentle hills, its bed covered in round rocks.

Beyond the river, atop a low rise, waited so-called King Mordred. Though he had come to surrender, he wore equal panoply to that of his father. Around him stood his own warriors. Arthur would not call them knights. They were a bunch of strangers. They seemed little more than brigands in fine clothes. Helms shone with polish, but within them lurked broken noses and rotten teeth and shattered honor. The brat had brought bullies to defend him.

Arthur clucked. It made no matter. They had not come to fight, but to surrender. If they tried anything—Arthur almost hoped they would try something—he had instructed his armies to attack. At first sign of naked steel, the brigands would learn how true knights fought. The armies of Benwick and Britannia would take back Camelot, and then there would be no terms. Mordred would die by Excalibur in the eye, or if he ran, he would die by the Lance of Longinus in his back. Whether by treaty or by war, Arthur would rule Camelot by the end of the day.

His steed splashed across the shallow ford of the Cam. It whickered softly at the cold, but soon gained the far bank.

Rasa and Lancelot rode close beside Arthur. Lancelot's eyes were eagle-bright. He was worried about this day. He had had a vision, and feared that despite all, it might come to pass. His gaze roamed the wintry wood behind Mordred. He did not look to the army arrayed within that wood, but to the tree boughs themselves.

"What are you looking at?" Arthur asked quietly, his breath ghosting on the morning air.

"I thought I saw something in the treetops," Lancelot replied urgently. "Not something, but someone."

"Who?"

Lancelot looked to his king, lips pursed tightly like the

mouth of a drawstring bag. At last, he said, "Morgan le Fey."

Arthur laughed loudly at that, as if to banish that dark name. "You and your visions."

The company of knights rode their stomping steeds up from the water. They mounted the frosty banks of the far side. Hooves bore them steadily toward Mordred.

Did he truly plan to surrender? Did he plan some ambush? If so, why would he stand so exposed in the vanguard?

Arthur rode up before his son and halted his steed. All around him, the knights did likewise. Breath rolled whitely from the king's helm. His eyes were ice blue as he stared at Mordred.

The usurper returned his gaze without defiance, without anything but repentance. "In surrender, I will sign our treaty and kneel to you, Father," he said sadly, "but must I kneel to your horse?"

Something in Arthur said, Yes, let him bow before my horse too. But this was his son—his bastard, wayward, traitorous son, but his son all the same. "Dismount," Arthur called to his company. As one, the king of Britannia and his knights stepped from their saddles.

The pretender king of Britannia and his warriors meanwhile dropped to their knees.

Mordred clasped his hands, and said, "Forgive me, Father."

Sadness and hope fled through Arthur. It was as though the window to the future had been thrown wide, and from it came a fresh breeze. Mastering himself, Arthur reached beneath his tabard and drew forth the final treaty Mordred had sent. He unrolled it and drew out a quill that had not yet tasted ink. He stepped to his son and held the items forth.

"In blood we will sign this, you and I, Mordred. Ink is not enough for such things. We must be blood-bound."

Still on his knees, Mordred nodded and took the treaty and quill. He reached down to his sword but did not slide it forth. Only his finger ran upon the blade. He lifted his hand. A red serpent of blood ran down his finger. Dipping the quill in it, Mordred signed his own name to the treaty. He flicked the blood from his hand and sucked his finger as he handed the scroll back to Arthur.

The king reached over his shoulder and slid his finger on the edge of Excalibur. He pulled his hand away, but there was no blood. The scabbard Rhiannon had healed him.

"Do you plan to sign in my blood?" asked Mordred from his knees. "Otherwise, you will have to doff your sword and scabbard."

"No!" cried Lancelot beside Arthur. "He will not doff them. He will not sign in his blood. He will sign in mine. I am as much to blame for sundering Camelot. Let my blood seal the pact between you."

Mordred smiled sickly, his teeth lined in red. He nodded his approval. His finger dripped upon the ground.

Lancelot reached for his sword. He would do as the other two had, cut himself without drawing steel, lest the armies see it. His hand fastened upon the hilt. His forefinger sought out the base of the blade.

Without warning, he drew his blade and lashed down between Arthur and Mordred.

Both kings fell back. Lancelot's sword cut through a red viper that had risen, hissing, from Mordred's blood. It was no mere phantasm. The severed halves of the snake writhed upon the ground between them. Lancelot hacked again, chopping it into three and then four. Still the serpent squirmed. His sword rose and fell. Mordred and Arthur stared at the bloody spectacle in shock and horror. At last, the chunks of viper lay still. Its horrid hiss was silent.

Only then did they hear the roar of armies converging. Across the Cam and in the woodlands beyond, warriors had seen naked steel and flying blood. They ran together.

Treaty turned to war.

35

The Battle of Camlaun

This was how it would be, Lancelot realized. Mordred had tricked them all. Mordred or his witchy mother. They had lured Arthur here and turned blood into a viper and turned treaty into war. This is how it would be. Very well, Mordred would die.

Lancelot's sword was the first drawn, the banner that brought all the other warriors running, and he would use it. He lunged at Mordred.

The pretender king threw himself backward from his knees and rolled. He clutched his lame hand against him and scuttled away.

Instead of skewering the pretender, the sword met steel. One of Mordred's thugs loomed up. Metal clanged on metal. A meaty arm rammed Lancelot's sword aside. The warrior charged.

Lancelot stepped away. He brought his blade whirling down on the brute's neck. It bit deep. Blood melted the frost. The man dropped nerveless—the first kill in a day full of killing.

This was not how it was supposed to be, blood and ice. At

least his vision had not been borne out. At least Mordred had not slain Arthur. If there was to be no treaty, let there be war.

Shouldering forward, Lancelot placed himself before his king. He swung his sword violently, warding off the blows of three warriors at once. Ah, this was more like it. They pressed their attacks. Lancelot bashed away one blade, and then another, and the third. He had to do more than defend. There were three adversaries and three basic strokes—parry, riposte, and attack. The man to his right jabbed at Lancelot. He caught the stroke and threw it back. The man to his left swung a decapitating blow. Lancelot tangled blades and wrenched his foe's sword free. The man directly before him stabbed at his belly. With a neat sidestep, Lancelot brought himself up before his foe and skewered him. Even as he crumpled forward, Lancelot slashed the first man across the neck. The other had dropped his sword and run.

Lancelot advanced into the space he had carved out. Traitors retreated before him, but someone shoved up alongside. King Arthur strode forward with Excalibur foremost.

"What are you doing?" Lancelot asked. "If they kill you, then this whole thing is over."

Excalibur responded for him, falling like a hammer and smashing a man to the ground. "I am a warrior king, Lancelot. I won my nation with my sword, and will win it again that way." He took another stride up the slope and cut a man in half.

Lancelot feared to see the king in that thicket of steel, but then he remembered Rhiannon. Arthur could not bleed while he wore the scabbard. More, as he watched his sovereign attack and throw back man after man without ever being struck himself, Lancelot knew that even without Rhiannon, the warrior king could hold his own. Laughing, Lancelot called out, "Just don't go so fast. We can't keep up!"

"I can't wait," shot back Arthur with a brutal grin. "I'm on my way to Camelot."

A charge began behind them. They heard hooves pounding the ground. Someone shoved Lancelot's shoulder, and he turned to see Rasa. The brilliant beast had urged Arthur's horse forward as well.

"If we are going to Camelot, let's go in style," Lancelot called, swinging up onto Rasa's back. The horse reared, his front legs bashing down a pair of rebels that charged the king.

Grinning, Arthur pulled himself into his saddle. "What is chivalry without a horse?"

Taking a cue from their king, the Knights of the Round Table mounted as well. They pressed the attack. Like men at the harvest, they hewed traitors. The treaty would be signed in blood this day, more blood than could ever mark a page.

As the knights rode forth to meet with Mordred's band, Guinevere waited in the woods. She marshaled the woodland folk. Dryads little liked the cold and emerged sluggishly from the ancient oaks where they lived, but they did emerge. Pixies glowed a little bluer in the frosty air. The spirits of the wood slumbered with winter. Only a few came forth to see the treaty signed.

The water spirits were easier to muster. While the river ran, they swam through it. Selkies, kelpies, naiads, and wee washers all watched in the depths while the horses churned across the ford. They bore an understandable interest in all things that splashed through their waters, but were reluctant to show themselves in full daylight.

Only the spirits of air—welkin walkers and spectres and winds—were eager to gather. Winter empowered them. Snow, sleet, frost, gales, and cold all were the weapons they bore, and they were eager to use them. Guinevere had had to convince them they probably wouldn't need to.

Then, Lancelot's sword flashed. It seemed he struck Mordred or Arthur—Guinevere couldn't tell. The blade went down clean and came up covered in blood. It rose and fell again. Mordred and Arthur both were falling back, and Lancelot's sword flung blood on them.

Guinevere gaped. What was happening?

Her question was answered by tens of thousands of mouths roaring and feet running. In a great tide, the armies of Benwick and Britannia rushed down the Camlaun. Their swords gleamed in their hands as they ran. They crunched across the river's icy bank and splashed through its rocky ford and climbed up the far side.

From the forest behind Mordred, another roar came. Swords flashed like moth wings among the boles.

They would fight, all of them. They would die, all of them.

"Come, children of the forest," Guinevere called urgently to them. "Come, fight!"

Though she had had trouble waking them, the roar of armies had done what she could not. From countless crevices emerged dryads, woody and slender. From mushroom rings came brownies armed for battle. Pixies poured out of every hollow to fly in agitated swarms around them.

Spreading her arms to draw them out behind her, Guinevere ran. In her wake came the forest folk, furtive in daylight, more dream than real.

Guinevere reached the Cam, not at the shallows where the army crossed but in the deep wells beyond. She plunged in.

Cold cut through her, but she swam. Her mind reached out through the waters to summon up the mysteries lurking beneath.

Rise, children of the waves. Come fight!

At the far bank, she pulled herself to dry ground. Water poured off her, but not all of it was water. Some were water spirits. Fluid and feral, water horses rose and champed. On their back rode selkie warriors, in their manlike semblance. Naiads, angular and angry, flowed in company around their mistress. The ranks of Otherworld creatures grew wider.

"Children of air," she called as she ran up the hillside. "Come! Fight!"

Out of the gray sky came blustering spirits. They whirled in frigid vortices and left trails of frost in their wake. Some had humanlike faces, wailing as they passed. Others were just presences that made hearts quail and blood run cold. All eagerly rushed upon the foe.

Guinevere had swung wide to strike Mordred's flank, and now she ran amid his grim-faced warriors like an apparition. Garbed in air spirits and water spirits and wood spirits, she was hard to see, but her touch was undeniable. Ice formed across warriors' faces, plugging their noses and freezing their eyes shut. Roots grabbed warriors' feet and pulled them down to be clawed to bits. Howls shattered warriors' ears so that the blood ran down and they staggered in a deaf daze. Guinevere raced among their ranks, trailing spirits behind her. The idle dreams of the folk became nightmares. For every one man slain by the fey, three more retreated, gibbering in dread.

It was horrible, but it was war. The land would not be ruled by strangers.

• • •

Arthur had not fought this way since he had been young, since he had first won Camelot. He had almost forgotten the blood-price he had paid to build his kingdom. Today he would pay the same blood-price to ransom it from Mordred.

Mordred. Where was he? If that one worm were to die, none of the rest need do so. It was not simply revenge now. Every moment Mordred lived was another gallon of blood.

Gazing out above the horrible press—Arthur and his knights had cut their way through Mordred's personal guard and now fought mounted warriors—Arthur glimpsed the erst-while king. He had scrambled back a quarter mile on palms and buttocks, and now was well beyond the fighting. He headed for a nearby vale, probably to hide beneath some rock.

With a loud growl, Arthur smashed back the sword of his most recent foe. He brought Excalibur down, cleaving the man cleanly from helm to heart. The body slumped from the shriek-ing horse. It was in Arthur's way, hemmed in by the cavalry behind.

In sudden inspiration, Arthur sheathed Excalibur and drew the Lance of Longinus. He leveled it over the horse in his path and struck the next rider, knocking him from his steed. "Yah! Yah!" the king cried, digging heels into the flanks of his mount. It reared, unable to move, but when it came down, a small space had opened before it. Bounding forward, the horse brought the Lance in range of another fighter. It flung him from the saddle, too. "Yah! Yah!" King Arthur drove his steed to a trot. He cleared the way with the Lance and shoved the riderless horses aside. Jousting in the midst of a throng, King Arthur rode until he reached a gallop. In moments, he had pushed past ten, and then twenty riders. The final few were not simply thrown down, but slain by the Lance. He yanked it from their fouling flesh and galloped into the open woods beyond.

This bloody business was a fight between father and son.

It had begun with them.

Let it finish with them.

With the lance still leveled, King Arthur charged over the ridge where he had seen Mordred disappear.

"Where are you going?" Lancelot shouted amid the clangor of sword blows.

Arthur rode like a madman through the traitorous cavalry ahead. He even used his lance rather than his sword. With it, he carved a narrow channel that opened just before him and closed just behind.

"Where is he going?" Lancelot called to the other knights. No one answered. They all had their hands full. "Wherever he's going, I'm following."

Rasa knew. He breasted the flood of riderless horses. There was no one to slay here, only horse heads darting, seeking escape.

Lancelot pushed among them like a drover among sheep. He had to lean to reach any traitors. Lashing out to his right, he caught a nearby sword and flung it away. The blade spun over once and clanged against the breastplate of another warrior. Stunned, the man did not see Lancelot's jab. It caught him in the shoulder piece, and he fell.

Craning above the crowd, Lancelot glimpsed the last flash of Arthur's mount. It galloped over a rise and down into the vale beyond. Worse, two of Mordred's cavalrymen turned their steeds from the pack and gave chase.

"Oh, no, you don't," Lancelot snarled.

Rasa bounded, bulling his way past the other horses. They shied from him, and his canter broke into a gallop. The final steed, a roan gelding, got the full brunt of a blow. Rasa's shoulder struck its hip, and the beast spun about like a crouching dog. It whickered its anger, but Rasa was already far beyond. He ducked his head. He dug his hooves into the frozen ground. Trees hurtled past, alarmingly close.

Rasa chose a clear path parallel to the trail left by one of the cavalrymen. With huge strides, the white stallion closed the distance. He pulled up alongside the piebald, a narrow screen of trees flashing between them.

The rider glanced over, expecting to see one of his own. His eyes grew wide.

Lancelot looked forward, judging the time to the next tree, and swung. His blade chopped shallowly into the man's neck. Lancelot hauled the sword back, simultaneously dragging the rider from the saddle. He fell in a tumble and crashed against a tree.

"Where's the other one?" Lancelot growled.

Rasa turned and bolted toward the second rider. He was a stone's throw away, nearing the rise where Arthur had disappeared. Hooves pounding, Rasa hurled himself on an intercepting path. Muscles corded and rippled beneath his white hide. He closed as if the other horse stood still. They converged. Lancelot hadn't even the chance to get his sword out before him. Rasa barged against the other beast. It screamed and fell. Horse and rider smashed against an ancient oak.

As they thrashed, Rasa ran on. He broke from the forest and slowed, circling back.

"What are you doing, Rasa?" Lancelot shouted. "We've got to find Arthur."

Rasa only snorted and pawed the ground.

Lancelot looked up to see three more of Mordred's cavalry heading their way. "Or, we make sure they don't," he said tightly. Still panting from their last ordeal, horse and rider bounded toward the three newcomers. Lancelot sheathed his sword and lifted his lance from its couch. "Might as well try it Arthur's way." He leveled the lance and bore in.

What had happened? What was that with my blood? Snakes don't come out in winter. Snakes don't form themselves out of blood. What was that? Mordred's mind reeled with questions as he scrambled away from the battle. Battle? Whatever happened to treaty, to shifting the fight into the court, where he could win? A small man with a ruined arm and a bloodthirsty father—what chance did Mordred have now? Why had any of this happened?

There was a single answer to all those questions. Morgan le Fey. She had summoned the asp. She had suggested the treaty, and she had broken it. But why?

Mordred would have answers. By Jesus, he would have answers. He was still king, after all, and what was his mother anyway? Just an angry witch. But to question her, he had to survive, and to survive, he had to get away from the battle.

He was far enough now from the main fight that he could turn and run. Mordred did, pelting over a ridge and down into a vale beyond. It was a rocky place, with great gray slabs of stone jutting from the broken earth. A creek fell down the hillside. At the end of the vale, it gathered in an ice-covered pool before trickling away. Some of the stone shelves had hollows beneath them, narrow caves. In other places, wedges of rock leaned together, creating triangular dens. Here, he could hide, perhaps indefinitely. Here, he could call down his mother.

Keeping low, Mordred scrambled down among trees to the crumbling cliff. He saw a likely space, narrow and dark and deep, and scurried back within it. Stone closed around him. It made his footsteps loud. He reached the end of it and crouched down. His heartbeat was loud too. At least it was dark. Only a long sliver of light shone from the world beyond.

Mordred hunched. "Mother," he whispered breathlessly. The sound was like a rasping cry. "Mother, what have you done to me?"

She always listened to what he said. She came. There was no need to knit herself from the darkness this time, for it was all darkness. She surrounded him. *Did you think you were the only one who wanted to win this war?*

"I thought you were on my side," Mordred replied. "I thought if I won, you won."

No. If you won, Arthur would return to Camelot, and rule until you killed him, and then you would rule Camelot until someone killed you, and then he would rule Camelot until someone killed him. Do you see how this is not what I want?

"You don't want someone to kill me?"

No. I don't want Camelot at all. I want no man to rule this land. I have arranged all of this not so that you will win or Arthur will win, but so that no man will win.

Mordred had not thought he could be more frightened until that moment. He couldn't help panting. "You want anarchy, utter destruction?"

How little you know me, Son. Before Camelot, Old Powers ruled the land. The Romans could not conquer them. They built Antonine Wall and Hadrian's Wall to keep them out, but that only blocked the Picts, the people who worshiped the Old Powers. Even the Celts could not conquer them. Then came Arthur and Camelot, founded upon the realm of fey, drawing upon the Old Powers, but marrying to them this new Christ.

Now Merlin is gone, now Guinevere is gone. All that remains are the Christian sword and the Christian lance and the Christian cup. The knights themselves are becoming monks. When Christ sits upon the throne of Camelot, the Old Powers will be dead forever.

"Mother, I would not turn to Christ!" Mordred protested.

All men turn to Christ, for he is a man's god. Better that no man rule Camelot. Better that there be no Camelot.

At last, Mordred understood. A strange calm came with that realization. "So you intend that this day will be the death of Camelot. The death of us all?"

No answer came. His mother was gone. Something moved beyond the space where Mordred hid. He peered out of the darkness and saw his father, King Arthur, peering in.

36

Death

Are you going to come out?" asked King Arthur, peering into the deep cleft. His son cowered in the darkness. "Or am I going to come in?"

Mordred pressed himself against the rock wall. There was no escape. "You would murder me in cold blood?"

The afternoon's gray light made Arthur's face seem the color of his beard, made him seem a statue. "You murdered me in cold blood, with that scroll you wrote. But no, I will not murder you in cold blood. I will kill you in hot blood. Come out and face me."

"You have Excalibur. How is it a fair fight when you have Excalibur?"

"You have a sword, Mordred. It is a fair fight."

"You have the scabbard Rhiannon. It heals you. You cannot be hurt."

"I will put the scabbard aside, and swear not to use it while we duel." He reached up and pulled the sheath and sword off his shoulder. He drew Excalibur, and tossed the scabbard away to lie on a nearby shelf of stone. His voice nearly roared with command. "Now. Come out!"

Mordred took a few more deep breaths. Then, still crouching, he scuttled forward through the cleft. "Back away, so I can get out of here and draw my sword."

Bowing slightly, Arthur backed away. "Why has it come to this, Son?"

"You tell me," shot back Mordred as he reached the edge of the cave. "You're the one calling me out to kill me." He dropped to the ground outside and stretched his back. "Never mind. It's too late for you to father me. You might as well kill me."

Arthur nodded grimly. "Arm yourself."

Mordred pulled his sword from its sheath—the first he had drawn it since the battle began. It was sharp, and he was quick with it, but his most deadly weapon was already in use. "As far as I remember, our relationship went awry when you decided to rape your own sister."

The king visibly winced at that stroke. He strode forward, lifting Excalibur.

Mordred backed away, his sword at its guard position. "I suppose you should be credited for not simply killing her once you were done with her. From what I understand, it is a tyrant's prerogative to rape and murder."

Excalibur descended in a blow that was more rage than precision.

Mordred stepped to one side and batted the sword away. It struck the ground, and he leaned nimbly in to lash Arthur across his jaw. Mordred withdrew before Excalibur could rise again. Blood wicked down the man's gray whiskers. It wasn't a killing blow—unless enough of the contact poison washed into the wound—but it was first blood, and it was infuriating.

Growling, Arthur advanced, but Mordred dodged side to side and scampered away across ledges of stone. The king followed. "Stand still, you whelp. Are you dueling me, or running tail-tucked again?'

Mordred leapt up onto a higher shelf and kicked loose a stone. It sailed across the air and cracked against Arthur's breastplate. "Dueling, I assure you, Father. But dueling my way."

The king climbed after him, tireless and serious. "Oh, yes, your way. The way of deceit, lies, trickery."

"It is a way," Mordred said as he leapt down suddenly beside his father and tried to jab him.

Arthur was too quick. Excalibur struck the sword, flinging it to one side, and then swung inward. The blade could cut through stone, and it severed Mordred's breastplate as though it were nothing. It cut the flesh beneath as well, an eviscerating stroke. Mordred's belly burst open, and he fell backward from the ledge. With a crash, he landed on a shelf of stone below.

"Damn it!" Arthur growled. He hadn't wanted to eviscerate his son. He had wanted a clean kill, but Mordred's antics had distracted him. Grinding his teeth, Arthur turned and leapt down to the lower shelf to finish the kill.

Except that Mordred wasn't there. Ragged breaths came from a hollow beneath the ledge.

Arthur leaned down and peered in. "Come out, Son. You'll only die of slow misery in there. Come out, and let's be done."

A sword hacked from the darkness. It chopped through Arthur's helm and cut into his skull. He reeled back, and the sword shrieked against the riven helm as it pulled loose. Arthur sat down, his hands catching him before he dropped off the stone. He couldn't see out of one eye. It was covered in a cascade of blood. Arthur reached up and felt the wound. Bone edges jutted from it, and his skull was partly caved.

He roared. The sound was strange in his own ears. It echoed oddly.

The roar turned into a laugh, his son's laugh. From the hollow came Mordred's voice. "It's a poisoned blade, you know. You can't cheat this death. Now, who's dying slowly?"

Arthur's arms trembled before him, and Excalibur shivered. "We're both dying, Son."

"No, Father," Mordred replied lightly, "because, you see, I have Rhiannon. You left it too near at hand. The scabbard is healing me. Once my belly is sewn back together, I'm going to come out there and give you the mercy of a quick death."

Arthur struggled to his knees, to his feet. He could hardly balance. He had to balance. He walked toward the edge of the shelf and lowered himself down. With his feet on the ground, he tottered toward his horse.

"So who's fleeing, Father?" came the mocking question. Mordred shifted in the cleft, apparently trying to stand, but his groan told that he was not ready. "Who's the coward, Father?"

Arthur reached his steed and stood a moment, steadying himself. He rested his head on its side. Blood ran thickly down the creature's pelt.

"You can't even get into the saddle, let alone ride away."

Arthur grasped part of the saddle and yanked. He didn't pull himself up, but pulled the Lance of Longinus from its couch. Grasping it in both hands, Arthur strode back toward the shelf of stone and the cleft above it.

More laughter poured out of the darkness. "Old fool. You cannot kill me, cannot even hurt me while I have your scabbard. That lance might have killed the Christ, but it will not kill Mordred."

Arthur climbed stiffly onto the ledge and clumped over before the cleft, making sure to stay out of reach of Mordred's sword. He leveled the lance, pointing it into the darkness. It always struck true. With another wordless roar, he lunged, putting all his weight against the spear. It rammed into its target and shattered it, with a resonant boom. Then came the glassy cascade of jewels from the sundered scabbard.

Mordred shrieked in rage.

Arthur backed up grimly, set his feet, and readied the lance.

Mordred hurled himself, sword first, from the cave.

The Lance of Longinus struck. It stove what remained of Mordred's breastplate, pierced skin and muscle, shattered bone, and ran through the man's heart. Out poured blood and water. Mordred's eyes went gray. He dropped his sword and slumped, dead, to the stone.

Arthur let go of the lance. He too fell. They bled together across the great dolmen, a pair of sacrifices.

Lancelot yanked his blade from the helm of the third horsemen. The man toppled. His steed shied as if to catch him. It ran upon a tree. The man struck the bark and slid down. More hooves sounded ahead.

Lancelot looked up. Five more traitors peeled away from the cavalry engagement. Their fingers jutted toward Lancelot, and they kicked their steeds forward.

Three, he could stop, but five? Wearily, he lifted his sword and said, "Rasa, let's go."

The horse did not respond. He only stood as the rumble of hooves grew louder.

It was more than hooves though. Something was breaking up through the ground—roots, saplings, vines, thorn brakes. A hundred thousand twisting tendrils cracked the frozen earth and rose. They twined around each other and wove a dense thicket between Lancelot and the charging cavalry. Among the boughs were other things, incorporeal things—fingers, arms, shoulders, faces, wills. The fey. The army of them had swept up to hem in the cavalry battle.

From their midst came a real creature. She stepped from the thorny tangle, changing from spirit to flesh, and ran to Lancelot. Guinevere's face was bone white.

"It's Arthur," she gasped, reaching to him. He pulled her up behind him on Rasa. "We've got to get to him."

Before Lancelot could speak, his steed was galloping toward the ridge and the vale beyond. The woods flew by, black lines against pitching planes of gray. Guinevere clung to Lancelot as they rode. Her hands were cold. Rasa topped the rise and plunged down into the vale. Iron shoes struck sparks on the shelves of stone as he descended toward the creek. Leaping across it, he rose up a berm on the far side and came to a horrible sight.

There upon a stone ledge lay Arthur and Mordred, father and son. Mordred had been impaled on the Lance of Longinus. It had burst his heart, and his blood made a pool beneath him. Arthur lay nearby, on his back. A deep cleft through helmet and head welled with blood. It filled the socket of one eye and poured in a steady stream down the king's temple. Through it all, he still clutched Excalibur.

Guinevere slid down from the saddle and climbed to Arthur. She fell to her knees at his side. Her hands moved quickly about the wound. "We have to get this helmet off," she said to herself, but the edges of the steel had crimped inside the wound.

Lancelot knelt and gingerly worked to slide the helm off. He couldn't. The metal held on like fingers.

"It's no matter. . . ." Arthur said weakly.

"You're awake!" Guinevere gasped.

"Mordred's sword was poisoned," Arthur said. "Even if you could get the helm off . . . you couldn't heal me."

Lancelot peered desperately around the ledge. "Where is the scabbard—Rhiannon?"

"Shattered," Arthur replied.

Despite the helm, despite the poison, Guinevere laid her fingers gently within the cleft. She began to sing. Her fingers trembled. Tiny motes of energy swirled within the bloody groove. They tugged at the severed flesh, struggling to reignite the spark of life there. Already, the tissue was necrotic. Already, the poison was sinking deeper, beyond the reach of her magic.

"Do you remember Mount Badon?" Arthur said with a sigh. "How I was laid open, and you knitted me . . . hours upon hours . . . ?"

"Yes," she said, trying to smile, though her eyes brimmed. She sang more.

"Do you remember the Bedgrayne? Lot nearly killed me. . . . Only you and Rhiannon saved me."

"We'll save you again," Guinevere said.

The king reached up and clasped her hand. He pulled it away from the wound. His own blood covered their fingers. "No. This is the end. You know it is."

Guinevere looked to Lancelot. "Lift him. I can't heal him, but Brigid—"

"Yes," said Lancelot. He placed Excalibur upon Arthur's chest, reached under him, and picked him up.

"There!" Guinevere said, pointing to where the creek emptied into an ice-covered pool. "There."

With the grace of his Tuatha blood, Lancelot carried his king across the stone ledge, down the slope, and to the pool.

Guinevere followed, pausing to yank the Lance of Longinus from Mordred. She dragged the thing across the rocks, lifted it, and rammed it into the ice, which shattered. Blood floate in the pool. She tossed the spear aside and clutched Arthur' hands. "To Avalon."

"To Avalon," the king said weakly.

They leapt into the icy water and sank straight away. Bloo crazed the liquid. The surface closed over their heads. Ice shard cracked together. Then even they were gone, and all was tum bling blackness. Arthur, Lancelot, and Guinevere bumpe through the cold veins of the world. In darkness, in chill, the clung to each other.

Suddenly, they stood beside the Lake of Avalon. It steame in the winter air. Ghosts of mist whirled about its mirror sur face. Within those veils, the isle stood, broad and beautiful i summer heat.

"Why are we on this shore, and not on the island?" Lancelo wondered.

Arthur's beard streamed blood and water, and his flesh wa gray. "Excalibur . . ."

"What?" Lancelot asked.

"Merlin first hid the sword here . . . hid it from the gods Rhiannon formed in the lake from jewel sacrifices. It hid Ex calibur. Now Rhiannon is destroyed. Now Excalibur must re turn to the waters . . . hidden from the gods. . . ."

Lancelot stared at the sword, the finest blade the world ha ever seen.

"Throw it in, Lancelot." Arthur said.

"No, I cannot."

"It must never fall into mortal hands again. Not until ther is a new Arthur, a new Camelot."

Lancelot shook his head, smiling. "We're not done with th old Arthur, the old Camelot."

"Throw it in, Lancelot. . . . It is the price of our passage."

Lancelot's breath washed across the silvery blade, lingering for a moment before fading to nothing. He lowered the king to the frozen grass at the lakeside. Pillowing Arthur's head on the reeds, Lancelot took up the sword. It was exquisite—light, powerful, perfectly balanced.

"Do it now."

Lancelot lifted Excalibur up over his shoulder. He drew a deep breath and hurled the blade. It flew through the air, sparkling like a star. End over end it went, cleaving mists and wrapping itself in them as in gossamer veils. The surface of the lake caught the image of the peerless sword as it plunged. A hand rose from the waters and caught the blade—a slender, powerful, feminine hand. The hand of Brigid. This was the price of their passage. Slowly, she pulled the blade down beneath the flood.

When its tip vanished, a barge appeared where it had been. Upon the barge stood two women—Brigid, resplendent in robes of light, and Morgan le Fey, resplendent in robes of darkness. Between them, the cowled ferryman poled the craft forward. Tiny waves streamed from the bow across the glassy waters. The barge seemed not to move at all, but was suddenly at the shore.

"Bring him," Brigid said simply. She opened her arms to the three.

As Lancelot bowed to lift Arthur, Guinevere said, "Why is Morgan le Fey here?"

Brigid's face was serene within her robes of light. "She is his half-sister, and part of the land's power. She has grown up to become my shadow, and is entitled to be here. She will do no harm this day. It is only right that we three, Guinevere, be here."

Cradling Arthur in his arms, Lancelot stepped onto the barge. Guinevere followed. The ferryman set his pole in the muck and pushed off. The barge glided away from the world. Already, the mists spun about it, enfolding the company.

"You can heal him," Guinevere said to Brigid. "You will heal him. Mordred's poisons can be nothing to you."

"This wound was struck long before Mordred, and its poisons are manifold and potent. Some wounds are mortal wounds."

Guinevere caught Lancelot's eye, and both understood.

The barge did not move, but they arrived. Avalon breathed her summery breath upon them, bearing the scent of apples, of clover and waterfalls, of home.

Lancelot drew the fragrances in. They filled him with a sudden, strange hope. He stepped from the barge onto the grassy verge and lifted his eyes. There, up the slope, was Brigid's cottage. He strode toward it, carrying Arthur as though he were but a child. Guinevere had to run to keep pace. They were smiling on those summer hills. How could Arthur of Camelot die on a day like this, on an isle like this? How could paradise allow the great king to slip away?

They reached the door to the hovel. Guinevere flung it open.

Lancelot strode in, striking his head on the lintel as he went. "Damn," he cursed softly, and blushed to see Brigid and Morgan already within.

Brigid now wore her old body, and the homespun dress Lancelot knew so well. She gestured to Lancelot's own pallet, lying half-made from when he had last slept there. "Lay him here. We will make him comfortable."

Morgan, who now seemed no more than a young woman in a fine black gown, watched as Lancelot set the king down. Arthur's head eased onto the pillow. The linen bulged up around the wound and wicked blood from it.

Guinevere pushed Lancelot back. "Let me near him," she said almost desperately, kneeling. "He's my husband."

Nodding, Lancelot drew back. He panted. It had been a long climb up the hill.

Guinevere ran her fingers along Arthur's jaw. She leaned over him and kissed his lips. She drew back, and her tears lingered on his face. Sobbing quietly, she said, "What am I going to do without him?"

"What will any of us do without him?" Brigid wondered.

Lancelot looked to his aunt. She held a shovel in her aged grip. She thrust it toward him and nodded.

With one last glance at Guinevere, weeping over her husband, Lancelot took the shovel. "Good-bye, good king." He ducked through the door and headed toward the apple orchard. There was a good place beyond, near to where he had buried the Saxon.

Lancelot stripped to his waist. It was hot work beneath the summer sun. Still, the soil was black and deep, and it came away in solid shovelfuls.

At first, he had bristled. He should have been there. He was Arthur's knight, his ally, his friend. But he was also Arthur's rival, and the man who had stolen Guinevere. That was the real reason Brigid had sent him away. Guinevere had to be free to grieve. She loved Arthur, loved him more deeply than Lancelot had ever realized. It was right that she should be the one with him.

The grave was half-dug—three feet deep along the whole course of it—when Guinevere shrieked below.

Lancelot planted his shovel and jumped from the grave. He took a few running steps down the hill before stopping himself.

It was reflex to come running when Guinevere was distressed, but he could not go to her now. She had to be free to grieve. Aunt Brigid was with her. No harm would come to her. She had to be free.

The shriek broke into piteous wailing.

No, Guinevere was fine. It was only that Arthur had just died.

Lancelot hung his head. Arthur had just died. The world had changed forever.

The hovel below went silent.

Turning on his heel, Lancelot strode back up the hill and dropped into the grave. He grasped the shovel and began to dig again. His own tears fell silently into the rich earth. This was how he could help. It would be a fine, deep grave, and he would get the miners to cut a slab of stone to lay atop it, and Lancelot himself would chisel the epitaph. This was what he could do.

The grave was shoulder-deep when Brigid approached. Grief lined her face. She walked slowly, using another shovel as a cane. Each step was leaden.

Lancelot called to her. "It's all right. I don't need help. I'm almost done. Go back down to Guinevere."

Brigid did not. She climbed the rest of the way to the grave site. Setting the point of her shovel in the grass, she leaned on it heavily and caught her breath.

"I said I'm almost done. You can hardly climb the hill, let alone—"

Setting her foot on the shovel, she dug down, lifted a clump of sod, and threw it aside. She positioned the point in line with her first shovel mark, sank the blade, and pulled out another chunk of earth.

"What are you doing?" Lancelot asked. "Can't you see that

I've already dug this down five feet? Now you want Arthur to be buried over there?"

Brigid chucked more soil. She had begun to cut a second grave, beside the first.

"Oh!" Lancelot groaned, falling to his knees. "Oh. Brigid. No!"

She did not respond, but only continued shoveling.

37

Only Little Things

The letters were the same size. That was important, not just the spacing, but the size, so that the two stones looked like they belonged together, which they did. The little things were important. There really weren't any big things anymore, so the little things were all-important.

Lancelot leaned down and blew across the new cut. He rubbed his thumb on the stone. It was smooth. No burs, no chips. The cut was fine and deep, five chisel strokes high, and three wide, with the width of the chisel between letters, and the whole thing straight because he'd used his own sword edge to line it up. This was the last letter, and it had to be right.

He positioned the chisel for the crossbar. The metal edge rang like a nervous bell on the stone. He steadied his hand and gingerly laid down the chisel. Stone dust clung to the sweat on his palm. His hands were as cold as the stone. He rubbed them together.

The witch had killed her. No. That was always his first thought when he let himself think, and always he answered no. Brigid wouldn't have let her. Besides, it was too easy to blame the witch. It was much harder to think that love killed her, love for Arthur, and harder still to think that love for her hadn't killed Lancelot.

These were the big things, and he was through with big things. The little things were what mattered, and there weren't even any big things.

He snatched up the chisel and hammer and with three strokes it was done. He didn't even blow the dust away. Let the wind do that, and the rain, and Time. Lancelot had done what he could do, and he was done.

He stood. His eyes passed over the words. He'd not even intended to read them again, but once you can read, words pour into you:

Here Lies Arthur, Once and Future King

and on the other slab,

Here Lies Guinevere, the King's Heart

Lancelot clutched the chisel to his breast. It cut him. He flung it away. He flung the hammer too. Let the stonecutters find them in the gorse or let no one find them and let Time do what it did to them.

"You're done." Aunt Brigid. He hadn't heard her come up or hadn't remembered if she had just been there. He didn't startle. When it's all little things, nothing's very startling.

"Yes," he said without looking at her.

"They look fine. You've done a fine job."

"Yes."

"Then why don't you come down to the cabin? There's cider ready."

"I'm not thirsty."

"Someone's waiting for you down there."

"I don't want to see anyone."

"Oh, yes, you do. You'll want to see him. Come on."

"I'm going to wait a while."

"Then you'll come?"

"I'll come, after a while."

"All right. I'll keep the cider warm."

"I'm not thirsty."

"In a while you might be."

She walked away. He heard her old feet on the stones. He still didn't look at her. Sounds told him she was gone.

He lay prone upon Guinevere's slab. His shirt was off because of the hot work, and the cold stone hurt at first. It felt like ice. He was freezing to it. He could feel the letters under his skin and knew they were imprinting. He was becoming her gravestone, except that everything would be backward. Even her name would be backward.

Perhaps he was dying of love as she had. There was a drifting, sinking misery all around him. With his eyes closed, there was nothing else.

He awoke, and the sun was low. The words were pressed into his chest. His wound had bled until the *G* of her name was full. He had not died of love.

Lancelot stood. He walked down the hill. Late sun laid a dazzling road across the water, but everything else looked the color of charcoal. The bees had given up the trees. They dropped one by one into their holes. Wind rolled restlessly on the dry grass. It might have been a night from his childhood. Everything was the same—sweet clover underfoot and breezes tugging like spirits at his hands and daylight giving itself over in a series of slow and colorful flashes to the starry night. Brigid was the same, in the cottage below, wood smoke crooking up from the chimney. Even Lancelot was the same. For the first time in decades, he was a single, pure thing, not torn by conflicting claims. Only the graves up the hill were different. Only the one grave made any difference.

These were big things, and he was through with big things.

Lancelot reached the hovel and opened the door and stepped inside. He didn't hit his head, hadn't for three days now. He used to walk with his head too high.

Brigid was there, stirring some stew. "I hope you'll stay," she said, looking up and smiling sadly. "As long as you want. I know you'll be needing to get back to Benwick, the Joyous Garde, Dalachlyth, and the Castle of the Rose, but they all can wait until you are ready."

He sat down. The place felt and smelled the same as always.

"You might even pop in at what remains of Camelot. With the armies decimated and the kings gone and the dukes and brigands doing their best to ransack—Camelot could use some help. . . ."

"Where is he?"

Brigid stared querulously at him. "Where is who?"

"The person who was waiting for me."

"Didn't you see him outside?"

"I didn't see anyone outside."

Aunt Brigid smiled and laughed. "You're not seeing much today. You'd better go out and look again."

Lancelot stood. He walked to the door, opened it, and ducked through. Gloaming sky met black earth in a distant series of ridges, like torn paper. Along that tear moved something white and fleet. It coursed across one hill and through the next swale and grew ever larger. Its coming set a glad rumble in the earth, and Lancelot smiled. "Rasa."

Brigid was behind him again. "I don't know how he came across, but he did. He came looking for you."

The stallion neared. He moved with supple grace across the dark hillside. His hooves, heavy though they were, did not tear at the grass. He tossed his mane in greeting and arrived at a gallop. Rushing past, he turned and reared and trotted gently in.

Lancelot held out his hand and stroked the fine white pelt.

"I shouldn't be surprised," Brigid went on. "He came from here. This is his true home. And his longevity tells of hidden powers." She watched gladly as Lancelot rubbed the steed's shoulder. "He'll bear you where you need to go—your four kingdoms and war-torn Britannia in their midst."

"No," Lancelot said. His hand stilled on the horse's back, and he breathed a gusty sigh. "No. Look at me. I'm not a king. I'm not a knight. I'm not Lancelot du Lac."

Brigid's eyes narrowed. "You are. Here's your knightly steed, and within is your armor and sword."

"This is my steed, but he was mine before I was anything, before I was even a warrior. I will keep him. As to the rest—armor and sword and honor and kingship—I'm done with them. Give them to your next Tuatha changeling." Still shirtless, he swung up into the saddle.

Brigid gaped at him. "What are you doing? Where are you going?"

He shook his head. "I don't know." Clucking once to Rasa, he turned the beast away. "Good-bye, Aunt Brigid."

"Good-bye, Lan—Good-bye, my child."

Rasa eased from a trot to a canter to a gallop, and they were gone.

• • •

"If you look a wee washer in the eye, you're dead before dawn," said Elias, the oldest of the three brothers. His long strides carried him quickly along the footpath. His eyes darted down amid reeds as if hunting frogs, although this night they had come for ghosts. "I doesn't matter if it's direct or in a mirror like with Medusa. Either way, you die."

The second brother, Aidan, had to jog to keep up. His red hair flopped in the dusk. "What if you don't keep both eyes open?" He clenched one closed to demonstrate.

"Then you get really sick," offered Gabe, the youngest.

"No, you die," said Elias. "I said, if you look a wee washer in the eye, you're dead. That's just one eye." He held up his index finger.

"What if you squint?" asked Aidan.

"Get serious. It's not like fishing when you go looking for ghosts, 'cause a fish doesn't jump on you and suck out your soul."

"They suck out your soul?" asked Gabe.

"Yep, and then you go around without a soul."

"What happens if your soul has already been sucked out and then they catch you again?" Aidan asked.

"Then they suck out something else," suggested Gabe, "like your spleen."

Elias snorted and stopped in his tracks. He wheeled on the other two, who ran headlong into him. He hissed, "Get serious. What's a ghost going to do with a spleen? They just need souls. Now, no more questions. They'll hear your questions and they'll know you don't know what you're doing and they'll come for you right away. They have instincts for that."

"Ghosts have instincts?" asked Aidan.

"Somebody's coming!" Gabe blurted.

All three went silent, and they heard it distinctly, the hollow thud of hooves on the path behind them. Ever since Camelot had fallen, none of the roads were safe from brigands.

"Get off the path—there, in those weeds. Get in there!" Elias said, shoving the other two. He was in charge, and if he got his brothers killed he'd be in big trouble. The bush was thick, and nobody would look there. He pushed.

"Ow!" Gabe said.

"Ow!" agreed Aidan.

"Quiet! He'll hear you."

"But this is sticker bush."

It was. Elias didn't realize it until he had pushed his way in, and the burrs stuck right through his shirt. The hoofbeats were really near now. "Quiet. Just hold still till he's gone."

"I can't," Aidan said. "I got one down my pants."

"I sw-swallowed one," gagged Gabe.

"Hold still!"

"Eye-yi-yi-yi!" Aidan whooped, leaping from the nettles.

Elias made a swipe for him but couldn't reach and dived, gratefully, out of the sticker bush. He caught Aidan's ankle and dragged him down just short of the path. Gabe clambered out atop his prone brother. All three lay there as the rider came up out of the darkness. The horse clumped to a halt. Three sets of eyes rose, fearfully.

It was a white horse—not just white but ghostly white, and too big to be real. Steam came out of its nose, and its eyes glowed red. Worse, though, was the rider. A savage, barefoot, with tattered breeches, and no shift. He had a scraggly beard that reached down to a bloody G drawn backward on his chest. His hair was matted, and his eyes were wild and stared down at them.

"Don't look at his eyes!" cried Gabe. "He's a wee washer!"

Aidan said, "He's not very wee."

Even Elias was having trouble mastering his fear. "What are you? Are you a man, or a ghost?"

The figure on the horse did not respond, which was response enough.

Elias went on, "Because none of us've got souls left. We already ran into one of you tonight, so, you're a little late."

Still, the figure was silent, his eyes lit with madness.

"How come his ghost horse smells like a real horse?" Aidan asked.

"Because he's not a ghost." Elias chewed his lip and addressed the man on the horse. "And you're not a brigand, unless you're a bad one. You've got no bags for loot, and not even any pockets. All we got that you might want is shirts, and ours are full of burrs." His eyes narrowed. "Wait a minute. You're a knight." He pointed emphatically at the figure. "You're Sir Lancelot! Lancelot du Lac. You're the King of Benwick! You're the one who married Guinevere and fought against Gawain and fought for Arthur. Everybody thought you died with him, but you didn't. Here you are! Lancelot du Lac!"

As Elias spoke, the red madness faded from the man's eyes. He seemed to be coming awake from a dream. He was remembering who he was, and it terrified him.

The horse flung its head back and forth as if to beat away a crowd of foes. It stamped and turned and darted. It ran down the path to where the Brue emptied into the Glastonbury swamps. Not stopping, the horse charged into the water. Fantails of muck hurled up in its wake. Deeper, and deeper, until water lapped its shoulders.

The rider stooped in the saddle and scooped up water and flung it over himself as if he were washing. He splashed his face and head and rubbed the muddy stuff in. Soon the horse was swimming out into deeper water, and the man splashed and splashed. He kept it up until they had swum out of sight in the darkness.

"Was that really Sir Lancelot?" asked Aidan.

Elias shook his head. "No. It couldn't have been. Lancelot was a great man. He wasn't like that. Not ever."

"Then what was it, and why did it run off like that?"

"I don't know what it was," Elias said. "I don't think it even knows what it was."

EPILOGUE

Forerunners and Harbingers

The mad horseman traveled world and Otherworld and came even at times to the Cave of Delights.

That morning, the sun shone just as Merlin had commanded it, and birds flitted through a firmament of blue. He and Nyneve, in their youthful semblances, took tea upon an ivy-vined portico of their palace. It owed more in form and style to a Roman villa than a British manor. Stationed at the brow of a hill, it peered down a rankling slope of wildflowers and scrub trees to a sparkling bay. All was as Merlin had ordained—all except for the madman who rode, dripping, onto the bank.

Horse and rider alike shook the water from their hair. They gazed around with dumb wonder.

In silence, Nyneve and Merlin watched the distant warrior. They showed no fear. They ruled this paradise and could hurl him out more easily than he had found his way in. Still, they watched him closely. It was rare they saw something they didn't expect.

At last the silence became unbearable. Merlin rubbed a

clean-shaven chin and remarked, "The tea is fine this morning."

Nyneve smiled, fastening her hair in a knot behind her head. "You should go down there."

"To blast him, I suppose," Merlin said lightly.

"He is lost, just as you were. He doesn't know who he is."

Merlin took a sip of tea. "He doesn't want to know. Lancelot du Lac has become Lancelot du Lethe. He washes away his memories."

"Have a little pity—"

"Pity the man who seduced Guinevere and destroyed the Round Table and killed Arthur and brought Camelot crashing down?"

Nyneve's gentle gaze wore away her husband's anger. "He's mad, Merlin. Of all people, I would think you would understand."

"Out of madness Camelot rose, and into madness Camelot fell," Merlin said. "I was a madman who became a god, and he a god who became a madman. We are opposites. There is nothing between us."

"You are reflections of each other. There is everything between you." She reached across to him and set a slender hand on his. "You built Camelot, yes, and he destroyed Camelot, yes. But what you are forgetting is that Camelot saved you, and it damned him." Nyneve leaned over and kissed him on the cheek. "Go to him."

"What am I supposed to say?" Merlin asked aloud, though already he was going. He shed his young body. His spirit fled down the tumbled hillside. He took new form—in fact, old form—below. With white beard and hair, tattered travel cloak, and rumpled hat, he stood directly uphill from the horse and rider. Hitching his mouth ironically, Merlin said, "Welcome."

Lancelot did not startle. He slowly turned his head. His

eyes had a strange quality to them, as though they were mirrors. "Where am I?"

Merlin shrugged, spreading his hands. "You're here. Now I have a question for you—*who* are you?"

Blinking placidly, Lancelot seemed to drink in that question. He lifted a hand to his chest—it bore a backward G, inscribed in blood—and he said, "I'm me."

Merlin had trouble not laughing. "Well said. You're you, and I'm me, and we're here."

"It seems a good place," Lancelot said, looking around.

"Oh, yes, very good," Merlin replied. Anger rose in him. "You know, there used to be another good place, a very good place called Camelot, with a very good king and a very good queen, but it's all gone now."

"All gone," echoed Lancelot.

"I don't suppose you knew such a place."

"No," said Lancelot quietly.

Merlin nodded. "Once, I wandered the way you do. For a century I did. A boy and a sword saved me. How long will you wander, Lancelot du Lac? Who will save you?"

Lancelot stiffened in the saddle. "I am not truly welcome here."

"No. You are not."

His horse stomped a fore hoof and headed back toward the bay.

Merlin watched soberly as the wild-haired man rode away. Water splashed, rising to fetlocks and knees. Merlin might not have heard what Lancelot said next, for he muttered it to himself, but Merlin was in the waters and knew what they knew:

"I'll wander until there is a new Arthur, until there is a new Camelot."